DEATH IN THE OFF-SEASON

Death in the Off-season

A MERRY FOLGER MYSTERY

Francine Mathews

William Morrow and Company, Inc. • New York

It is the policy of William Morrow and Company, Inc., and its imprints and affiliates, recognizing the importance of preserving what has been written, to print the books we publish on acid-free paper, and we exert our best efforts to that end.

Library of Congress Cataloging-in-Publication Data

Mathews, Francine.
Death in the off-season : a Merry Folger mystery / Francine Mathews.
p.   cm.
ISBN 0-688-13443-2
1. Women detectives—Massachusetts—Nantucket Island—Fiction.
2. Nantucket Island (Mass.)—Fiction.   I. Title.
PS3563.A8357D43   1994
813'.54—dc20   94-8594
CIP

Printed in the United States of America

First Edition

1   2   3   4   5   6   7   8   9   10

BOOK DESIGN BY LINEY LI

This book is dedicated with love to my mother,

Elizabeth MacEntee Barron,

who always believed

Acknowledgments

M Y GRATITUDE GOES FIRST and foremost to the people of Nantucket, who patiently bear the onslaught of summer visitors, traffic, litter, and noise to share their beautiful island with authors like me, whose books only encourage *more* tourists, traffic, litter, and noise; and to the Nantucket Police, who were kind enough to answer a lengthy series of questions by mail in 1991 regarding everything from the makeup of their force to the color of their uniforms. Any errors or fabrications (such as a father-daughter relationship between the chief and one of his detectives) are entirely my own. Thanks as well to Ocean Spray Cranberries, Inc., who supplemented my research into cranberry farming with informational literature and encouragement.

No book is the product of one person. Mine was helped along by Kay Fanning, who had the temerity to send her daughter-in-law's unsolicited 450-page manuscript to an agent of her acquaintance; and by Rafe Sagalyn, the agent in question, who actually read it. His energy and dedication in marketing an unpublished author went well beyond what many in his profession would consider necessary; to him I owe far more than 15 percent of my good fortune.

Adrian Zackheim and Marjorie Braman, formerly of William Morrow and Avon Books, respectively, encouraged me immeasurably by

Acknowledgments

believing the book should be published; and Rose Marie Morse and Bob Mecoy, who followed them on the project, saw the manuscript through to publication with thoroughness and patience.

To all those who read this book in its incipient stages and offered valuable criticism—Laurie Mathews, Mark Mathews, Betty Barron, Cathy Barron, Jo and Tony Del Negro, Pat Anthony, Charles Sibre, Frank J. MacEntee, Bill Ferretti, Philip Carroll, those at the CIA who prefer their names unmentioned, and most important, Liz Ferretti, who should edit books for a living—my sincere thanks. You helped prevent some egregious errors and some very silly ones; and if others remain, they are entirely my fault.

DEATH IN THE OFF-SEASON

Prologue

A PERFECT NIGHT FOR FEIJOADA. The thought came to him unbidden as he stared through the windshield at the fog, a fluid blackness wrapping the car like a mourning sheet. *Feijoada.* Pungent rice and black beans, the bits of pork and tomato and sausage drenched in their depths, and Susanna's fat black arms gleaming with perspiration as she stirred the pot. A food intended to comfort—like most of his life in Brazil's decaying paradise.

His life. The car creaked into a pothole, lurching like a water buffalo on its ravaged shock absorbers, and the motion sent blood pounding into his temples. He was exhausted, and his thoughts darted like fish in a disturbed pool; the nine-hour flight and the night ferry were catching up with him. He shivered in the creeping dampness. *His life.* He had to hold on to it, despite the insidious enemy, the threat coursing through his veins. He had to do more than escape. He had to win.

He'd always hated this island. Hated the fog, the way it masked his sight, made him stumble, and turned the familiar into something threatening. He felt vulnerable on Nantucket, something no Mason could ever endure. Masons destroyed the vulnerable, for God's sake.

The car came to a stop, engine idling, its headlights picking up the glint of the livestock gate's gray metal bars. He stared at it an instant, taking in the words "Mason Farms," painted in a red semicircle on a square white signboard; and then he bared his teeth at the family domain.

"Get out and open it for me," the driver said.

"Why?"

"Because that's how you were raised."

He hesitated an instant, then opened the door. The car was filled with the smell of salt and pine. He stepped tentatively into the opaque night, breathing his discomfort in quick bursts, the fog smoothing his brow with a wet hand. Only a few steps to the gatepost and the wire loop holding the bars closed against the sheep.

He crossed in front of the car, feeling exposed and backlit in the headlights, and glanced over his shoulder. The glare blinded him momentarily, as he had known it would, and he blinked, thinking for an instant that the car's sudden movement was a trick of the light, something to do with the fog, and not the hurling of wheels and metal toward his body. The first stab of fear and understanding came just as the hood of the car crashed into his spine, throwing him up and backward, snapping his skull against the windshield.

He skittered left off the roof into a darkness that was filled with searing pain, unbounded by the edges of his body. *The fog,* he thought, fighting for sense even as it left him; and knew with anguish that he was lost.

Chapter 1

WILL AWOKE, as he did every day, a few seconds before his mother turned from the muffins she was mixing in the kitchen two floors below and walked to the stairs. He lay still, his eyes closed in the semidark, listening for her voice.

"Will! Will, it's past six!"

Labor Day. He hugged the stillness of the early morning to himself for a few seconds longer; tomorrow he'd be torn from sleep and thrust into the long tedium of the school year. With it would come winter—shorter days, fewer ferries to the mainland, and the disappearance of the summer people, whose energy and strident voices broke the island's isolation for a few months.

"Tomorrow, and tomorrow, and tomorrow," he murmured sleepily, and then stopped, self-conscious. His voice had changed a year ago and its new depth still had the power to startle him. He thrust his head deeper into his pillow and groped for the strands of a dream that had drifted across his brain an instant before his mother's voice turned night to day. No good; it was gone. His eyes flicked open.

The attic room high above the restaurant faced east, into the morning sun, but today a livid white light filtered through the shade, and the groan of horns, human and suffering, rose off the water. That meant

13

fog, his favorite weather. He felt a rush of satisfaction as he threw back the bedclothes and swung adolescent legs, lanky and beautiful, onto the rag rug. It was boom day at the bog, and Peter would need him early to work the flooded cranberry beds.

He pulled on a pair of jeans and a sweatshirt and ran down the two flights, three steps at a time, passing his mother's second-floor living area and the freshly painted dining rooms at the stairs' foot. The kitchen sat at the back of the house, down a length of narrow, aged corridor that smelled of dry rot; the off-islanders considered it quaint. He pushed open the swinging door and a rush of air blew his dark bangs back from his forehead.

His mother turned from the sink and gave him a brief smile as he slid a stool over to her butcher block. She'd already set out his blueberries and cream. He threw himself down before them and yawned hugely. The kitchen windows were shut against the damp, and the heavy smell of sausage fat hanging in the warm drafts from the stove reminded him of winter. His face creased uncontrollably in another yawn. He could feel his mother's eyes on the back of his head, and dug into the berries.

Tess Starbuck studied her boy an instant, and then pulled up another stool.

"Get enough sleep?"

"Yep."

"You were up until all hours. It was twelve-thirty when I fell off."

"I was reading," he said. "That book on the Egyptian campaign is really good."

"Peter lend it to you?" she asked, reaching for a towel. Her fine hands were reddened like a waterman's, or a chef's. She had been both, among many things. Will loved his mother's hands. He dropped his eyes to his breakfast.

"Yeah. He's got awesome books out at the farm. I could spend a week there."

"You could spend one in bed, too, by the look of those circles under your eyes. Read all winter, Will, when there's nothing else to do on this godforsaken island."

Will gave her a doleful look from his dark blue eyes, and then grinned. Despite herself she grinned back, looking suddenly younger than her forty-two years, more like the pictures of the college girl in his father's wallet, who had come to Nantucket for a summer's waitressing and never left. His mother's hair was reddish-brown, and she had golden eyes that made her look like a tiger, Will thought. Now, at the end of summer, the freckles stood out clearly at the end of her Irish nose and her arm had a broad white band from wearing her watch at the beach. He knew that however she cursed Nantucket, Tess loved the island as he did and his father had, a native love deep into the bone.

At the glancing thought of his father, Will felt the familiar burst of pain shoot through his gut, and breathed deeply to push it away. When would it stop?

He wiped his mouth on his napkin and shoved back his chair. "It's boom day, Tess," he said. "Gotta get out there."

She kissed him swiftly on the cheek and brushed a hand across his forehead, needing to feel the silkiness of the hair spilling into his eyes. Fifteen. Growing up and away from her, and she'd never have another. "Take a change of clothes. You don't want to ride back in wet jeans."

He was already out the door.

·   ·   ·

HER BROW FURROWED, Tess followed him through the kitchen window as he swung a leg over his bike and sped off down Quince Street. One of these nights, maybe he'd be able to sleep without dreaming, she thought. Until then, she'd have to live with the dark circles, the pallor underneath his late-summer tan, and have faith that the passage of time would ease his nightmares.

She watched as the fog rolled up from the harbor, silent and unstoppable, blotting out the gray shingle of the neighboring house, and crossed herself, once, for luck. Then she shook her head angrily and turned back to her pans.

She rarely indulged the pain of Daniel's death, one way she and Will were very much alike. She had mourned the man she loved from

15

the night his body was found on the beach at Siasconset until she buried him three days later; then she had turned her energies to survival. She could brood, cultivating the terrors of the unstable future, and go slowly mad in the emptiness of her queen-sized bed; or she could cook until she was mindless and weary. Tess had undertaken to feed the island.

Daniel's partner had bought out her share of the scalloper. God knows it was worth less these days than when Dan had mortgaged his soul three years ago to buy it. But his partner had pitied her, something she hated and bore because she had no choice; he had given her enough to clear the debt and get out from under the bank. She had thrown Dan's insurance money—how little she'd thought of actually having to use it, the day they went to the Allstate booth at Sears—into a professional kitchen, moved her life upstairs, and opened for business three months after the storm that killed her husband. The Greengage was a home away from home for the men who fished Nantucket's waters, and it was a tourist find as a result. Tess had been so busy from the day she opened that the nights she had feared—the stillness in her room, the dread reckoning of all she had lost—had been consumed by exhausted, dreamless sleep. Now she steeled herself against the arrival of winter, when the crowds fled, the island battened down against endless wind and damp, and she would have only Will, fighting his own demons, between herself and the memories.

The oven's timer shook her out of sadness. She opened the door and breathed deeply of bursting cranberries, then glanced at her watch. Four hours to the lunch crowd.

· · ·

WILL COVERED THE MILE and a quarter from his house to the rotary at the end of Orange Street in about five minutes. The bike was a three-year-old Trek 1100, one of his prized possessions and a gift from Peter, who had bought a new Cannondale early in the spring. Tess had almost made him give it back, too proud to take charity from one of the Masons, but Peter had told her it was a fair exchange for Will's help at lambing. Peter had hired him outright after that, paying eight dollars an hour. Will was saving his money for college.

The tall captains' houses that lined Orange Street were silent this morning, their backyards blotted out, the colors of the late dahlias bleached and flattened by fog. Already most of the summer people who owned or rented them had left the island, beating the rush for spots on the car ferries at the end of the season. A few hardy souls waited until the shops closed in late September, but the ones with kids his age, bound for school tomorrow, were long gone. Farther down the street, lights glowed from the Nantucket Bake Shop and the smell of warm bread drifted out the open screen door. Will drew in his breath sharply as he passed, his mouth watering despite his sturdy breakfast, then threw his head down to pedal harder. At the rotary at the end of Orange Street, he took the Milestone Road bike path toward Siasconset, not trusting the road in the fog.

He had close to four miles to pedal before the turnoff to Altar Rock, through the gently rolling moors whose wind-gnarled scrub, on clearer days, had begun to show the first of fall's intense color. Here in the middle of the island, beyond the town's closely huddled houses, the heath stretched almost unimpeded to the sea. The occasional gray-shingled saltbox, rising amid the moor like a ship cresting a wave, was invisible now in the fog.

The bike path was empty. Up ahead, a single gull huddled in the middle of the road, its feathers fluffed into a ball against the damp, examining an indeterminate roadkill flattened on the macadam. Will felt moisture clammy on the back of his neck, already warm with exertion, and shivered. Even in the height of July the island had weather like this, but today the air bore the scent of dying grass and beach plum past its prime, the stamp of summer in decay.

He slowed the bike, anxious lest he miss the turnoff in the fog, but his sense of timing hadn't failed him. Ten yards ahead a swirl of sand showed where the road to Altar Rock cut through the heath into the center of the island. Will stopped the bike and glanced to either side, wary of cars looming suddenly out of the mist, then shot across. His thin tires, crafted for racing, made slow and wobbly work of the rutted road, and it took him fifteen minutes to travel the mile and a quarter before Altar Rock loomed on his right. He stopped the bike an instant to look at it, but today the granite peak was lost in fog. The radar station, his earliest memory of alien technology, hovered nearby. Most days, at ninety feet above sea level, this was one of the best spots for viewing the whole island. He turned around and looked north, toward where the harbor should be. The rise and fall of foghorns, a lament steady as his own breathing, carried across the moors from the sea a mile to the east.

He pushed the sleeves of his sweatshirt higher above his elbows and labored slowly on, past Altar Rock to the intersection of three sandy trails. He took the right-hand fork—less than a mile now to the farm. He felt a sudden burst of happiness at the thought of the day ahead. Wet harvesting was much more fun than dry. This year, Peter would give him a beater and let him wade through the flooded bog, the whirling machine sending a carpet of blood-red berries bobbing to the surface in his wake. Will was just young enough to relish having water up to his knees. To be paid for it was too much to be believed. Lunch would be something hot, given the coolness of the day and the drenching nature of the work: quahog chowder, maybe, with corn bread and fried scallops, followed by blueberry pie. Rebecca, the housekeeper who was old enough to be Peter's mother, would serve him second helpings. Then they'd haul in the booms, skimming acre after acre of red berries from the water.

Will felt a shifting current of air graze his cheek, and the fog cleared slightly: he'd passed the entrance to the farm. He thrust out a leg to stop the bike, his heel kicking up a whorl of damp sand, and studied the tangle of scrub pine to his right. No wonder he'd almost missed it. The aluminum gate that stood closed most of the day—to keep the sheep from roaming too far—stood wide open this morning. Rafe must have been out early. Will's forehead wrinkled slightly in puzzlement. Then he put his head down and pedaled up the unpaved drive toward the old saltbox.

A mouse darted from the undergrowth to his right and shot in front of his wheel. He clutched at the hand brakes so suddenly that the bike skidded to a stop, throwing him off balance. In a desperate bid for stability, he dropped his left leg; but the bike went down. He slid on his side in the sand perhaps five feet before his momentum ceased, and then he lay, slightly dazed by the early hour and the sudden panic, staring at the gray sky. He hoped devoutly that the mouse wasn't ground to a pulp beneath his left hip. When he thrust the bike upright and eased himself to a standing position, slapping his jeans, his hands came away bright with smears of blood from one torn knee. Great. Now he'd have to tell Tess, and she'd never believe he hadn't been reckless.

A bobwhite called its name from the undergrowth opposite, and Will glanced up. Water lapped at the edge of the cranberry beds running along either side of the drive. The vines were completely submerged. A fragment of bright fabric, caught on a large piece of driftwood half sunk in the shallow pool, drew his eye. He walked closer and strained to make out its shape.

And then he cried out, hands over his mouth to stifle his terror. He turned in panic and dashed back to his bike, scraped leg forgotten, screaming for somebody.

• • •

RAFE DA SILVA SURVEYED the flock of merino sheep bunched up around the hay bale and counted them mentally. Fifty-three, ewes and lambs, with the ram fifty-four. Not a major concern, but not a shabby bunch, either. With this year's shearing—and a good price from Nantucket Looms, their major customer—they might begin to pay for their keep. Not that Peter cared; Rafe knew the sheep would stay whether they made money or not. Peter raised the merinos for the same reason he did everything on the farm: for the love of it. The sight of sheep dotting the moors around the bog satisfied Peter's sense of history, the way his life in the two-hundred-year-old saltbox seemed a direct link to Masons dead and gone. Rafe didn't question it, and he didn't waste much time thinking about it. He understood very little of Peter's class of people, but everything about Peter's way of life.

The dog Ney sauntered toward him, his tongue hanging out lazily now that his work was done and the sheep were busy eating. Part cattle dog, part bearded collie, Ney looked like pure mutt. Peter had picked him up in the parking lot of the South Street ferry in Hyannis, where the bewildered pup had been circling a crowd of embarking Nantucketers waiting patiently in the rain. Peter had watched as Ney herded the passengers into a tight knot next to the gangplank, and then he'd grinned. He had been on his way to the Boston Marathon. He hadn't needed a dog. He'd thought about an animal shelter, and then he'd thought better of it. He could usually find a use for strays.

"You and me both, fella," Rafe said to the dog. He dropped his hand to Ney's snout and scratched either side of it, knowing the dog loved it. Ney thrust his nose deeper into the man's hand and snorted deeply.

"Come on, pup." Ney pivoted as though joined to Rafe's body, then loped off ahead, disappearing into the fog.

Rafe strolled without hurry toward the barn where the bog equipment was stored. He and Peter had opened the shunts of the reservoir across ten of the farm's fifty acres at sundown last night and flooded them with several feet of water. He glanced up at the gray weather. Not pretty, but not bad. There were worse things than a cool day of farming.

He stopped suddenly and cocked his head, listening. Since well before dawn he had been half conscious of the moaning of foghorns, a sound he had known from birth; but now a long, thin note spiraled through the air. Ney was howling, a high-pitched keening Rafe had never heard in the three years of the dog's life. It came from the driveway. He broke into a run.

•   •   •

"I THINK IT'S PETER, Rafe," Will said. He was bent over, staring at the bog, one hand on his knee and the other on Ney's collar. Rafe glanced at the boy's ashen face and then back at the body floating facedown in the water, seized by the same fear. The hair was Peter's dark brown, the body long and muscled. The man was dressed in khaki shorts and a rugby shirt, black-and-orange, that looked vaguely familiar. The calves were discolored with what at first glance appeared to be splotches of grease, but as Rafe moved to the edge of the bog and put one foot up to his knee in water, reaching for the man's hair, he realized the legs were badly bruised. He lifted the head. Wide and staring, the dead eyes looked toward the bank.

"It's not Peter, Will," he said gently, and let the corpse fall back into the water. "Let's get back to the house."

"You're not going to leave him here, are you?"

"It's better not to move anything until the police arrive. I shouldn't even have touched it." Rafe shook his wet hand and felt suddenly sick, not wanting to dry it on his own clothes. He shot a look at Will. The boy was watching him, his eyes filled with worry. And something else, Rafe thought—the memory of old pain.

"I'd tell you if it were Pete, Will. Believe me. Come on, let's get to the phone."

•   •   •

IT WAS NOT UNUSUAL for Peter Mason to be out of the house early. He spent a good part of his nonworking hours on his bicycle or running through miles of Nantucket's moors. A light sleeper, he'd been awakened at five today by the horns off the water. He'd stared at the beams running across the low ceiling of the upstairs bedroom, unable to doze. At six, abandoning all hope of sleep, he'd thrown on some clothes and headed out the back door for an easy run. An hour later he was making the turn for home at Altar Rock when he heard the sirens.

The ambulance and police car came up behind him suddenly in the fog, driving him into the underbrush as they went by. He narrowed his eyes and slowed to a near-walk, assessing what the sirens meant as they diminished in the distance. Then he began to sprint.

Chapter 2

Detective meredith folger surveyed the trampled drive, the
flooded bog, the bent backs of the two police sergeants, and Rafe
da Silva standing silently in the distance; then she ran her fingers
through her choppy blond bangs and tugged on the ends nervously.
Barely seven in the morning, and no evidence to speak of. Her first
murder might have been kinder to her.

For a few moments after arriving with the crime scene unit, she had
held on to the chance that the sodden body might mean nothing more
than a drunken slip and a drowning, or even an inglorious suicide. She
had dismissed those options fairly quickly. The bruises on the dead
man's legs and the broken underbrush raised too many questions. The
burden of finding the answers was causing her some panic. What to do
next?

She fished in the depths of her shoulder bag and came up with the
slim packet she was looking for: her half-glasses. Useful for detail
work—and maybe they'd even lend an air of professionalism to her
face. She perched them on the tip of her delicate nose and walked in a
half-crouch to the end of the drive, stopping to study the spot where
Will's bike had met the mouse. Then she surveyed the unpaved road
that ran perpendicular to the Mason Farms entrance. Multiple car
tracks—a heavy four-wheel-drive and several passenger cars of varying

sizes—had crisscrossed its sandy surface. She walked back along the road several feet, following the intertwined treads closely, and veered left. Near the right-hand verge a car had gone off the road, stopped abruptly—spraying gravel on the grass—regained the road, and continued on its way.

Merry crouched motionlessly above the scattered gravel an instant, thinking, and then stood up. She removed her reading glasses and stuffed them into her coat pocket, staring abstractedly at the roadbed. Then, impatiently, she pulled out the glasses again and retraced her steps.

Bent double, hands on her hips, she walked slowly along the bog's edge from the turnoff to where the body still lay in the water twenty feet down the drive. Then she paced back along the driveway more carefully, and was rewarded: a small wooden object, tossed haphazardly in the high grass by the bog's edge, caught her eye. She dropped to the ground.

"Clarence!"

Clarence Strangerfield, head of the crime scene unit, was up to his knees in the bog, camera poised, taking multiple shots of the corpse from various angles. He glanced across the drive at Meredith. "Ayeh," he said.

"C'mere. I found something."

Clarence hitched up his trousers with one hand, balancing his camera in the other. "What is it?"

"Looks like—" Merry hesitated. "Looks like a small wooden rat. I need a shot of the way it's lying. Make sure you get the pattern of the breakage in the underbrush all around here, too."

Clarence was pushing sixty, and he enjoyed his wife Emmeline's dinners; with a grunt of effort he pulled one bog-laden boot out of the water and heaved himself onto the bank. He took one last shot of the dead man from above, and then ambled down the drive toward the detective.

Her hands were on her hips, and her dark brows, always so startling in contrast to her tow-colored hair, were furrowed. "Looks like an oversized charm from a bracelet. Any ideas?"

Clarence eased his bulk down onto his work-worn knees and hovered over the scrap of wood. There was a pregnant pause. Then he cocked an eyebrow gravely at Merry. "Ayeh," he said, "thaht's as sure a raht as evah was."

"Never mind, Clare," Merry said. "Just shoot the thing." When he had finished, she reached into her purse for tweezers and a plastic bag, and lifted the rat from the grass.

"Okay," she said. "We have a button. With a thread of yarn still stuck in the buttonhole—looks like it's from a sweater. The wood's smooth enough to dust for prints back at the ranch, just in case." She slipped the button in the bag and handed it to Clarence for labeling. "You'll probably want to vacuum the corpse for matching fibers, too."

"Or any fibahs, for that mattah, Marradith. I know how to do mah job. Ah've been doin' it, you know, since yahr dad was about as uppity a young fellah as yahrself. Now get along and ahct like a detective. It impresses folks, pahticularly summah types. They've all been raised on television, ah believe."

Merry turned toward the spot at the side of the driveway that she could no longer avoid: the corpse, floating gently on the water's surface. She took a deep breath and forced herself to walk over to the broken underbrush and the lifeless body, wondering for an instant at the way the outflung arms seemed to embrace death. She had expected murder to look less thankful.

"You've triangulated the position of the body?" she asked Clarence.

"Used the gate and thaht tree ovah there," he said, "and I've had young Coffin sketch the scene." If he was aware of any irony in the surname of his chief assistant, Nathaniel Coffin, the crime scene chief did not betray it. "We're 'bout ready for Doctah John, I should think. He's already seen the cahpse *in situ*. Told me to bring it to the van when you wahr done. Guess he doesn't want to get his trousahs wet."

Dr. John Fairborn was the island's medical examiner. Merry glanced over to the rescue squad's white van, useless now to the man floating in the flooded cranberries, and caught the doctor in the act of discarding a cigarette as he lounged against the truck's open back door. She made a mental note to pick up the butt—to prevent Clarence's boys from cataloguing it as evidence—and wondered again how doctors could smoke after studying cancer in medical school. A God complex, probably. She turned back to Clarence. "We'll need Coffin's help," she said.

Clarence motioned to his assistant, who came at a run, and the three of them stepped up to their knees in bog water and vines. "Let's lift him out and over the bank, Clare, and carry him directly to Dr. John," Merry said.

"Yah know he'll look rathah bahd," Clarence said carefully. "The blood'll have pooled in his lowah tissues."

Merry nodded impatiently. "Let's get it over with. He's beginning to stink."

She took hold of the man's sodden rugby shirt just under his left armpit, while Clarence took his right; Coffin placed himself near the corpse's pelvis and legs.

"On the count of three," Merry said. "One, two . . ."

Protesting like a sleeper torn from his dreams, the body lifted free of its watery bed. They staggered, foot over stumbling foot, to where Dr. John lounged.

The medical examiner slapped his hands together in mock glee. "The iceman cometh," he said. "I'll let you know how long he's been dead, give or take a few hours, in a couple minutes."

Merry wiped her wet hands on her khakis and opened her mouth to say something, then thought better of it and turned away. She had always liked Dr. John, and in the past she had taken his black humor as one of the survival techniques of police work. Today she felt differently. The dead man must have been loved by someone; perhaps even now a wife or a friend was dialing the station frantically, wondering why he hadn't come home last night. He might be someone she'd bumped into exiting a shop, apologizing as he held open the door for her before moving on in his separate life. That life was over.

She forced herself to look at the purple face. "Any idea who he is, Clare?"

Clarence's ample stomach rumbled. He had missed his breakfast because of this call, but Merry was crawling toward the end of the night shift at eight-fifteen. On a normal morning they'd have met over coffee and doughnuts at the Downeyflake. "A-no, I don't. You?"

She shook her head. "What a lousy way to die. He's not much older than me, for Chrissake." She paused, looking at the crime scene chief, her arms folded protectively across her chest, and then looked away. "Think about it, Clare. We're supposed to help people. And while I was sitting in the station last night, killing time, this guy was out here dying in the dark. *Violently.* I couldn't stop it. How could I know? It's not like we can be everywhere at once, patrolling the back roads and the beach and the middle of the moor."

"But it makes yah feel like yah failed," Clarence said. "Like yah lahst a contest yah didn't know had stahted."

"It makes me angry, Clare."

Merry stood still for a moment in front of him in her red slicker, the cheery color belying her weariness. When she was this tired, her strongly molded cheekbones stood out sharply beneath her skin, making her seem even thinner than she was. Clarence, who had a streak of the mother hen in him, would want to throw an arm around her and send her home. To forestall him, she rolled her neck a bit to ease her muscles, and then moved past him toward the white van where the murdered man was lying. Clarence fell into step beside her. She could feel his worry nipping at their heels like a small dog. He was uneasy about this body. First of all, it was on Mason land—and though Clarence would consider them "summah people," the Masons had been powerful islanders for more years than Merry could remember. Secondly, the corpse hadn't died by itself, and that meant Merry had some difficult days ahead of her—or as Clarence would put it, she was due for "some rough weathah." She had years of training behind her, but no actual experience investigating violent death.

So what, she thought. I'm a Folger. That's always stood for competence on this island.

"Maybe he's a tahrist," Clarence said matter-of-factly.

Merry shook her head. "What tourist would be this far out of town, alone at night? Doesn't make sense—"

"—and it's *too easy*, in yahr opinion," Clarence finished.

Merry smiled at him wanly. *It's too easy* was her father's favorite phrase, as Clarence well knew. She shook herself slightly, throwing off her abstraction, and turned toward the crime scene chief. "I'd like you to shoot the spot out on the road where the car went into the grass, Clare. There's a faint set of footprints you might be able to lift. Then, as soon as you can, get somebody on the Mason car, or cars—particularly the bumpers."

Clarence's face grew sober. "The bruises on the legs."

Merry nodded. Her eyes drifted back to the dead man, and Clarence saw her blink rapidly. "When you're done there we'll deal with—"

"Baggin' him," Clarence said.

· · ·

HE HAD EXPECTED THEM to pull up in front of the house, and so he ran right into the official knot gathered behind the yellow police barrier.

"Peter!" It was Will's voice, young and filled with relief. Peter looked for the boy and saw instead a blond woman in a bright red raincoat, her booted feet firmly planted in his bog. Then he found Rafe, standing next to Will by the police car, and started toward him.

"What's going on, Rafe?"

"That's what we'd like to know, Mr. Mason."

Peter turned. The woman ducked under the police barrier and walked toward him, fumbling in her pocket for a badge. She flashed it half-apologetically at him. "Detective Meredith Folger, Nantucket police."

Peter held out his hand. "Peter Mason."

She seemed to shake it for a fraction of a second longer than was necessary, as if she found his hand comforting and didn't want to let go. He registered wide-set eyes the color of moss, heavy dark brows, and a high forehead. A face an artist would love, all bones and angles beneath a translucent skin. She was made for the forties, he thought, made for Cecil Beaton to photograph. She wore no makeup. Probably smart—if she did, the station house would explode.

"I'm afraid we've got some bad news, Mr. Mason," she said. "Someone's been killed in your cranberry field." She cleared her throat and swallowed. "Under the circumstances, I'll have to ask you some questions."

"Killed? Who?"

"He's carrying no identification, and I'm afraid he's a stranger to me and everyone present. Did you have any guests on your property last night?"

Peter started to brush past her, headed for the ambulance parked near the farm's entrance. She laid a hand on his arm. "Answer the question, please."

He stared at her a moment, as if considering whether she were worth obeying. The green eyes were hard and steady. "No," he said. "I didn't expect anyone, and nobody dropped by the house." He turned to Rafe. "Any midnight callers?"

The foreman shook his head. "And I've never seen this guy before, Pete," he said. His voice held a note of uneasiness that might almost be fear.

Peter's eyes narrowed. "But what, Rafe?"

Rafe crossed his arms over his chest and dropped his gaze. "The guy looks familiar. Maybe you know him."

Peter felt an involuntary chill strike at the base of his spine, and for an instant, his instinct was to run in any direction. Rafe was afraid for him. He took a deep breath, glanced at Merry Folger, and walked toward the black body bag laid on a stretcher. A lanky paramedic was in the act of zipping it shut.

"Wait a minute," Peter said, leaning past him. He pulled back the edge of the bag and looked hard at the dead face. The eyes had been closed. He was sharply aware of the smell of his own sweat, vividly alive, as he studied the blue lips. He drew in his breath, and the hand holding the bag began to shake.

"Finished, sir?" the paramedic asked.

Rafe was standing next to him suddenly, one hand on his back. "Who is it, Pete?"

"It's Rusty."

Merry Folger looked up sharply. "Rusty?"

Peter nodded, his eyes bleak. "My brother."

Chapter 3

"C AN YOU TELL ME what happened, Will?" Merry said. She was
trudging with the boy and Rafe da Silva, a police summer intern
in tow, up the quarter-mile of sand-and-gravel drive to Peter Mason's
saltbox on the moor. They had left Peter behind with the paramedic.

Will looked imploringly at Rafe, who seemed to have retreated into
himself. He was striding purposefully toward the house, head down,
lost in thought.

Merry followed the direction of the boy's eyes and glanced at the
foreman, whom she had known all her life. She recognized his brand of
abstraction. The routine walk over familiar territory allowed him to
think without interruption, and the careful lack of expression on his
Portuguese features camouflaged a very active anxiety. *He's worried not
about the body, but about what it implies,* she thought.

This close to Rafe, she felt a rush of terror that had nothing to do
with the murder investigation that had brought her onto his turf; she
bit her lip and wished he would look at her. He frowned and studied
the ground, as if determined not to meet her eyes.

She gave up and turned back to Will. He was walking between the
two of them, slightly bent as he held firmly to the collar of a large,
indiscriminate dog. He looked peaked and too old for his fifteen years,

and something tugged at the back of her brain. She did not know the Starbuck family well—in fact, she knew Tess Starbuck only by sight— but there was something about the father's death that she knew she should remember.

Will cleared his throat. "I wouldn't have seen it if it weren't for the mouse," he said.

Merry nodded encouragingly, not understanding him in the slightest. "Let's start before that. Why were you here at all, and so early?"

"I was coming out to help Peter with the harvest. That's why the bog's flooded. We're wet-harvesting today." At the prospect of the promised job, Will's face brightened momentarily, then clouded as he remembered his morning. "It was pretty foggy, you know, so I had to ride really slow. I almost missed the drive, because the gate was open, which it never is, and in the fog you couldn't tell there was a road there, even."

Merry made a mental note to ask Rafe about the gate. "And so?"

"There was this mouse on the driveway—it ran out in front of the bike, and I tried to stop and couldn't. The gravel makes it hard with the brakes. Anyway, I wiped out." He stopped.

"And that's when you saw the body?" Merry asked gently.

Will's head dropped to his chest, and he shrugged. "I didn't know that's what it was, right away," he said. "I thought somebody's T-shirt had got caught on a piece of driftwood, you know? In the fog, nothing looks like it should."

"Or maybe when you don't expect a body to be there, your eyes tell you it's something else," Merry said. "You didn't touch anything? Didn't pick anything up?"

"Nope." Will was studying his running shoes as he walked. "And then Rafe came."

At the sound of his name, Rafe looked over Will's head at Merry, a warning in his eyes. "Ney was howling," he said carefully. "That's something he never does. So I got there pretty quickly." Merry nodded slightly and looked down at the ground. Rafe was protecting Will. From what?

Rapid footsteps crunched along the gravel behind them, and

Peter's tall frame loomed suddenly out of the fog at Merry's side. His tanned skin gleamed with moisture, part sweat and part condensation. He reached urgently for her elbow. "I need you to talk to the paramedic," he said. It was a command, not a request.

"What's wrong, Mr. Mason?"

"He won't let me go with Rusty's body. He wouldn't even let me search his pockets."

"I'm afraid that's police procedure," she said, not unkindly, and waited for him to drop her arm. She had expected something like this from Peter Mason. Next-of-kin rarely took a death well; and they all handled it differently, the men being the most unpredictable.

"Well then, change police procedure," Peter said.

Merry lifted her purse higher on her right shoulder and drew herself up to her full five feet ten. She still had to look up to him. "Mr. Mason," she said, "you're probably feeling grief and a bit of shock. Maybe even anger. I know I would in your place. I'm sure your brother meant a lot to you, and the idea that he's been killed is pretty difficult to accept—"

"I don't need you to tell me what to feel," Peter said, his anger in his voice. *"I need you to talk to the paramedic."*

Merry stopped short and stared at him, feeling less intimidated by his family's importance and more annoyed at his manner. His strong chin, jutting brow bones, and sweep of jet-black hair were attractive, certainly—if a hawk is attractive; his gray eyes held intelligence, even when he was in a rage. But he was decidedly arrogant—an attitude she put down to off-island wealth, years of family authority, and the male desire to run things. It was hard to know whether he felt any sorrow. Probably that would come later. Now he was in a mood to take charge, as generations of Masons had done before him. Just her luck to draw the Mason card for her first big case. Merry felt a knot form in the pit of her stomach. She glanced over at Rafe and Will, the one looking wary, the other, confused; and knew she'd have to fight this one alone.

"I'm afraid I can't change police procedure, Mr. Mason, because the body is evidence," she said firmly. "There will be an autopsy. A coroner's report. We'll probably have to send fluid and tissue samples to the

31

state police crime lab in Boston. After a while, a couple of days at a minimum, we can release your brother to you for burial. We'll do our best to speed the process along, but you're going to have to live with some delay and some red tape."

"I don't have to like it," Peter said. "Rusty may be evidence to you, but he happens to be my brother." He was staring straight ahead of him, furious and unwilling to meet her eyes, his lips compressed. "I want the name of your chief," he said.

Despite herself, Merry felt the faintest finger of amusement tugging at the corners of her mouth. Her chief, indeed! "I guess that'd be Chief John Folger," she said. "He'll be in the station in another hour or so. But I'll save you the trouble, Mr. Mason. He's a bigger fan of the book than I am. He's not likely to tell you anything different."

"Folger? Is he—"

"Any relation? Yeah. He's my dad. Police work is kind of a Folger tradition on the island." She turned and began to trudge up the drive, glancing at Mason from the corner of her eye to see how he was taking it. Momentarily checked, but not beaten. He'd want to run this investigation alone. One of these days he'd probably tell her that murder needed a man's mind to solve. She'd been hearing talk like that most of her life. Well, this was her case, and she intended to solve it by herself.

If she could just persuade her father to let her keep it.

They reached the saltbox's geranium-colored door, and Peter turned the knob. The dog bolted out of Will's grasp and into the house, bound for the kitchen with the boy in pursuit. Peter stood back and waited for Merry to enter. She stepped inside the low-ceilinged entrance hall. A smell peculiar to the island—pine, salt water, roses, the fragrance of the moors, and something else she could only describe as the odor of time—drifted up from the floor. The house reeked of finished lives and the passage of years.

Peter led them to the study at the back of the house and sank into an armchair. Rafe took up a leaning position by the door to the kitchen. Merry refused a seat and stood squarely in the middle of the sea-blue rug, rummaging in her purse for her notebook and half-glasses. The intern, a Northeastern criminal justice student named Howie Seitz, stood a reluctant three paces behind her. Seitz was six feet two and his limbs were straining out of his regulation blue uniform. He had abandoned his hat, and his tanned face under an unruly mop of dark curls managed to look bored and exultant at once. He had spent his summer internship on a bicycle in Siasconset, giving directions to day-trippers and making sure some senator's kid didn't get run over on the way to the beach. Now, in his final week, he had something to talk about.

Merry abandoned her slicker, revealing khakis and a pale green crew-neck cotton sweater above the black rubber knee boots she still wore. She flipped her hair behind her ears and seemed not to notice when it slid just as quickly back down her cheekbone. An old boy-friend, in a burst of ill-advised fervor, had told her once that the soul of Medusa lived on in her hair. Her most striking feature—dark brows over eyes the color of a mountain stream—had caused her endless grief in her younger years. She had tried to bleach them blond in high school, and had suffered the horrors of orange eyebrows for a good six months. Chiefly because of the shame they had caused her, Merry thought them awful and herself just short of ugly. Those who did not know her well mistook her shyness for aloofness and thought her proud. It was one of the many miscalculations made about Meredith Folger.

She dropped her bag on the floor next to the sofa and after a second decided to sit down. She was starting to feel the hunger of an all-nighter, like a crab clawing its way out of her stomach. She shut her eyes momentarily, took a deep breath in an effort to quell her nervous-ness, and said a quick prayer that she wouldn't forget to ask anything important. Then she glanced around the study. Old maps in bird's-eye-maple frames flanked the fireplace. A partner's desk occupied one corner, while a flowered chintz sofa and a russet-colored leather chair were drawn up to a table with an inlaid chessboard. The chess-men were soldiers of some kind, and there was a game in progress. Books were everywhere. The room—comfortable, expensive, and en-tirely personal—was Peter Mason's defense against the world, and she had invaded it with her officiousness and her death. She felt light-headed, and swallowed.

As for Peter, even at rest in his chair, his body conveyed grace and power, qualities that Merry assumed were part of his genetic material. Masons had walked the world for centuries with just his brand of self-assurance and ownership; it was their birthright. His chin was resting on one palm, and he seemed to be gazing at nothing, his mind working furiously. Time to ask him some questions. She clicked the top of her pen briskly.

"Since no one recognized him, I take it your brother doesn't live here, Mr. Mason?"

He laughed suddenly, shortly, and looked at Merry. "No, my brother did not live here, Miss Folger."

Merry hesitated, then decided to press a point for authority's sake. "I prefer Detective, Mr. Mason."

"Detective. I prefer Peter, but perhaps you have rules about calling victims by their first names."

"Victims, in my experience, are beyond being called anything," Merry said. "I prefer to maintain a professional relationship with those involved in an investigation, if that's what you mean."

Peter's expression of bitter amusement widened. "So now I'm under investigation? That's perfect. And just like Rusty." He rose and crossed to the bookcases that lined one wall, filled helter-skelter with old leather-bound editions and dog-eared paperbacks, and reached for a bottle of Glenfiddich doing duty as a bookend.

"I'm sorry, Detective Folger. I'm not being very helpful, and now I'm drinking before eight in the morning." The door next to Rafe opened, and Rebecca, the housekeeper, entered on a tide of warm air and comfort. She carried a tin tray with a coffeepot, five mugs, and a basket of cranberry bread. Will followed with the cream and sugar. Rebecca pointedly ignored Merry and Sergeant Seitz as she set the tray on the low table in front of the fireplace.

Peter downed the scotch, neat, and sighed as the liquor hit his empty stomach. "Thanks, Rebecca," he said.

Rebecca shook her closely cropped gray head disapprovingly at the drink, but, showing unusual self-restraint, said nothing and disappeared back into the kitchen.

Peter crossed to his chair and sat down again, eyes alert, face in control.

"When did you get up this morning, Mr. Mason?" Merry asked.

"About six."

"How do you know?"

"I didn't check the clock, if that's what you're asking. I awoke about five—which I know from long experience of what five o'clock feels like—and couldn't get back to sleep. I lay in bed awhile and then decided to go for a run."

"Do you often run at that hour?"

"I always run at that hour. The afternoons are for biking or swimming."

Merry suppressed the impulse to ask him when he got any work done, and shot a glance at Rafe. The force behind the farm, obviously. "Did anyone see you leave?"

"Rebecca was in the kitchen. I said hello to her as I left."

"Did you call to her, or did she actually see you?"

"Why does it matter?" he said irritably.

Merry didn't answer.

"I left by the kitchen door. I assume Rebecca saw me out of the corner of her eye. She was standing with her back to me, at the kitchen sink."

"So you left the house in the direction of the moors," Merry said. "You didn't come around the house and take the drive? Perhaps leaving the gate open as you ran?"

"No. If I'd wanted to go in the direction of the drive, I'd have used the front door. I'm sorry I didn't make it easy for you and discover the body myself, but I'm a creature of habit. I run through the moors."

"Where did you go?"

"First north, toward the sea, and then down the Polpis Road toward town, and then back up the Milestone Road bike path to the Altar Rock turnoff. I was just beyond there when you roared past me in your 4×4."

"Did you see anyone while you were running?"

"No. It wasn't a morning conducive to sightseeing. More to breakfast in bed, I imagine."

"Mr. da Silva," Merry said, dismissing Peter and turning to Rafe, "could you describe your movements this morning for me?"

Rafe's lips twitched at the use of "Mr. da Silva." "I guess I got up about five-thirty," he said, "and saw to the sheep."

"Meaning?"

"Meaning I got the dog and we herded them up off the moors and drove 'em in to feed. Came in for breakfast after. That'd be about six."

"And did anyone see you?"

Rafe gave the ghost of a smile. "Herding's nothing to get up for, unless you own the sheep," he said.

"And then?"

"I went back out to the barn to check out the harvesting gear. That was when Ney started terrorizing the neighborhood. I ran up the driveway and—saw Will."

"When would that be?"

"Six forty-five, thereabouts."

"What did you do at that point?"

Rafe looked uncomfortably at Peter, and then at the floor. "We wanted to be sure it wasn't someone we knew, so I lifted the head a bit outta the water, just enough to see it wasn't, and then we left everything and came back to the house."

Peter's gaze was riveted on Rafe. "Who found the body?" he said.

"I did, Peter." Will's voice was very small and seemed to come from a farther distance than his cross-legged position in front of the coffee tray.

"Oh, Will," Peter said, turning to the boy. "Not you." He paused, looking at Will's white, stiff face.

Will flinched. "Like it matters who found him, Pete. I don't care." He stopped suddenly, and the set lines of his face crumpled and reddened. "I mean, I'm—I feel really awful about your brother, Pete, I do. I'm really sorry."

"I know, Will. It's all right." Peter held the boy's eyes, then glanced at Merry, who was watching, and waiting. She adjusted her half-glasses on the end of her nose.

"If you could give me your brother's address, Mr. Mason—"

"I'm afraid I can't help you, Detective. Rusty left the country ten years ago, and we fell out of touch. I think he was living in Brazil at one point, but I can't even be sure of that."

36

"Brazil?" She was momentarily startled, and showed it. "What was he doing in Brazil?"

"I've no idea," Peter said.

Rafe drew in his breath sharply, and Merry glanced at him. He thinks Mason is deliberately stonewalling, she thought. She turned back to Peter.

"Had he contacted you recently?"

"No."

"How about anyone else in the family? Who else is there, by the way?"

"My mother lives in Hobe Sound, Florida. I have a sister—Georgiana Whitney—who lives in Greenwich, Connecticut."

"And they said nothing about your brother coming home?"

"I think if either of them had heard from Rusty, I'd know about it. Particularly if he had it in his head to come here." Peter was staring at the floor again, his left leg crossed on his right knee, one hand nervously drumming on the tanned skin of his thigh. As if suddenly conscious of his fingers, he stopped the staccato and reached for a mug. "How do you take your coffee, Detective? Black or white?"

"White, thank you. No sugar. In other words, all of this is a bolt out of the blue."

"Yes." He was pouring the coffee very carefully, willing his fingers to stop shaking.

"Not just your brother's death, but the fact that he showed up here at all," she said, accepting the mug.

"Right. In fact, I would go so far as to say that any news of Rusty, alive or dead, would come as an unpleasant shock." Peter sat back and stared straight at Merry for the first time. His eyes were gray ice, and there was a challenge in them. Whether for her or his brother she couldn't say. An appalling thought entered her mind at that moment: Peter Mason wasn't sorry his brother was dead. In fact, the very sight of his brother seemed to have made him furious. It was incomprehensible. The body that had filled her with a sense of the fragility of human life, and the abrupt finality of death, had only made him resentful.

"Mr. Mason," she began, and stopped. It must be faced. She took a swig of coffee and felt the crab in her stomach retreat. "How well did you get along with your brother?"

"I can't see that that has anything to do with this, Detective Folger."

"When a man's been murdered, it has everything to do with it," she said quietly. "I don't think you're stupid, Mr. Mason, so I won't bother to point out that bad blood between brothers was good enough for Cain." She waited. Mason said nothing, an answer in itself, she thought. She glanced at Rafe, whose face was carefully wiped clean of all expression. *Either he knows more about this than he's telling, or he's turning it over in his mind,* she thought. She made a mental note to talk to Rafe later, alone.

"I'm afraid I have to ask you, Mr. Mason, whether you killed your brother."

Peter closed his eyes, as though suddenly weary. "It's the obvious question, isn't it? No, Detective, I did not."

"Even without meaning to? By accident, or on the spur of the moment?"

"If I had, would I have left him there in the ditch for anybody to find? Give me some credit for intelligence, please!"

"I've tried to do that. I'd ask for the same in return," Merry said, exasperated. "It's pretty hard to believe that your brother's been gone for ten years, and you didn't know he was going to show up the night he got murdered. It looks, as we'd say down at the station, like an implausible explanation."

Peter said nothing, his face darkening.

Merry flipped through her notebook as though searching for Rusty's life somewhere among its leaves. She waited, knowing Peter Mason would offer nothing further.

"Did anyone here at the farm know your brother?"

He set down his coffee cup and cleared his throat. "I think we've established that Rafe and Will never knew him," he said. "Rebecca's in the kitchen. You're welcome to talk to her on your way out. But to my knowledge she's never seen Rusty. She's only worked here since I moved back to Nantucket permanently, ten years ago. Rusty was here every summer as a child, of course, as I was. But as an adult he lived in Manhattan and rarely visited the island." He took a deep draft of coffee, wincing slightly as it burned its way down his throat. "Tell me something, Detective, if you're allowed to. How did he die?"

Merry paused an instant, weighing her answer. Her training warned against allowing Peter Mason to ask the questions. But at the moment she was wracking her brain for an opening to all that he was withholding, and maybe some give and take would help. "I think your brother drowned, basically, but how that happened I don't entirely know."

"Couldn't it have been an accident? A stumble in the dark, a blow to the head, a roll into the water, something like that?"

Meredith pulled her glasses away from her face and met Mason's eyes. "I doubt it. The crime scene unit is wrapping up its work right now, and we won't have the autopsy report for a couple of days. But from the bruises on the body when we pulled him out, I'd say he was struck with some violence behind the knees and thrown backward onto a hard surface. His skull is cracked."

Peter's eyes narrowed. "Struck by what?"

"A car bumper, I'd guess."

"A hit-and-run?" Will's voice broke as he spoke, and when they turned to him he looked suddenly ashamed and miserable.

"I don't think so," Merry said. "At least, not in the sense of an accident, which is what I think you mean, Will. There are no tire tracks coming to a sudden stop anywhere near where you found the body. He wasn't hit on the drive."

"You said he drowned, Detective," Peter said.

She nodded. "I'd like to wait for the coroner's report, of course, but it looks to me as though he was struck squarely by the middle of the front fender—a few feet down the road from the drive—went into the air, and slammed his head on the hood of the car. He'd have rolled off to one side. It's clear he didn't go under the tires—there's no sign of crushed bones, as there would be if the car had actually driven over him. I'd bet he was knocked senseless by the impact."

Peter looked at her levelly. "So whoever ran over my brother deliberately placed him facedown in the water and left him to die."

There was a small silence. "That's about it," Merry said. "He didn't walk into the bog. There's a fairly distinct drag mark, as though someone had pulled the body up the drive by the shoulders and rolled it into the water. Fragments of gravel from the drive are stuck on the fabric of your brother's shirt. It's possible there are microscopic paint chips from the vehicle that struck him lodged in the fabric as well. We just don't know yet. There's also a nice, deep set of footprints on the soggy edge of the bog that I'm having my colleagues cast right now, and a single print out on the main road. They were made by the same shoe. A set of what I think are Rusty's prints are near some tire-track patterns on the road, but there are none of his anywhere near the bog itself."

Peter stood up and crossed to the diamond-paned window that took up most of the study's far wall. Roses, coming into their end-of-summer bloom, trailed from the low eaves beyond it. The window looked out on the vivid moor, but today the view was obscured by fog.

"Are these bogs always flooded, Mr. Mason?" Merry asked.

"No," he said, "just at certain times of the year—in fall, for wet harvesting, which is harder on the berries than dry. Wet-harvested product goes to processing; dry, to the grocer. Then in winter, we flood the vines slightly and the water freezes over them. It's a form of protection. Why?"

"Could anyone have anticipated that the bogs would be flooded today?"

Peter turned to look at her, pausing to think. "We hire a team of day laborers to wet-harvest," he said, "but it's Labor Day weekend, and half of them are on the Cape shopping for their kids' back-to-school clothes. Rafe and I decided to start on a few acres today without them. As far as I know, only we knew the bog would be flooded—and Will, of course, and his mother presumably. And Rebecca," he added, as an afterthought.

"Once these things are under water, can they be drained off again?"

"I suppose so. Why?"

"I'd like you to do that. Some of your brother's effects may have sunk to the bottom. We should do a thorough search."

Peter's jaw set. "That'll delay my harvest, Detective."

"Not by much," Merry said shortly. "I think you can spare a day.

Use it to plan a funeral." She pulled on her glasses again and re-addressed her notebook. A wave of blond hair obscured her expression from Peter Mason's sight. "How many people work here at Mason Farms?"

"You're looking at the staff, Detective, with the addition of Rebecca. She lives in the cottage out back. Rafe lives over the barn. Will, of course, just comes over when he can spare the time."

"I'll need to know where each of you was after eleven P.M. last night," she said.

"I can't even drive!" Will's face was white, the blotchy shadows under his eyes that much darker.

"I didn't think you could, Will. Were you in bed at home?" she asked.

Will nodded, swallowing.

"Rebecca and I were here," Peter said, "but of course, we could be covering for each other." Merry ignored the acid in the remark and turned to look at Rafe. He was leaning forward over his work boots, studying the patches of mud on the worn leather laces.

"I'd guess I was at the Greengage until eleven," he said carefully. "Dod Nelson ran me home in his truck."

"Did he drop you at the door?"

Rafe shook his head and smiled crookedly. "At the end of the drive. And he didn't run anybody over doing it. But I guess you'll want to see his bumper."

"Will said the gate was open when he arrived. Did you close it after you last evening?"

Rafe hesitated, then nodded. "And I didn't open it this morning."

"Notice anything unusual as you walked up the drive?"

"Not a thing."

"Did either of you hear anything out of the ordinary last night—a car jamming on the brakes, a cry, a fight of any kind?"

The two men glanced at one another, but said nothing. Will Starbuck hung his head and pulled at the threads of his torn jeans.

"It's a half mile to the road, Detective. When you're inside, it's hard to hear much," Peter said.

"Is the dog loose at night?"

"He stays in the loft with me," Rafe said.

"Did he bark last night?"

Rafe shook his head.

Merry glanced down at her pad, stalling for time, wondering if she'd missed anything. She looked up and thought she saw a small expression of amusement cross Rafe da Silva's face. Her stomach contracted. "What time would you say you turned in?"

"Around eleven-thirty, or near enough."

Peter nodded. "All tucked in, Detective. Not that that lets us out. We sleep alone, after all." There was a bitterness in his voice, Merry thought suddenly, that had nothing to do with his brother's murder. Peter turned back to the fog beyond the window. "I wish I could tell you why Rusty was here and why he died," he said. "But I haven't a clue."

Merry closed her notebook. "I'm not sure that's true, Mr. Mason. It's possible you know more than you realize. I'd appreciate it if you'd think about who'd want to kill your brother on this island where no one supposedly knows him. You say he spent some time here as a kid. Maybe it's something from the past." She crossed to the leather chair and picked up her red slicker. Sergeant Seitz pocketed his notebook.

"I'd like to talk to Rebecca now, if I could."

Peter nodded distractedly, his back to the room.

As though I were invisible, Merry thought. One of the domestic help.

"Detective Folger," Peter said. "Please keep me informed."

It was not, Merry reflected, a request.

Chapter 4

Peter Mason continued to stare at the blank view through the study window, his arms folded across his chest. Rafe and Will did not intrude on his thoughts. Rafe crossed to the coffee tray and picked up a mug, tousling Will's hair as he reached past him. The corners of Will's mouth flicked upward in a poor attempt at a smile. "Have some bread, kiddo," Rafe said. Will shook his head. His knees, showing through the torn jeans, were drawn up to his chin and his arms were wrapped tightly around them. Warding off the bogeyman, Rafe thought.

"Rafe," Peter said, "do me a favor and run Will home in the Rover. We're not going to harvest today."

"But school starts tomorrow, Peter!" Will protested. "I'll miss everything!"

Peter turned to look at him and then crossed to his armchair. He sat down and leaned toward Will, his eyes intent. "You heard the good cop, Will. We're not harvesting anything for the next few days."

"Can I come over after school and help?"

"If your mom thinks you've got the time, sure," Peter said carefully. "Now run home and spend the last day of summer vacation the way you should." He looked up at Rafe, who was staring at him over Will's head.

"Go say goodbye to Rebecca and meet Rafe at the Rover," Peter said, clapping the boy on the shoulder. Will rose reluctantly and headed for the kitchen, casting a doubtful glance backward at the two men.

When Will had disappeared into the kitchen, Peter sat back in the armchair. "What is it, Rafe? Think I killed my brother?"

"Of course not, Pete," Rafe said. "But somebody did, and I don't feel that great about leaving you alone."

"What do you mean?"

"I know you. You'll head right out of this house to look for Rusty's killer. You know a lot you're not telling, and it's going to get you into trouble." He stopped short and took a swig of coffee. "That's one theory. The other's simpler, but it's much worse."

"Meaning?"

"Meaning someone's going to be surprised as hell when you show up in town today. And not very happy."

Peter ran a finger around the edge of his mug. The coffee was cold. He frowned in distaste and set it back down on the tray.

"You mean the person who thought he was killing me when he killed Rusty," he said. "I thought of that, too. But it doesn't make sense, Rafe. Who'd want to kill me?"

"Who else would they be trying to kill? Never mind why your brother showed up here last night. That's weird enough. It's too much of a coincidence to think he could get himself to your place and killed all in one day." Rafe threw himself down on the sofa and leaned forward, elbows on his knees. "Pete, the fog hadn't come in yet last night when I got home, but believe you me, you can't see the end of your nose at the end of that drive after sundown. It's black as all get-out. Anybody who caught Rusty in his headlights, wearing a Princeton rugby shirt like yours, hit the gas thinking it was you they were mowing down. *Betcha.*" He stood up and fished for his keys in his jeans pocket. "Remember that when you go looking for the guy."

Peter glanced up at his foreman and smiled crookedly. "Thanks, Rafe," he said.

The vehemence faded from Rafe's heavy features. "Aw, hell," he said. "You're not going to listen to me. But you better watch your back." He pulled open the door to the hallway. Merry Folger was saying goodbye to a friendlier Rebecca at the front door. He ducked back inside the study. "Nantucket's finest is on her way out," he said. "Think I'll give her time to get on down the drive."

Peter smiled again, genuinely this time, and Rafe grinned back.

Rafe knew very little about Peter's life before his return to the island. The youngest Mason had purchased the land with its abandoned saltbox ten years earlier, when he was just twenty-four, and had spent the next four years waiting for his fifty acres of cranberry vines to bear. He hired Rafe as foreman after that first harvest, and Rafe had been happy to stay. Over the past five years the Portuguese waterman and the Ivy League farmer had forged a deep friendship, born of common labor and love for the island. Rafe respected Peter's intelligence and strength, and counted on them to steady his own life. He was grateful to him for giving his days some structure and purpose, and he would sacrifice much to preserve Peter's peace. That Peter needed peace Rafe understood very well. He felt, rather than knew, that Peter carried a weight he never spoke of, something unhealed and festering from the past. On days when simple work and hours spent outdoors drained him of energy, the ghosts were far away. But during the winter months, when the islanders were housebound and farm work was less demanding, Peter withdrew into his books and his memories. Rafe was perhaps more necessary to him then, as friend and silent presence. Peter often wondered how he had survived the winters before Rafe came.

"Well, you're right," Peter said. "Whether I'm supposed to be dead or not, I need to find out why Rusty is. And to do that, I have to find out why he was here."

"You could let the police do their job, Pete," Rafe said.

Peter laughed. "You mean the blond bombshell?" he said. "I don't think so. The closest she'll get to figuring this out is what she told us this morning: how he died. She won't have a clue as to why."

"I'm not so sure." Rafe's voice was quiet. "She comes from tough stock."

Peter looked up. "You know her?"

"I grew up with her. Heck, everybody knows the Folgers. Her grandpa was chief before her dad."

Peter put his head in his hands abruptly in mock dismay. "Her grandfather. I *knew* Folger sounded familiar. Oh God, I put my foot in it when I asked for the name of her chief, didn't I, Rafe? The Mason family throws its weight around with the local force."

"Well, she told you pretty straight that it wouldn't get you anywhere, Pete."

"Round one to the Folgers."

"Her brother Billy was probably my best friend," Rafe said. He thrust one large hand through his mop of black hair awkwardly and looked down at his work boots. "He saved my life in Nam, and died doing it."

There was a short silence. Peter nodded. "I'll try not to disparage the local force, of whatever gender. Perhaps, if the local force displays some talent for investigation, I'll even work with them." He closed his eyes, his face suddenly weary. "But if we assume I'm the one they want to kill, I'd be an idiot to sit here and wait for them to try again. Action may be my only means of survival."

"Or a flare gun for the killer."

Peter appeared not to have heard him. "When you get back, we'll pull out the pump and start draining the fields," he said. "Wouldn't want to obstruct justice."

"Or have the cops do it for you, and ruin the fruit," Rafe said. He sighed heavily as he stood up. Merry Folger was probably long gone, and Will would be waiting patiently by the Range Rover. He'd better get the boy back to Tess. "Whistle if you need me," he said, opening the study door. Peter nodded in dismissal. The door closed quietly behind Rafe.

•　　•　　•

PETER STUDIED THE CHESSBOARD in front of him for a few seconds, and moved Napoleon—the king piece—one square to the left. Marshal Ney, his horse rearing, was about to be taken by a Russian hussar. He could not let that happen. It seemed blasphemous to fight the Russian campaign over and over again on this circumscribed board, particularly with casualties that hadn't occurred in history, but he loved the opposing chessmen. A gift from his father, two years before his death, one of the many tokens by which Max Mason had tried to show he understood his son.

He straightened Ney's horse, and then stood up. He needed a shower. Then he had some phone calls to make. He considered waiting until he had a funeral date before contacting his mother and George, wanting to delay the inevitable; and then decided against it. Rusty had the right to be mourned by someone other than himself.

Chapter 5

MERRY FOLGER GLANCED OVER at Will, sitting beside her in her Blazer. She had spotted him waiting patiently for Rafe and had seized the opportunity to take him home herself. Howie Seitz was hunched in the backseat, crammed next to Will's bike, his head shaking rhythmically to the rap music coming through his Walkman. Merry was relieved. She had expected him to cross-examine her interrogation technique during the ride back to town, and she was at a loss how to justify it. She asked the questions that occurred to her as they entered her mind, and had never done it any other way. After six years as the only woman on the Nantucket force, having worked her way up to detective, she wasn't about to follow the suggested guidelines in one of Howie's college texts. She had learned that stuff, retained what was important, and forgotten the rest. Not that you could argue with Howie. Massachusetts spending cuts had whittled the Nantucket budget for Summer Special Officers from fifteen down to one—Seitz—and he thought he was God.

They were almost to the house on Quince Street when Will spoke. "They were trying to kill Peter, weren't they?" he said. "Nobody wants to say so, but I guess that's what's going on. No one knows his brother. It doesn't make sense they'd run him over."

"They?" Merry asked. She assessed Will's profile. He was still too pale, and his brooding fascination with the horizon wasn't encouraging. "Who's they?"

"You know. Whoever did it. The murderer." He turned and looked out the side window, apparently riveted by the shop windows on Centre Street.

"I don't think we can say anything yet about who killed Rusty or why," Merry said carefully. "But that's an interesting idea, Will. Why would someone want to kill Peter?"

"I dunno. It's not like he's got any enemies. Everybody thinks Peter's terrific. Maybe it was somebody who can't stand him for that. It's how things work—if they're going well, you can't trust it. You've got to watch for trouble all the time, or it'll find you when you're not looking."

Merry pulled into the gravel drive in front of the Greengage and put the car in neutral. "Will," she said, and waited for him to look around at her. He did. She was struck by the raw worry suffusing his face. "If you can think of anything that might help me find out who killed Peter's brother, come see me." She fished into her slicker pocket and found a scrap of paper. Her pen was in her purse on the car floor. She reached for it. "Here's my phone number. You know where the police station is on South Water. Call first to see if I'm around, and we'll talk."

She opened the door and stepped out. "Howie," she yelled, trying to penetrate the rap. "Help Will get his bike out of there." Howie unfolded his bulk from the backseat and lifted the bike from the cargo area. He was good for something.

Tess Starbuck was standing at the kitchen door, holding the screen open with one hand and a towel with the other. Merry looked up at her and waved in a friendly fashion. Tess nodded coolly back.

Will took the bike from Howie and held out his hand. "Thanks, Officer," he said, and turned the wheel.

What a pathetically sweet kid, Merry thought, and then reminded herself that he was entering his sophomore year of high school. He seemed both younger and wiser.

She followed him to where his mother stood and smiled at Tess. "Don't worry, Mrs. Starbuck, Will hasn't gotten into any trouble."

"Oh, Lord, you had a fall," she said, bending down to examine his torn knee. "And these are your new jeans for school." She was exasperated, and showed it.

A spot of color came out high on Will's cheekbones, and he pushed past her into the kitchen, clearly a teenager now. "It's nothing," he said. "Torn jeans are cool."

Tess Starbuck looked inquiringly at Merry. "He was on his way to Peter Mason's cranberry farm," she said. "He left not two hours ago. Where did you come across him?"

"Could I come inside for a moment, Mrs. Starbuck?" Merry asked. "I'd like to have a word with you."

"Of course, of course."

Merry turned back to where Howie Seitz stood by the jeep. "Take the car back to the station, Howie," she said, "and start typing up your notes. I'll walk over later." He assumed his bored expression and walked around to the driver's side. She tossed him the keys.

Tess led her into the kitchen and motioned to a chair. She was clearly in the midst of prep work for the noon meal. Live lobsters, their claws bound with rubber bands, struggled to climb the sides of a galvanized tin bucket. Chopped melons and fresh mint stood near a bottle of balsamic vinegar on the butcher block counter, and the smell of a corn chowder filled the air. "I was just making some melon salsa for the swordfish," she said, motioning to the counter. Will was nowhere to be seen.

Merry sat down, the kitchen's odors reminding her sharply that she hadn't eaten in twelve hours. She shrugged herself out of her slicker. The morning had turned humid, and the coat was too heavy.

"Will did have a fall, Mrs. Starbuck, but that's not why I brought him home. I'm afraid he found a body."

She was unprepared for the impact her words had on Tess Starbuck. The woman's weathered face drained of color, and Merry was afraid she was going to faint. She pushed back her chair and reached for Tess, but the woman motioned her away and groped for the stove behind her for support.

"I'm all right," she said. "It's just that what you said, almost word for word, is how I heard of my husband's death." Tess looked down at her hands and clasped them tightly together, to keep them from shaking.

"Will found him, you see. Dan was washed overboard during that nor'easter last year. It took a week for him to turn up on shore." Her strange golden eyes sought Merry's. "The boy was frantic. I couldn't keep him in the house. He never stopped looking for his dad. And by God, he found him." She paused, staring sightlessly at her own reddened hands. "He's never spoken of it to me. I don't really know what he saw, how Dan looked. They took Will's word as identification. But he's never been the same since."

Merry knew now what she had tried to remember about Will Starbuck. A body lost in the ocean for a week wasn't a pretty sight, and it smelled like nothing on this earth. Will hadn't spoken for a month after his father's funeral, it was said. Tess had sent him to the mainland, to a cousin who was a psychiatrist, and Will hadn't finished out the school year. "I'm so very sorry, Mrs. Starbuck," she said.

"My God, I haven't even asked you," Tess said, coming suddenly back to the present. "Was it someone he knew?"

"No—at least, not really. I think he may have thought it was Peter Mason at first, but it turns out the man was his brother."

"Peter's brother? He has a brother? I didn't know."

"Apparently no one did. He hadn't been to the island for a while."

Tess Starbuck looked anxiously toward the doorway to the hall and the stairs leading to Will's attic room. "It must have been a horrible shock," she said, "if he thought it was Peter. He adores Peter. He's been like an older brother to Will."

Merry rose. "I won't take any more of your time, Mrs. Starbuck." The woman seemed not to hear her. "I'm sure he'll be okay," she said, with a cheerfulness she didn't feel. Just in time for school to start again, she thought, and he had to be the one to find the body.

Tess showed her to the door. As Merry walked down the gravel

51

drive she turned and waved. The woman raised one hand, a gesture eloquent in its loneliness. Such a small island, Merry thought, and yet so full of hidden pain.

As she turned into Centre Street, a red Range Rover sped past her, headed for the Greengage. Merry looked over her shoulder. The Rover jerked to a halt, and Rafe da Silva got out. Tess met him at the door. Merry saw the woman crumple and begin to weep, her face buried in Rafe's shoulder. His arms came up around Tess's back.

And suddenly, her face crimson, Merry turned and walked quickly toward Water Street and the station. She felt ashamed, unsettled, and dared she admit it, hurt. She thought she had forgotten Rafe da Silva.

• • •

PETER TOWELED OFF HIS HAIR and picked up the phone. He had called his mother and discovered she was in Capri, temporarily out of reach. He left a message to call him as soon as possible, and dialed Georgiana's number in Greenwich, hoping she, at least, was around. She had sense and compassion, and he had always valued both.

Four rings. The machine clicked on. The voice of his youngest niece, charming and almost unintelligible at four, came across the line. "Please—leave—a message!" Much giggling followed. Casey had clearly been coached. He sighed inwardly and waited for the beep.

"George, it's Peter. I need to talk to you ASAP. If I'm not here when you call, tell Rebecca when and where I can—"

The recording clicked off and George's voice broke into his words. "Peter! Darling! It's your own gorgeous George. Sorry about the machine, but I can't get a thing done unless I turn the phone off and answer the calls later. Not to mention weeding out the ones I've no intention of calling back. So. Tell me. How's the island? Miss us?"

The entire Whitney clan had descended on the Mason ancestral home, high on the Cliff Road, for the month of July, and Peter had played surrogate father. Hale Whitney, a director of Salomon Brothers, flew in for only two of the four weekends, while George spent much of the time at work on her travel writing. So Peter built sand castles, led bike caravans to Surfside, and rented a boat for the boys' first bluefish-ing. He had loved every minute of it. Yes, he missed them.

"George, I've got bad news." He felt rather than heard her small silence on the other end of the line, and knew she was gathering strength for calamity.

"Is it Mother?" she said.

"No. Rusty."

"Rusty?" She sounded decidedly relieved. "What's he done now? Led a coup in Central America?"

"He's dead. His body was found here at the farm." Peter shut his eyes and waited for her response.

Unexpectedly, she laughed. "But that's impossible. What would Rusty be doing on Nantucket?"

Peter said nothing. Georgiana was silent for a moment, then said, "You're not kidding, are you?"

"No," Peter said. "He was murdered, George." Another small silence. "Listen, you hadn't heard from him lately, had you?"

"Me? Rusty hated me. Why would he get in touch now? No, I hadn't heard a thing. My God, murdered? That's just like him."

"I know," Peter said, and reflected that only Georgiana could understand that essential fact about Rusty: he'd victimize them all if he got the chance. "But as you can imagine, it's made things rather awkward. Rafe seems to believe someone was trying to kill me, and got Rusty instead."

"Not likely," George said. "I imagine some of his unsavory friends followed him up here and knifed him in the back. He probably welched on a drug deal. Was it a knife, by the way?"

"No, the bog. He was run over by a car and left to drown, apparently."

George was silent for an instant. "And Rafe thinks whoever drove the car intended to wallop you," she said. "Do be careful, Peter. Do you need me to come?"

Peter thought of the ringing noise level of the Whitney household, weighed it against George's energy and intelligence, and said regretfully, "I'll let you know when the funeral date's set. Don't worry about anything until then."

"Peter," George said, and paused. He waited for the inevitable. "Have you talked to Alison since—"

"No," Peter said. "Listen, I've got to go."

"Don't you think perhaps you should—"

"I'll be in touch." He set down the receiver before she could continue, and stared in front of him. It had to be faced, and sooner rather than later. But first he would talk to Sky.

Chapter 6

HEAD DOWN, MERRY WALKED from the corner of Quince over to Broad Street, where the last of the season's tourists were setting out from the Jared Coffin House in tennis shoes and cotton sweaters. Probably headed to the Whaling Museum, she thought, to hear about Great-Great-Great-Great-Grandpa Ezra and the rest of the famous Folgers who'd made fortunes, built houses, and left their names on the island's streets, before kerosene put an end to fishing for oil. Museum business was invariably brisk when the island was fogbound; the horns and the shifting damp drove home the threat of the sea and invested the whaling past with a glamorous power. Glancing up at the gray sky, Merry decided that the island was mourning summer already; from now on even the brilliant days of September would have a note of sadness in them. She had lost her summer in relentless hours of work, compensating, she told herself, for the state budget cuts and the smaller staff. On sleepless nights, she admitted she was trying to prove something else: that she merited her promotion to detective, regardless of her father's influence or any unspoken quota for women the force might entertain; and she would keep it.

She turned to watch her reflection ripple in the storefront windows that lined Broad Street. The expensive goods catering to the off-island trade were plastered with sale stickers. Another week, and the shops on Main and Centre would be closed for eight months. Her steps slowed as she approached Mayling Stern, the New York designer's island store, which she had never entered but could not pass without surveying. No sale stickers here. The window display had changed from late summer to early fall, with a collection of hand-knit sweaters spilling out of a scarred iron-and-leather trunk. She peered into the shop, not yet lit for the day's business, and decided that if she ever became extremely rich she would buy everything inside. Her eyes strayed back to the sweater display. Perhaps if she solved the Mason murder she'd spend her fall clothing budget on one of them. But which? Merry enjoyed choosing among impossibilities. She looked closer.

Someone had propped a discreet card, penned in calligraphy, against a glass vase full of cattails: *Island Wool from Mason Farms*. Of course. With his family's retailing connections, Peter Mason's fleeces would go to nothing less than a New York designer. She eyed a mulberry-colored cardigan. An abstract geometric pattern in mustard and sage trailed across one shoulder and ended on the right front edge, where a leather toggle caught a single button.

Merry's jaw went rigid, and she felt a wave of heat wash over her. The button was of wood, cunningly made to look like ivory, and carved in the shape of a pig's head. A quick check of the other three cardigans draped across the trunk's edge revealed similar buttons, all of them representing different animals—a rabbit, a cat, and something she could only call a dragon. In her mind's eye she saw a similar button, carved in the shape of a rat, half hidden in the grass by the side of an unpaved road. She dodged around the window to the door and tried the knob, unsuccessfully, only then noticing that the shop opened at the reasonable hour of ten. She turned abruptly away from the shop window and headed toward the police station on Water Street, lost in thought. She had glanced at it only briefly, but she would swear the button she'd picked up by the dead man in the bog had been one of Mayling Stern's.

" 'The fact of the matter is, Noah Mayhew,' I said to him, 'you've not enough faith in the necessities of the Lord. Sure it's true that Hurricane Bob came through and tore your garden to pieces. And it cannot be denied that I was fortunate enough to have harvested my tomatoes two days before. But let us not forget that I listen to the radio, while you'll not have it in the house, and so were caught with your proverbial drawers down. There's no cause to hold a grudge because you're too dim to see a hurricane coming, even when it leaves calling cards all up the coast.' " The monologue was followed by a rich burst of laughter.

Merry stopped and turned around. "You're talking to yourself again, Ralph Waldo," she said.

The white-haired man striding briskly along behind her looked up and smiled. "I thought I was talking to you, Meredith Abiah. Why are your feet taking you to the station? In my day, a man thought one shift was enough."

Merry waited until he reached her and then stood on tiptoes to peck him on the cheek. She was tall, but her grandfather was over six feet, with a trim white beard and deeply tanned cheeks. "Habit, I guess," she said. "I figured I'd better write up my report before I turned in."

"Well, that explains it. In my day there was never much to report," Ralph Waldo said, and laughed heartily once again.

Merry gave him a slow smile and slipped one hand through his arm. "Walk me to the dump?"

"Only if you'll stop at the Downeyflake first. Had breakfast?" Merry shook her head, and her grandfather nodded decisively. "Thought you looked peaky. Can't write on an empty stomach."

It was after nine o'clock, and the Downeyflake had a line of break-fasters out the door. "Let's get coffee and Scotch oatcake and eat it by the wharf, Ralph," Merry said. "I need to talk to you."

He shot her a sharp glance from under his thick eyebrows—her eyebrows, as she well knew—and said, "Half a moment." She watched as he edged past the tourists waiting for tables and made for the counter. He stood upright and distinguished despite his eighty years, khaki trousers clean and pressed, his shoulders broad in a teal-blue Patagonia fleece pullover that sharpened the whiteness of his hair and the darkness of his skin. During the Depression, before he'd returned to the island and joined the force, he'd trained as a Shakespearean actor. Traces of the stage were visible still in his bearing and the cadences of his speech.

Bertha Shambles, who had ruled the Downeyflake counter for decades, beamed at him. There wasn't a woman on the island who hadn't carried a torch at some point for Chief Ralph, as he was still called, even after his son had taken over and he'd begun to talk to himself, spending his hours growing tomatoes, or scalloping in Madaket harbor. Merry wondered if he recognized his charm, if he was conscious of his minor eccentricities, and felt a fierce love for her grandfather grip her abdomen. *What the hell is the matter with me today?* she thought impatiently. *I must really need some sleep.*

"I guess you're starting to need your sleep," her grandfather said, appearing at her elbow.

"Reading minds today, Ralph Waldo?" She scowled at him and reached for one of the steaming coffee cups he held precariously in his right hand. "Don't bother, with women," he said. "You write it all on your faces." He led her to the marina that bounded the Downeyflake. Most of the boats were safe in their slips, gleaming palely in the fog. Ralph eased himself stiffly onto the dock, his legs dangling over the side.

"For instance?" she said.

"For instance, something momentous occurred on your shift, Meredith Abiah, and you are in need of advice. Either that, or you've fallen in love, but I tend to discount that possibility."

"Yeah, it'd be a shock to me, too." She sat down next to him and breathed deeply of salty sea, boat tar, and rotting fish. Rafe's face rose unbidden before her eyes, shimmering like a trick of sea-light on the water. She thrust him aside with effort.

"There's no one on the island capable of engaging your fancy, my dear, and we both know it." He took a long draft of coffee and sighed appreciatively. "I'll take Bertha's percolator any day over these auto-drip gadgets and cappuccino whatsits the current world makes so much of."

"So Ralph," Merry said, marshaling her flagging energy, "I need you to dredge your brain for Mason family history."

He cocked one eyebrow at her and took a massive bite of Scotch oatcake, chewing ruminatively, before he answered her. "I assume you're not asking idly. Masons, Masons. So many stories to tell, so little oatcake. Hang on, I'll go get us some more and think about it on the way back." He rolled to his feet before she could protest, and left her to glance at her watch and appraise the quality of the fog. She never managed to sleep during the day before a night shift, and at this point she had been up for twenty hours. A Forster's tern glided to a landing on a piling five feet away from her and eyed her cake. She broke off a bit and tossed it to the bird, knowing Ralph Waldo would disapprove.

She considered the button. If the designer and Peter Mason did business, it was possible it had been dropped long before the murder, during some sort of fashion consultation. Or Rusty Mason could have been killed by a wealthy socialite who favored Mayling Stern clothing. Or, she supposed, Mayling Stern could have taken a sudden, violent dislike to Mason Farms wool and decided to kill Peter, but had gotten Rusty by mistake. None of it seemed even remotely plausible. Perhaps she needed more coffee.

"I got you some more coffee, too," Ralph Waldo said, sliding down beside her, "which I recommend you get inside of you. Eat this piece of oatcake instead of feeding the gulls. How far back in Masonry do I have to go?"

"You can skip the founding of the island," Merry said, "but not the founding of the empire."

"That would be somewhere around 1840, I do believe, and canny John Paul Mason. Saw the handwriting on the wall when kerosene was discovered in 1839 and got his money out of whaling. By the time the rest of the island figured it out, about ten years later, the sandbar had started to block the harbor, and a lot of fortunes went out with the tide. By then, John Paul had moved to New York permanently and his clothing store was quite the rage. Pretty much ignored Nantucket for the rest of the century, except for visiting relatives. He was married to your great-great-great aunt Hermione, by the way, which makes us some sort of relation."

"You're kidding. Masons related to Folgers?"

"Masons had been marrying Folgers for two centuries at that point. But once the two families' fortunes parted ways, what with the island economy in decline and John Paul moving Hermione to New York, the habit kind of died out."

"I suppose so," Merry said shortly, thinking of the quiet, but clearly moneyed, elegance of Mason Farms. "I can't imagine two more different worlds." She felt oddly cheated. She had disliked Peter Mason enough to readily suspect him of murder. Knowing he was a distant relation brought her up short. She wondered if her antagonism was solely in response to his arrogance and apparent lack of grief—or if she had been intimidated by his status and her own lack of experience. That thought made her uncomfortable.

"Next we come to Fletcher Mason, and his son August—Fletcher's first wife died childless and then he married a German girl around 1890, but he only lived a few years after August was born. The family fortune, by the way, diversified and multiplied and revivified and whatnot. I think they set up the newspaper chain around the turn of the century. Anyway, August went off to World War I and came back a flying ace, only to die in the influenza epidemic of 1919. Poor kid. His bride was pregnant at the time and was sent off to Saratoga to avoid the flu."

Ralph chewed his oatcake ruminatively and cocked a bushy white eyebrow at his granddaughter. "Sarah Mason was a pistol, I'll tell you that, Meredith. She was a spirited young thing with a steel-trap mind who grew into a grand old dame. She ran the Mason empire—no minor feat for a woman in those days—and sent her son Max to learn the business on the retailing floor. You didn't fool with Sarah."

"You knew her?" Merry asked, startled.

"She kicked off the family habit of summering on Nantucket. Bought the ancestral home on the Cliff Road and had it restored—I'd say Sarah Mason single-handedly launched the island's tourist trade, what with all her New York society friends steaming in for those summer parties. Max and I learned to sail together."

"Ralph Waldo Folger, you do *not* sail," Merry said severely. She put down her coffee cup and turned to gaze at his profile. "And if you do, how come you never taught me?"

Her grandfather broke off a bit of oatcake and, contrary to philosophy, threw it to the Forster's tern. "Owning a sailboat and knowing what to do with it are two different things, young woman," he said. "Somehow I never managed to scrape together the price of the whistle."

Ralph Waldo viewed Ben Franklin—and his aphorisms—with affection, in part because Franklin's mother was a Nantucket Folger, albeit of cousinage much removed. He had insisted Merry's parents give her Abiah Folger's name, and disliking it, they'd compromised and placed it second. He was the only one who called her by it, and in fact one of the few people alive who knew what her middle initial stood for. Merry exhaled gustily, her breath lifting the stray strands of blond hair plastered to her forehead, slightly clammy from the fog. "Tell me about Max," she said.

"Max." Ralph Waldo steepled his fingers and thrust his long, knife-like nose into their midst. "Max is—was—a chip off the old block. Meaning Sarah, not August. He was a proud and lonely youngster, always wandering off into the moors by himself with a book and a sack of lunch, like as not gone for hours. I think, when I look back on it, that I was his only real friend; and that, probably because I accepted the friendship on his terms."

"I don't understand," Merry said.

Ralph Waldo turned and looked at her fondly, if somewhat speculatively. "No, I daresay you wouldn't, dear heart," he said. "No one is ever likely to make you conscious of your class." He laughed shortly and clasped his arms around his knees. "Max knew he was several levels above me on the social scale. He chose me to be his tagalong, as a lord might enthrall a vassal. I was happy enough to be sword-bearer and general dogsbody to the highest liver on the island. Lord, we had fun. We raced around the island in his boat and swam naked in the surf; we buried pirate treasure in the Hidden Forest, made maps, and dug it up again; we ate cranberry tarts purloined from Mrs. Hodge's window and gave the miller fits with loosening the windmill sails. For a couple of years I got through the island winters just by making plans for the summer when Max would be back. The play-acting lasted until we were suddenly too old for it."

"Meaning?"

"Meaning," Ralph said, "until women and real money entered the picture."

The tone in her grandfather's voice made Merry angry, and she was uncertain why. She mentally thrust Max Mason away and said, "You got the girl, right?"

Ralph Waldo smiled. "More or less," he said. "He went off to Princeton. Smack dab in the midst of the Depression. I took to the road and hoofed it a bit, did some vaudeville, spouted Hamlet. It was a lark while it lasted. Then I came home, married your grandmother, Swedish beauty that she was, and took a dose of real living." He glanced around him for his coffee cup, which Merry saw was empty. He raised it to his lips anyway for something to do.

"What'd Max do after Princeton?" Merry asked, relentless.

Ralph Waldo cleared his throat. "Well, he didn't marry for another twenty years, matter of fact. Guess he carried a torch for a while. Came into his fortune, which, carefully shepherded by his wise and lovely mother, had made money while others lost it. He won a contract for military uniforms in 1941, took the company public after the war, and never looked back. And we never really spoke again. Oh, once in a while, if we passed on Main Street in one July or another, I'd raise a hat and he'd nod." He paused. "I never asked your grandmother if she had any regrets."

"You know she didn't, Grumpus," Merry said, giving him the name of her childhood. "He sounds like a real prick."

Her grandfather threw back his head and laughed out loud, a clear and joyous sound that came from his depths and washed away her weepiness like a sudden wind. Merry began to laugh herself, slightly giddily, and Ralph Waldo threw his arm across her shoulders.

"Oh my, yes," he said joyously, "as his poor brood no doubt discovered."

"Why didn't you ever tell me any of this?" Merry asked him.

"I don't like to talk about my failures. And, somehow, Masons never had much to do with our lives."

"They do now," Merry said. "One of them got himself killed last night."

"Not young Peter?" Ralph Waldo turned to her with real concern on his face, and Merry felt a spark of jealousy.

"Don't tell me you're in love with him too," she said. "And he's not that young."

"So he's all right, then."

"If you consider being a suspect for murder all right, I suppose he's in the pink. A local kid found his brother drowned in the Mason Farms cranberry bog, and Peter isn't talking."

"Rusty dead. Well, well. And it couldn't have been an accident?"

Merry shook her head. "Not that Mason cares. I've never seen such indifference in a next of kin."

"He's probably being strong and silent," Ralph Waldo said. His voice held a note of reproof Merry knew was meant for her. "His kind of people don't show emotion to strangers."

"He made it very clear that he hadn't seen his brother in ten years, didn't know why he'd turned up, and couldn't care less that he's dead; and he doesn't even seem to realize that makes him look guilty as hell."

"This begins to get interesting," Ralph Waldo said. "Peter and Rusty were inseparable as boys. Peter was younger, of course, and trailed around after his brother with that pathetic adoration most teen-agers exploit unmercifully—you did it to Billy, remember, and he had you washing his car every week until your mother found out—"

"—and lectured me about feminism for the first time in my life," Merry interjected.

"I'd have thought Rusty's murder would be a terrible blow. Sure he wasn't in shock?"

"Shock my foot."

"But he was surprised?"

Merry shrugged, somewhat grudgingly. "Yes, to be fair, I'd say Rusty's body was the last thing he expected to run into this morning. My gut says he had no idea it was there." Merry met her grandfather's eyes, her own troubled. "But I can't ignore the impression I got that he hated his brother. Particularly when his brother's dead. You think this falling-out's for real?"

Ralph Waldo gave her a long look. "Meaning, he could be trying to put as much distance between himself and the corpse as a good story can buy him? I grant you, it's possible, but not likely. I've watched Peter for years, and he's never given cause for worry. Rusty, now . . ." He paused, stroking his jaw. "Rusty's the last person I'd expect to end up dead. But then, I've been wrong about Rusty his whole life."

"You know, Ralph," Merry said, "it's safest, as a general rule, to assume we'll all end up dead."

"Rusty would have argued that point, my dear. He understood power. Maybe he confused it with immortality, I don't know. He certainly pursued it relentlessly. If you'd asked, I'd have said Rusty Mason would rule the world one day, whatever world he chose. I had him pegged as Max's successor—Peter wasn't enough of a shark." He dusted his hands free of loose oats, his fingertips gleaming with butter. "I figured Rusty would eventually enter politics—not electoral campaigns, you understand, but the sort of back-room influence that means real power. A cabinet member, maybe, or a presidential adviser. I never thought he'd die young. He must have lost his hold on Fate." The lines in Ralph Waldo's skin settled more deeply into his face. He had watched over a number of untimely ends.

"What else were you wrong about, Ralph?"

"Well, he didn't succeed Max, for one thing," Ralph said. "I can't tell you why. And he's never been back to the island since the heart attack that killed his father. That'd be about nine, ten years ago now, which squares with Peter's story."

"The island's Living Memory, Ralph Waldo Folger," Merry intoned. "I didn't even recognize the guy this morning. What was he like? Beyond being power-hungry, I mean?"

Ralph hesitated. "I could say one thing or the other, and they'd both be partly right and partly wrong," he said finally. "Rusty was a tricky customer. Very good at the poker face and the unemotional voice, and next to impossible to know. He was bright in the way that's clever more than brainy, if you know what I mean—good at seeing people's vulnerabilities and using them to get what he wanted."

"Your basic privileged snake," Merry said.

"That's too easy, Meredith," her grandfather said sharply. "It ignores his most useful skill—his charm. People would do anything for Rusty. That's what made him dangerous."

"Stop indulging your dramatic side, Ralph," Merry said.

"I'm not, young woman. I'm telling you what I've seen. I ran into Rusty once or twice on what I thought was the wrong side of the law, and was never able to pin him down to it."

"Like?"

"Well, there was one bad month in the summer of '75 when the Mason household petty cash disappeared and Martha Shambles, Bertha's niece, was dismissed for it. I think Rusty took it."

"But the Masons are made of money," Merry broke in.

"Sometimes there are things you don't want to ask for," Ralph Waldo said. "Like fixing a girl's trouble when you've caused it."

"That happened? You knew that?"

"There's knowing, and there's proving," Ralph Waldo said. "Let's just say that when a sixteen-year-old summer kid started hemorrhaging one night, and had to be rushed to Mass Gen in a helicopter, some of us started to think about the Mason theft. Rusty had spent a lot of the summer with the girl, and the timing fit pretty well. But rumors never washed much with Max; he stood by his kids, I'll give him that." Ralph Waldo fell silent, as Merry turned over his words in her mind.

"And you say Peter never gave any trouble?"

"Classic case of a completely different personality admiring, in his older brother, all that he wasn't. I can't blame Rusty for his crafty ways, all the same. I saw some of his problems—his love of money, and the way he had of manipulating people to get what he wanted—as Max's fault. Max believed kids their age had too much money and too much freedom, so he kept them all on a short rein. Peter and the daughter could take it. Rusty fought it any way he could. I thought that was youth, something he'd grow out of."

"Like you think Peter's innocent now," Merry said.

"Perhaps. At my age, I'm allowed to want tragedies to have happy endings."

A deep-throated horn blared across the harbor, dominating the voices of other craft obscured by the fog. Somewhere beyond the curtain of damp, the Hyannis car ferry was rounding Brant Point. Merry shifted restlessly. Her backside was numb from sitting on the dock. "The thing is, Ralph, I'm of two minds, and I've got to pull them together if I'm going to move on this investigation."

"Sounds like sense."

"I can assume Rusty was the intended victim, and try to find out who would want to kill him, what possible motive he could have after all this time, and how he happened to know Rusty would be back on the island last night after so much time."

"Or?"

"Or I can look for a killer who thought he got Peter Mason and killed Rusty instead. You can see there's a certain sense of urgency in that."

Ralph Waldo meditated an instant, then slapped his knees, hoisted himself to his feet, and extended his hand to Merry. "Can't think of anyone who'd have any reason to kill young Peter," he said. "There's not a fellow with more integrity and sense on the island. No, Meredith Abiah, there is a tide in the affairs of men, which, when taken at the flood, can send entire families spinning off into separate eddies. Something snaps the line that binds them together. Maybe there's a tug when it happens, maybe it's so gentle it just slips apart. But mark my words, it's the severed ends of the rope you're looking for."

Merry stood up and mechanically dusted off the seat of her khakis with one hand. When had the tide taken Rafe da Silva? Somewhere in the jungles of Vietnam, or later, in a holding pen in New Bedford? A sudden wave of dizziness washed over her, and she closed her eyes, stars bursting against her lids. When she opened them, Ralph Waldo was gazing at her sternly.

"I'm going down to the wharf to buy bluefish, young woman, and I expect you to turn right around and head for home. Forget your report for a few hours and get some sleep." He pulled her close in a rough embrace. She yawned hugely against his shoulder.

"Can't, Ralph. I've still got to deal with Dad."

"I was wondering when you'd mention that," he said carefully. "Let me know if you need reinforcements."

Chapter 7

MAYLING STERN SAT CROSS-LEGGED in the red leather Adam Tihany chair, looking at the sea. She was susceptible to weather; today the gray of water and air had driven her up and down the studio in restless pacing or left her huddled wordlessly, mug in hand, before the enormous and woeful sky. The house sat high on a bluff overlooking Siasconset, its front facing into the island's past and the back addition looking out at limitless sea. Mayling had furnished each half as befit its age, seventeenth-century and twenty-first, two faces of her divided soul.

She had awakened with a groggy head, the foghorns reverberating in her skull, and stumbled for the shower. She would get nothing done today. Desultory sketches that trailed off the paper, unfulfilled; much sighing and snapping of charcoal; the knowledge that her season's creative burst was done. Time now for the decayed and stinking face of New York, smacking of life, of brilliant harlotry, of details too rapid to absorb.

She wore black, her best color, suited to the quality of light and the richness of the chair. In her lap were the discarded pages of a letter. She had profited from Sky's early-morning urge for surf casting: waiting until he disappeared into the mist; lighting a burner for the cold, full, kettle; and then, tea in hand and the envelope flap carefully steamed, opening the letter with her nail file. She had read it three times and knew the words by heart.

At the sound of the light footsteps springing up the staircase from the ground floor, she shot to her feet, scattering the pages. A black head rounded the doorway, and she gave a small gasp.

"Peter!" She shut her eyes and reached for the back of the chair.

Peter's smile of greeting faded. "Mayling," he said, crossing to her side. "What's wrong?" The color had drained from her face. "Sorry I scared you. I knocked, but you probably can't hear me up here."

"Forget it," Mayling said, opening her eyes. "I'm fine. I startle easily when it's foggy. Everything's both muffled and louder than usual, if you know what I mean."

"Let me help you with those," Peter said, as she bent quickly to pick up the discarded letter.

"I said I'm *fine*," she said sharply, glancing up at him. Her brown eyes were furious, and he flinched as though he'd been slapped. She scuffled the loose sheets into a pile, found the envelope beneath the chair, and left the room.

•   •   •

PETER SAT DOWN ON AN OTTOMAN, stifling the impulse to follow her. Mayling was moody enough, but rarely without reason. He was convinced she had thought he was someone else. Who? Sky? And what could be so important about a letter?

He glanced around the studio, his eyes adjusting to the dim light, wondering why she hadn't bothered to turn on the bronze lamps that hovered, UFO-like, in the space of the vaulted ceiling. He stood up restlessly and wandered over to the drafting table, where a single black spotlight threw a pool of brightness onto the paper. He had lied when he told Meredith Folger no one on the island knew Rusty. But he was determined to talk to his oldest friends first before he subjected them to her questions. They deserved to hear of Rusty's death from him alone. The detective could grill them in a few days. Maybe by that time he'd know who had killed his brother.

He glanced down at the drafting table. Mayling hadn't done much. A heavy red cross was drawn through the only sketch on the page. He leaned closer to examine it, curious, and saw that it was the last thing he had expected: a wedding dress. He felt suddenly self-conscious, as though he'd gone through her drawers, and turned away from the table. She'd never done a bridal line before. There was no hint of one in the works when he surveyed the bolts of silk and wool from her winter collection, stacked in the studio's corners. He reached out to finger a length of mohair the color of oxblood and smiled involuntarily. He was starting to speak Mayling's vernacular. Her names for colors—Anthracite, Ming Blue, Pomegranate—had never come naturally to him.

She had recovered when she returned to the room, her eyes clear and her smile carefully sustained. He decided not to probe.

"I hope I haven't missed Sky," he said.

"No, but only just. This is a twenty-four-hour trip—he's flying back tonight."

"He may not be going anywhere if the fog holds."

"That'd be nice, Peter. I'll hope for it. It's good to see you," Mayling said. "Every summer I envision weeks of things we can do together, and then summer disappears." She threw herself down on the chair and swung her legs over one side. "It's gone for good now, and I'm ready to be back in New York. It happens that quickly. I may go back with Sky."

"When I was a kid I hated this weekend," Peter said. "Because it meant loss—the end of my time here and the start of ticking off the months until I could return. I never really felt home was anywhere else."

"Except Princeton," Mayling said.

"Except Princeton. At night, when the past and the ghosts were all around you."

"You're a romantic, Peter. A romantic with sense."

"That sounds like a fast trip to hell."

"No!" Mayling protested. "You have sense enough to know when you're at home, and stay there. Most of us hunt for it all our lives." She looked wistfully out at the sea. "Sky is fishing," she said. "You can't see him from here because of the fog."

"Up or down?" Peter said.

"I assume toward Sankaty Light. It's one of his haunts." She looked back at him and for the first time seemed really to see him: the exhaustion around the eyes, the smile on the lips not reaching above them. "This isn't a social call, is it, Peter? Is something wrong at the farm?"

His gaze met hers, slid away. "Yes," he said carefully. He looked behind him for the mate to her chair, and eased himself into it. "It seems Rusty came back to Nantucket last night. His body was found in the bog early this morning." He paused. "I figured Sky was the person to tell. No one else here knew him as Sky did."

"Or loved him like that," Mayling said. Her voice sounded as though she found it difficult to breathe. "I'll come with you."

Peter looked at her narrowly, and then laughed, a short, harsh sound. "Nine out of ten people would have asked two questions, Mayling," he said. "What was he doing here, and how did he die. But not you. You've already gone mentally ahead, to Sky, and you can feel what he'll feel. You're saving your worry for him. What is it like to lose yourself in someone that completely?"

"You should know, Peter," she said. "You lost your soul to Alison years ago."

He saw that she regretted the words as soon as they left her mouth.

"I'm sorry, I've been impossible all morning," Mayling said in a rush. "Just let me get a sweater."

"Don't, Mayling," he said, reaching out his hand as if to pull her back. "Don't. I'd like to see him alone, if I could."

"I said I was sorry, Peter."

"I know. But I want to talk to him by myself. The death is only half of it, Mayling. You can deal with that later. It's the murder I've got to discuss with him now."

.   .   .

Schuyler tate-jackson's jeans were rolled up to his knees, a mark of the skinniness of his long legs. The Atlantic Ocean swirled around his calves and numbed his toes, raising gooseflesh he disregarded in his eagerness to land a bluefish. Never mind that they preferred deeper

71

water. His line, cast twenty yards into a wave, was taut as a bowstring, and his rod was curved into a question mark pointing out to sea. Something, blindly, had taken the hook, and Sky was determined to know what it was. He played the fish, letting it tire, praying the line would hold. In his teeth he clenched a pipe. The wind had ruffled his hair into a feathered mess of gray and black. He wore the oilskin hunting jacket Mayling had given him for Christmas, and he looked, Peter thought, completely happy.

Peter stood just out of line of Sky's peripheral vision a few seconds longer, avoiding what he'd come to do and wishing that his friend's day could continue as he'd planned it. This is how God feels the second before a car swerves into an overpass, he thought, or the instant before a heartbeat stops; the desire to suspend time and keep it somehow from grinding to its natural end. I've made myself the marker between now and whatever comes after.

Unexpectedly, Sky turned and saw him. He pulled the pipe from his mouth with his free hand. "Peter!"

So much for controlling fate. Peter kicked off his Top-Siders and walked splashily into the surf.

"I think I've got a big one," Sky said.

"This the new rod?"

Sky nodded and shoved the pipe back into his mouth. The fish was almost done, its darting runs less vigorous and panicked, as though a gear inside were running down. Sky reeled it in, stopped, reeled some more. "It's coming," he said around the pipestem.

Peter watched in silence, and then bent for Sky's net. As the fish came into the shallow water he scooped it up, gills heaving, eyes blind in the waterless air, its body jackknifing in the mesh. Sky threw down the rod and carefully lifted the blue out of the net in triumph. "All summer," he said, "*all summer,* and not a one. You free for dinner?"

"You'll have to catch more than that if you're going to feed three, buddy," Peter said. "I think I'll let you have it all to yourself." Sky bent down and started working the hook free from the fish's mouth.

"I need to talk to you," Peter said.

Sky hefted the fish in his hands, estimating its weight. "Something wrong with the farm?"

"No."

Sky looked up and focused for the first time on Peter, his teal-blue eyes wide and steady. He waited.

"It's Rusty."

"Rusty. He got in touch with you." He said it as if it were expected, although he knew Peter'd never given his brother an address.

"He didn't. But he may have been trying to," Peter said. "Sky— somebody killed him out at the farm last night. We found his body this morning in the bog. The police think he was run down by a car and left to drown. We'd flooded the cranberries yesterday for wet harvesting, you see."

Sky stared at him wordlessly for several seconds, the fish dangling. "Rusty," he said again. He sat down in the surf, salt water cascading over his jeans, and stared at his hands. "The bog?" He looked up at Peter, and his face contorted horribly. "My God, what was he doing there? You say he drowned?"

Peter nodded. Sky looked down at the fish, its gills still fighting for air, and suddenly threw it back into the water. He turned his head aside and vomited.

Peter waited until Sky stopped shuddering and then extended a hand to help him up. He groped in his back pocket for a handkerchief and then remembered he never carried one. Sky filled his hands with salt water and doused his face. He kept his hands over his eyes a moment, feeling the cold shock of the water, wanting it to clear his head. Then he stood up.

"Peter," he said, somewhat unsteadily, "tell me you didn't do it, for God's sake."

"I didn't do it," Peter said. "I've given you cause to think me capable of anything. But I didn't do it, Sky. Never."

Sky nodded, and looked around vaguely for his fishing tackle.

"I'll walk you back," Peter said, picking up the rod and net. "I've already told Mayling."

"I always thought if there were news of Rusty," Sky said, "that I'd be the one telling you. I was the one he talked to, the one who got the letters. Why was he on the island? Why didn't he call me?"

"I was hoping you could tell me, Sky," Peter said. "That's why I'm here."

Sky looked ruefully at his jeans, which clung to his body like a wet-suit. "Let's get back to the house. We can talk after I change."

· · ·

THE STATION ON SOUTH WATER STREET had the air of a retail store on Christmas Eve: the end of the high season was almost in sight, with peace and sanity hovering on the horizon. Labor Day meant the summer people were on their way home—all excess thirty thousand of them. Another week and the island population would settle into its winter numbers, with the drug dealing and the drunk driving, the boat thefts and the petty shoplifting, receding for another year. The traffic that choked Main Street would trickle away; the boatloads of day-trippers would dump fewer and fewer tourists in need of directions, public bathrooms, and first aid. Errant bikers going the wrong way on the town's one-way streets would have fewer head-on collisions with New York lawyers' BMWs. Off-island teenagers would cease brawling in alleys on Saturday nights. And after a week of relief, the force would be restless and bored.

Ten of the island's finest were lounging around their desks like runners at the end of a race, some with their feet up and their chairs tipped back, others preparing to head out onto the streets for the season's final patrol. They were deeply tanned, solidly built, fresh-faced, and fairly young; most were off-islanders to begin with, and few stayed on the island longer than five years. They were all male. Several pairs of eyes glanced casually at Merry as she walked into the main office, then looked down. Word of the murder was out.

The division of criminal investigation had eight officers assigned to it. She knew Randy Garrett was following up a case of arson; Wendell Case was on leave for the next two weeks; Phil and Tom Potts, brothers and islanders, were about to close a sting operation targeted against cocaine dealers working both Nantucket and Martha's Vineyard from a fleet of yachts. Everyone else was too junior. She could make a case.

Merry threw her red slicker over the back of her desk chair and dumped her large, shapeless plastic leather bag on the floor. She locked her fingers together and thrust them toward the ceiling, stretching to her full height and looking more than ever like a lean and fine-boned cat. It was important to seem relaxed, confident, instead of exhausted and nervy as she really felt. To ignore Matt Bailey—*the snake*—sitting twenty feet away and staring at her over his coffee cup, as he calculated her chances of holding on to the case. She picked up her notebook and then felt around vaguely for her reading glasses. She'd left them in the pocket of her slicker. She reached for them and smelled the fog—wet macadam, damp car interiors, the animal odor of soggy hair—rising from the coat.

"Thanks for the legwork, Mere," Bailey said. "When you get the notes typed up, leave a copy on my desk."

Merry turned. Matt had finished his coffee. He was leaning back in his desk chair, his dark head cradled in his arms and his feet up on his desk. He was grinning. She felt her face begin to flush crimson.

"What the hell are you talking about?" she said slowly.

"The Mason murder. That call you logged around seven A.M."

"I know when I logged the call, Matt. You were still in bed."

"Yeah, well, you can head home and get some rest. Your dad gave me the case. I'm glad you went out there, Merry—none of the guys types as well as you do."

"My *dad* is Chief Folger to you, Bailey," Merry said through her teeth. She slammed her chair into her desk and turned away from him in a rage. She made straight for the glass-walled office in the corner of the room where her father sat reading the paper over his second cup of coffee.

Matt watched as the glass door shook behind her. Then he chuckled softly.

•   •   •

"YOU CAN'T KEEP DOING THIS to me," Merry said. She was shaking with anger, and her hands were braced on the edge of her father's desk. He

75

looked up at her over his paper, and his light blue eyes were flat and icy.

"Control yourself, Meredith. I have nothing to say to you—"

"The hell you don't."

"—until you can speak in a normal tone of voice. Let's try this again. Good morning, Detective Folger."

Merry turned away from his desk and yanked one hand through her blond bangs, tugging at them in frustration. She reached for the door-knob and then dropped her hand. She folded her arms, took a deep breath, and turned back to face him. "Good morning, sir. It looks like a fine day, sir. A perfect day to resign, sir."

John Folger's expression didn't change. He motioned to the wooden captain's chair shoved stiffly against one wall. Merry hesitated. She felt more powerful standing. Her father didn't blink. She took the chair.

"Now tell me about the Mason case," he said.

"You mean the case you took away from me?" Merry said bitterly.

"I didn't know I'd assigned it to you."

"Yeah, well, anyone else who was first on the scene, and who had my seniority, would be allowed to the keep the case. Not to mention that I'm the only one free right now. Or did you take Bailey off the Atwater vandalism?

"Bailey expressed an interest in handling a murder. Vandalism isn't up to his talents."

"What about mine?"

A muscle in her father's cheek twitched. He was beginning to get angry. But otherwise, his face betrayed nothing. He had a talent for suppressing emotion that had served him well as chief—particularly when dealing with his daughter.

"Your talents are considerable, Meredith. So are your vulnerabili-ties. I don't think you're ready for murder."

"No, that's not quite true. You just don't think *any* woman is ready for murder."

"I wonder if the public is ready for a murder investigation headed by a woman, but that's different. I don't have any control over the con-fidence of the public. I *can* control my officers' caseloads. I gave the case to Bailey because I think he's tougher than you are." As Merry started to protest, her father raised one hand. "The Masons draw a lot of attention, on-island and off. They're also the sort of people who demand results fast. I'm not sure you can handle the pressure."

Merry swallowed, remembering her nervousness that morning. Still, she had overcome it, and asked Peter Mason some tough questions; her heart cried out that she deserved her father's trust. "I've got two years' seniority on Bailey. I've logged more hours of training and crime scene unit experience." She began to pace back and forth in front of the chief's desk, and then stopped, glaring through the glass wall at Bailey, whose feet were still propped on his desk. He seemed less than eager to pursue her case. "Hell, I've got more balls than that guy, Dad!"

"Meredith!"

She turned back to him, and this time forced herself to face the hard blue eyes. "My problem is that I've got my father for a chief. I've got a boss who's so worried he'll be accused of favoritism that he treats me as if I'm the worst officer on the force." She placed her hands on the edge of his desk and leaned over him for emphasis, not caring, now, how he might respond. "I had to fight you to get promoted to detective. Now I've got to fight you to be allowed to do my job. Well, I'm not sure it's worth it. I've been proving myself to you for so long I'm beginning to wonder if there's anything that could convince you I'm as good as I know I am. Maybe I need to move off the island and work for somebody who'll treat me fairly."

John Folger shot out of his chair, and the pencil he held in his right hand snapped in two. He threw the ends down on the desk. "I'm going to assume you need sleep, young lady. I'm going to send you home to get it and overlook what you've just said. And I'm giving you two weeks off to get your head on straight."

"I don't need two weeks off," Merry said. "I need a break." She met his eyes and held them. "I need you to stop protecting me from the ugliness in the world, Daddy. I need you to let me do my job."

"And you think murder is your job," he said.

"Solving crime is what I've been trained to do. I've known that for years. When are you going to accept it?"

John Folger glared at her. Then he cleared his throat and sat back down in his chair. There was a pause while he carefully fitted one shattered end of the pencil into the nub of the other. "I never wanted this for you, Merry," he said. His eyes flicked up to hers, and she could see his pain. "Your mother didn't want this for you."

"Oh, God, how long is that going to matter?" Merry cried out in exasperation. *"I'm your daughter, too.* I'm not Mom. I'm not going to go nuts when things get tough!"

She stopped abruptly, appalled at what she had said. Her father's face had turned to stone, and his hands were trembling slightly.

"Get out of here, Meredith," he said quietly. "Just go, now."

Chapter 8

S KY'S STUDY WAS IN THE OLD HALF of the house. It was a small room, and dark, overlooking the 'Sconset street—a room better suited to lamplit reading on cold November nights, of a kind Sky never spent on the island. Mayling had used cherry silk for the drapes that hung against the mahogany wainscoting, and picked up the warmth with a paisley print on two large easy chairs drawn close to the fire. An orange-and-black banner hanging on one wall proclaimed Sky a member of the Princeton class of 1979.

Peter slouched against the massive desk, idly looking at pictures, while he waited for Sky. Mayling's face shone out of one frame; in another, she stood next to a fashion runway, a slightly bewildered expression on her face. Peter imagined that she was searching beyond the lights for Sky, even as he had taken the picture.

He picked up a black-and-white shot of a Princeton rugby game, an exhausted Sky throwing his arm around an exultant Rusty. Peter remembered that year, his first at college. He had stood on the sidelines and watched the senior god, his brother, and known then he could never play rugby at Princeton. He set the frame down and frowned.

When Rusty disappeared, Sky had tried to transfer his friendship to Peter. He had not been completely successful. Hurt and lost without a brother he'd once loved, Peter had resented Sky's efforts to take Rusty's place. As he had gotten older and come to know Sky better, he understood that Tate-Jackson had needed him to fill a void, and that he had failed him. Mayling, who had never known Rusty, was necessary to both of them, a buffer against their memories.

"What do the police think? They've been out, of course."

Sky stood in the doorway. Peter turned, his fingers tracing the inlaid fruit on the desk's surface.

"They practically woke me this morning."

"You found the body?"

Peter shook his head. "No, that's the real tragedy. The one person who should never have seen it—Will Starbuck—had to be the one to find it. Rafe called the police. I had gone out for an early run, and only got back after the ambulance and whatnot had arrived."

Sky threw himself into a chair and reached for the box of foot-long matches. "And?"

Peter sat down and pressed his fingers against his eyes. "They think he was struck by a car sometime after eleven P.M., knocked out by the blow, and then dragged to the bog, where he was left facedown to drown."

"A car?" Sky stopped short in the act of lighting the fire, startled, then assumed his professional mask of concentration. In the time it had taken to change his clothes, Sky had managed to distance Rusty's death in order to assess it as Peter's lawyer. His mourning was something only Mayling would see, and then only when he could contain it no longer. "Who's handling the case?"

"A Detective Folger. A woman."

Sky's eyebrows shot upward. "What's she like?"

Peter shrugged. "A little abrupt. She struck me as tentative and somewhat nosy, but maybe that's my discomfort with being a murder suspect. She's not very old—maybe thirty. Rafe says she's competent."

"And what do you think?"

There was a pause. "I think she's beautiful and doesn't know it, or doesn't care. And yes, if she'd been a man I wouldn't have commented on her looks. So shoot me."

"Peter—"

He threw up his hands. "I don't know! For God's sake, I've never done this before. I don't know how to rate detectives."

"This is important," Sky said, and his tone was in deadly earnest. "She's going to want to know why Rusty was here."

"And I can't tell her that, Sky," Peter said evenly. "I don't know. I may never know, now."

"If the extent of your—falling-out—were known, it could place you in an awkward position. You realize that, of course."

"Yes," Peter said impatiently. "But right now it's not the main thing on my mind. I know I didn't kill him, and I don't much give a damn if the Nantucket police aren't convinced. That'll sort itself out. Right now, I've got to figure out why Rusty was killed. Because there's a strong chance he was killed by accident. Someone may have thought he was me."

There was a pause. Sky gazed at the fire, which was catching slowly, the wood too green. His long, thin fingers were loosely clasped in his lap. "You don't believe that, Peter," he said. "No one has the slightest reason for wanting to kill you."

"I agree. Personally, I think it far more likely that Rusty was the target. It's possible he was fleeing whoever killed him when he came to the island. An animal gone to ground. I need to know more about what he was doing, Sky, if I'm going to figure this thing out."

"Was he carrying anything that might help? Luggage? Any—documents, or letters?"

"Not even a matchbook, apparently. Although it's possible the police aren't telling me much. They should be back in a few days with the results of the autopsy."

Sky shifted in his chair. "If you're concerned about the quality of the police, we could call in an investigator. The firm uses a number of them."

"This isn't like tracking an adulterer."

"Our firm has never handled domestic disputes, you know that," Sky said. His tone was sharp. "Nor personal injury."

"Just corporate graft on a grand scale. I know. That's not the point." Peter stood up and began to turn back and forth in front of the fire. "Listen. The fact that Rusty came back here to die means something to me, Sky. He was in trouble, and for whatever reason, he needed to talk to me. The fact that he didn't get in touch with you only confirms it. Rusty was a proud bastard, you know that. Nothing but desperation would have brought him back to this island, and nothing but mortal fear would bring him to my door."

"Unless your premise is wrong," Sky said.

Peter stopped. "Meaning?"

"Perhaps Rusty was returning in triumph. Perhaps he'd come back to settle an old score, from a position of strength. And perhaps, without realizing it, he strayed into the path of a killer who thought he was you."

"So you haven't ruled that out," Peter said.

Sky gave him the ghost of a smile. "I'm a lawyer, Peter. I consider the case for both sides. Have you stopped to think who might want you dead?"

Peter looked away, embarrassed. "I'm not that interesting."

"No rival cranberry farmer who'd kill for your market share?"

"The only other bog is a collective on preservation land, you know that. You drew up our agreement for sharing the water rights to Gibbs Pond. Nobody connected to it has any reason to want me dead. Dollar for dollar, I spend more maintaining the sluice gates than they can afford to."

"Scorned any women with bad tempers and big cars?"

Peter smiled crookedly. "I'd have to look at them first, and you know I haven't done that in years."

"Pity," Sky said, then added swiftly, "If I remember correctly, Georgiana's children are the main beneficiaries under your will."

"I left some stock to Princeton and the cost of an Ivy League education to Will Starbuck."

Sky studied him a moment. "I'd put that at about one hundred and fifty thousand dollars by the time he's ready to go," he said. "Does his mother know you did that?"

"Come on, Sky, Tess isn't the type to hang around my gate at midnight hoping I'll just happen to walk in front of her pickup," Peter said.

"Did she know her son would benefit by your death?" Sky persisted.

"I may have mentioned I'd like to help him with college at one time or another," Peter said grudgingly, "but I never told her I'd remembered him in my will. I've discovered how proud she is."

Sky grunted. "That would be incentive to keep you alive, then. I suppose we can rule out material gain as a motive. Barring a psychopath, we've come up with nothing."

"A big *nada*," Peter agreed. "Which brings us back to Rusty. And all that you know and I don't."

Something in the line of Sky's shoulders stiffened, and the set expression he adopted for particularly difficult clients came over his features. "If you mean the background to Rusty's business ventures, Peter, I probably know very little more than you do," he said.

"Rusty's dead, Sky. You don't have to protect the sacred flame any longer. I need you to tell me what you know."

Sky stared wordlessly into the fire. "I've said that I know nothing. And I'm not sure that knowing will satisfy your curiosity anyway, Peter. You're still the little brother, aren't you? Wanting to share his secrets? They're probably not pretty. I'm glad to live in ignorance."

"But he told you something," Peter said. "About that last break with my father."

Sky shrugged. "He showed up in Cambridge, in a snowstorm, the night it happened," he said. "But he wasn't talking about details. By that time, all he wanted was to get out of the country."

"Max and Rusty never got along that well," Peter said. "Both of them knew Rusty was bound for the business; Max needed him and Rusty was good at what he did. He had that kind of brain. But they were always looking at one another out of the corners of their eyes, like two guys stopped at a red light, waiting for green. They were ruthless, they both had a will to power, and neither trusted the other."

"I know," Sky said. "Max loved you, and feared Rusty. I don't think Rusty ever forgave him for trying to keep him down as a kid."

"Why do you think Max cut him off from the business and the family? What could he have done to warrant that?"

Sky looked up at him. "I suggest you ask your mother."

"I did. She doesn't know. Neither does George."

"Whatever it was, it was ten years ago. I can't believe it has anything to do with Rusty's death."

"But on the chance that it might, you've got to tell me what you know. I'm the one person who can piece this together. You don't have the time to spare away from New York. I'm here, I can follow things up and work with the police."

"I think you were the one person, above all, that he never wanted to know," Sky said. "How ironic it is. What's the time, Peter?"

Peter glanced at his watch. "Ten of three."

Sky cocked an ear toward the Atlantic, his entire body listening. The faint bellow of horns drifted into the stillness of the room, and a log in the grate hissed. "The fog persists," he said. "They'll have closed the airport anyway—I'm not going to get out tonight. Where do I start?"

"How about December 1982," Peter said. He sat down in the chair next to Sky and stretched out his long legs. His calves ached from the aborted run earlier in the day; amid the confusion and police, he'd forgotten to stretch.

Sky gave him a sidelong glance. "After Alison. Very well. December 1982. That palmy time in the halls of trading. Rusty had been working for three years at Salomon. He had made an enormous amount of money for someone twenty-five years old." Sky stood up and poured himself two fingers of sherry, his favorite drink when fog engulfed the island, and began a slow procession back and forth in front of the hearth. The wine's gleaming depths threw back the light of the fire as he lifted the glass to his lips. "But '82 was a recession year, you remember? It hit the market hard. Rusty decided to bail out and was applying to business schools for the following September."

"I remember. I was filling out law school applications around the same time."

"Fortunately, you didn't mail them," Sky said, and for an instant the expressionless mask shifted and he smiled at Peter. "The world would be much diminished without Mason Farms."

"Thank you. I would be, too."

"I think he intended to sit the economy out for a couple of years, earn a degree, and then join your father at Mason Enterprises." He paused, swirling his glass, then looked searchingly at Peter. "But maybe that began to seem too safe. I don't really know what he was feeling or thinking at the time, I only know what he did. Can you understand that?"

"Perfectly. I always felt that way about Rusty. He was impossible to read."

"He kept himself under tight rein. When he was in the grip of some passion, he was extremely volatile. I'd seen it for years, under different circumstances: before a really big game, or when he was about to pull off a major deal, he'd have an air of genius—and of danger, of instability. During those moments, or weeks, I used to feel he'd gone beyond me, somehow, that anything he'd felt for me had receded in his mind, and that I didn't really know Rusty at all. But to be around him then was the most exciting living I've ever done. He could enslave anyone in that mood. December 1982 was one of those times."

Peter shifted uneasily in his chair.

"How much did you know about the family business in those days?" Sky asked. He got up and walked over to the desk, fishing in a cubbyhole for his tobacco and a cherrywood pipe. His restless progress through the room struck Peter as the restrained man's method of warding off fear. The muscles of Sky's back were tensed and wary under his chamois shirt.

He shook his head. "I was never an heir presumptive, Sky. Mason Enterprises has always gone on around me, like the postal system or weather reports."

"Happily for ME, somewhat more efficiently."

"I wasn't in particularly good shape anyway, that Christmas. I'd spent most of the autumn holed up alone in the Cliff Road house, musing on fate and my wounded soul."

"That's right, you would have been. I suppose Rusty lived dangerously most of that year, didn't he?" Sky turned back to the fire, looking, Peter thought, curiously relieved. He sat down. "But Alison was nothing next to power."

"What do you mean?"

Sky struck a match and cupped it closely over the bowl of the pipe. Peter waited.

"I don't know the details," Sky said, "but I think he tried to profit from a merger Max was planning, and it went awry."

"Rusty didn't work for Max."

"Exactly," Sky said. "From what he said before the whole thing blew apart, he got wind of a deal Max was putting together and tried to buy a chunk of stock."

"Insider trading?"

"Basically."

Peter studied the fire as he mulled over this information. Then he looked up at Sky, somewhat impatiently. The lawyer was consciously avoiding Peter's eye. "I figured out that much on my own, Sky. It had to be insider trading, given the business Rusty was in and the fact that a lot of traders got in over their heads around that time. Even though the federal grand jury came down with a sealed indictment once he bolted the country, it was pretty clear that securities fraud was the issue." He paused. "But that's not enough. Max would have fought something like that with the best lawyers he could buy. He'd have loved the challenge, even if it was ME stock Rusty'd played with. Instead he cut his son's legs out from under him and went home to die. Can you see what that means?"

Sky drew on his pipe and said nothing.

"It must have happened before Christmas," Peter said. "I remember. I'd gone back to Greenwich for the holidays and when Max showed up that night, Rusty wasn't with him—I flattered myself that he was avoiding me. But I'd never seen Max look like he did that entire holiday. He was in the grip of a cold, white-knuckled fury. On Christmas Eve he stood up and raised a toast to Masons dead and gone, and he added Rusty's name to the list. That was it. A flat announcement that he'd cut my brother off. My mother went nuts. But he never told her anything."

Sky's face was wooden.

"Once Rusty left the country, Max wouldn't even hire a lawyer on his behalf, despite the grand jury that investigated his personal trading. Max died that January, you know," Peter said. "A massive heart attack. No one knew how to reach Rusty to tell him."

"It's a year we've all tried to put behind us."

Peter chose his next words carefully, studying Sky's face. "We got almost no information out of that grand jury. We weren't even allowed in the room. But you were deposed by the prosecuting attorneys, Sky. What did you tell them?"

He reached up and pulled his pipe out of his mouth, then slapped the tobacco into the grate. "Nothing but what I've told you, Peter. Rusty didn't tell me much. Probably didn't want to incriminate me."

"I've thought for years that it must have involved a personal betrayal so deep, and so monstrous, that Max could never bear the sight of Rusty again. It seemed the only thing that could explain the rage— the profound bitterness—that marked his last months."

"They're both dead," Sky said sharply. "None of this has anything to do with what happened last night."

"Wait. Let's think for a minute as Rusty would have. It's 1982. Max has a deal going down—no surprise, he lived and breathed them, but this one is special. What could it have been? Let's suppose it was something risky, and big; something Max was betting the store on." He stopped, his brows knit in concentration, gray eyes seeing deep into the past. "Let's call it a hostile takeover. Here's Rusty at Salomon—Max's major underwriter. Let's suppose Rusty has the sort of information a trader would die for—he knows when Max is going to move, he knows the target, he knows the status of negotiations with the banks; he stands to make big money on commissions."

"I think we've already established that," Sky said.

"We're not going far enough. Think, Sky. If you had that sort of information, and you were Rusty, what would you do?"

Sky said nothing. Peter leaned back in his chair and stared at the ceiling thoughtfully. A section of the top log popped and showered the grate with sparks. Sky jumped. Peter looked at him intently, his eyes flat and cold, and opened his mouth to speak.

Sky preempted him. "This doesn't get us anywhere," he said, and stood up restlessly. He was telling Peter, in his well-bred fashion, to get out of his house.

Something in Peter's face changed as he looked at him. Then he drew in his breath and let it out slowly. "Maybe you're right."

"I know I'm right. This was ten years ago. Rusty was spooked by a brush with the law and he did a stupid thing—he ran. If you want my opinion, it was the running Max couldn't forgive. And Rusty couldn't stand the embarrassment of coming back."

Peter got to his feet and turned his back to the fire. The late-summer day was ending prematurely, the sun lost in the fog, and the old house felt drafty. "You're right, of course. None of this tells us why he was here when he died."

"I find it hard to believe this murder has anything to do with the past. No one knows the facts of what happened, other than your father. And he's dead." Sky looked at him suddenly, a wave of surprise stealing over his face. "They both are, aren't they," he said.

Peter turned and reached for his light jacket. Sky thrust his hands in his pockets, swaying a little back and forth on his long legs as if about to say something, then changed his mind and made for the door.

"I'd think about taking the back way home, if I were you," he said, one hand on the polished cherry doorknob. "There's going to be a lot of press at your gate. You're the closest thing to the Kennedys Nantucket's got, and people love a scandal."

· · ·

PETER TOOK SKY'S ADVICE and made for the Polpis Road, the frame of his aluminum bike bucking stiffly over the occasional stone and his progress swift in the windless air. He pedaled unconscious of the effort involved, past Sesachacha Pond, his mind wrestling with the dark tangle of his brother's past. He was certain Sky knew more than he would say. He dismissed the reasons for his silence—loyalty to Rusty, a lawyer's innate discretion, fear of some kind; they could wait. More important was the thread he had picked out of the woof of the past, the fragile link between all that had gone before and the blood on his doorstep.

Rusty had traded on information about a merger before that merger had occurred. Well and good. Peter was convinced the merger had been of Max's planning, between ME and another company. Why had this particular deal drawn Rusty's attention? He forced himself to think as his father and brother would have: making money wasn't the point, power was. Money was a means to the real end—ruling the course of markets, world economies, and lesser men, controlling those chained by fear and doubt.

And suddenly, as he neared the Polpis Harbor Road, it seemed obvious. This particular deal must have given Rusty power over Max. How did he find out about it? Not from his father; the control of information was one form of protection, and Max tried to fool others about his intentions. Peter considered Salomon briefly, and ruled it out. When ME went to its underwriter, it counted on Salomon's practice of encoding clients' names—to limit the spread of information among insiders and shield it from speculators.

"There must have been a source," Peter muttered to himself, the wind generated by his passage tearing the words from his lips and throwing them over his shoulder. Someone close to Max, someone vital, who had betrayed him for a reason and lived to regret it. Once Rusty had the knowledge he needed, the source's credit with Max would be worthless. Had he tried to salvage what he could by telling Max what he'd done? Had that been Rusty's undoing? And had the source then lost everything—his job, Max's trust, and maybe even his freedom?

A motive for murder, perhaps, once Rusty reared his ugly head on American shores.

Peter slowed the bike to take the left-hand turnoff past Almanack Pond and down toward the farm. He knew now what he had to do. There was one man who might be able to help him—Malcolm Scott, Max's former chief financial officer, who was spinning out his remaining years patiently at home in Westchester County. He would pay Malcolm Scott a call.

He dove for his driveway neatly, slowing the bike as it hit the unpaved surface. The wheels steadied and he looked up, then came slowly to a halt, his right leg dropping to the ground for balance. The dim bulk of parked cars loomed through the fog. Sky was right. He had company.

Chapter 9

THE SLAM OF THE KITCHEN DOOR woke Merry abruptly from a dream that she was underwater. She had been pushing her way through brackish weeds in a swimmer's crawl, her eyes clouded by mud, searching for something. *The bog,* she thought hazily, and opened her eyes. Her Swedish grandmother used to say it was bad luck to dream of water. From the shifting patterns of leaves thrown on the wall by the beech tree beyond her window, she judged it to be five o'clock. She lay back on the pillow, eyes closed, and listened to Ralph Waldo humming among his vegetables in the yard below. Her father's face rose in her mind, and with it, the residue of anger filling her head like bad gin. She opened one eye, groped for her watch on the bedside table, and discovered it was past six. She was fuddled with daytime sleep.

By this time, the bog would be drained and the crime scene unit would be crawling among the sandy vines searching for anything manmade that might have belonged to Rusty Mason. Bailey would be with them. A wave of anger washed over her, and then remorse stabbed at her gut. Her father would never forgive her for the scene she'd made today. She'd have to resign. But where to go? Back to New Bedford? It was too much to think about. She yawned and fell back on the pillow.

The Folger house sat on Tattle Court, one of the warren of lanes that sprang from Fair Street. It was a Federal-style cottage of six rooms, with a slate-blue door placed asymmetrically in the clapboard facade—a "three-quarter" house in Nantucket parlance. The shingles that sheltered it from salt air and the island's winter winds had mellowed to a soft charcoal over the years, and on the shady north side, sea-green moss grew thick on some of them. The white trim was peeling and the windowpanes were clouded with age. The house sat close to the street behind a white picket fence, whose gate opened onto the driveway running along one side and snapped shut with the weight of an iron ball and chain staked in a bed of dahlias. In the backyard, hydrangeas and herbs were ranged in riotous disorder around a mirrored lightning ball. Ralph was a desultory weeder.

Inside, the house was a mass of clutter. Boxes of junk mail, never opened, but hoarded over decades, sat on the dining-room table. The living-room curtains—removed for cleaning before her grandmother's death three years earlier—lay folded over a wing chair whose silk upholstery fell in tattered streamers around its legs. Wrought-iron blacksmithing tools, owned by some nineteenth-century Folger, stood in the corner of the stairway. An easel sporting a half-finished canvas straddled the hallway next to a large Boston fern.

Merry descended the stairs, stepping over Tabitha, the calico cat, and her latest litter of kittens, and picked her way through a collection of prewar ladies' hats on her way to the kitchen. Ralph Waldo had raised her father here, and when Merry's mother and brother died, she and John had moved back into the house. The clutter drove her father mad. The prospect of clearing it away, however, was too daunting. Every winter began with a vow to sort through the accumulation of years, and every spring found the house in its usual state. Nothing had changed; it had merely increased.

"What's for dinner, Ralph?"

Her grandfather, splendid in a red butcher's apron, held a fillet knife in one hand. There was a smell of lemons and freshly ground pepper. Ralph turned and smiled when he saw her.

"Bluefish. With tomatoes and basil. Potato salad. Iced tea with mint. There may be some ice cream left, but then again, you may have eaten it when I wasn't looking."

"I'm starved. Got any cheese?"

91

"You can look."

Merry considered the icebox, which sported the profusion and decay of the rest of the house, and gave up. She pulled out a rush-seated chair and slumped over the table, feeling cranky.

Her grandfather raised an eyebrow and turned back to his fillet. "You're looking cranky, Meredith. We'd better start with the iced tea."

"Dad gave my case away."

Ralph stopped his work on the fish and shook his head. "That boy," he said. "Never fails to lay the wrong foot."

"So you think I could have done it?"

He looked at her: her mouth wistful and uncertain under the cool green eyes, hair tousled like a child's from sleep. He never failed to see the eight-year-old she had been, and his heart ached for an instant as he noticed the lines of her thirties beginning to crease her wide tanned forehead.

"Of course you could have done it. I intend to tell your father so when I see him."

"Don't play favorites, Ralph. This is important. I was nervous as hell out there today; I almost couldn't look the corpse in the face. Do you think I'm tough enough to handle a murder?"

"Toughness has its downside, Meredith. It can keep you from feeling. Assurance is what you want; and it's something that'll come with experience. If you believe in yourself, that is." He shot her what she called his wrath-of-God glance from under his white eyebrows.

"I have to get Dad to believe in me first."

"I *do not* agree," he said firmly. "Work on your self-confidence, and you'll give him a reason to back you. You've never quite believed in your abilities, Meredith Abiah, and for the life of me I cannot see why. You're smart, you're dedicated, you're thorough—and better than that, you've got the best instincts I've seen in a long time. I flatter myself they're hereditary." He pulled out a chair and sat down opposite her, one gnarled hand supporting his chin and the other stroking her blond head. The unruly waves were springy beneath his fingers, like ferns or feathers. "What is it you're so afraid of?"

She laid one cheekbone on the table's scarred surface and let herself be a child. With Ralph, she was open as she never could be with her father. "Of failing, I suppose."

"Failing to solve your first murder, or failing to fill your brother's shoes?"

Her head shot up, and she held his blue eyes for an instant, considering. "There's some of that," she said slowly. "I think there's always an underlying thought that Billy would do my job better if he were here."

"Why? Because he was a boy? That doesn't sound like you."

"It's hard to shake off, Ralph—that feeling that Dad would be prouder of a son. I'm always struggling to be what I'm not."

"Rubbish! Not to speak ill of the dead—but you're more your father's child than Bill ever was. A great lad, make no mistake, and one of the loves of my heart; but you were too young when he died to remember him with anything but a child's eyes. He had your mother's romanticism, her impetuousness, her tendency to act without thinking." He lifted his gaze from his granddaughter and stared at the opposite wall, seeing the painful past. "One reason he enlisted so young, and jumped on a grenade as it went off." Ralph Waldo's eyes flicked back to Meredith's and grew tender. "You're too stubborn and willful and rational to be a hero. Or a fool. Good thing, too. Your father's got the same cussed nature, and look where it got him. He's ruining your life."

"This isn't funny, Ralph." She sat back in her chair and fiddled with her fingers, her eyes downcast and obscured by the dark brows. "I blew up in his office when he told me I couldn't handle a murder. I was probably on a caffeine-and-sugar high from the Downeyflake."

"So we'll call it my fault," Ralph said. "And I wasn't laughing at you, Meredith Abiah. I meant every word I said. I think you've got a future that'll be a credit to the family and the force. Your father needs a talking-to. Getting stiff-necked as a Down Easter with all his authority. He's too young to act like an old man. I'll have a chat with him."

"Well, it won't matter, I can tell you. He mentioned Mom, and I said something stupid." Merry ran her finger around the rim of her iced tea tumbler, her face flushing as she spoke. The tea was the color of mahogany and smelled like the inside of a cedar closet. She drank deeply and sighed.

Ralph rose at that, and busied himself at the counter, saying nothing. When Merry felt guilty her face looked exactly like his dead wife's, and the sight always caused something deep in his chest to break with emotion. He cleared his throat, set down his knife, and wiped his hands on his apron. "How bad was it?" he asked.

"Pretty bad. He said that he'd never wanted a police career for me—that Mom had never wanted it—and I told him I wasn't Mom and I wouldn't slit my wrists the first time things got rough. Or words to that effect." Her voice was very small. "I thought he'd punch his fist through the door."

Ralph blew out his breath in a gust and turned back to the fillets. "Well, Meredith, you have had more intelligent moments. And more noble. Your mother was the sweetest woman who ever lived."

"You think I don't know that?" she burst out. "You think I don't feel like a worm? Like I disowned her? The truth is that he's partly right. I'm not tough enough for murder. I nearly flunked out of my forensic anthropology class. I can't stand to look at 'human remains.' I hate the smell, the bloating, the obscenity of a murdered body." She glanced up at him, and he saw the pain on her face. "Never mind that this is the first murder to happen on my beat—I read the newspaper articles about all of them, all over the state, with a sort of horrible fascination. Dad thinks I'm morbid, Ralph. Other cops seem able to depersonalize murder—they talk about the statistical group the type of killing falls into, or they compare the modus operandi of this case to one last year—but I can't. I think about the victim. What his life might have been like. What he must have thought as he was dying. Whether he died in fear and pain, alone. And I think about how I'd have felt if it happened to me."

Merry took a deep breath. "That's why I can't understand Peter Mason's reaction. He's so cold, Ralph. It's as if he's dismissed the fact of his brother's death and moved on to worrying about his harvest. It's not normal. In fact, it makes me angry. So why am I in this business?"

" 'Any man's death diminishes me, because I am involved in mankind,' " Ralph Waldo mused. "You're in this business because you can't turn away from all the pain. I don't think that's bad, Meredith. I think

94

it's a form of grace too often lacking in police work."

"Dad tapped into my worst fear—that I'll fall apart when things get tough."

"That's something you'll have to live with to overcome, Meredith Abiah. And when you do fall apart, get up and pull yourself together. A caring heart can live with a cool head. You're a Folger, and you'll learn to trust in your strengths—even when they look like weaknesses," Ralph said.

The backyard screen door swung open abruptly, and Merry looked over her shoulder. John Folger stepped into the kitchen, nodded to her wordlessly, and handed a brown paper bag to Ralph. "Picked up some melons from the produce truck in town this morning. Whole office smells like them."

"Thanks, son," Ralph said. "Well, I'd better get these fish on the fire." He slathered the fillets with mayonnaise and then disappeared into the foggy yard, where a charcoal grill smoked gently.

Merry screwed up her courage.

"I'm sorry for what I said this morning. All of it. You're probably right to give the case to somebody with more experience. I was just so tired, so—"

"—fed up with banging your head against the wall," her father said. "I know. I used to have to fight Ralph for every case I worked on. I should be better at it than he was." He dropped his keys on the kitchen counter and stood looking at them blankly for an instant. "But we don't learn, Merry. I look at you and I see the little girl who used to make me bury dead seagulls in the backyard. I see the girl who dragged around for months when her brother didn't come home from war. Death makes us careful with our children. I don't want anything, ever, to happen to you. You're all I've got left. Hell, you're not just all I've got left. You're the most important thing in my life. And so I protect you too much." He reached for her head as she sat in her chair, and held it against him gently. She put her arms around his waist. "Don't resign, kid. I'd be lost without you."

"Sometimes it seems like the only thing left to do, Dad," she said.

He released her. "You could try working on your first murder instead. I told Bailey I can't spare him from the vandalism case."

Merry looked up at him. "No!"

He nodded. "But this is a trial thing, Meredith. You're a rookie on a murder investigation, however much experience you've got on larceny and vice. If you're not making progress in two weeks, I'll review the case."

Merry said nothing, her breathing suspended, hoping he wasn't kidding.

Her chief kissed the top of her head lightly, something he rarely did. "Now eat your dinner and get back out there." He made his way through the cluttered kitchen to the stairs, cursing as his shin met the edge of a blacksmith iron.

Merry shot out of her seat and thrust her head around the screen door. "Ralph! I've got the case! What in the *hell* do I do now?"

Upstairs, as he folded his discarded uniform and reached for a towel, John Folger smiled.

Chapter 10

Two HOURS LATER, bouncing over the sandy trail through the moors to Altar Rock, Merry made a decision. Peter Mason's safety was paramount, and therefore she would have to operate on the assumption that he was the killer's intended victim and his brother an unlucky double. If in the course of investigation she was proved wrong—if Rusty in fact was the target—she'd have erred only on the side of caution.

She had done the obvious where Rusty Mason was concerned—furnished a description of him to the ferry service, the taxi stands, and the airlines in the hope that someone would identify him and she could trace his movements. She had stopped by the station and heard the results of the bog search from Clarence Strangerfield. Three hours of combing an area within a hundred-yard radius from the body, with a party of three sergeants on hands and knees, had produced fifty-six cents in pennies, nickels, and dimes; a multitude of scratches; a rusted piece of metal, presumably from Peter's harvesting equipment; crimson juice stains on four uniforms; an ancient beer bottle; and colds in several heads. Clarence had vacuumed the clothes and body for fibers before they were sent to the forensic center on the mainland. The pockets were empty, as though Rusty Mason had left Brazil with the clothes on his back. His watch, however, had stopped at two forty-seven.

"That doesn't mean he went into the water then, Merry, only that the movement stopped at that point."

"Fine," she'd said impatiently, wondering why anyone would travel to an island with nothing—not even a ticket stub—in his pockets, and deciding it was unlikely. The murderer must have disposed of Rusty's belongings. Clarence had developed a set of prints from the wooden button; they did not match the dead man's, nor those taken from Rafe da Silva's and Peter Mason's fingers that morning. "So we've got a non-suspect ident," she'd mused. A set of prints from an unknown person— who might be the murderer. Or might not.

"Ah'll be searching through the files tomorrer mahning," Clarence told her, "but the likelihood of findin' a mahtch is pretty remote."

Finally, there were the photographs taken at the scene. She lingered over the shot of Rusty Mason's dead face, revising her earlier opinion of his resemblance to Peter. His hair was a brighter brown, shot with red where Peter's tended to black, and the lines on the face were deeply etched.

"Looks like he lived hard, Clare," she'd said.

Now, as she guided the car along the still-foggy trail through the moor toward Peter Mason's house, it was Rafe da Silva she was thinking of. The prospect of bumping into him gave her a thrill of terror and nausea coupled with wild hope. Despite the smallness of the island, the two of them had been out of touch for years—because Rafe wanted it that way, she suspected. She had tried to pump her grandfather for information over dinner, to little purpose.

"Ralph, you know anything about how Rafe da Silva wound up out at Mason Farms?"

"Nope. But I imagine like most folks he answered a want ad."

"The da Silvas are watermen. Not farmers."

"In this economy, you're lucky if you're apt for more than one trade. Mason Farms pays a salary, and I'll bet the board is thrown in. Shoot," Ralph had said, as he caught a bone from the bluefish. "You know old Jose hasn't spoken to Rafe since he got back from New Bedford, Meredith. He's not likely to have him on his boat. The best Rafe can hope for is that the old coot'll kick off one of these days and leave him the scalloper. Not that I wish the man ill. Still, I get tired of fellows who've no time for their own sons. Death ends enough conversations without men doing it for themselves."

"They just seem like an odd pair," Merry had said. "Mason and Rafe, I mean."

Ralph had grunted assent, his attention on the beefsteak tomato he'd pulled off the plants next to the fence. He'd held it in the palm of his right hand, a paring knife in his left, and sliced the dark red flesh into wedges. Tomato juice had run over his fingers and dripped to his elbow. He'd mopped at it with his napkin. "You thinking Rafe went for Peter and got his brother?" Ralph had said.

"Ralph! That's crazy. Rafe's not the killing type, whatever people think."

"I know that. I'm just wondering why you're worried about what the man does for a living."

.   .   .

BECAUSE I WANT TO KNOW *why he's gotten so chilly toward me,* Merry said to herself. *It's all part of the changes in his life since Nam, since nothing seemed right to either of us with Billy gone. I'm just worried about him. And I don't like him so close to another murder, either. He's got some pretty deep scars.*

Somewhere behind the fog, the sun was in decline. Merry switched on her low beams and saw the air solidify in front of her, dual arcs of opacity thrusting into the darkness past the radar station. Her police radio squawked static suddenly into the quietness of the car, and she jumped involuntarily in her seat. She reached over and turned it off, then thought better of it and turned it back on, at low volume. A car passed her heading back to town, its high beams flooding a wall of fog, the motorist hunched over the wheel in a desperate effort to see. *Tourist,* Merry thought. Nobody used to fog would throw on the high beams. Must be lost, too; there was no good reason to be driving back in the moor tonight. Other than Mason Farms, the road led only to

Nantucket Conservation Foundation lands. As she approached the driveway to the farm, she frowned, puzzled. A crowd of vans and cars had pulled up, helter-skelter, near the turnoff.

"Great night for a barbecue, Mason," she said to herself. She made the turn into the driveway and came to an abrupt halt. A crush of people with cameras were huddled near the yellow police cordon, flashes exploding in the darkening fog. Merry threw the Blazer into neutral and pulled up the handbrake, searching for the Nantucket police sergeant Clarence had left on duty. He was nowhere to be seen.

As she got out of the car, a knot of excited gawkers broke from the spotlit area in front of a television crew and moved toward her in a wave. Merry stopped dead. "Seitz," she muttered. "Of course."

Howie Seitz was in the midst of his fifth exclusive interview, his trademark smile in full force. He stooped slightly to hear the questions posed by a breathless blond in red linen, who held her earphones in one manicured hand and a microphone in the other. Merry glanced at the camera crew's call sign. A Boston station. The station must have helicoptered them in when the news hit the wire.

She marched over to the charmed circle, reached out a hand, and said, "Sorry, ma'am, we've got work to do here. Seitz!"

"Detective Folger! Hey, Madeleine, this is the woman who's handling the investigation!"

The blond newswoman turned to Merry eagerly and shoved a microphone next to her chin. "Could you comment on the death of Rusty Mason, Detective? Were drugs involved? Do we know whether this was an accident, or murder?"

"We'd know a lot sooner if you'd let us do our job," Merry said, scowling. "Now turn that thing off and leave my sergeant alone."

"Cut that, Steve," the blond said coolly, turning to her cameraman. "We'll have to go with the kid."

Merry turned to Howie, took him by the elbow, and marched him over to the Blazer. She reached into the back and pulled out a bullhorn. "Start talking with this," she said. "I suggest the phrase 'Clear the area.' It generally works. If you're talking to anyone, anyone at all, do you understand me, when I come back down this driveway, you're fired."

100

"I'm going back to school at the end of the week anyway, for Chris-sake," Howie said.

"And you can leave without a recommendation, too," Merry shot back. She turned on her heel and pushed her way through the crowd.

The quarter-mile of driveway was relatively clear. At the geranium-colored door, however, another knot had gathered, hoping for a glimpse of Peter Mason. Merry glanced at it and paused, thinking. Then she turned and drove around the house to the barn. A light glowed from the loft.

After the chaos at the gate, the barn's stillness seemed unnatural. Merry paused at the huge, half-open doors, allowing her eyes to adjust to the dimness of the interior. The sweet smell of hay blended with the mustiness of sheep's urine and old wood rising from the floor. She sneezed once, and then again. A chair scraped against the flooring over her head, and heavy footsteps crossed the platform. From the barn's far corner, Merry heard the unoiled hinges of a door whine open. She turned in the direction of the sound, and saw a staircase leading from the threshing floor to the hayloft.

"Rafe," she said, her voice tremulous. "It's Merry."

He paused, a dark outline against the glow of the doorway. "Hell," he said, "thought you were a tourist."

•   •   •

RAFE'S ROOM STILL LOOKED like the hayloft it had once been. He showed her the bolted trapdoor in the flooring, partially covered by a trunk that served as his coffee table. A single bunk in one corner was neatly made up, and a desk across the room was strewn with papers—feed orders, wool counts. The lamp hanging from the low rafters sent swinging shadows against the walls, but threw steady light on the arm-chair Rafe had clearly just vacated. Next to it on the floor stood a beer bottle and an open book, facedown. The windows cut in three walls were bare of curtains. She imagined the sun pouring in on clear morn-ings, slanting across the sharp planes of Rafe's face, causing his dark brows to furrow over crinkled lids, and then corrected her mental pic-ture. The sheep on the property meant he'd be up long before dawn, something farming had in common with fishing. Maybe his new life wasn't so different from the old after all. As if he felt her eyes on him, Rafe turned and looked at her, and she dropped her gaze awkwardly. The sight of his face undid her.

Rafe waited for her to speak. When she didn't, he motioned to the chair. "Have a seat," he said, and pulled out the desk chair for himself. He straddled it backward, arms folded along the top rail, and waited again. Rafe was accustomed to silence, and it did not compel him to speech. He'd learned long ago that if you didn't rush to fill a gap, people were likely to fill it for you. He'd learned a lot by not talking.

"How long have you been here, Rafe?" Merry asked, with effort.

"Bit over five years."

"It doesn't seem that long." Since we both left New Bedford, she meant, but didn't say.

"Time goes."

Merry nodded, and looked around the room again. It looked as though no one really lived there, much less for five years. She glanced back at Rafe, hugging his chair like a safety barrier. It had been months—maybe a year and a half—since she'd had a reason to say more to him than hello. With a sense of shock she saw that he looked older than she remembered. She did a quick calculation and realized Rafe was forty-one, Billy's age if he'd lived. His body was still fit and powerful, his perpetually copper face and deep brown eyes as controlled and calm as ever, but lines of weariness ran from the corners of his mouth to his nose, and the mink-brown hair was shot with gray. It seemed inconceivable to her that she had touched that hair once, that he had cried in her arms like a child. Since New Bedford he'd opened a steadily widening distance between them. Merry realized he was aware of her appraisal, and suddenly self-conscious, she looked away from him. "It's really good to see you. I'm sorry it takes a murder to get me out here."

Rafe didn't answer. He reached for the beer bottle and took a long drink. "What can I do for you, Detective Folger?"

As if they were strangers. "Well, Rafe, you could talk to me like a friend, for starters," Merry said. "What's wrong?"

A muscle in Rafe's cheek twitched. "Let's just say it's been a long day, and the morning comes early. If you need something from me, let's get it over with."

Merry looked down at her hands, which were tightly clenched, and forced herself to loosen her grip on her fingers. "I thought you might have some ideas about what's going on here."

"I think Peter's brother bought it last night. What do you think?"

"I think you're being hostile for no reason," Merry burst out, exasperated. "And I think if Peter Mason winds up dead one of these days, I'm going to be asking you some pretty tough questions."

Rafe's face darkened, and he set the bottle down with a quiet clink that somehow managed to sound ominous. "So ask 'em now," he said.

Merry felt her stomach clench. This meeting wasn't going at all as she'd intended. "What do you know about Mason's life? Any reason somebody'd want to kill him?"

"No."

"That's not good enough, Rafe."

"Maybe not, but it happens to be the truth. I've watched the guy for five years. He's got no personal life. No women. He's not growing controlled substances down on the farm. He's a nice guy trying to make a living out of Ocean Spray."

"Know anything about his brother?"

"Didn't even know he had one."

"Has Mason seemed okay lately? Not preoccupied?"

"He's been fine. He works out like he's always done, sees his friends, runs the farm. Plays a lot of chess, and that music of his. He keeps to himself."

"Who normally gets the mail around here?"

"Whoever goes into town first. There's a PO box there. What're you getting at?"

"Just wondered if he'd had any upsetting news lately, but if you don't see the mail every day you might not know."

"I don't hold it up to the light, either, when I do get it," Rafe said sharply.

It was remarkable, Merry thought, that someone you loved could become a complete stranger you no longer knew how to talk to. She thrust her fingers through her bangs and tried again.

"No weird phone calls? Nothing out of the ordinary? Nothing that might have been a sign or a code from his brother telling him he was due in town?"

"They teach you espionage and witchcraft at the police academy, too?"

"Answer the question, Rafe." Her voice had a pleading tone she disliked.

"No. Not so's I noticed." Rafe appeared the slightest bit abashed.

He's protecting Peter Mason, Merry thought, and he's afraid of me. What an extraordinary thing. "Rafe," she began, and then stopped, dreading his coldness. But there was no way to repair this. She'd have to keep forcing Rafe da Silva to talk to her. "Do you like Peter Mason?"

For the first time, Rafe dropped his gaze, and his face became carefully expressionless. "Yeah, I like him. He's a good guy. The best. Why do you think I'm so worried?" He stood up and started to pace around the loft. "I'm pissed as hell that I didn't hear something last night. That could've been Pete out in the bog, you know that, Merry? And I heard nothing."

"Can't take care of everybody, Rafe," Merry said gently.

He stopped in his tracks and looked at her, his dark eyes shadowed. "Yeah, well, it'd make a change from everybody taking care of me," he said. "But I'll be ready tonight."

"Meaning what?"

"Meaning if the clown comes back, he's going to run into me. Me and Smith & Wesson." He gestured toward a Browning nine-millimeter that stood on a gun rack next to a twelve-gauge shotgun.

"I didn't know you kept an arsenal."

"They're Pete's. He wants them stored in the barn, not the house."

"So you can't think of who'd kill Mason, or why, but you think he was the target just the same."

There was a silence. "Nothing else makes sense," he said.

Merry shifted in her chair. "Rafe, is he the kind of guy who could kill his brother?"

"Not a chance." He gave a short bark of laughter, but he was angry, not amused.

"Listen to me, Rafe," Merry said, leaning forward. "Mason looks like the only guy in town—besides Ralph Waldo—who remembers Rusty exists. And he isn't hiding the fact he couldn't stand him. That says to me he's probably the only guy with any interest in whether Rusty lived or died. Convince me I'm wrong."

Rafe took a turn around the room while he ran his left hand over his stubble. "There's something there, something with the brother," he said. He turned to Merry and sat down on the floor near her chair. "He carries this thing inside him, you know? I don't know what it is, but I know it when I see it. I could see it today. The man's got a grudge. The thing is, he won't talk about it, Merry, and it bugs me."

"You're afraid he killed him," Merry said slowly. Her green eyes were very still.

"Maybe I am. Aw, shit, listen to me. Peter'd never kill anybody. It's not how he does things." When Rafe looked up at her, Merry almost reached out a hand to touch him. He looked that worried.

"How does he do things?"

"Right. He does them right. If he makes a promise, he'll keep it, even if it kills him. He doesn't even tell white lies. He pays his bills on time. He'd never tell a woman he cared about her just to get laid, you know?"

Merry nodded. "And where Rusty's concerned, maybe none of that makes any difference. Could he have done it, Rafe? Would either you or Rebecca know if he left the house in the middle of the night?"

Rafe studied his hands and said nothing.

"Rafe."

He looked up at her. "I'd hear a car, wouldn't I?" he said, but there was a note of defiance in his voice Merry understood.

"Not if he met Rusty somewhere on foot—a prearranged spot, fixed in a letter you never saw or a phone call you didn't hear."

"Rusty was killed on the road, walking toward the gate," Rafe said.

"Maybe Peter offered him a room at the house, and insisted on driving because of the fog and the strangeness of the roads. And when they got to the gate, Rusty got out to open it, as any passenger would. Something inside Peter snaps—whatever it is he's been holding on to for so long. Maybe Peter hits the gas."

Rafe sat silently for a minute, then shook his head. "If Peter wanted to kill him, why would he wait until he got home to do it, and then leave the body in his front yard? And where did he put Rusty's car? If he has half the brain I think he has, he'd kill him and leave the body and the car together. You're working overtime, girlscout," he said.

Girlscout was a name from childhood she'd almost forgotten. She felt the memory of her brother wash over her in a sweet, painful rush, and shut her eyes. "Okay. I just wanted to hear what you thought," she said. "So when he sees people, who does he see?"

"Oh, a few islanders, some off," he said. "The off-islanders are old family friends. Guy named Sky Jackson and his girlfriend. She's part foreign, makes clothes. Has a shop in town."

"Mayling Stern," Merry said. Rafe nodded.

"Then there's Lucy Jacoby, the English teacher at the high school."

"How's he know her?"

Rafe shrugged, looked down. "And the Starbucks, of course. He was a friend of Tess and Dan's first and got to know Will when Dan passed away. He's been good for the kid."

"Like you've been good for the widow," Merry said, and bit the words back too late.

Rafe's head came up and his eyes narrowed. "You watching what I do, Meredith Folger? You got a squad car following me?"

Did he think she was jealous enough of Tess Starbuck to stoop that low? "No, Rafe," she said, hurt. "I don't have to. I just checked on your alibi for Sunday night. Dod Nelson spent Labor Day weekend on the Cape. He must've come a fair piece to drive you home from the Greengage."

Rafe said nothing, but hung his head.

"Next time think before you panic," Merry said gently. "You spent most of Sunday night with Tess Starbuck, I'd guess. You just couldn't say so in front of the kid and your boss, could you?" She waited, but he wouldn't look at her. "I think that's why you feel so guilty about Rusty's murder. You'll never know if you could have stopped it, because you weren't even here."

"Man, I am so sick of being tailed by police," Rafe said. His voice was low and taut with contained anger. "It's like I'm always guilty until proven innocent. God knows my dad thinks so. And you're the worst, Merry Folger. Somehow you're always there, like a bad omen." He stood up and crossed to his chair, wrenching it around and thrusting it between his legs as he spoke.

Merry felt tears start into her eyes and hated herself for her weakness. Damn Rafe. Damn all men who made her love them and then blamed her for it. "Don't hold out on me again, Rafe, not when there's a murder involved," she said, more loudly than she'd intended. "It doesn't help you to falsify an alibi." She was blinking rapidly.

"I'll do as I goddam please," he said. "You seem to think you're my self-appointed parole officer and grandma all rolled up in one. I bet you think I killed him myself!"

"If the body had a knife wound, maybe I'd consider it," Merry shot back, and then stopped, horrified. "Rafe, I'm sorry, I didn't mean it," she said.

Rafe's face was impassive. He seemed not to have heard her. Then he stood up quietly, without looking at her, and crossed to his desk. He rifled through the feed orders and wool counts. "Yeah, Meredith, but part of you will always think it," he said. "I can never change that. Whenever I see you I'm back in a holding pen in New Bed. And it gets harder and harder to take. So just get out of here, will you?"

Chapter 11

MERRY STUMBLED IN THE DARKENED YARD as she made her way from the barn to the drive, and the sharp stab of pain in her turned right ankle unleashed the tears she'd barely held back in Rafe's presence. "You're such an idiot, Merry Folger," she muttered furiously to herself as she massaged the bone, limping. She had screwed up again, reminding Rafe of something he'd never done and a shame he couldn't change. He didn't miss her, didn't want her, and didn't need her; he just wanted to be left alone. She looked up, searching for her bearings. The night was moonless, the fog still holding, and the yard had no spotlights.

A dog gave voice suddenly close at hand. A dark, moving shape hurtled around the corner of the house and shot directly toward her. She stopped short, reaching for the service pistol she carried but had never had to use, her heart beating fast with fear.

"Ney!" A man's voice called through the darkness, followed by a whistle. The dog slid to a halt just in front of Merry, jaws snapping and ears back, holding her until his master approached. She froze. A man's hand came down over the dog's collar, and just as suddenly as he had appeared, Ney fell silent, sat down, and turned his nose upward to look at Peter Mason.

"The sideshow is closed for the evening, ma'am, and you're tres-passing," he said, not recognizing her in the darkness. "I'd appreciate it if you'd leave the property."

"That's some dog, Mr. Mason," Merry said shakily. "How come he didn't go into action last night, when a murderer was running around?"

"He probably would have, Detective Folger," Peter said, "if I didn't keep him inside at night. I was just taking him over to Rafe's. The crowds have been driving him nuts, so I locked him in the kitchen all afternoon. He's a little jumpy. Thank God that cop at the end of the drive finally cleared them out." He paused. "Wait here a minute and I'll be right back."

He walked off in the direction of the barn, Ney moving with him like a shadow against his leg. Merry breathed deeply and closed her eyes. The last thing she wanted now was an interview with Peter Mason, but his requests had a curious way of sounding like commands, and she didn't have the energy to fight him. She heard Rafe's door whine open, and after a pause, whine shut. She waited for the light footsteps through the long grass to reach her and then turned. Mason was looking at her quietly.

"Let's go inside."

He led her around to the back door into the kitchen. A single light burning over the sink gave it the deserted feeling of a midnight raid on the refrigerator. Rebecca had tidied up after dinner, leaving pots and a coffee cup to drain in the dish rack. As Merry passed it, the dishwasher cycle kicked into rinse with a roar, flooding the drain with a rush of water. The sound was vaguely comforting.

She followed Mason into his study, catching a glimpse of a neat laundry room off the kitchen and, on the other side, a small, brightly painted dining room with a portrait of a woman in oils on one wall.

"My grandmother, Sarah Mason," he said, following the direction of her glance. He gestured toward the sofa and took his favorite arm-chair in front of the fireplace, where pine logs were burning brightly.

"It's early in the season, I know, but the fog cuts through you," Peter said. "The fire's half for mental comfort." He scanned her face now that they were in the light. Her eyes were red-rimmed. He considered Rafe's uncharacteristic surliness when he'd handed him Ney for the evening, and followed a hunch. "How does tea and sympathy sound?" he said.

Merry's smile conceded defeat. "Tea would be fine."

"The cognac's on the shelf," he said. "I'll be right back."

· · ·

ACROSS THE ISLAND, in Siasconset, Mayling Stern stood by her studio's wide window, looking out at nothing, and shivered. Foghorns were booming over the night sea from the international shipping lanes to the southeast. Off to her left, up the beach, Sankaty Light sliced its powerful beam through the sky, but its reach was truncated by fog, its passage illuminating nothing but a moving cloud of darkness. With one hand she drew her sweater closer around her slender body and with the other closed the vertical blinds against the fog and the night. "I hate this island in bad weather," she said. "It feels as though all the lost souls in the world have converged in the air above us, and are waiting."

"For what?" Sky asked.

"For Rusty to join them, perhaps." She shivered again, and turned to look at Sky. Sitting in the red leather chair, he was backlit by the glow of her drafting-table spotlight, and she could not read his features. It occurred to her that he wanted it that way. He had turned off the overhead lamps when he entered the room.

"The first and last sign of an off-islander," he said. "Arrive with the sun, leave with the fog."

She had willed him to reach for her, and instead, he offered her scorn. She waited.

"Mayling," he said, "Did Peter tell you how Rusty died?"

She shook her head. "He was angry when I didn't ask."

"He was run down by a car, then dragged to the bog unconscious and left facedown to drown."

Mayling said nothing, and folded her arms across her chest protectively.

Sky sat perfectly still for the space of several heartbeats. Then, "Don't drive the Mercedes," he said. "Keep it in the garage. We'll get it fixed later, after all this has blown over."

110

Mayling searched for his eyes in the gloom, gave up, and turned back to the draped window. "Take me home to New York with you, Schuyler," she said. "I can't bear to be here alone."

• • •

"RAFE TELLS ME you two go back a long way," Peter said delicately, as he handed Merry the tea.

"I'm surprised he remembers. Most of the time he treats me like summer people, instead of a woman he knows as well as his own sister."

"I see." Peter settled back in his chair and reached for the cognac. "I didn't realize there was that much history. What happened? Irreconcilable differences?"

"That, and probably everything else that can drive two people apart."

"When did you two get together?"

She hesitated, took a sip of tea, and gave Peter a long green look from under her dark brows. "We began to be close friends when he got back from Vietnam—Rafe's sort of the last link to my brother, Billy. But we didn't start seeing each other—romantically, I mean—until about five years ago. Probably right before he started to work for you. I'm not surprised you never heard of me—Rafe cut his losses pretty quick where I was concerned."

"And you didn't?"

She laughed—harshly, bitterly. At the sound, Peter realized he'd never heard her laugh before; and he wished suddenly that he could bring joy into her voice instead of sorrow.

"Let's just say I haven't dated anybody since."

Like me, Peter thought, carrying my perpetual flame for Alison. What a waste.

She swirled the tea bag in the mug, staring into its depths as she gripped it with both hands. The room was very quiet.

"I think oracles use loose tea," Peter said.

She looked up. "The future's not really worth knowing about ahead of time, anyway, is it?"

"No. No, I don't suppose it is. If happiness awaits you, it would lose some of its significance with foreknowledge. And if the years hold only pain, knowing that won't equip you any better to meet it."

Merry gazed into the middle distance. "Your brother, now. If he'd known he was going to die last night on this island, would deciding not to come have saved his life?"

"Rusty would have come anyway, convinced he could beat even death. That's how he was. I think that's what fate really means: that we're consigned to live our lives with the personalities we're given, and our actions are dictated by the impulses that are native to us."

"Meaning, people are people, and things don't change. I suppose that's Rafe and me in a nutshell," Merry said. She pulled out the tea bag and laid it on the plate Peter had provided for the purpose. "How did you get to know him?"

"Rafe?" he said, momentarily distracted by thoughts of Rusty. "I needed help around the time of the first harvest, in 1986. Dan Starbuck said Rafe needed a job. He'd been crewing on and off for Dan, but the scalloper couldn't really support another guy, and Rafe knew it. The harvest turned into a series of things around the place—I was rebuilding this house, putting the addition on the back there for the kitchen and laundry room—and Rafe became a fixture. Then the sheep came in 1989. At this point he's indispensable. I live in terror of the day he decides to marry or buy a fishing boat, and I lose him."

Merry nodded, and sipped her tea. She grimaced as the hot liquid coursed down her throat.

"You've known Rafe forever, I suppose?" Peter said casually.

"It's a small island, Mr. Mason. When you're a kid here, going through the school system, it's pretty hard not to know everybody and their brother. In my case that's exactly what it was: Rafe was my brother's best friend. The two of them went to Nam together in 1970, when they were eighteen."

She set down her cup and sighed deeply. "They were just kids. By 1970 nobody in his right mind was going over to that war. But not Rafe and Billy. They'd been fighting battles for years on the moors, and this seemed like a good time on government money. I was around ten when they left, and thought they were heroes, you know? But now, when I look back on it, eighteen was so young. They were boys out of high school. And Billy died over there."

"Rafe told me," Peter said soberly. "It's a war that didn't even touch my family. Rusty and I were too young."

"Your dad would've gotten you out of it anyway," Merry said matter-of-factly. "I can't imagine a Mason would ever die in a ditch for a bad reason." She looked up, caught the flash of something in Peter's eyes, and remembered the body in the bog. Color flooded her face. "Geez! I'm sorry. What was I thinking of? This is my night for foot-in-mouth disease if ever there was one. I should just go home." She turned to search for her shoulder bag and half-rose from the sofa.

"It's okay," Peter said gently. "I'd like to talk about what's troubling you."

"Why?"

"Because I care about Rafe, and he's in a pretty foul mood tonight, too."

"I see," she said, amused "I get the tea and he gets the sympathy." She eased back onto the sofa and thought for an instant. Then she looked up at Peter, her eyes like cool mountain water under the darkness of her brows. He saw, as if for the first time, the contrast of bone and hollow that formed her face, a harsh composition that was nonetheless arresting. He wondered whether Rafe had ever told her she was beautiful—a separate thought as he waited for her to speak; as a man considering the business deal he will negotiate at the end of a flight will notice the cloud formations beyond the airplane window.

"How much do you care about Rafe, Mr. Mason? Enough not to fire him for something that's over and done?"

"I'd never fire Rafe."

Merry looked down at her hands. "Because I don't know you, and you can never tell, with people. One minute they're thick as thieves, the next . . ."

Peter sipped his cognac and stifled the impulse to laugh at her earnestness. "I don't sell out my friends, Detective."

"Even if they've been tried for murder?"

Peter choked on his drink and set down his glass in a hurry. "What?" he said.

"In 1985. New Bedford." She paused, assessing his reaction. "Rafe

113

was working there on a fishing fleet owned by some Portuguese cousins. It was a real mess. A real media circus."

"Tell me about it," Peter said.

"It was pretty ugly. But then, they all seem ugly to me. I'm too sensitive for this business." She shot him a glance. "You seem to handle death a bit better."

"In these times, indifference is the only way to live a coherent life," he said, somewhat stiffly. "And how I feel about my brother's death is, as I said before, more my business than yours, Detective." He looked past her, at the fire. "I don't take the violence I read about in the papers very personally. For me, it's an abstract, and it's a statistical impossibility it will ever touch my life."

"Until today."

He looked at her then, his eyes very careful and very neutral. Then he nodded once. "Where Rusty's concerned, statistics mean nothing," he said. "But you were telling me about Rafe. Please go on."

Merry took a deep breath and shut her eyes, as though trying to remember a movie she'd seen a long, long time ago. "Three guys had been drinking in a bar. One of those waterfront places the New Bed fishermen hang out in. Turns out one of the guys—it had to be the guy with a petty rap sheet a yard long, a reputed wife-beater, and the ringleader of the group—was about to lose his boat to the bank. So the more the guys drank, the louder and angrier they got, the more vows of group honor and solidarity they took, the more obscenities they threw at the rich banker types in their BMWs who've never fished a day in their lives."

"Rafe was one of the three men?" Peter asked.

Her eyes flashed open and she shook her head. "No, but as luck would have it, he was in the same bar. And he had to go and get into a fistfight that night with some smart-aleck thug. Later, as many people thought he was with the three guys as didn't."

"So what happened?"

"The fishermen got tired of the beer and left, looking for some trouble. They found it about three blocks away."

Merry stopped and took a swig of tea. It had cooled. The slightly metallic flavor tasted like the stale nausea she'd felt in the courtroom every day of Rafe's trial. She looked at Peter. His patrician face was expressionless. How could he know what it had been like?

"There was this couple pulled up to a money machine. The street was pretty deserted—it was three in the morning. The guy was working his card while the woman sat in the car looking at her makeup in the visor mirror. It happened to be a BMW. At a bank. The three guys went nuts. The wife-beater had his gutting knife in his jeans pocket, and he held it to the guy's throat while he withdrew the maximum allowable on his card. Then they forced him into the car, drove to an empty warehouse, and made him watch while they raped his girlfriend. All three of them." Merry paused and looked at her hands. "Then they slit both their throats. And went home to their wives to sleep it off, I guess."

She fell silent. Peter sat back in his chair, dazed. He remembered the incident dimly, but he rarely followed crime stories in the news; they had so little to do with his life. "Where does Rafe come into all of this?" he said.

"He was accused of the crime."

"By whom?"

"The dead woman's kid sister. You see, Rafe had taken the victim out a few times. She was from a Portuguese family—it's a pretty tight community in New Bed, you know, and they can close ranks around their own. The woman's death had them screaming for blood. First they accused a local homeless man of the crime, but that didn't work. Then the woman's sister came forward and said Rafe had been in love with her, and out for blood when she left him for this Anglo guy who had money and a great car."

"Why in God's name did she do that? She had no reason to believe it was true, did she?"

Merry looked at him and paused. "You know, when you hear stories like this it's easy to say men are animals. They're sick. But women are worse, sometimes. Because what they can't do physically they manage to do emotionally. The girl who testified had a crush on Rafe and was insanely jealous of her sister. Rafe never looked at her. So she brought him down. That's my theory, anyway. Don't try to understand it."

Peter sat back.

"Turns out Rafe didn't have a very good alibi. He lived alone, and all he could say was that he'd left the bar and gone home to bed. Enough people knew that he'd been angry when the woman sent him packing for her new rich boyfriend. A bunch had seen him hit a guy in the bar that night. The prosecutor even used the fact that he was a Vietnam vet to make it look like we were all just lucky he hadn't taken out a McDonald's with an M16. It didn't look good. What saved him— the backbone of the defense, in fact—was that his sperm and hair samples didn't match any of the three found on the woman's body. Thank God. He was acquitted. But for months, until the wife-beater was picked up for something else and fingered the other two, half of New Bedford believed he'd done it. He was thrown off his cousin's boat, and when he came back to Nantucket, his dad refused to see him or speak to him. He was probably pretty desperate around the time you came looking for help."

Peter nodded and studied Merry, puzzled. "How do you know all of this, Detective?"

"New Bedford was my first posting after I got out of the police academy. I wasn't on Rafe's case—too junior—but . . ." She hesitated. "I think that's when I fell in love with him. I watched the whole thing, day after day. I've never been so terrified in my whole life. I decided then that the difference between the wrong man going to jail and the right one was good detective work, and that's what I wanted to do."

"When did you come back to Nantucket?"

"I followed Rafe back." She laughed shortly and looked down at her linked fingers. "Pretty pathetic, isn't it? To fall in love with a guy because he's wrongly accused of murder? I've been here ever since. And Rafe has put just about as much distance as possible between us."

"The irreconcilable differences," Peter said gently.

"He's the sort of person, Mr. Mason, who thinks if he's vulnerable, he's weak. And he can't stand to feel weak—it strips him of his self-esteem. Of his identity. I saw him at his most vulnerable; I thought it would bring us closer, that he'd need me," she said wistfully. "Shows you how self-deluding you can be if you want to. The truth is, whenever Rafe's around me, he remembers himself as vulnerable—and he can't get past it. At a time when I thought I was indispensable, he grew to hate the very sight of me."

"I think I can understand that. Rafe's got a lot of pride. And he's been hurt pretty badly," Peter said.

"Yeah, well, I've been hurt too," Merry said. "The worst of it is, he thinks I wasn't sure, all that time he was in jail and on trial. He thinks I wondered if he'd done it. And I was the only one in New Bedford who knew it was impossible for Rafe da Silva to kill anybody, especially after what he'd seen in Vietnam."

Peter blew out his breath in a great gust and stared blankly at his chessmen. Then he stood up and poked at the logs with the fire tongs. Merry studied his face apprehensively, searching for a sign that he was ready to march over to Rafe's barn and turn him out on his ear. His gray eyes were expressionless, but his lips were compressed and his jaw was locked in an aggressive fashion.

"What a nightmare," he said, jabbing viciously at a log so that a shower of sparks exploded into the chimney. "And to feel that there was nothing one could do. The powerlessness, and the fear he must have felt." He stood up and put one hand on the mantel, thinking, then set down the tongs and turned to Merry. "I've never really known him, have I?" he said.

"I wouldn't say that, exactly. I'd say you know the man he's become, not the man he was. And maybe that's a good thing. I know it is for Rafe. He hasn't kept a lot of the friends he knew in his old life. Billy was the best of them, and Billy's long gone. He's trying to build something new here—and whatever friendship you have probably means a lot to him. In fact, he'd hate it if he knew I'd told you about all of this. He'd never forgive me. I'd appreciate it if you didn't tell him."

"I don't see any reason to." He sat down again and looked over at her. "It never fails to trouble and amaze me how much sadness we cultivate, and hide, and carry with us into the future."

Merry hesitated, and then plunged in. "You're thinking of your brother?"

Peter met her eyes, then looked away. "Perhaps. Tell me something, Detective Folger: how do you sustain your belief in living when you spend your days digging into our collective unhappiness?"

"I was asking myself that this morning," she said, "although not exactly in those words. I've never really had to face it before, on a personal level, you see. Nantucket doesn't witness a lot of violent crime. Although it's risen in the past decade, of course—and drugs have moved onto the island with the rich summer kids. But murder's rare. Not much grand larceny, either. Too hard to get cars or large valuables off the island once you've stolen them." She paused. "Anyway, it really hit me—this being my first murder."

Peter's reserve dropped for one startled instant, then he recovered, and said, "Mine, too. But I hope it will be my last. You can't say the same. Something you said a few minutes ago—that good detective work is the difference between the right man and the wrong one paying for a crime—is true. But I think good detective work must take a significant toll on the good detective. I respect you for trying to do it." He leaned toward her and looked down at his hands, clasped and dangling between his knees. "I've thought a lot about Rusty's murder," he said. "I don't know what your working hypothesis is, but I thought I'd tell you mine."

"Does that mean you're 'working,' too?"

Peter looked up quickly and met her eyes, his face sober. "Well, yes," he said.

"Go on."

"My brother was something of a black sheep, Detective Folger. He was cut off from my family over ten years ago for reasons that I still don't understand completely. But his general character and behavior lead me to believe that he was the likely target of last night's attack, not me. I think it possible that some of his business dealings in Brazil went awry, and that he was followed here and killed when he thought he was finally safe. I thought perhaps if you checked Interpol, it might be a start."

"I've already contacted Interpol, Mr. Mason," Merry said quietly.

"You have?"

"When you mentioned he'd been living down there, it seemed the logical thing to do. If there's anything in the response I think you should know about, I'll fill you in. And by the way," she added, "did you know the Department of Justice has a sealed indictment outstanding against your brother? He should have been picked up wherever he entered the U.S. Which says one of two things to me: he used a fake passport, or he entered illegally. We found no passport, fake or otherwise. Not that that means much. He could have had everything in his luggage, and the killer might have taken it with him and gotten rid of it after he'd finished with your brother. It seems kind of odd to me that he'd leave Brazil without even a change of underwear, so I'm betting on that one."

Peter nodded slowly. "I wondered about that myself," he said. "What's next?"

"Suppose we talk about your role in this investigation. What do you see it as?"

Peter sat very still. "To help in ways that only I can," he said.

"What does that mean? As patron of the criminal arts?"

"I'm sorry?"

"Could you explain how you envision helping? Because if it means you're going to wander around asking random people where they were last night, or you're planning to fly to Brazil and hunt up your brother's old buddies, or if you're going to pay to have the harbor dragged in a search for his luggage, I'm going to have to ask you to stay home and let us do our job." Merry stood up and set her tea mug down on the table. She looked around the room for her raincoat.

Peter's face darkened, and he sat back in silence, arms folded, watching her. After a moment he said, "I hung it in the coat closet. I'm not going to get it until you listen to me."

Merry stopped and looked at him. Then she sat down. "All right. I'm all ears."

"I happen to believe I'm uniquely qualified to help. Since this is your first murder investigation—I'm not questioning your ability, I'm only stating a fact," he said, as she started to rise—"I suggest you take all the help that's offered. I promise not to butt into your methods. I won't screw up your investigation. I am merely intending to supplement it, where such might be helpful. With my knowledge of Rusty's personality, his contacts, and his history. I happen to think his death has long roots in the past."

"What do you mean?"

"It goes back to the family matter I mentioned. Forgive me, but I'd rather not go into it fully with you now. The press attention on this has been a little too high."

"The severed ends of the rope," Merry said.

"Excuse me?"

"That used to hold your family together. Somewhere it snapped, right? You know, you can't be much help if you don't trust me and you're not willing to talk," she said gently. "And there's another factor. You could be the murderer's real target—or, to be frank, you could be the murderer yourself. We just don't know. I can't stop you from delving into your brother's death—you're a free man in a free country. But I must warn you that it could have consequences for your safety and perhaps your personal freedom."

There was a heavy silence as Peter turned over the idea that he was a suspect in the murder investigation. It was nothing he hadn't anticipated.

"Detective," he said, "I didn't kill my brother. And I don't think I was the intended victim." His eyes were as brilliant as gray ice. "But if you think either might be true, it's only more imperative that I get involved. Have you considered that it might be to everyone's benefit if we worked together?"

"Meaning, I tell you what I find out, and you plead family confidentiality?" Merry said.

"I promise you that anything pertinent to Rusty's death will be turned over to you immediately," Peter said stiffly. "I'm just unwilling to disclose the family's private affairs when they may have absolutely nothing to do with this murder. You might discover Rusty's killer without needing to know any of it."

Merry stood up to go. "I can't stop you from running around in a Sherlock Holmes suit, Mr. Mason," she said. "Or from telling me only what you feel like, although I might mention that withholding information is a punishable offense. But I'd watch your back while you're searching for clues, okay? Now may I have my coat?"

Peter hesitated an instant, and then capitulated. "I'll get your coat," he said. "I just don't see any reason to air the family's dirty laundry unless it's absolutely necessary. Why can't you accept that?"

"Maybe I don't like being mistrusted," Merry said, "and maybe that's what this feels like. I should never have told you this is my first murder investigation."

"I don't care how many of these things you've done. It's the first one that involves my family. That changes things."

"Because the Masons have always played by different rules, Mr. Mason? I'll have to remember that. Thanks for the tea."

· · ·

SKY STOOD UP AND OPENED the drapes Mayling had closed, and stared for a moment out over the Siasconset bluff. The sea was obliterated from view, and no stars were discernible above. Unlike Mayling, he found this comforting. Some nights, the knowledge of the sea lying just beyond his sleep, ceaselessly eating away at the shoreline, restless and powerful in the dark, struck his dreams with malevolence and sent him tossing through the hours until dawn. The bluff had been Mayling's choice. Left to himself, he'd have moved into town, or built something solid and comfortable on the moors outside of Madaket. A house on peaceful Madaket harbor, perhaps, with a view of furled sails and faded wooden docks to ease the mind before bedtime. The sea off Siasconset was never calm in the dark. It stretched to the horizon, to Europe, over the bones of the *Andrea Doria* and other ships that had fallen to wrack in centuries of storms since the New World's discovery.

Nights like this, alone in the dark with the sea obscured, Sky knew what had set him apart from Rusty. Violence of feeling, violence of action, the night sea or the turbulence of the upper air tossing a small plane—he avoided these whenever possible. Rusty had thrived on them. And violence had ended his life.

Sky leaned toward the broad window and rested his forehead

121

against the glass. He closed his eyes. The image of the Mercedes's mangled front end hung in his brain. *The fog,* she had said. *I hit a deer in the fog.* "The police would have understood that, Mayling," he'd said. "Why didn't you tell them? Never, never leave the scene of an accident again."

That was a conversation from this morning, before the news of Rusty lying in the bog, his legs bruised from the front end of a car. This morning, before he'd had a reason to doubt her. And what reason, after all, did he have? Mayling had never known Rusty. She had no reason to end his life. Sky pushed himself away from the window and jerked the drapes shut. He turned in the darkened room and pounded his temples with clenched fists. What reason! It was madness. No reason to kill Rusty. An accident, then. Mayling striking something, panicking, and leaving the scene. But no, an inner voice reminded him, Rusty died facedown in the water. Whoever did this knew what it was he—or she—did. Sky stopped and stared sightlessly in front of him. What if she thought it was Peter?

He sat down in the Tihany chair and threw his head in his hands. He had to get Mayling away from here. God help him, he couldn't face what it all might mean.

"Forgive me, Rusty," he whispered.

•   •   •

WHEN MERRY FOLGER's Blazer had disappeared down the driveway, Peter drew closed the study curtains, turned off the tole lamp that sat on the desk, and put his head in his hands. It seemed a year since he had pulled open the body bag and seen Rusty's face.

He pressed his fingers to his eyes. In the darkness behind the closed lids the image of Alison's face rose unbidden, and involuntarily, he stiffened. Whenever he thought of her, his head whirled with emotion and he pulled back, afraid of the chaos. One long winter before Rafe came, when his anger had wavered and he thought he would go mad if he did not hear her name, he had written her sister for news. Molly had told him everything and nothing: Alison lived here and there, doing this or that, neither happy nor unhappy; but she was alone, it seemed, and she never spoke of him. He had tried since to shut every memory of her into a sealed chamber in his mind, and he did not want to open it now.

But George was right. She deserved to be told of Rusty's death, and her knowledge of his life in the last months of 1982 might prove invaluable. A rush of excited nausea welled in his throat. To see her—! The agony of it, the fury, the extraordinary sweetness. To see her was to lose his soul, to surrender the pride and loneliness that had held him steady for the past ten years; at what cost, Alison, he thought, at what cost? Is finding Rusty's murderer worth the loss of my splendid isolation?

A foghorn blew plaintively across the distant water, and he hesitated an instant, listening. Then he mounted the stairs to his room, the old house creaking around him in the darkness. He lay sleepless, well into the long night.

Chapter 12

"I   T'S NOT JUST THE IMPACT of the clothes, you know," Mayling said,
as she settled into the curve of the chintz sofa and crossed one slim
golden leg over the other, "it's me. I'm essentially alien to everything
on this island. You should walk around Main Street with me sometime
off-season and notice how people stare. I think I'm the only Asian in
town—barring the family that runs the Chinese restaurant. Not to
mention one of the few Jews. It turns them off my clothes—the islanders, I mean. Too foreign, too New York. I have to content myself with
catering to the summer trade."

"But you like it enough to come back every year," Merry said.

Mayling laughed, and the sound held a note of self-mockery.
"Well, it *is* one of the most beautiful places on earth, and I've never
been one to deny myself beauty. And, too, I suppose I come for the
peace. The very thing that sets me apart here—my ethnic difference—
causes New York to erupt in violence on a daily basis. On the island I
can't imagine that kind of ugliness."

"How do you explain what happened to Rusty Mason, then?"

Distress clouded Mayling's black eyes for the barest instant. "I
can't," she said. "It's utterly inexplicable. What do you make of it, Detective? Or aren't you telling?"

Merry said nothing. Mayling drew on her cigarette and then released the smoke in a long blue sigh, her gaze fixed on the distance over Merry's left shoulder.

"At a certain point every April I begin to crave the peace here, my drafting board overlooking the sea, the luxury of not having to see the same crowd of people at all the same shows—and then, around the end of August, I can't be gone quick enough. Another few days and you'd have missed me, Detective."

"Could you tell me what you were doing the night Rusty Mason died, Ms. Stern?" Merry said.

Mayling's gaze snapped back to meet her own, but her face remained immobile. "I presume I was in bed," she said.

"Alone?"

One of Mayling's nostrils flared as a thin trail of cigarette smoke wafted upward from her right hand. "In any other circumstances I wouldn't say. You police can be rather impertinent, can't you?"

Merry smiled faintly, but the warmth failed to reach her green eyes. "Be glad I'm a woman. These questions sound even worse when a man asks them. Were you alone?"

"No. Sky arrived earlier in the evening."

"By ferry?"

"Plane. From New York. A quick-turnaround trip, so he could say he'd had a Labor Day weekend. I picked him up at the airport at eight-thirty, or thereabouts. You can check his flight."

"And that evening the two of you—?"

"Stayed in. Like the dull married couple we're not."

Merry looked at Mayling over her reading glasses. The designer's voice had an ironic edge Merry knew she was not supposed to miss. She decided to ignore it for the moment.

"How long have you known Peter Mason, Ms. Stern?"

"As long as I've known Sky." She paused, and did some mental arithmetic. "That'd be eight years this past August. I met Peter my first summer on the island. He and Sky spent more time together then."

Merry lifted one black brow inquiringly, her pencil poised above her pad. Mayling shifted on the sofa and uncrossed her legs.

"This was about two years after Rusty'd broken with the family, of course, and Peter was just starting to pull his life back together. He'd come into some money when Max died, and he'd bought the land out on the moors. The bog was dredged and the runners set, but he wasn't living in the farmhouse. It was pretty much an unrenovated shell. He was camping in one wing of the old place on the Cliff Road, and we were renting in town, on Centre Street, so we just saw more of each other."

"You're one of the few people on this island who actually knew Peter Mason had a brother," Merry said. "Did he talk about him much?"

Mayling studied her for an instant, then looked down at her fingernails. "The first time he spoke of Rusty in my presence," she said, "was to tell me that he was dead."

"Does that strike you as odd?"

"No," Mayling said, and she smiled, half amused, half saddened. "It's completely typical. You don't know Peter Mason, Detective, so I'll try to be very fair to him." She looked over Merry's head, as though, Merry thought, she couldn't see her and think at the same time.

"Peter is capable of great love, and thwarted in that, I think he has turned his energies inward. He can be very focused, very driven. That made him a *summa cum laude* graduate of Princeton once; it makes him a dedicated farmer and a good athlete now. But sometimes it gets in the way of his living. As much as he thrives on being alone, he seems to envy other people's togetherness. And envy makes him sound bitter, sometimes." She stubbed out her cigarette. "And yet, at base, he's one of the dearest people on earth. He possesses integrity—which is a vanishing quality, in my life, at least. I'd trust him with a great deal."

She paused.

"But I'd never trust him in the same room with his brother."

Merry stopped writing and looked up from her pad. A curious end to a glowing testimonial. What was Mayling after? "Is he capable of killing a man?"

Mayling shifted again in her seat and glanced over one shoulder at the sea, a bright blue line capping the edge of the sunlit bluff behind the house. All of the designer's movements were abrupt, Merry reflected, in contrast to her carefully chosen words.

"I don't know," Mayling said. "I think both Sky and I have been wondering. But neither of us has been willing to say so to the other. He had the opportunity, surely, and probably the means. God knows he had the cause. I just can't decide if he had the will—not to commit the act, but to sustain the deception."

"You mean he'd crack under pressure?"

Mayling shook her head. "It's more that he's too honest. The way he's acted since the murder would be utterly uncharacteristic if he'd committed it himself. He'd be much more likely to kill Rusty in a fit of violence and then turn himself in to the police."

Merry's glasses were dangling speculatively from one corner of her mouth as she listened. She dropped her pad, stretched out her legs, and pulled her glasses briskly onto the top of her wavy blond head. "Let's talk about the cause," she said. "Why did Peter hate his brother?"

"He hasn't told you?" Mayling said, startled.

"I haven't asked."

"Well," Mayling said, and paused. "I suppose Rusty's death renders it all pretty moot, anyway. And I've been frank enough in talking about whether Peter might have killed Rusty; I suppose I can talk about why. It all goes back to Peter's engagement, Detective."

"A woman."

"The source of original sin, as we're forever reminded."

"When would this have been?"

"Summer of '82. Right after Peter and the girl—Alison Miller—left Princeton. They'd been dating forever, probably since freshman year, and Peter asked her to marry him at a big Fourth of July party the Masons threw at the Cliff Road house. Sky was invited."

1982. Her senior year at Cape Cod Community College. Merry realized, with a start, that she was the same age as Peter Mason. A slight chill ran up her back. All these unknown lives, progressing for years in parallel to her own, intersecting suddenly with a death in the dark and fog. She had passed the Masons a thousand times on the island's streets in the past three decades and never known whether they were islanders or summer people. Or cared.

She usually spent Fourth of July on a blanket in the back of a truck, a beer in her hand, watching the fireworks off Jetties Beach. Up above her on the Cliff Road, the Masons would have watched the same thing from the terrace of their perfectly mown back yard, hidden behind ten-foot boxwood hedges, the women in brightly flowered sundresses with bracelets on their tanned arms. The men would be in open-collared pastel madras shirts and vivid blazers, and their white teeth would flash in the glow of the colored sparks falling from the sky. They would drink Tanqueray and tonic. The night breeze off the sound would ruffle hair still wet from a last shower before dinner. Perhaps there had been a tent, a striped and poled affair with potted hydrangeas ranged around the tables.

Maybe, as she'd tipped back a longneck that night for another swig of beer, she'd even heard the distant strains of music, a phrase from a life that had nothing to do with her own. She had been twenty-two, and this summer she'd had her thirty-second birthday. She had worked straight through this past July Fourth. When had she stopped growing up and started aging?

"That was when Peter's mother still spent every summer here, and the kids all came home for three months, except Rusty, who was work-ing in New York," Mayling said. Merry shook herself out of reverie and met her gaze. The designer was studying her as she spoke, conscious Merry had only half heard her. "They'd fly up on weekends."

"Pretty tight-knit family."

"Perhaps. Or maybe wealth just has its routines, like everything else. I don't know."

"So did something happen at the party?"

"Nothing that gave anyone a clue as to what was coming, no. But Rusty met Alison. And then he came back to Nantucket for two weeks in August. He told Sky he needed a vacation, but it's clear, looking back, that it was Alison he was after."

"She was living at the house?"

"Yes."

"What was she like?"

"From what Sky remembers, pretty unexpected," Mayling said. "Anything but the New York debutante who'd hooked a good Establishment boy. She was solidly middle-class. Probably a lot like me," she added, to Merry's surprise.

"I think we might define 'middle-class' differently, Ms. Stern," she said. "Could you explain what you mean?"

Mayling looked slightly nettled. "I grew up in the garment district of New York, Detective. I went to public schools. My father was a wholesaler, a Jew raised in Queens, and my mother was a Chinese immigrant who worked as a seamstress in his back room. They killed themselves just to get by. That's what I mean by middle-class. Alison went to Princeton for the degree, not for the deb balls. She came up to the island and got a job waitressing while she figured out what she wanted to do next—apply to grad school, or work for a few years first."

"Thank you," Merry said. "That helps. And Peter?"

"He was pretty aimless that summer, too, Sky said. Good at knowing what he didn't want to do—work in the family business—but unable to hit on an alternative. He took a job as a lifeguard at Jetties Beach and spent his off hours reading self-help career guides. *What Color Is Your Parachute*, that sort of thing."

Merry searched her memory for a youthful Peter Mason lifesaving on Jetties Beach, and gave up. She found it hard to picture him young. He seemed incapable of its essential silliness.

"So the farm wasn't even a thought at that point?"

"No. I think he was toying with law school. Sky's influence, probably—he was approaching his third year at Harvard." Mayling pressed her hands against her eyes.

"You okay?" Merry asked.

"Fine," she said. "I've just had these splitting headaches lately. End-of-season blues, probably." She glanced up, her black eyes unfocused, searching for the thread of her thought. "Peter. Yes. He had a lot of time to think it over during the winter."

"Alison left him?"

"By Labor Day. To do her justice, she probably never stood a chance. The way Sky tells it, Rusty was a competitive bastard. He measured himself against every guy he came in contact with. Even his brother, even though he was four years older and Peter, up to that point, adored him. Rusty never failed, Sky said, to get anything he decided he had to have. He set out to seduce Alison, and so of course he was successful."

"So in Rusty's mind, it was just a passing fling?"

"Hard to say, because of everything else that happened. It might have lasted, who knows? She left the island with him and lived in his Manhattan apartment until he had to flee the country later that year. I don't know if she went with him."

"Rusty fled the country. Why, Ms. Stern?"

Mayling avoided her eyes and bent toward the coffee table for her pack of Dunhills. She shook one into her palm with delicate fingers and held it to her mouth. Gaining time again, Merry thought. There's something no one wants to talk about here. A sealed indictment is nothing to sneeze at, but would that shut up an entire family?

"I don't know," Mayling said, shaking out a match and exhaling. Merry winced. The smoke was starting to get to her. "I don't think Sky knows, either. And he said once that Max—Peter's father—refused to mention Rusty's name or anything to do with his crime. The same with Alison. She's never mentioned by the Masons, any more than Rusty is. So I've no idea what happened to her."

Merry set her reading glasses back on her nose and fished around for her pad. She picked up a pencil and wrote "Alison Miller," in her rounded, left-handed script, on a clean page. "So Peter's been nursing a grudge for all these years because a college love affair went sour?" she said. She underscored the name on the pad heavily, twice.

"Peter's never given Alison up, not in any visceral sense," Mayling said. "That's not particularly healthy, but I don't believe he has any control over it. And he felt betrayed by Rusty, Detective. By the brother he adored. He could never forgive Rusty for that. They were both Masons, and the Masons are excellent haters."

"And now the object of his hatred is dead," Merry said slowly.

Mayling nodded. "If any good is likely to come of Rusty's murder, it's that Peter finally may give up the bitterness that's been ruining his life."

But, Merry wondered, would killing his brother get rid of the hatred? Or had it become so necessary that he would hold on to it at all cost? Did hatred make him less likely to end Rusty's life? "You said Sky met Alison. What did he think of her?"

Mayling considered her answer. "He had only a partial sense of her, I'd say. She was smart as a whip, of course. He said she was very verbal."

"Meaning?"

"An effortless vocabulary, the sort of wit that takes the form of puns and double entendres. Sky seemed to consider her good at drawing people out. He said the Masons—Julia, George, Max—were entirely charmed by her. And Max had been against Peter's engagement; he thought he was too young. As perhaps he was." She stopped abruptly, and thought further. "One thing Sky said made sense to me: he said Alison and Peter seemed to fit. He couldn't explain what he meant. But I understood. I have felt it myself, about Sky, that he's an extension of myself and I of him. They were probably two people who completed each other."

"And yet she left him after two weeks of Rusty?"

"Peter had found Rusty irresistible for most of his life. It makes sense to me that someone as close to him as Alison was would react in exactly the same way."

Merry cleared her throat. "Has Peter seen anyone else on the island since? Or off, for that matter?"

"You mean, has he been emotionally involved? I don't know, really. I can't say I'd be the first person he'd tell. He spends a lot of time with a schoolteacher here on the island, Lucy Jacoby. But there never seems to be much between them. Except companionship. It's too bad, really. Peter has so much to offer. He just doesn't seem capable of feeling, anymore."

Merry shoved her blond hair behind her ears and flipped closed the cardboard cover of her steno pad. "Thank you, Ms. Stern. You've been very helpful."

"Not at all."

Merry assessed her for an instant, liking her more as she left than she had when she arrived. "I must say, as an islander, that I love your clothes," she said. "I just can't afford them. The other day I was glued to your window by some incredible sweaters you've got there."

"The Chinese New Year sweaters," Mayling said, and smiled. Merry felt rather than saw the tension in her body relax. "I'm glad to hear you like them." When Merry looked puzzled, she added, "It's the animal buttons. The Chinese lunar calendar—the zodiac, if you will—runs according to a twelve-year cycle, each year represented by an animal."

Comprehension broke over Merry's face. "The Year of the Dragon," she said.

"For instance. Yes. Or the Horse. Or the Chicken, to take a less exalted example. When were you born?"

"1960."

"You and me both," Mayling said. "The Year of the Rat."

The image of a wooden button, meant to look like ivory, like a raw bone, flashed before Merry's eyes, and her face must have changed. Mayling laughed. "It's not that bad, really," she said. "You're not supposed to resemble the animal of your sign."

"I didn't happen to notice whether you had a rat sweater in the window," Merry said. "Did you make many of them?"

"Oh, I could find you one, don't worry. They've met with varying degrees of success. So few people know the sign of their birth year; they scooped up the ones with the rabbits and dragons, and left those with the rats and pigs. Unfortunate. I'll have to give them away."

"Do you happen to know if anyone on the island bought one?"

"A sweater? Of course. Scads. Although they sell better in New York. Everything does." Mayling stubbed out her cigarette and gave Merry a long look. "What's going on? Was Rusty wearing one?"

Merry reached into her pocket and withdrew the plastic evidence bag that held the button she'd lifted from the grass by Peter Mason's driveway. "No, but his murderer was," she said. "There were some prints on it. We haven't identified them."

Mayling reached for the bag and turned it over in her palm. "It's from a rat sweater, all right," she said. "I should know; I wear one myself."

"Could I see it?" Merry asked, her voice carefully neutral.

132

Mayling looked at her swiftly. There was a moment's pause. "Of course," she said, and rose to go upstairs.

She returned in a matter of seconds with a cardigan made of heathered wool in the shifting colors of the sea, and handed it wordlessly to Merry. A solid row of rats marched up the left edge.

"Looks like the real thing," Merry said. "Does any other manufacturer use this type of button?"

Mayling shook her head. "They're a unique design."

The sweater formed a soft weight in Merry's lap, like a sleeping cat. She shook it out and held it above her head, noticing the creases remained, as though it had been folded some time. A faint odor of plastic clung to the wool. Either this sweater had been stored unworn for some time, or it was fresh from the manufacturer's carton. She doubted it had come from Mayling's drawer. "It's terrific," she said. "When did it come into the store?"

"About mid-July. The color would be wonderful with your hair, you know."

"Is there any way you could trace the sale of specific sweaters?"

"I could try, I suppose," Mayling said slowly. "But I'll be honest. It's highly improbable that either the New York or the island store noted the type of sweater sold in most cases, if they did at all. And with the number of New Yorkers who come to Nantucket, the button lost at Peter's could have been owned by almost anyone." She folded her arms under her breasts protectively, as though feeling a chill. "Detective— this probably is irrelevant, but—"

"But what?"

"I sold one to Peter, you know, rather early on."

"To Peter? For himself?"

She shook her head. "It was a birthday gift. To Lucy Jacoby."

When Mayling Stern had shut the door of the house on the bluff, Merry walked to the Blazer without looking back. She imagined the designer standing just to one side of a window, too intelligent to pull back a blind and betray her watchful gaze, but following her progress down the hydrangea-lined path just the same. Merry glanced at the passenger side of the car, and saw with relief that Seitz was inside, his head rocking to inaudible music. She yanked open the driver's side door and jumped in. Seitz's head hit the Blazer's roof with a little jolt of surprise.

"Find anything in the garage?" she said, as she started the car.

"Just a mangled front end," he said. "Got some great pictures. Some soil and paint samples, too."

Chapter 13

THE BOYS—PERHAPS FORTY OF THEM—faced off in two lines on the muddy field, and hurled themselves at each other on the coach's command. Their bodies, some gawky, some newly powerful, collided in a shuddering of bone and curses that was audible across the field where Will Starbuck stood. He had been poised on the slight rise between the high school parking lot and the football field for an hour, an oversized T-shirt rucked up around the hands he'd shoved in the pockets of his jeans, waiting for something. He did not know exactly what.

The coach blew piercingly on his whistle, and the grappling bodies fell apart. "Okay, okay, work it out, work it out," he shouted. The crowd of muddied uniforms, with their bulging pads incongruously large for the breadth of the players' bodies, turned toward the far goalpost in unison and began to lap the field. One boy cast a glance over his shoulder and, it seemed to Will, saw him for an instant. Then he turned back and trotted on. Sandy Stewart, who had been his best friend. Will stood still, the familiar shame and nausea burning in his gut.

The coach was walking toward him, whistling something that might have been "Ninety-nine Bottles of Beer on a Wall." He was short and powerful, a bulldog of a man who had once been a nearly great defensive linesman for an obscure college. Now he lived for the single game the Saturday before Thanksgiving, when his boys took on the high school from Martha's Vineyard in one of the age-long rivalries the islands cultivated. His team was an acknowledged powerhouse among the ten small-town high schools that made up the Mayflower League. The Whalers had won two games to every one the Vineyard had managed to pull out over the past several decades, despite the fact that Vineyard High had twice Nantucket's talent pool. The coach made the most of the kids he had. Roughly one quarter of the two hundred–odd students at the school were on the football team. He had shaped the perspectives of generations of Whalers.

He grunted as he took the slight rise toward the school, throwing his back into it. He seemed unaware of Will standing motionless above him.

"Hey, Coach," Will said.

The coach glanced up as he crested the rise, and nodded coolly. "Hello, Starbuck."

"Listen, Coach—" Will began, somewhat desperately.

"You want to play football, right, Starbuck?"

Will stopped, looked down at his shoes, and nodded.

"Then where were you three weeks ago, when practice started? Every other kid out there managed to get himself to the field in August."

Will looked up and met the coach's eyes, and the man was startled at the boy's expression. He looked as though he had been slapped. A sensitive kid. The kind that drove him nuts. "Look, I've got to see some commitment before I can make a place for you on the team," he said. "There's no freeloaders on the Whalers, you understand? None of this on-again, off-again business." He paused, and pulled out one of his favorite phrases. "You don't win games with a short attention span."

"I know," Will said.

"Maybe next year you'll take the time to come over early. Talk to me then." The coach turned as a horn blared at his elbow, and saw a Nantucket police Blazer pulling up behind him with a woman inside. She rolled down the window, leaned out, and waved cheerily at Will.

The coach looked back at the boy, who flushed.

"Trouble follows you around, doesn't it, Starbuck?" he said. Will didn't answer him. He was waiting for the coach to walk away before he approached Meredith Folger. She turned off the ignition and opened the car door.

"Hey, Will, how's the first day of high school?" she said.

He thought of the frozen faces of his home room, the guys who'd looked past him. Thought of the word "fruitcake" that had been scrawled on his locker door in pink highlighter, faint but unmistakable, the period before lunch. Thought of how he'd eaten alone, nearly choking on the peanut butter and jelly Tess had packed for him, while a table of girls tittered and giggled across the aisle, pretending they weren't talking about him when he met their eyes. Thought of Sandy Stewart slouched in front of his buddies, stone-faced and remote, saying, "Yo, Starbuck. You're back," and then walking past him to sit somewhere else. He was a pariah. A refugee from the funny farm. A kid with a padded cell.

"Couldn't be better," he said to Merry Folger. "It's gonna be a great year."

She smiled brightly and then looked past him to the football team, now finished its laps and laboring wearily up the rise to the parking lot. The guys surveyed the squad car and Will standing uneasily next to it, and nudged one another. Sandy Stewart met Merry's eyes and nodded once, curtly, then looked away. The entire group fell silent as they passed her, until one kid in the back started humming the "do-do-*do*-do, do-do-*do*-do" of the *Twilight Zone* theme and the rest of them burst out in snickers. She turned back to Will, her smile gone and a slight furrow between her green eyes. "Not a group with triple-digit IQs, huh?"

"They're okay," he said defensively. "What do you want?"

"Nothing much," Merry said. "I just came over because I saw you. I'm looking for Lucy Jacoby."

"Miss Jacoby? The English teacher?"

"Yep."

"She's not here."

"Darn, I thought I'd catch her," Merry said, and pulled out her keys. "You don't happen to know where she lives, do you?"

"Actually, yeah, I do," Will said. "Out at Tom Nevers. Off the Chuck Hollow Road, right around where it intersects Jonathan Lane. She's got a pink door. But I think she's sick."

Merry stopped in the act of opening her car door. "Didn't she come in today?"

Will shook his head. "It didn't really matter, since all they do the first day is pass out books and stuff," he said. "But it was a weird way to start the year. And she didn't get a substitute—they usually do if they know they're going to be out."

Merry nodded thoughtfully, one foot on the car's doorsill. Then she looked at Will. As usual his fine-boned face was pale, and the dark circles under his beautiful eyes seemed, unbelievably, to have deepened. He must not have slept the previous night. "Want me to run you home?"

He shook his head. "I've got the bike. I thought I'd drop by Peter's and see how the harvest is going. But thanks."

• • •

THE DOOR WAS CLOSER to old rose than pink. The cottage nestled between two big-shouldered, obviously new houses thrust forward on the Chuck Hollow Road, windows looking blankly south into the Atlantic. Summer people, Merry decided, gone back to the mainland for the winter. Lucy Jacoby's house would be the only one with lights on these fall evenings, but come spring, the bulk of her absent neighbors' houses would shield her somewhat from the ceaseless winds. The house looked cozy for a woman living alone.

For a moment, Merry imagined what it would be like to have her own house, an ordered refuge from work, instead of living amid the jumble on Tattle Court. Then she stifled the impulse. She was lucky even to be able to live on the island. Most of the kids she'd grown up with had been priced out of the housing market and had moved to Boston suburbs. It was the single ones like her who could stay, taking rooms with aging relatives and clinging to a life that was swiftly vanishing. The alternative was to sell the plots of undeveloped land passed

down through generations, buying security with a fast real estate killing. She knew of people who had done that, and she couldn't reproach
them. She just couldn't see doing it herself.

There was a Folger lot just outside of Surfside, but she never
thought of it as marketable. Someday she would build a house on it,
something she could call her own. But for now, Ralph Waldo and her
father remained her only relations in the world, the two who had made
home for her whenever she needed it. While they lived, she would stay
at Tattle Court.

Merry parked the car to the side of the road in front of the house
and walked up the drive. A knockoff of a Nantucket lightship basket
hung from the door, a few uncollected letters still sitting inside it. She
pushed the bell and waited. After about thirty seconds, she pushed the
bell again. Perhaps it was out of order. She knocked firmly on the door
and listened, holding her breath, for some movement inside the house.
Where was Lucy Jacoby if not home sick in bed?

She turned and walked back down the path, then stopped and
scanned the house, her hands shielding her eyes. No lights shone from
the windows on either side of the door. The eaves of the roof sloped
down to the first floor; there were no dormers cut in the loft space
above. The house looked blank and unoccupied. Merry took the path
leading around the left side of the house to the yard, hesitated in front
of the gate, and then opened it.

The garden was carefully plotted and groomed, with semicircular
beds ranged around a center square of roses in riotous bloom. Merry
stopped in respect. Roses like these—hybrid teas rather than the hardy
island ramblers that covered fences and cottage roofs—were extraor-
dinarily difficult to grow. The damp climate encouraged black spot.
She walked over to them slowly and reached out a finger to touch an
enormous Peace rose, pink and yellow and cream, awed that something
so beautiful could be hidden away behind the house. Lucy Jacoby was
either a pro or engaged in a labor of love.

Merry started as a patchwork cat made a four-point landing on the
large sundial in the middle of the rosebed, curled its tail around its
body, and gazed at her soberly.

"I don't belong here, do I, but you're too well-bred to say so."

The cat flicked one ear and looked away.

"No, you don't," a woman said.

Merry turned. The slight figure standing under the loggia that ran the length of the house took a step backward into the shadows under the vines. Merry strained to make out her face. "Miss Jacoby?" she said.

"Of course," the woman said impatiently. "Who are you?"

"Detective Meredith Folger," Merry said, walking toward her, "of the Nantucket police."

Lucy Jacoby turned to the steps leading up to her back door and sat down abruptly. She put her head in her hands.

Merry stopped short. "They said you called in sick today at school," she said. "You okay?"

"Yes, yes, I'm fine," Lucy said. She pressed her hands against her head once, briefly, as if adjusting a hat, and then looked up at Merry. "I was—expecting someone else."

Merry stared at her wordlessly. Expecting? Or avoiding? She had imagined Peter Mason's sometime girlfriend would reek of off-island elegance—the sort who knew how to assess wine and hoist herself out of a limo without her dress hiking up for the camera; the kind who could attend auctions and bid without anyone knowing she was there. Lucy had all the elements of a beauty, but she was crumpled on her doorstep like an emptied sack. Her eyes told Merry she had braced herself for pain, and beseeched her to make it quick.

"I only wanted to talk to you for a few minutes," she said, "but if now's not a good time—"

"You'll come back?" Lucy said, a note of panic in her voice. "No! Just say what you have to say now."

Merry shifted awkwardly in her Top-Siders and glanced around the yard. The crash of surf at Tom Nevers Head came faintly up from the shore, and shades of crimson and orange crept along the horizon to the west. The calico cat arched its back against her bare knees and slid around her leg, meowing soundlessly. Lucy reached for her and pulled her into a huddled lump against her cheek.

"Can we go inside?" Merry asked.

Lucy hesitated, then nodded and stood up. She turned toward the house, holding the screen door open behind her.

The cottage held only two rooms, a small kitchen and an open area that served as living room, dining room, and study. A large easy chair and ottoman facing the fireplace still held the imprint of Lucy's body. An open bottle of wine and a half-filled glass stood on the end table next to the chair. Against the front wall sat a desk cluttered with papers and a computer, and next to it was a wine rack holding about thirty bottles, Merry guessed. She glanced up at the open vault of the ceiling, clear to the second story, and saw skylights cut in the roof on the garden side. The railing of a loft topped the partition to the kitchen: Lucy's sleeping area, probably. The walls—as in Peter Mason's study—held shelves of books from floor to ceiling. Merry wandered over to them and scanned the titles while Lucy Jacoby ran a glass under the tap. *The Perpetual Orgy: Flaubert and Madame Bovary*, she read. *The Great Cat Massacre. Gilgamesh. In Search of Lost Roses.*

"Why'd they send a woman?" Lucy said, as she walked into the room. "Did they think I'd talk to you more easily?"

Merry turned. "Talk about what?"

"Whatever it is you want to know."

"This is a great house," Merry said. "Somebody did a terrific job of gutting and renovating the space."

"Thank you," Lucy said. She set her glass down on an end table and hugged her elbows. "Call it therapy. I spent the winter after my divorce tearing out walls. A fitting metaphor, I thought."

"You did this? Wow." She scanned the room with respect.

"There's no end to my ingenuity, Detective. I surprise even myself with what I get away with."

Merry turned and looked at her. "Have a seat," Lucy said. "And say what you came to say." She remained standing, braced for some onslaught, in the middle of the room.

Merry sat down on the ottoman, a trifle gingerly, feeling as though she were sitting on someone's unmade bed. For all its simplicity, the room was a place of richness and wealth. The wool throw on the back of the chair was from Nantucket Looms, as was the deep purple rag rug, and both had cost a fortune. "I'm told you're a friend of Peter Mason's, and I'd like some information about him, if you're willing to offer it."

Lucy stood still for an instant, as if the words she had been waiting for had yet to come. Then she seemed to crumple slightly, and reached for her glass. She took a long drink. "That's it?" she said. "That's why you're here?"

Merry nodded. Lucy closed her eyes, and Merry could almost feel the relief that suffused her body.

"You were expecting something else," Merry said.

Lucy's eyes flew open, and a warning flashed for an instant in her face. Then she shrugged and turned to sit in a chair. "I'm sorry, Detective," she said, "but when you've lived with someone as violent as my ex-husband you stop expecting trouble to be somebody else's problem. Even after five years, I'm afraid of what I'll hear. Now, what's happened to Peter?"

"His brother was found dead over at the farm," Merry said, "and we're making some routine inquiries of his friends."

Lucy sat very still, and all expression left her face. Then she crossed to the fire and picked up the tongs, busying herself with the screen as she spoke. "How awful. I must call him right away."

"He hasn't told you?" Merry asked.

"Why should he?" Lucy said, turning toward her. She looked faintly defiant, as if she were challenging Meredith to say what she was thinking, that it was odd Peter Mason hadn't sought her out for comfort at his brother's death. "He must be terribly upset. And death is a family matter first, not something you share with friends," she said. She smoothed her wild curls and turned back to the fire. As she lifted a log with the tongs, Merry noticed, her hands were shaking.

"How long have you known Mr. Mason?" Merry asked.

"Why does it matter?"

"Let's just say that anything could matter. In fact, it might keep Peter from being murdered."

"Murdered? But that's ridiculous. Why would anyone want to kill Peter? And the brother's death was an accident, surely?"

Merry hesitated. "Rusty Mason—that was his name—was murdered, Miss Jacoby. You can trust me on that. The problem is, he hadn't been on this island in ten years or so, and there's a chance he was killed by mistake. We have to work to some extent on the assumption that the intended victim was Peter Mason. That's why I'm talking to you."

Lucy put the tongs down and gripped the mantel, leaning against it as she stared into the flames. She took a deep breath and then expelled it, slowly. "All right," she said. She pulled out the desk chair and sat down, propping her feet on the ottoman near Merry's leg. "Shoot."

Merry pulled her pad and her half-glasses out of her purse. "Start with when you met," she suggested.

"Five years ago, the first winter I came to the island."

Merry looked up, pen poised, and waited. Lucy looked at her steadily and said nothing. Finally she looked away, at the fire, and capitulated.

"We met in the Nantucket Bookworks one dreary February evening, when the light was gone by five o'clock and I was certain I wouldn't last out the day if I didn't talk to someone. I threw on something and drove into town, drove anywhere, half-mad because it was an island and I couldn't get off. I'd been running away for so long, I'd gotten used to the feeling, you see. If there'd been a ferry I'd probably have left everything and never come back. But there was a light coming out of the bookshop. Peter was reading."

She stopped. Merry hesitated. "And had you read the book or something?" she said.

"The book? What book?"

"That he was reading. You know, like, 'The good part is on page sixty-seven,' or something like that."

Lucy Jacoby smiled faintly. "*Reading.* He was reading his poems aloud. You didn't know he was a poet?"

"Of course not," Merry said. "I don't know anything about him. That's why I'm here."

"He's quite a talent, in fact. Lyric, tortured, very dark; and always—*always*—impassioned with words. I keep trying to get him for my senior class, but he's so damnably shy about his poetry." She ran a thin finger around the rim of her glass, an impatient gesture that covered her rapidity of thought. "He only reads during the winter, when the off-islanders have gone home, you know. And as for getting him to publish . . ."

"And so you struck up a conversation?"

Lucy looked down at her hands. "I don't know if you can understand what I was like that winter," she said. "Nothing could make me whole again. I swung between a giddy euphoria and the blackest gloom. I used to lie awake nights and either thank God I was free—or imagine ways I could kill myself. And then there was Peter, reading, and every word he spoke was a lifeline thrown out to me. I clung to it. I stood by a bookshelf and listened to poem after poem, struck dumb, incapable even of clapping when he finished. Everyone left, in the dribs and drabs of people who really don't want to go home again, out into the wet. I was more honest. I stayed. He looked up from the papers he was gathering together so carefully with those strong hands of his, and saw my face. I had tears running down it. I must have looked like an idiot. He became very still."

Lucy met Merry's eyes, and her own were filled with tears. "I can't describe it. He nodded once, and said, 'You were *listening*, weren't you?' I knew what he meant. We've been friends ever since."

Merry shifted uncomfortably, aware that she was out of her depth. "And he never mentioned his brother?"

Lucy started, and shook her head. "I've met his sister, George, and the children; but other than his mother he never mentions family. He doesn't seem to be involved with anyone, either."

"Involved?"

"Emotionally. Sexually. What you will. There are no women in his life." Her head was up, daring Merry to ask her why she wasn't.

"How often do you see Mr. Mason, Miss Jacoby?"

She didn't hesitate. "Three times a week."

"Every week?"

"Absolutely. We do interval training together at the high school track on Mondays, Wednesdays, and Fridays. Five o'clock. He rarely misses."

"Intervals?" said Merry, bewildered. Peter Mason did altogether too much with his time.

"Wind sprints. A quarter mile fast, a quarter mile slow," Lucy said. "Increases your speed and your distance. Not that I can keep up with him; he just likes the company. And lapping me, of course," she said.

"I see. Did you run yesterday?"

Lucy Jacoby dropped her eyes and then looked away. She swallowed. "No," she said. "I couldn't make it. I left a message to that effect with Rebecca." Her eyes drifted toward her wineglass and Merry thought she would reach for it, but she restrained herself and leaned forward. "How is any of this likely to help Peter, Detective?"

"His friends might know if he'd been threatened, even if he couldn't admit it to himself." Merry thrust her fingers through her bangs, forgetting that today she had clipped them back in a barrette; the hair caught and snarled, and she let out a sound of annoyance.

"Is there anyone on the island likely to gain from Peter Mason's death? Anyone who'd be happy if he were injured?" she said.

Lucy pondered the question for several seconds, and then her eyes narrowed. "I can't answer that specifically," she said, "but I'd be willing to bet there are a number."

Merry had expected a flat negative. "A number?"

"He's a Mason, Detective. When you're as powerful and driving and hungry as that family has been, you breed violence and you attract it in return. If Rusty's the first to die, they've been lucky."

Merry reflected that the English teacher had a flair for the dramatic. Her gloom probably made for difficult living as well. Lucy was staring off into space, lost in thought, her thin legs drawn up under her chin. The cloud of auburn hair curling around her face and the lines running from nose to mouth gave her the look of a terrible angel, an avenging creature of wings, sword, and fire. She had wrestled her demons to the brink of the abyss, her face seemed to say, and perhaps had thrown herself into it with them.

"Ms. Jacoby," Merry said, "where were you Sunday night?"

Lucy Jacoby turned her head slowly and gazed at her without recognition. Then she shook herself slightly. "What time?"

"Oh, between, say, dinnertime and breakfast."

Lucy said nothing for several seconds. Then, "So you think I killed Rusty?" she said. "Why in God's name would I do that? How could you even think it possible?" Her voice rose with a slightly hysterical edge.

"I'm asking purely as a matter of routine, Ms. Jacoby. In case you saw or heard something that might help us out."

"Well, I didn't," Lucy said angrily. "If you want to know, I wasn't even here. I was over on the Cape shopping for clothes at the Labor Day sales."

"When did you get back?"

"I had dinner, saw a movie, and then caught the last ferry home."

"The one that gets in at ten-thirty P.M."

"Yes."

"Had you parked your car in the day lot?"

"Why does it matter?"

"I wondered how you got home. If you took a taxi, you'd have a witness," Merry said. Her voice and her eyes were hard. Lucy Jacoby's discomfort made her uneasy.

"Well, it's just too bad, isn't it, that my car's been in the shop for a week. I rode my bike to the ferry and I rode it back. I'm sorry that doesn't suit your purposes."

"I have no purposes," Merry said, "only procedures. I'm sorry you've been having car trouble. A week sounds serious."

"The clutch died," Lucy said distractedly. "No surprise in a seven-year-old American car."

"One last question," Merry said. "Peter Mason gave you a birthday gift, I understand."

Lucy looked puzzled. "The sweater."

Merry nodded. "Have you lost one of the buttons, by any chance? Perhaps after visiting Mason Farms?"

"I've never worn the sweater, Detective."

"Really." Merry was startled, and showed it. If she'd owned one, she'd never have taken it off.

"It was the buttons, actually. I have a phobia about rats. I can't stand them—I never could, even as a child. I gave the sweater away to a clothing drive, and I didn't have the courage to tell Peter. Why are you interested in his sweater?"

"It's not important. You wouldn't happen to remember the clothing drive?"

Lucy hesitated, and reached for her wineglass. "Our Lady of the Island," she said. "For their bazaar. Sometime around the first of August, I think it was. My birthday is July fifteenth."

Merry took off her glasses and stood up. "Thanks for your time."

"Not at all," Lucy said automatically. She looked, however, like a wounded animal. Merry felt vaguely guilty. Lucy led her to the door, and turned, one hand on the knob. "If I can help in any way, don't hesitate to ask. But do call first before you come out," she said. "I won my sanctuary, Detective, and I guard it jealously."

.   .   .

As she drove away, Merry wondered why Lucy Jacoby had no interest in knowing how Rusty Mason died. And what had compelled her to drink so heavily that she had missed the first day of school.

Chapter 14

PETER HOOKED ONE HIP-BOOTED LEG over the side of the flatbed truck, reached his hand into the shifting mass of cranberries, and let the wet beads run through his fingers. A day's harvest, he thought, a piling up of summer's wealth, and with it a certain sadness. The crop was a good one, a relief after the disease that had swept New England's bogs in recent years, and he felt lucky. But the flatbed truck, bound for the ferry and an Ocean Spray depot, represented the end of the growing season—so exuberant in its ripening, and yet so quickly gone to death. It was a need for rebirth that had driven him into farming in the first place; now the promise of spring, the chance to witness a yearly renewal, kept him in the business. In a few months, the tight mat of red-black vines running over acre after acre of his land would settle into a protective layer of ice; he and the farm would endure a winter vigil that always seemed to last too long. He shook off his hands and jumped down to the ground.

Rafe sat on the running board of the truck's cab, a beer resting on one bent knee. A spreading map of sweat stained the shirt under his heavy overalls. The dog Ney was sprawled on the wet turf next to him, muzzle on forepaws, his clear, light eyes following every movement the two men made. A yellow metal wet-harvesting machine—called a beater because of the egg-beating effect of its blades in the water—was propped at rest where the waterlogged vines began, just beyond the truck. When propelled through the flooded fields, the whirling blades knocked the berries off their vines and sent them bobbing in a blood-red tide to the surface. The beaters were large and awkward, like early forms of the velocipede, or nightmarish insects; but they were simple improvements on a harvesting process that had changed little through the first century of cranberry cultivation.

That morning, Peter had summoned the crew of harvesters and, avoiding the acreage where Rusty had died, moved to the land on the other side of the driveway. They had opened the sluice gates of the channels that ran from Gibbs Pond to the farm and flooded the bog for a wet harvest. Peter liked to start the season that way: taking the fruit intended for processing first, and leaving the perfect berries, bound for the grocer, to be hand-picked last. Striding with the beaters through thigh-high water had given them all a sense of purpose and shifted some of the weight of Monday's violence.

"I think we've made us some money, Pete," Rafe said.

"Yeah, we'll survive the winter." He sat down next to Rafe and reached for the foreman's beer. The two men grinned at one another. Ocean Spray paid the growers in its cooperative about fifty-five dollars for each hundred-pound barrel. The Mason Farms bog yielded an average of 190 barrels per acre. They had harvested five acres to date, and had forty-five more to go. The revenues for the year would be over five hundred thousand dollars.

Peter tipped back Rafe's bottle and took a long draft, then wiped his face with his T-shirt and sighed deeply. The suspenders of his overalls hung down to his knees. "I understand why nobody ran marathons fifty years ago," he said, fondling Ney's ruff. "No farmhand in his right mind would move if he had the option of sitting for an hour. Much less taking a nap. I feel like an old man."

"You *are* an old man, son," Rafe said, and slapped him on the shoulder. "Just can't face it. All that training of yours is one pathetic denial. You'll run tonight and you won't be able to move tomorrow. But I'll be out here working."

"It's Wednesday, Rafe. Can't disappoint Lucy."

Rafe snorted and took back his beer. "Yeah, well, don't come whining when you can't pedal home, you hear? Because I'm already gone. Taking the Rover with me."

"No ride, no sympathy. Got it. How's Tess?"

"Same as always, pretty much. She won't relax until the kid starts to look normal and acts more like it. He's too peaky, too quiet, keeps too much to himself. He's lost that kid look."

"The unself-conscious immersion in his world."

"I s'pose."

Peter braced himself on Rafe's knee and stood up. As if on cue, Ney hauled himself to his feet and waited, tail up, for his master to choose a direction. "Should he be coming out here all the time after what happened Monday?"

"Can't keep avoiding places. Rate the kid's going, he won't be able to leave the house." Rafe shielded his eyes with his hand as he looked up at Peter. He stood backlit in the slanting rays of late afternoon, his dark hair a bright helmet. "Besides, he's happy when he's here. Doesn't matter if he's harvesting, like yesterday, or sitting with a book in the house, he's doing something other than moping, and that's all to the good."

"If Tess thinks there's anything that might help . . ."

"She'll tell you. The girl's proud, but she ain't shy."

• • •

LUCY JACOBY STOOD with her hands braced against the goalpost, one Lycra-clad leg bent and the other stretched firmly behind her. She was lost in thought. Occasionally a passing member of the track team would wave and smile at the English teacher—Lucy's athleticism was an oddity among the faculty, and her running tights something of a sensation—but she didn't notice. Shifting from one stretched leg to the other, she went through her pre-run warm-up with the mechanical precision of long familiarity. She was thinking of Will Starbuck. There was something too casual and studied in his questions about Madame Bovary, the book she had assigned the advanced sophomores. He was intensely interested in Emma's suicide, and doing a poor job of hiding it.

A sixth sense compelled Lucy to turn suddenly and scan the high school parking lot. She was rewarded with the sight of Peter turning his racing bike in from the Surfside Road. As he rolled to a halt, he clicked his right shoe out of the bike's clip and swung off the saddle. Lucy raised one arm in greeting. He looked up and saw her.

She set off at a slow trot toward the parking lot, cutting across the track and the field, while Peter changed from bike to running shoes. Her sweatshirt would be too warm, she decided. The day had started cool, with a hint of fog, but the sun had burned through by noon and the September day was hot.

"Hey," she said. "I wasn't sure you'd come."

Peter looked up from locking his bike and smiled at her. "Training. My substitute for God."

"I thought that was me."

"No, you're what keeps me honest." He stood up and bounced from one leg to the other, unaware that her face had drained of color. "I wouldn't be here today if you weren't waiting. Turn around."

Lucy obediently presented her back. Peter braced himself against her shoulders and stretched his calves. "Thanks for the flowers, by the way."

Lucy was thankful he couldn't see her. "Not at all."

Peter released her and stood up. "Ready?"

"I mean, no, forget not at all," Lucy said, turning around to face him. "That's a stupid convention. I've been feeling so inadequate. Your brother dies—is *murdered*—and I don't even hear about it for two days. And then I send flowers. It's so ridiculous! I feel like such an idiot! I've never known how to deal with death."

"It's okay," Peter said. "The flowers were nice."

"*Nice*. Nice is not what you need when you're facing a funeral. Why do we do these things? Why couldn't I just come over to your house and talk to you?"

"Because the car was in the shop?"

"I was even afraid to call you, Peter. I'm such a jerk."

"You're not a jerk," he said, awkwardly reaching one hand to her elbow. She stiffened at his touch, and he remembered they were at the school. He looked around. No one seemed remotely interested in them.

"I should have called you," he said. "I'm sorry. You said Friday you were going to the Cape to shop, and then when everything happened Monday I completely forgot about running. Yesterday I just wanted to get the harvest started—"

"I've just been asking myself why normal expressions of feeling are so hard for us to say to one another. They always have been, always will be, I think. We're both so bad at it."

"Are we?" Peter said, surprised. He thought for a moment. "I suppose we are. I am, certainly." He hesitated, and looked away from her. "I don't know whether I just can't talk about emotion or whether I don't feel deeply enough to express it. And I'd rather not debate the question, most days."

Lucy looked down at her shoes. "Anyway, I'm sorry it had to be something as trite as flowers. I could have called, at least, and asked if you were okay."

"I'm okay," Peter said. "Really. There's no question something as brutal and unexpected as a drowning in the front yard has the power to unsettle me. I'd be lying if I said it didn't. But that's over. I can turn my energy to finding out who did it."

" 'I am a rock,' huh? Reason over emotion?"

"If you like. It's how I live." His words were clipped and his voice held an edge.

"Fine. Fine. Forget I even brought it up."

"You didn't. I did. Now let's run."

They set off for the field in lockstep, neither looking at the other. Peter's gray eyes had gone flat as a rainy day. Lucy sighed audibly and then stopped in midstride.

"Look, could we skip the sprints today and just take a long, slow run? I've been cooped up inside for a couple of days and I'd really like to get off this track."

Peter turned and studied her for an instant. Her eyes had heavy shadows under them and her cheekbones stood out prominently under the cloud of auburn curls. "Are you eating enough?" he asked. She nodded impatiently.

"I was out sick yesterday, that's all."

"Sick?"

"Just under the weather."

It was unusual for Lucy to indulge her blues on a weekday. She rarely missed school. She saw the concern in Peter's eyes and looked away.

"What happened on the Cape?" he asked.

"Nothing." She stirred the asphalt dust with her toe. "Really. The Cape was fine. Got a terrific dress, saw a movie, bought four boxes of seconds at the Cape Cod Candle factory—"

"Lucy," Peter said, reaching for her shoulders and shaking her slightly. "Don't do this. What happened?"

"I saw someone I used to know," she said, straining away from him. "On the ferry."

"From Italy? From the old days?"

She nodded, and tears formed in her eyes. She did not want him to see her cry.

"Did he speak to you?"

"What do you think? It's a goddam ferry, you can't get off!" she burst out. "I thought I'd go insane. I kept moving, I kept changing my seat, but he kept following me around the boat. I swear, Peter, I was this close to jumping over the side."

"What did you do?"

"I ducked into the women's room and stayed there until the boat docked."

"For two and a half hours? Is this guy on the island?"

"I guess so. I didn't see him when I got off. But I've wanted to hide ever since. I keep thinking I'll run into him in town. What's he doing here, Peter? What else could he be doing but looking for me? I keep waiting for something to happen. I keep expecting a knock on the door."

"Why didn't you tell me?"

153

Lucy said nothing. Peter brushed the tears from her face and pulled her into a rough embrace. This time, she was oblivious to all observers. While she sobbed he rocked her gently, stroking her hair. Lucy's demons were too real, and even an island couldn't protect her forever.

"I think we should mention it to the detective," he said. "Call it harassment, call it anything you like, and get the guy picked up for questioning. If he's who you think he is, he won't be able to get off the island fast enough."

"No!" Lucy said, rearing back. "Promise me you won't talk to that woman!"

"What's wrong with Meredith Folger?"

"Nothing's wrong with her. Just don't tell her anything about me, do you understand? You say a word, and I never speak to you again. I'll deal with this myself. I've got to, sooner or later."

Peter made as if to speak, then nodded. "Okay. Just do me a favor. If anything comes up, call me. There's nothing wrong with having a bit of protection. Promise?"

Lucy nodded. She rubbed her hands across her eyes and gave him a watery smile. "I really am an idiot, aren't I?"

"A very dear one," Peter said. "Now, it's getting late. Are we going to run?"

．　．　．

IT WAS A RELATIVELY QUIET afternoon at the station. John Folger's tanned forehead had a slight wrinkle in it, and his left thumb moved backward and forward across his salt-and-pepper mustache. He was reviewing the Mason murder scene summary for the third time. His eyes flicked up from the folder on his desk and focused on Merry, seated beyond the glass wall of his office in her cubicle, engrossed in a volume of federal securities regulations. There were two more stacked on her desk, one put out by the Securities and Exchange Commission, the other a case law textbook edited by a Stanford professor. Their spines bore the catalogue numbers and faint bleaching of dust from the Nantucket public library. His daughter's expression was obscured by the fall of tow-colored hair down one cheekbone, but from the set of her head he knew she was confused and near exhaustion. The chief sighed and slapped the folder shut. Time for him to go home. Much as he wanted to run this investigation for her, the last thing she needed was her dad looking over her shoulder. He would wait another few days before he asked his questions.

· · ·

MERRY PULLED OFF her reading glasses and thrust her arms up over her head, stretching painfully. She had been plowing through the volumes in quick succession and found none of them riveting. She was convinced that somewhere in the legalese lay the clue to Rusty Mason's sealed indictment, but she was beginning to feel intimidated by the mass of material on securities convictions springing from the 1980s. A quiet cloud of gloom, familiar from her days at Cape Cod Community, had settled over her desk. "There's got to be a video somewhere on this stuff," she muttered out loud. "Too many white-collar types have made too much money for it to be this dull."

"Hey, just what the world needs. Another lawyer. You looking for a new career, hotshot?"

She looked up and met Matt Bailey's eyes, cold and hard above an unfriendly grin. He was leaning on the edge of her desk, his face thrust forward, challenging her. No forgiveness or goodwill there; he was gunning for her to blow the case. She resisted the impulse to slam a reply down his throat, and smiled at him. "It never hurts to have a fallback."

"Or Daddy looking out for you," he said. He pushed himself away from her desk before she could answer, and she felt the anger in the trembling wood. Bailey was vicious. She should never have refused a date with him six months back; he'd taken it too personally. Then again, the thought of having saved even one evening from his company made her feel a slight sense of victory. All the same, she'd have to watch her back.

Bailey turned and stopped dead as he found himself suddenly face to face with Chief Folger, who stood silently in the doorway of his office.

"Haven't you got anything to do, Bailey?" John said. "Do I pay you to work, or to run your mouth?"

Matt backed toward the door, speechless, and scrambled through it.

The chief slapped his hand against the frame of the door in frustration. "Damned if I do, damned if I don't," he said. He looked around the room. The few heads present bent immediately to their paperwork, pens scribbling. He nodded, to no one in particular, and turned out the light in his office. He said nothing to Merry as he left the station. But she smiled at his disappearing back.

•   •   •

HALF AN HOUR LATER, she was the only one left in the office. The quiet in the room was so absolute, and her concentration so deep, that she jumped several inches off her chair when the phone rang, and then, furious, reached for the receiver. It clattered out of her hand and over the end of the desk. She could hear the caller squawking incomprehensibly from his disembodied position three inches off the floor, and for an instant she thought about leaving him there. Then she slammed the textbook shut, reached over the sickly Sansevieria plant dying slowly under the lamp, and hauled the receiver up, hand over hand, to her ear.

"Meredith Folger."

"Ah, Detective Folger. Just the woman I need. You seem to have dropped me."

"Yeah, well, people were beginning to talk," Merry said.

A puzzled silence filled her ear. She thrust her forehead into her free hand and closed her eyes. "What can I do for you?"

Her caller seized on normalcy with relief. "Dr. Whitlow, state crime lab. Your medical examiner sent over a body two days ago. Number 37552."

Whitlow. She imagined a balding, pasty-faced guy with a nose that twitched like a rabbit's and a white lab coat smelling perpetually of formaldehyde. "Yes, that's right. Rusty Mason."

There was another pained silence. Apparently the coroner's office preferred to avoid names. "The autopsy was witnessed by your Clarence Strangerfield," he said, "but I'm faxing a copy of the report for your files. Mr. Strangerfield was exceedingly unhelpful in the matter of the body's disposition. What do you want done with it?"

"I'll have to get back to you on that after I talk to the next of kin."

"So Mr. Strangerfield said. It's so much more helpful if the final disposition of the corpse is noted on the committal form."

"I thought the state crime lab felt fortunate when it *had* a next of kin, Dr. Whitlow," Merry said briskly. "Is there anything unusual in the report I should know before you send it?"

Another silence. A rustling sound came over the line, as though Whitlow were fumbling in a paper hospital gown. She shut out the image and decided he was flipping the pages on a clipboard chart. "Rigor was just coming on at the time of the body's discovery, according to the medical examiner at the scene, making it likely that death occurred six to twelve hours previous. There were abrasions on the rear of the calves—bruising occurred prior to death, of course—suggesting a forceful blow; further bruising on back of head and shoulders indicating victim somersaulted when struck. Cranium fractured, presumably when victim fell backward following the blow from the lower rear, but inadequate to cause death. Grains of sand driven into the back of the skull and surface clotting of blood, somewhat reduced because of the water in which victim was immersed. Death was by drowning. Impossible to set the exact hour due to the immersion of the body, which would affect the onset of rigor; probably within eight hours of discovery. Tissues of the nasal passages inflamed and cartilage partially eroded from repeated exposure to a chemical agent, presumably cocaine. Traces of cocaine found in the follicles of deceased's hair and in the sinus passages. Deceased carried antibodies for the hepatitis B and HIV viruses—"

"What?" Merry said, startled.

Silence. Whitlow disliked interruptions. "I'm faxing you the report," he said.

"Whoa, whoa—just a minute, here. You're telling me Rusty Mason was HIV-positive?"

"Over a million Americans are, Detective."

"Yeah, well, they're not getting killed in my backyard. How advanced was he?"

Whitlow cleared his throat. "It's hard to say. The effects of autoimmune deficiency vary from case to case, you know."

157

"I'm sure you can do better than that."

"His T-cell count suggests he was in the early to middle stages of the disease," the coroner said grudgingly. "Not yet at full-blown AIDS, but probably suffering from fatigue, night sweats, repeated bouts of flu-like symptoms."

"Think he knew he had it?"

"He knew he had it, all right. Lab sampling turned up AZT in his system."

"Dr. Whitlow," Merry said, "there's no way this guy could have bonked his head, gotten a little confused, and dragged himself to the bog, is there?"

"Are you asking if he committed suicide?" Whitlow was unenthused.

"Right. Say he passed out after he hit the water."

"Highly unlikely. The force of the blow to the back of the legs was strong enough to send him head over heels, fracturing his skull as he rolled. One doesn't do that to oneself. And the presence of AZT indicates a desire to live for a while longer—it's expensive stuff."

Chapter 15

PETER MARKED HIS PLACE IN *War and Peace* with a forefinger and threw his head back against his chair. The sweeping strains of Rachmaninoff's Second Piano Concerto filled the room, a faint breeze stirred in the darkness beyond the open window, and Ney lay at his feet, warm and relaxed, whiffling softly in his sleep. Usually Peter required nothing more than these—good books, good music, a day of hard work followed by an evening of solitude—to feel complete contentment. But tonight he was restless and uneasy, his concentration broken by the slightest sound. He pressed the palms of his hands against his eyes. There would be no peace until Rusty's killer was flushed out of hiding and the past could return to dust.

The night had been broken more than once by the insistent ring of the telephone, bringing Ney to his feet with his tags clinking. The first caller was Merry Folger, telling him the state crime lab was done with Rusty's body, and what did he intend to do with it? He'd thought for a moment and told her he'd call her back. The second call, from Georgiana, came through with exquisite timing a mere ten minutes later. She had reached their mother in Rome, listened with forbearance while Julia Mason screamed and moaned, then agreed to meet her plane at JFK the following afternoon.

"When's the funeral, Peter?" she had asked.

"Whenever we like. The autopsy's over."

"What did they find?"

"The woman handling the case said she'd talk to me when I got back from Greenwich."

"So you're coming here?"

It was like Georgiana, he thought, to accept Merry Folger's gender without hesitation. His mother would have been appalled. "It's easier for everybody to reach, and it seems like the only place Rusty really thought of as home. We're certainly not going to haul everyone out here."

There was a small silence, then an equally small sigh. "It's just that I'm dreading this so much," George said.

"All the more reason to be close to the kids and Hale. We got through living with Rusty, and we'll get through burying him."

"It will rain. You *know* it will rain. We'll be gathered around a sodden hole in the ground some idiot has attempted to disguise with Astroturf. The flowers will be hideous. Mother will make a scene. People will ask repeatedly how he died, and where he's been all these years. I can't bear it."

"I've been thinking, Georgiana," Peter said. "What if we have the body cremated? Take the *Seventh Wave* out into the sound and commit him to the deep. It seems cleaner, somehow. And sailing that boat was the only thing that ever freed him from himself."

"It's an idea," she said slowly. "We'd have to persuade Mother. I can call Dr. Pritchett—he's the yacht club chaplain—and ask for something private, a bit simpler than the usual solemn public ceremony he stages. A burial at sea might be just the thing. We could have a quiet memorial service, just the family, and skip the graveside horrors. I'll never be able to swim in the sound again, of course."

"To my knowledge, you haven't dropped a toe in Long Island Sound in fourteen years."

"Barring the occasional capsizing," Georgiana said. "Not if I can help it. Peter, there's something beastly about being able to speak so lightly of all this. Of Rusty, I mean. I suppose it's because I'm not there that it doesn't seem real to me."

"No," Peter said. "It's because Rusty has seemed dead for years. And we've been just as glad. There's a vacuum of feeling where his life used to be. That's what's so horrible. And there's nothing we can do about it, now."

"It's been rather bad for you, hasn't it?"

"Yes. But I'm hoping it won't get any worse."

Georgiana was silent a moment. Then, "Do they know who?" she asked.

"I don't think so."

.   .   .

HE HAD CALLED THE STATION and only then realized Merry wasn't on duty. The idea that she had a home—a life separate from her official capacity—was a revelation. He found himself wondering idly whether she lived alone, or knew how to cook, and if she had bookshelves, what she kept on them. It occurred to him that his tendency to see only pieces of people—the pieces that related to himself—was one more sign of how detached he'd become in the isolation of the farm. He failed to connect. He shook himself out of his thoughts and debated calling her at home. Then he redialed the station number and left a message that he would reach her in the morning.

The final call was from Sky Jackson.

"Have they come up with anything?" he asked, by way of greeting. He sounded nervous and tired. Peter imagined him standing fifty-eight floors above New York in his office, his back carefully turned to the two vertiginous walls of glass that formed one corner.

"Malcolm Scott," Peter said. "Name mean anything to you?"

"Men's clothing designer?"

Peter snorted.

"Golf pro?"

"He was ME's chief financial officer in Max's time. Retired now, splits his year between Chappaqua and Boca Raton. I caught him just before he left town for the winter."

There was a pause as Sky digested this information. "The point being?" he asked cautiously.

"Scott will see us Friday afternoon, if you can make time. I think he

161

knows every dollar Mason Enterprises spent, and amazingly, he remembers why. He's our key to the M&A fiasco Rusty tried to pull off."

"Peter—" Sky began, and then stopped. He was strung as tightly as a wire and close to snapping. "Digging up the past isn't going to do diddly to help this investigation. You're wasting your time. Concentrate on getting the harvest in and let the police do their job."

"I'm picking up Rusty's ashes in Boston Friday morning," Peter said, "I can catch a shuttle and be at your office by one o'clock, if that suits."

"I'm not sure I'll be able to make it," Sky said shortly. "Who decided on cremation?"

"I did. Ashes to ashes, dust to dust. We'll need you at George's Saturday for the memorial service."

Another pause. Then, "You're a cold bastard," Sky said, and hung up.

•   •   •

THE LAST NOTES OF THE CONCERTO reverberated in the air and the CD whirred to a halt. He closed his eyes in the silence for an instant and then reached down to restart the piece, wanting to hear again the opening chords. The last measured steps of a man on the verge of passion, he thought. He hadn't listened to Rachmaninoff in years. He told himself it was because the Romantic composers wore poorly with time; that intellectually, he had outstripped the music he had lived for in college; but the real reason was that Rachmaninoff was indelibly linked to Alison. In his mind he saw her outlined against a moonlit window, her lithe frame impossibly graceful in the darkness, her eyes picking up the faint white light slanting through the leaded panes. She was listening to the music, head up and thoughts far away, her dancer's body unconsciously swaying in time. The opening chords drew him toward her, step by step, until he stopped, poised on the edge of the sonorous plunge.

"All the dark, impassioned, Russian night," she said, turning toward him. "Do you feel it, Peter?" And then the music swept him into her arms.

He stabbed the machine into silence. He'd sold his college records long ago. Something in the horror of the past few days, and his own blind need for comfort, had compelled him to reach back into the past. He'd bought the CD.

Ney thrust his cold nose into Peter's ear and whined softly.

"What, you want to hear the rest, too?" Peter said, fondling the bristling dome of the dog's head. "Or do you find Bartók more challenging?"

He stood up and stretched. His legs ached with the pleasant memory of that afternoon's long, slow run through the moors. A low growl came from his feet, and he looked down in surprise. Ney's ears were pointed toward the open window, and the hair on his back stood up in a vicious ridge. Suddenly he barked and shot over to the screen.

The dog loved to chase a pair of nocturnal cats that lived wild on the moors. Peter reached for Ney's leash and snapped it on, something he rarely did at night, but he had no desire to race after the dog while he tracked a mangy animal through the heath. Ney whined feverishly.

"Hey, pup," he said, opening the screen, "don't get your hopes up. You're headed for the hayloft."

The breeze had picked up and blew freshly from the northwest, sending the scent of scrub pine and bayberry off the cooling countryside. He glanced up at the sky, where a new September moon shot in and out of swiftly moving clouds. "Might get some weather tomorrow."

Ney trotted in front of him, conscious of the indignity of the lead, his ears up and his bark caught in his throat. The cat he'd scented must have gone downwind. Peter's bare feet in his Top-Siders were slick with dew from the stubby ends of the grass, left high all summer, then mown and baled a few weeks before the cranberry harvest. A few crickets sounded, already marked with the lethargy of cooler nights, the most mournful note of late summer; and Peter shivered suddenly. Ney reached the barn door and turned to look at him, tail wagging.

Rafe was gone, probably to the Greengage, but his light was on and a magazine left open on the desk. Ney trotted over to the dog bed in one corner of the room and flopped down, secure in the comfort of his routines. Peter unhooked the dog's leash and smoothed his ears once before turning to go. As he did, he glanced at the magazine on the desk and his eye was caught by the face of a famous baseball player, endorsing a mutual fund. Peter bent closer, a line between his brows, and flipped over the cover. An investment monthly. What did Rafe have to invest?

He shook away his curiosity and reflected that Merry Folger had shown him two nights ago how little he knew about Rafe. The man could have a personal investment analyst on retainer at Morgan Stanley for all Peter knew. Or cared to ask.

He pulled shut the door and clattered down the stairs. The wind had grown stronger, and the barn door he'd left ajar was shuddering in the sporadic gusts. He considered leaving it open for Rafe and the Rover, then heaved it closed and made for the house, head down and hands in his pockets. He felt completely alone tonight and tired to his bones. Perhaps he should have gone with Rafe to the Greengage. But the next few days would exact an emotional toll, and he knew he'd better get his sleep.

George was right; his mother would make a scene. She was a strong-willed and self-blinding woman who had never accepted her son's flight, just as she'd never forgiven his father for driving Rusty to it. That last Christmas had torn open the abyss between his parents, one Julia had been digging for years. She was white and silent at Max's funeral, her unvented fury leaving her impotent and speechless; at Rusty's memorial, she would be terrible in her rage and unappeased in her loss.

A twig cracked somewhere in front of him. Peter looked up, pulled out of his thoughts, and stopped. A dim figure in a coat and a shapeless hat, pulled low on the brow, stood in the darkness just beyond the kitchen doorway. He was reminded suddenly of the detective, as she had stood two nights ago, fending off tears. Perhaps she'd come to talk about the autopsy. To his surprise, the thought of her presence made his pulse quicken.

"Detective Folger?" he said, walking forward. "Merry?"

He saw the brief candle's flare of the gun as it went off and instinctively jumped aside, conscious of the shot's report coming a second

after the stinging pain, and thinking with a certain separate wonder-
ment of the speed of such a small piece of metal, hurled beyond mere
human perceiving into a trajectory of death.

The blood was on his hands and he had touched them to his face.
He had never been able to stand the sight or smell of blood. As he
crumpled to the ground he heard Ney, barking wildly in the barn, and
knew that his assailant was running toward him.

Chapter 16

THE HEADLIGHTS OF THE Blazer pulled up on the shoulder of Codfish Park Road threw Merry's shadow across the night sand almost to the waterline of Siasconset beach. She stood with her hands on her hips and her back to the light, staring at a waterlogged leather gym bag that sat like a grotesque jellyfish on the sand just above the high-water mark. Howie Seitz, his arm around a girl and his feet planted firmly next to the bag, was grinning triumphantly, and, Merry thought, with reason. He was out of uniform, and his eyes, caught in the headlights when he looked up at her, glittered like agates. His success and the rightness of his air of virtue annoyed her, and she scowled until her face was all black eyebrow.

"Tell me you haven't destroyed the evidence, Seitz," she said.

"Hey, you trained me, Detective. No way I'd screw up evidence. I just opened the thing to see if there was an ID inside, and that's when I saw the passport. I stayed with the bag while Deanna ran up to call you."

"Good of you," Merry said shortly, nodding toward the girl. She was a lithe summer kid, maybe all of seventeen, with the requisite mass of hair and buttery dark skin. She was clearly undecided whether this hiatus in an evening's grope on the beach was an excitement or a bore.

She flicked her hair over one shoulder impatiently and huddled closer to Howie. Merry walked over to them and squatted down next to the bag. It smelled vividly of rotten fish. She pulled open the top flap and saw why. A large clump of seaweed wrapped around the gills of something indeterminate was decaying quietly in the bag's depths. Just like Howie to leave it there for her. He'd probably been hoping she'd retch. She calmly scooped out the stinking mass and laid it on the sand at his feet, then wordlessly extended her hand. He slapped her palm with his flashlight. The bleached white shape of a rat gleamed suddenly at her feet, and she jumped, dropping the light.

"The sweater," she said through bitten lips. "I'll be damned." She picked apart the tangled sea-blue wool of Mayling Stern's sweater and scanned the button edge. Sure enough, one of them was missing. Her heart pounding, she dove back into the sodden bag and pulled apart its contents, laying them out on the sand. Howie uncharacteristically said nothing, but waited to be released, his hand running up and down the girl's shoulder. The wind off the Atlantic was brisk, even in August, and she was probably freezing.

"Looks like some clothes, some bottles—shampoo and stuff—and some papers. Hey, there's his passport. Brazilian. That explains the FBI's failure to pick him up at the border. No doubt it's waterlogged and indecipherable by now. Let's hope Clarence can pull something up." She flicked the passport cover open under the light for Howie to see, revealing an evil-looking photograph of Rusty Mason. "These things never fail to look god-awful. He might as well be dead in that picture."

One more piece of paper lay at the bottom of the bag. Merry reached in and extracted a blurred black-and-white photograph. She passed it under the light curiously, brushing away some grains of sand that clung to its surface. "Now what's so important about this, I wonder," she said thoughtfully.

The black-and-white photo had been old and worn well before its submersion in seawater. A sepia haze had leached through the photographic paper, clouding the image. A woman stood on a city sidewalk, leaning toward the open window of a limousine, apparently taking

167

leave of its occupant, whose face was clearly visible in the center of the frame. A dark-haired man well past middle age, but distinguished and arresting; the sort of face that commanded attention. The woman's face was half hidden by sunglasses, but her carriage and clothing suggested elegance, and from the length of stockinged leg braced on the sidewalk, Merry concluded she was rather young.

"What's so important about this picture that you bring it six thousand miles in a bag with a change of clothing?"

"Maybe it had some sentimental value?" Seitz said.

"Thank you, Howie. Advance to senior year. Do not collect two hundred dollars as you pass go." Her moss-green eyes flashed in the light of his torch as she shoved her blond hair behind her ears. "When do you get off this island, anyway?"

"Saturday morning. And man, it won't be fast enough," Howie said joyfully. Deanna stiffened and shot him a look. Too late, he caught himself. She wriggled out from under his arm.

"Yeah, well, like I've got a life here in high school too, you know, and I've got better things to do on a weeknight than freeze my ass off out here on the beach," she said. "Later, Howie. Call me when you know what it's worth." She shot off across the sand, hair streaming furiously in her wake.

"Car thirty-four," the Blazer's police radio squawked suddenly in the darkness, and Merry jumped, sitting back on the cold sand. That was *her* car. She looked at the swiftly vanishing teenager. "You can go catch up with her," she said to Howie. "You're not on duty. I'll handle this." She stood up and brushed off her pants.

"You're not on duty, either," Howie said.

Merry hoisted the water-soaked bag, crossed to the Blazer, and picked up the handset. "When has that ever mattered? Get out of here. And Seitz . . ." She leaned back around the doorframe to thank him, heard another burst of static over the line, and thought better of it. "Car thirty-four," she said, clicking on the radio. "Over."

Howie watched her an instant, then thrust his hands in his jeans and shrugged off in the direction Deanna had taken. It was then Merry began to swear ferociously. The sound carried over the surf and stopped

Howie in his tracks. He had just turned back to her when her car roared past him, hell-bent for the Milestone Road and town.

•   •   •

THEY HAD PETER ON A GURNEY behind a hanging plastic curtain at the Nantucket Cottage Hospital. His arrival by ambulance had caused a sensation. Gunshot wounds, however common to urban emergency rooms, were a rarity on the island. Only two of the seats in the waiting area held patients—an elderly gentleman who propped a swollen wrist on his knee and a small girl with a candy wrapper stuck deep in her ear—but they were mesmerized by the activity behind the curtain. The television set, propped high on a shelf in the corner, ran baseball scores unattended. The two patients looked up at Merry hopefully when she tore through the emergency room's swinging doors, sensing the arrival of Chapter Two in the unfolding drama, but she glared at them furiously and they shifted attention back to the curtain.

"They're taping him up, Detective."

Merry turned and saw Rebecca, the housekeeper, standing in front of the reception desk. She was in the midst of filling out the paperwork for Peter's admittance, and her gaunt frame looked more than ever like a perpetual question mark as she hunched over the counter. She wore no makeup, and her iron-gray hair was clipped short all over her head like a man's. She would look, Merry thought, as efficiently somber as a funeral director were it not for her tendency to chew her inner cheek as she wrote. Her bony right hand was shaking despite her deliberateness.

"Where was he hit?"

"Left arm. Bullet went in and out, took a nick of bone with it. If the poor fool weren't so skittish around blood, he'd have walked here, maybe. He'll be fine." Rebecca's head came up, and her eyes were angry. "What I want to know is, how are folks supposed to sleep nights when you cops can't keep 'em safe, hey? Enough to make a body pack a gun."

Merry tossed her purse on a chair and walked over to the curtain.

Peter, naked to the waist under a white sheet, was staring at the acoustic tiles of the ceiling. The yellow fluorescence of the room was not kind to his face, which had turned gray under his tan. The skin seemed to have shrunk over the jutting bone of his nose and the planes of his forehead, throwing his skull into sharp relief. His light eyes were not so much unfocused as too focused, Merry thought, as if the tiles mattered to the exclusion of everything else, so deep and pointed was his concentration. He seemed oblivious to her presence at the foot of the gurney.

The doctor bending over Peter's left shoulder ignored her as well. His fine, long-fingered hands were engaged in pressing white adhesive tape onto the ends of a bandage that encircled Peter's deltoid muscle.

"Hey, Peter," Merry said, unconsciously using his first name, something she had never done.

His eyes flicked over to hers, and he lifted his head slightly, a gleam of welcome flashing for an instant on his face, and then he fell back into his original position. The doctor straightened up and nodded to the nurse positioned at Peter's head. She smiled cheerfully down at him as though he were a child and said, "Just a short roll, Mr. Mason, to your room, and then we'll give you something to sleep."

"You're keeping him here tonight?" Merry said to the doctor. She felt oddly relieved.

"Normally I'd send him home. But he's lost a bit of blood, and the sight of it makes him light-headed anyway. Wouldn't want him fainting again." He studied her an instant and said, "You the girlfriend?"

Merry flushed, felt annoyed because she did, and pulled out her badge a trifle belligerently. The doctor's face cleared and he said, "You're Detective Folger. I didn't think to look for a woman. A Clarence Strangerfield, from your station, wants you to call him."

"Thanks. Listen, is Mason able to talk?"

"I think so. Nurse?"

The woman turned in the act of rotating the gurney toward the hallway's swinging doors and looked inquiringly at the doctor.

"Hold up a minute. Ms. Folger? I mean—Detective?"

Merry crossed to where Peter lay in front of the threshold and smiled down at him briefly. She restrained an urge, surprising in the extreme, to reach out and smooth his forehead. She noticed again how deeply set his gray eyes were, how the jutting browbones gave his face the look of a hawk. "Did you see anything?"

He nodded, then frowned. "Not enough. I saw the woman and the gun. No face. Just a coat and hat."

"But you thought it was a woman."

His eyes flicked upward and held her own. "I thought it was you," he said.

Chapter 17

"**W**HAT HAVE YOU GOT FOR ME, CLARENCE?"

"Looks like a nine-millimetah, prob'ly from a Browning," Clarence said. After an hour of combing the grass, he had just managed to retrieve the casing under a pine tree some thirty feet from where Peter had fallen. Now he was crouched near the barn's double doors, holding a bit of wood between thumb and forefinger. The slug had entered the barn door, and Nathaniel Coffin was busy extracting what remained of it. Clarence pulled the plastic bag that contained the casing out of his evidence case and offered it to Merry. "No prints on the casing—the fellah was wearin' gloves, ah believe. Nice set of footprints ovah there, howevah. Nice set. Not that you can see them at the moment."

Merry turned to where another of Clarence's boys was pouring plaster of paris into a wooden frame set over the prints, near a clump of pines just beyond the far side of the house. She crossed to them carefully, hating the necessity of disturbing the grass and hoping that Clarence had studied it thoroughly. She crouched down. Dew glittered on every blade of freshly mown stubble under the floodlights the crime scene unit had rigged up. She reached for her half-glasses, and while she settled them on her nose she allowed herself an instant to inhale the comforting scent of wet earth. Then she studied the ground. Slight indentations showed where the killer's heel and toe had sunk into the sandy soil as he waited for Peter to walk toward the barn, leave the dog, and walk back into firing range. Her eyes narrowed. Peter might be right. The prints—narrow and long, with a pointed toe and shallow heel—suggested a woman's shoe rather than a man's. Something turned in the back of Merry's brain. What did the print remind her of? She shook her head and closed her eyes, concentrating. Boots. Low-slung, cuffed suede boots worn with stretch stirrup pants. Off-island boots.

"Ah've only found the one casing. No sign of the weapon, eithah."

"Clarence, I want you to send somebody up into the barn loft."

"Thaht Woman got the dahg, Marradith."

Thaht Woman was Rebecca. Clarence had borne the brunt of her tongue.

"It's not the dog I'm thinking of. Find out what's missing from the gun rack."

Clarence turned and shouted for Coffin. He came at a trot. Clarence sent him to the loft.

Merry hunkered on her heels in the grass, trying not to touch the ground surrounding the prints. "I almost forgot. Mason's bag is in the back of the car."

"So now yahr haulin' his luggage?"

"Not Peter's, Rusty's. Howie Seitz found it washed up on the beach at Siasconset."

Clarence rolled his eyes. "Ah'm thaht wahrn out, Marradith, I wish he'd thrown it back into the muck."

"There's papers, a passport, some clothes and stuff in the bag. You'll want to take a look at it."

Clarence's bulk loomed over her. "And they call this the off-season." He snorted. "If the bag washed up at 'Sconset, Marradith, ah've got a good idea where it went into the watah."

"You do?"

"Ayah. And thaht means somebody screwed up."

"It does?"

"Carhse it does," he said impatiently. "Yah don't think they wanted it found, do yah? They consigned it for burial to the deep, and that's wharh it was intended to stay. The ocean's a hahndy place to dump evidence, but it doesn't always behave prop'rly." He looked at her with pity. "Yah don't sail, do yah?"

Merry shook her head.

"No college geology, eithah?" Clarence sighed, then summoned his patience. "Most of 'Sconset beach owes its existence to the teeth of the Atlantic gnawin' on the south shore, Detective—it's been shoving sand left and right for years, dumpin' it on Smith Point to the west and on 'Sconset to the east. If something washed up there, it was prob'ly thrown in the watah somewhere below Surfside. It looks as though things should drift out to sea around there, but they don't do it directly."

"Surfside," Merry said thoughtfully. "Not exactly near the scene of the crime, but not very far away, either."

"It was done with a cah, remembah," Clarence said gently. "With a cah, yah can get the evidence wherever yah want it, and fast."

"The car, again. Whose car?" Merry said with exasperation.

There was a delicate silence. Clarence was aware that one car, at least, had a damaged fender; and he was itching to vacuum that car for fibers and other forensic samples, but Merry wouldn't permit him to invade Mayling Stern's garage without a warrant—and serving a warrant, without enough evidence to charge her, might only startle her into flight. For now, they had paid one of Clarence's numerous 'Sconset cousins to keep an eye on the garage, with strict instructions to report immediately if the car was moved or the garage was the site of inordinate activity. Thus far he had witnessed frequent comings and goings on the part of the house cook, usually in pursuit of armloads of groceries, bouquets of flowers, and the *New York Times;* but she drove a battered station wagon, and never remained in the garage longer than was necessary to start or park the car. Clarence's cousin Aubrey said the Stern woman must be keeping a low profile; she hadn't poked her head around the front of the house in days.

"Shahrt of doin' a house-to-house search, I doubt yah'll find it," Clarence said.

"Thanks, Clare," said Merry shortly. "I hadn't realized that." She looked down at the prints. "I guess you've got an idea about these, too."

"Ayeh. The gunman is standing half hidden under the tree here, and he watches Mason leave with the dahg and walk tawrd the bahn. He waits till the dahg's shut up and Mason is walkin' tawrd him, and then he shoots. He doesn't know Mason's going to faint when he sees blood, so he thinks the guy's dead when he crumples to the ground. He takes off."

Merry nodded. Then she shook her head. "It's all wrong."

Clarence waited.

"I came over here a couple of days ago and the dog came around the house, heading for the barn, like the Hound of the Baskervilles. It all but lunged for my throat. Tonight, the dog trots to the barn without a peep. Rebecca says so. It was the dog's barking after the shots were fired that caused her to come running."

"Which means no one was here when he walked to the bahn?"

"Possibly, but I doubt it. It's more likely that the dog didn't bark because it recognized the killer's scent. He or she—I'm betting on she—stood here, sure that neither the dog nor anyone else would disturb her. She knows Rafe goes into town most evenings and the dog gets locked in the loft at night. Even if the dog decided to pick up on her existence, she's a friend, right? So she greets the dog and skips the shooting this time around. But if Ney gives her a miss—this is the one time of day she's got a clear shot at Peter Mason without Rafe coming at a run. She knows the routines of the place, Clarence. Just as she knew a few days ago that the bog would be flooded for the first time in months."

She stopped. Clarence was silent. Merry stood up creakily and pulled off her glasses, fumbling for the pocket of her coat as she stared toward the spot where Peter Mason had fallen. "Another thing. Look closely at the marks on the grass. She ran over toward the body, stood there an instant, and then veered back into the moors. Why? Why walk up to Peter and then leave without firing another shot? She must have seen that he wasn't dead. Why not kill him while he was passed out? Doesn't make sense, Clare."

"Maybe Thaht Woman scared her off," he said.

"Maybe. For lack of a better answer—"

A long shadow, grotesque under the stark lighting, advanced across the dew toward them. Coffin was done with the loft.

"No pistol on the rack, sir, no handgun of any kind, for that matter," he said. "Just a couple of rifles—not that that's unusual for a farm—and all of them are registered."

"Thanks," Clarence said. "Yah dusted the rack faw fingerprints?"

"You won't find anything," Merry said sourly. "This is not a dolt we're dealing with. Inexperienced, perhaps. Stupid, no. Coffin, there's a soggy piece of luggage staining the backseat of my car. Haul it out and take it back to the station with you. Everything in there should be tagged as evidence in Rusty Mason's murder."

When he had trotted back toward the front door of the saltbox, she turned to Clarence Strangerfield. The crime scene chief was down on his hands and knees, studying the faint marks leading from the prints to the body. "Ayeh. I missed it, Detective," he said regretfully. "My sincere apologies."

"They're pretty faint," she said absently. "Forget it. Listen, Clare— there was a pistol on that rack the last time I saw it."

He stopped his survey of the ground and turned to her. "Get a look at what type?"

"Oh, it was a Browning. Nine-millimeter. In fact, it was the weapon used tonight, I'm sure of it. The killer knew what he—or she— was dealing with. She knew where to find the gun. She must have entered the loft tonight after Rafe left, taken the Browning, and then stood here waiting for Peter to wrap up his evening. Pretty cool stuff."

Clarence cleared his throat. "Why is it so impawtant that the killah be a woman?"

She looked down at him, interested. He stood up and brushed off his knees. "The prints are narrah. But they're still within a fair range of shoe size—it could be a flaht oxford type with a slight heel and a pointed toe, or a kid's bucks, faw instance. Or cowboy boots—like the ones that Rafe da Silva wahrs when he's paintin' the town red." His eyes looked out from under his brow somewhat warily, as though he expected her to take a swing at him.

"What're you saying, Clarence?"

"I'm just wonderin' why Rafe's always fah from home when the trouble hits, that's all." He turned and stomped off toward Coffin and his camera equipment.

· · ·

THE GREENGAGE WAS CLOSING DOWN for the evening when Merry walked in. A few diners were still sitting at two tables near the Federal-style mantelpiece, where the last embers of an early-fall fire fell quietly into ash. The honey-colored wood floors and muted bayberry walls, hung with framed prints of whaling ships, gave the room intimacy and peace. The restaurant looked like a sure thing, Merry thought—a tribute to Tess's will and instinct, a measure of her canny perseverance. There was an air of bravery about the Greengage nonetheless: financing this first year could not have been easy. The reconstruction of the rooms alone represented a capital outlay Tess Starbuck must still be struggling to recoup. And what would the winter, and its loss of tourist revenue, mean for her and Will? Merry shook herself out of this train of thought, hardened her heart, and looked around for Rafe.

He was in the bar, an inviting room adjacent to the dining area where local fisherman—Dan's old friends—held pride of place. They were pulled up to tables near a second fire, legs stretched out in front of them, heavy boots quickly taking the shine from the recently sanded and refinished floors. Merry recognized a group of three men who sat with Rafe, arms carelessly draped across the backs of their wives' chairs, and understood with a shock why he spent so much time at the Greengage: these were his people, the friends of a lifetime, kids who'd gone to school with him and her brother Billy. A world his father had cut out from under him when he threw him off the da Silva scalloper.

The group turned to look at her as she stood in the doorway, and abruptly fell silent. Rafe thrust himself back from the table and stood up, his chair scraping across the floor harshly in the quiet. "Hey, Merry," he said.

Merry nodded toward the table of inquiring faces and wished for a heart that beat less fast. "Can I talk to you for a second?"

Rafe looked around at his buddies and drummed one hand on the table. "Sure. Sure. Everybody was taking off, anyway." He slid past the gathered chairs and shoved his hands in his jeans, rocking slightly on the heels of his dress boots. Clarence was right. They weren't far off the prints in the Mason Farms front yard.

The assembled fishermen eased out of their seats and threw on light jackets, clapping Rafe on the back as they passed him, the women reaching on tiptoe to peck his cheek. Rafe belonged. Merry felt curiously relieved as she watched the unconscious display of brotherhood, and knew that her anxiety for Rafe was broader than she admitted; she was concerned about the fabric of his life, not just that part of it that might have included her.

He motioned her toward a chair. She shook her head. "I stopped by to tell you Peter's in Cottage Hospital. Somebody took a potshot at him tonight."

Rafe slammed his palm down on the table, shoved a chair over on its side, and then stopped short, his fists clenched in futile anger and his head hanging. Conversation at the last table of diners in the neighboring room ceased abruptly. After an agonizingly speechless instant, he bent to pick up the chair and looked at her. "He okay?"

"Just nicked. Upper part of his left arm." She almost reached a hand to Rafe's cheek, and stopped herself just in time. She ran her fingers through her hair instead. "The doc kept him there overnight anyway. Seems he faints at the sight of blood."

Rafe turned his back to her, folded his arms against his chest, and slumped against the edge of the table.

"I knew they were after Peter, not his brother. Why the hell didn't I stick close to him?" He studied the dying fire in the barroom's stone hearth.

"So you'd have an ironclad alibi, maybe?" Merry said quietly. She steeled herself for his reaction.

He stiffened, his shoulders coming up, but refrained from looking at her. "I'm gonna ignore that asinine remark," he said.

Sometimes she hated this job. "Where were you about an hour ago?"

"Here."

"And half a dozen people can back you up. Okay. Where was Tess?"

That brought him around to face her. "Why would it matter?"

"Please answer the question, Rafe."

"She was in the kitchen cooking. Same as she is every night."

"Who's the chief waiter around here?"

Rafe nodded toward the outer room. "Sammy. Sammy and Regina. Sometimes Will fills in as busboy, but not tonight. Had homework."

Merry turned on her heel and walked into the dining room, seeing the man who had to be Sammy almost immediately. He wore a white shirt and a black waiter's tuxedo vest over black tuxedo pants. He was propping himself against the far wall with one raised foot, a napkin in his hand, alert to the whim of the last diners. "You're Sammy?" Merry said. He grinned, pushed himself away from the wall, and came over to her.

"Kitchen's closed. You can get sandwiches in the bar until midnight, though."

"Detective Folger, Nantucket police. About when would you say the last food order went back to the kitchen?"

His eyes flicked from the badge to her face. "Geez, it was a while ago. These guys have been sitting here all night, talking and drinking brandy. But they were the last table I sat. Must have sent the order back around nine."

"And you brought it to the table when?"

He shut his eyes and wrinkled his face, seeing the meals in his mind's eye. "The pork loin took a little while, and so did the bluefish in parchment. Tess held up the scampi. Say, nine twenty-five, maybe."

"Who's normally staffing the kitchen?"

"Tess. She runs the place herself. During the summer she had Otis Carmichael helping her—*sous-chef*, she called him—but he just comes in on weekends now. Weeknights she handles it alone, and Regina and I help her assemble the plates. It's still kind of a shoestring place— that's why we've only got twenty tables."

Merry looked around the room and nodded. Then she glanced at her watch. Eleven-thirty. It was just enough: Tess could have sent out the last meals, hopped in the Rover parked outside, and made it to Mason Farms by nine forty-five. On the off chance that someone from the farm noticed the car's arrival, she would look like Rafe heading for bed. A quick trip into the barn for the gun and then a brief wait in darkness, alone under the pine trees, as Peter and Ney took their bedtime walk. She could have been back in the kitchen by ten-fifteen.

"Did they order anything else?" she asked, nodding toward the last table. Sammy looked at her curiously. "Yeah, they had dessert," he said. "And coffee. Why?"

"So you'd have gone back into the kitchen around what time?"

"Geez, I dunno."

"Try and think."

"Nine forty-five, or thereabouts," a voice said behind them. Merry turned and saw a girl in her late teens, her long blond hair braided into a coil around her head.

"You're Regina?"

The waitress nodded. "I know it was nine forty-five because my boyfriend stopped by to see if I was ready to go. The kitchen technically stays open until ten, but weeknights after Labor Day we're usually cleaning up by nine-thirty. Tonight there were still two tables—remember, Sammy? You called me in to help with the dessert plates. You couldn't find the rum cheesecake."

"That's right, I did," he said. "Tess had stepped upstairs."

"You know she was upstairs?" Merry said swiftly.

Sammy shrugged. "Where else would she be? Probably took Will some pie. Hey, you're not moonlighting for the Board of Health, are you? The place is clean as a whistle, believe me."

"Could I say hello to Tess?" Merry asked.

"Come on back."

"I'll take her, Sammy," Regina said. "You clear the last table." For a girl of her age, she had a commanding air. Sammy didn't argue.

Regina led Merry back through the bar to the kitchen. Rafe had left the table by the fire, probably to find Tess, Merry thought.

"You're Chief Folger's daughter, aren't you?" Regina said.

"That's right."

"Must be nice to have your dad for a boss."

"That's not the first word that comes to mind."

"You working on the Mason murder?"

"You guessed it."

"It's not a guess. My boyfriend's a cop, too." Regina turned and held open the kitchen's swinging door, waiting for Merry to pass in front of her. "Matt Bailey. You know him?"

The malice in the girl's eyes was so blatant that Merry shivered slightly as she walked past her. "Yeah. He strikes out with women his age," she said.

•   •   •

TESS WAS ALONE in the kitchen, a slim figure struggling with a towering mass of dirty pots and empty plates. She wore heavy pink rubber gloves, and her auburn hair was beaded from the cloud of steam sent up by her spray nozzle. She brushed back a wisp from her face with one gloved hand, and her shoulders slumped. Any twinge of jealousy Merry felt died away. It was clear that the elegant rooms beyond the kitchen were purchased at great cost: Tess Starbuck was bone-tired. At that moment she turned to place a cleaned pan on a dish rack and saw Merry. She smiled. The lines of weariness disappeared suddenly and she looked as she must have been when Dan Starbuck married her—as Rafe must see her, Merry thought. Then the smile faded and with it the illusion of youth.

"Should I grab a towel?"

"Nah, don't bother. These can drain. We use them too often to bother putting them away. How're you doing, Detective? Making any headway?"

"Only backwards," Merry said. "I stopped in to tell you Peter Mason was shot tonight. Don't worry," she added quickly, as Tess's face went white, "he's fine. Just nicked in the arm. But I didn't want Will to hear about it in school."

"That's very kind of you," Tess said. Her words were barely audible over the running water. She shut off the tap, pulled her hands out of the gloves, and reached for a towel. But instead of drying her hands she rested them on the edge of the sink, staring at the tile wall in front of her. "This gets worse and worse, doesn't it?"

"Seems like it," Merry said. "Did you do a lot of business tonight?"

Tess seemed to hear her from a great distance. She sat down in a chair and put her head in her hands. Merry thought of Will, and knew where he got his brittle strength, his intelligence—and his vulnerability. His mother raised her head and met Merry's eyes. "Yes, thank God. But I'll be glad to get to bed. I've been standing in this ten-foot-square area for eight hours."

"Where's Will?"

Tess motioned toward the back stairs that led from one corner of the kitchen to the second and third floors. "Homework. Rafe's with him now."

So Rafe would break the news. He was becoming the boy's surrogate father. Merry thrust away the surge of pain that came with the thought of him, shifted from the table edge where she'd been leaning, and turned to go. She had time for a last probe. "Well, at least you got out to see the moon," she said. "You've got some sand on your shoes."

Tess stared at her as if she had spoken gibberish. Then she looked down at her cuffed, narrow-heeled ankle boots and ran one finger over the clay-colored smears just above the sole. "I've got to stop smoking," she said, and laughed hollowly. "I've tried and tried and can't quit. I have a no-cigarettes rule in the kitchen—think it's dirty. So I duck out every half hour to take a drag by the back door. Stupid, isn't it? For a woman my age. I'd almost kicked it. And then Dan died."

"Some habits are hard to break, Tess," Merry said gently. "Say hello to Will."

.   .   .

AS SHE LET IN THE CLUTCH and backed down the drive, Merry could see Rafe's shaggy head silhouetted in the window of a third-floor room. Standing guard, she thought, until she was safely gone. Will's was the only window lit that high up in the house. She imagined the yellow light spilling over the desk, and the boy with the long, dark bangs pretending to study, while he stared at nothing. Not even Rafe's strong presence could keep fear from that room tonight. She wished, very hard, for evidence that would clear Rafe and Tess completely. And wondered how much money they could expect from Peter's death.

Chapter 18

"So the name JOSE LUIS RIBEIRO doesn't mean anything to you?" Merry asked for the second time. She was sitting in Peter Mason's brightly lit study, the hum of an overactive bee slightly distracting from beyond the open window.

"I think in Portuguese it's about as common as Joe Smith, Detective. Sorry."

"Your brother was traveling under that name on a Brazilian passport. Or so we assume. His picture's in it, and there's no other travel document in the bag, so we're fairly confident it's the passport he used. I suppose that's why his entry—there's a Miami control stamp in the passport—didn't ring any bells in the federal computer system. In true name, his indictment, sealed or no, would have guaranteed him a welcoming party."

"You're very chatty today," Peter said. He was stretched out on the chintz sofa in a patch of morning sunlight, and looked as though he were feeling a lazy sense of well-being, probably born of light-headedness and a good breakfast. Or perhaps of having escaped death. Unlike Rusty.

She studied him an instant, her eyes very green in the sunlight. "Is that a polite way of saying your arm is throbbing and you wish I'd shut up?"

184

"No. It's merely an aside."

"I see. I talk a lot when I've got a lot on my mind. Or when I'm nervous. I'm both, today."

"I fall deathly silent when I'm nervous. Habit of childhood—I used to hope I'd turn invisible when my mother found out."

"Found out what?"

"Whatever evil I'd done that day. Do you live alone, Detective?" Peter asked suddenly.

"No," she said shortly. "I live with my family. And if you're going to ask whether I've had it easy because my dad is my boss, don't bother. I've answered that question *ad nauseam*. You didn't know I knew that term, did you?"

"What an interesting pronunciation," Peter replied. "It took me a second to interpret what you were saying. Never mind. Do you have bookshelves?"

"Last time I checked." She thrust her fingers through her bangs, her fingers snarling in her curls.

"What do they have on them?" Peter persisted.

"Potted plants. Among other things. At my house, everything from Great-Aunt Mitchell's underwear to back issues of nineteenth-century feed catalogues are piled on the shelves." She gave up discussing the case and knit her black brows, staring at him. "You're pretty chatty yourself."

"And I've got nothing on my mind at all, as it happens. Too little blood has gone to the brain in the past twelve hours. What exactly is making you jumpy? Afraid they won't miss, next time? Concerned for your career? Wondering whether Dad's beginning to think you take after Mom's side of the—" He broke off at the sight of her face, which had frozen, gone white, and then red.

"Whoa, I'm sorry," he said, sitting upright. "What did I say?"

"What have you heard about my mother?"

"Nothing!"

"Has Rafe talked about her, or what?"

"Why would he? It was just—"

"—an aside. Right. Please keep your asides to yourself, Mr. Mason."

"From now on, I will." The laziness had vanished, but the light-

185

headedness was back with a vengeance. He had apparently sat up too quickly, and quickly slid back down. "If I trespassed on private ground, I'm sorry."

Merry paced the room like a caged animal, her reflexive response whenever she felt claustrophobic. At the moment she was fighting both an unexpected urge to cry and a desire to flee the house. She had lost sleep the past few nights—tossing and turning with a cloud of bickering voices in her brain. She had hoped to be at her most rational, and instead she was a morass of feeling—fear that Peter Mason might be killed, and that it would be her fault; anxiety about whether she could solve this case; foreboding about Rafe's involvement in it; and a longing for his lost warmth and affection that had become acute since their encounter in the barn. Near-exhaustion and tension had her close to snapping, something she would die rather than let Peter Mason see. And now he threw her mother in her face. Better to deal with it head-on. She turned and faced him.

"My mother killed herself, Mr. Mason. After my brother came home from Nam in a body bag."

"I'm sorry."

"*Don't say that,*" she said furiously. "It always sounds so inadequate. She was an artist, you know—painted portraits. One night after dinner—she wouldn't have left us without a meal on the table for anything in the world—she filled my grandfather's waders with stones and walked into Madaket harbor. With my dad being police chief and all, he basically organized the hunt for the body. It was pretty public when they found her the next day. He handled it really well, actually."

She sat down in the armchair, a cascade of blond hair hiding her face from Peter's view. "I probably didn't. I was ten when we got the word about Billy and Mom started acting strange. I'm over thirty years old now and I'm still trying to show my father that I'm not going to crack up when the pressure gets tough. Isn't it pathetic?"

Peter pushed himself off the sofa with his good right arm and went to her awkwardly. He reached for her shoulder and then stopped as one slim hand came out, warding him off.

"Could we just deal with the evidence, please, and leave each other's personal life out of this?"

186

"Absolutely," he said, backing away.

Merry closed her eyes for an instant, gathering herself, and then turned to a pile of papers that stood on Peter's desk. She thrust her hair away from her face and settled her expression into an efficient mask.

"There was this picture, along with several letters signed by Rusty. We think. All of them were pretty water-damaged, I'm afraid. Recognize anyone?"

Peter studied the faded black-and-white figures under the sepia cloud. "The man in the car is my father."

"The woman's your mother?"

Peter studied the sleek cap of dark hair, the elegant form, and shook his head.

"You're sure? She's wearing shades, after all."

Peter turned to look at her. "I can pick my mother out of a crowd, five hundred feet in the distance, by the way she holds her head," he said. "I'm certain this isn't she."

"No thoughts who she might be?"

"None."

Merry nodded briefly. "We think it may be important, since Rusty chose to bring it with him." She handed him the photograph and flipped through some sheets of paper. "Okay, the letters may be copies, or practice for something he never sent. Or maybe he was waiting until he got to the U.S. to send them—the mail's probably better. Regardless, they're all remarkably similar." She looked from the letters to Peter's face. "I'd say they represent blackmail."

Peter looked up from the photograph with sudden interest. "You think Rusty came back here to raise money?"

"Maybe. Maybe he's been raising it for a while. Who knows? He had a very good reason for needing it, Mr. Mason." She paused, debating how to tell him, and decided that to be blunt was best. "According to the coroner, your brother was carrying the virus that causes AIDS. He had a lot of pretty pricey health care ahead of him, the kind that's harder to get in Brazil. Probably the kind he couldn't pay for, although we can't swear to that yet. We've cabled the Brazilian police to search for bank accounts under this name, or under his own, using the address on the passport."

Peter was staring at nothing, the eyes under the hawklike brow flat and unreadable. He picked up Rusty's passport and stared at the face. "Jesus God," he whispered, and abruptly sat down. "How far along was he?" Peter was still studying the photo. A line had sprung up in the tanned skin of his forehead.

"Not very," Merry said gently. "He had the virus but not the disease. And having learned a bit about your brother, I'd say he intended to fight it every step of the way." She passed him the letters. "Our crime scene unit typed up the text from the originals—they had to be examined under a microscope. The ink was almost completely gone after a couple days in the Atlantic, but the pen made enough of an impression in the paper that the words could be traced."

Peter seemed not to have heard her. He bent to read the first sheet, then looked up. "This is to Sky," he said.

Merry nodded. "We figured that meant Tate-Jackson. Nobody else with that name. You should see the next one."

Peter flipped to the second page. "Sundance?"

"Sounds like a Woodstock reunion, doesn't it? All we need is an Aragorn or a Galadriel. Or somebody named Love. The third one could be anyone—a guy named George."

"That's my sister."

"Keep those and take your time reading them. I want you to think about what they mean and get back to me if you've any ideas. With you getting shot last night, it looks like Rusty's death was an accident. But blackmail is a pretty strong motive for knocking somebody off. Money in any form, if it comes to that. Much more solid motive than love."

"How sad."

"Is it? You'd rather be killed by someone you love? Or loved once? I don't know. If it's going to be ugly, I'd rather it be about dollars and cents than about my place in the universe. Which reminds me: I've got to ask you a nasty question."

"Shoot."

She paused in midspeech, and looked at him. "You've got a weird sense of humor, Mr. Mason."

"Chalk it up to the loss of blood."

"Or that heady feeling of having beaten death."

"That too."

"What are the terms of your will?"

The question brought Peter up short. Sky had asked nearly the same thing, and he'd dismissed the thought as irrelevant, so convinced was he that Rusty had been the intended victim. He leaned back in the sofa cushions and raised one hand to his brow. Merry watched him closely.

"I leave my books and belongings to George, for her four kids; except for the collection of nautical architectural drawings—they go to Sky." He paused. "It felt morbid to write a will. Talking about it out loud is positively awful."

"Go on."

"I leave Mason Farms to the Nantucket Conservation Foundation—I'm hoping they'll run it in conjunction with the neighboring co-op. At the very least, it won't be developed, and that's something."

Merry walked over to the study window and gazed out at the bog. Still flooded for harvesting, it stretched like red porridge to the edge of the moor. She glanced back at Peter. "What's a place like this worth, anyway?"

He smiled faintly. "More than it looks."

Merry waited.

"I came into some money when my father died, Detective. The cost of the land was around three million—I had to beat out a developer for it, you know, who wanted to turn it into a hundred half-acre lots." Peter was gazing into the middle distance as he calculated. "Then I invested thirty thousand dollars per acre to set up the bog—that's a million and a half over fifty acres. The established vines have doubled the worth of the investment—call it three million now. Then there's the renovated outbuildings, the house, the ten acres of moor where the sheep graze—call that another million and a half or so."

Merry swallowed. She was at a loss for words.

Peter's gaze shifted back to her, and his grin widened. "I barely kept my head above water, despite the way it sounds now," he said. "If it weren't for some trust-fund income and the profits from ME stock, I'd have drowned in debt long ago. The place didn't make a nickel for four years—it takes that long for the vines to bear. Then there's the routine maintenance, Rafe's salary, the seasonal workers, the equipment—it mounts up. Technically, I haven't even earned back the cost of my initial investment. But I'm in it for the long term."

"And you've left all this to the NCF," she said woodenly.

"I hate the thought of those hundred half-acre lots."

Merry sat back down in the chair opposite Peter. She picked up her pad and tried to focus again on his will. "What about money?" she said.

Peter shifted, and jarred his arm uncomfortably. "You want to see my bank book?"

"I want to know what your life is worth to somebody who's desperate," she said.

"I didn't leave anything to Rusty, if that's what you're asking. I'd written him out of my life—and my death. The bulk of the fortune— what a grandiose word for stock and trust-fund income—goes to George's children, in trust once again. The Mason family trusts have always been handled by our New York lawyers and bankers. That part of it was pretty automatic."

"I'm going to have to ask you for a ballpark figure."

"My net worth?"

"If you like."

Peter was looking increasingly uncomfortable. Masons detested talking about money at home. "I'd say, all things considered, I have about ten million to play with. Does that give you an idea?"

Merry swallowed. "Yeah." She adjusted her glasses and wrote the figure down on her pad. All because some early Mason figured out whale oil wouldn't last forever. History sucked. She looked up. "How's your sister doing for cash?"

Peter smiled. He probably didn't intend to patronize her, but the amusement on his face felt like condescension, and she stiffened.

"These are routine questions, you understand?" she said.

"Completely. At my father's death, George inherited about the same amount as I. He'd disinherited Rusty. Everything else went to Mother."

"Your sister hasn't gone through it all, or anything like that?"

"I don't think so. Her husband, Hale, would hardly let her. He's a director at Salomon Brothers, the New York investment banking firm."

"Where Rusty worked."

"Yes—Hale probably got him his job when he was first out of college. They worked in separate sides of the house, however—Hale does corporate finance. Rusty is—was—a bond trader."

"Your sister work?"

"She's a freelance travel writer."

"And the kids? They know you left them your money?"

"I doubt it. And the oldest is only nine. They're far too young to even travel alone, much less purchase guns. I think we can rule them out."

"Maybe. I'll have to check. Anything else go anywhere else?"

"Odds and ends. I leave Rafe the price of a fishing boat—about a hundred thousand. Can't tell what it'll cost when I go. Then I leave one hundred fifty thousand to Will Starbuck for his college tuition. He's very bright, you know. I don't know if Tess realizes what he could do in the proper environment in a couple of years."

"Tuition? *That's* tuition? I got through Cape Cod Community on one tenth of that," Merry said.

Peter looked at her steadily. "I know what I'm doing," he said. "Included in the will is a letter of recommendation to Princeton. I intend to write one for him anyway. But if by some fluke I'm not around to do it, Sky—he's my executor—will send it on."

"So, if you died, would the money go to Will immediately?"

"No. There would be a trust until he was twenty-one. Tess would handle the money on his behalf. Will's education means everything to her, Merry."

"I bet," she said. "And if you're alive, you'll just pay the school bills as they come in, is that it? The trust only happens if you're dead?"

"Of course."

So Peter Mason dead was worth a great deal. Peter Mason alive wasn't worth the shorts he was wearing. "Does Tess know about this?"

Peter shook his head. "She's very proud. I don't want her to know about it until Will's college-bound. I may even figure out a way for it to look like financial aid from the university. Whatever university he chooses. I haven't worked that out yet."

The spark of an idea flared in Merry's brain. "Who witnessed the will for you, Mr. Mason?"

"Two of the family attorneys in New York."

The spark flared and died.

"Rafe is the one who suggested I keep Tess in the dark originally," Peter offered. "He came up with the idea of paying Will a fixed wage for his work on the farm, too, because she was so upset when I gave him the bike."

"Rafe," Merry said. "He knows about the terms of your will?"

Peter nodded. "At least, the tuition bequest. Yes. I wanted him to know he didn't have to worry about Will's college." He stopped, suddenly sensing the awkwardness of what he was about to say to Merry, then plunged on. "Rafe may be Will's stepfather one day. He doesn't make much, Detective. Tess's restaurant, Will's education—it can all look like a financial nightmare. I didn't want money to keep him from following his heart. Tess could use someone of Rafe's strength and intelligence."

Merry's breathing was suspended, and the circulation in her legs seemed to have stopped. She was numb from her waist to her toes. Good God, she thought, he doesn't even realize that he's giving Rafe a motive for murder.

To her surprise, Peter grinned. "So it's not much to write home about, Detective. And if you go looking for love as a motive, you'll come up even more empty-handed."

"I'll settle for money," she said. "It's what makes you different from a lot of other people, and what's different about you may make you a target. I don't know. I'm kind of groping, here. But we need to talk about your friends, Mr. Mason."

"My friends?"

"Yeah. Mayling Stern, the clothing designer, and the guy she lives with."

"Schuyler Tate-Jackson. He's my attorney."

"What a mouthful that is."

"Why do you think we call him Sky?"

"I'd really like to talk to that guy. What's the problem between him and Ms. Stern?"

"Is there one?"

"I'd lay even money on it. She was fishing for me to ask her why they're not married. Any ideas?"

The design for a wedding gown, crossed out with red ink, rose in Peter's mind. Something he'd seen in Mayling's studio the day after Rusty's murder. Still, what did that mean? He shook his head. "Not really. I consider that their business, and not something I'd ask them."

"So your friendship doesn't include trading secrets? No feelings, no personal stuff?"

Peter looked perplexed. "Why should that interest you?"

"Just wondering if you've got enough sense of either of them to be able to judge their characters, that's all."

"I consider myself a good judge of character, Detective, regardless of whether I know the secrets of a person's soul."

Merry's green eyes looked at him with amusement. "Yeah, well, whether you're accurate or not is another question. Let me ask you this: does Ms. Stern lie?"

"Does she lie?" Peter closed his eyes. The throbbing was becoming more intense. "I suppose we all lie, if the reasons are compelling enough. Why don't you tell me what you're aiming for, and I'll try to help you."

"Mayling Stern's Mercedes has a bashed-in front end. The cop who looked it over while I was talking to her says it's pretty recent. The weather's so damp here that anything older than a week would rust already. But she doesn't mention it when I ask her what she did this weekend, and there's no accident report on file at the station."

"Is that so unusual?"

"When her life-mate's being blackmailed by his old friend, who just happens to end up on somebody's front end? Yeah, I think it's a little strange."

"Mayling never knew Rusty."

"And another thing." Merry fished in her pocket and pulled out a plastic bag. The rat button dropped onto Peter's lap. "I've been carrying that thing around so long it's started to feel like a good-luck charm."

"What is it?" He turned it curiously.

"A button from one of Stern's sweaters."

His face cleared. "The Chinese New Year ones," he said. "I bought one for Lucy's birthday."

"Did she like it?"

He looked up. "I think so," he said. "She seemed to."

"Would you know if she was faking and really hated it?"

"Why?"

Merry took the plastic bag from his hand. "I found this near the body. The sweater it came from turned up in Rusty's bag on the beach. I figure whoever murdered him got blood on it and decided to dump it with his stuff. I don't know whether he—or she—realized one of the buttons had been lost."

"And you think the sweater you found is Lucy's?" Peter said quietly.

Merry shrugged. "Mayling Stern owns one exactly like it. And if I believe Lucy, she hates rats, and gave your gift away to a clothing drive a little while after she got it. Which means anybody who went to Our Lady of the Island's bazaar might have picked it up, worn it to murder Rusty, and dumped it in the ocean. If we believe Lucy. The people who ran the bazaar have no record of individual items or purchasers. I checked. That's why I'm asking if you could tell if she liked it or not. Does the story make sense?"

"Yes and no. I thought she liked it. But if she hated rats, she'd never tell me in a million years, and it would be like her to get rid of the sweater quietly and charitably behind my back." His lips twitched at the thought.

"So minus the bazaar and the mystery shopper, we're back to Mayling Stern's sweater."

"You think Mayling killed Rusty?"

Merry shrugged. "I dunno. I really don't. It's just one of those threads I keep following in my mind."

"She's sold a lot of these sweaters. Anybody could have worn one. Let's talk about the other threads you're following in your mind. They may prove more fruitful."

Merry shoved herself away from the edge of the desk where she'd been leaning, legs crossed, and sat down on the wing chair. "Let's talk about Lucy Jacoby. Why's she so scared of strangers?"

Peter hesitated.

"I went to talk to her the day after the murder, and she had trouble inviting me in. Kept acting as if she expected bad news. You'd think she'd killed Rusty herself."

There was a short silence. Merry waited for Peter to fill it. He didn't disappoint her.

"You can rule out that possibility, Detective. Lucy is a friend of fairly recent acquaintance. She never knew my brother, nor did anyone she cares about."

"Except you."

He looked up at her quickly, a fleeting expression of pain crossing his features, and Merry realized that he knew Lucy Jacoby was in love with him, and that the knowledge was not a source of happiness.

"She's not the sort to murder," he said quietly. "She's the sort who takes her suffering, as though it were expected, and fades away."

Merry looked down at her hands. "Let's suppose she didn't know it was Rusty," she said. "Any reason Lucy'd want to kill you?"

Peter laughed, an unpleasant, harsh sound that reminded her of the first day she had met him over the body of his brother. "I'm sure she's felt like it many times, Detective, but it's never that simple for Lucy. She's a woman of great passion, and a woman who has seen too much pain; she's been nearly throttled by thwarted love. And now she shuts off as much as she reaches toward."

"Any idea why she skipped the first day of school?"

"One or two," Peter said warily. "Why?"

Merry shrugged again, affecting casualness. "I talked to her that afternoon. I think she'd tied one on the night before."

"You've got to be kidding."

"Well, I'm not the island expert—that honor goes to my dad—but I've seen a few hungover people. She gets my vote."

Peter stood up from the sofa slowly, his good hand massaging his brow, and walked toward the window. He stopped, turned, and took a few unsteady paces back to the sofa. Unused as he was to weakness and inactivity, he'd overestimated his strength. He sat down rather heavily. "Lucy was probably searching for courage. She's on her own out there at Tom Nevers, literally and figuratively, and sometimes it probably gets too much for her."

"Any idea why she was drinking the night Rusty was killed?"

"I can see you think it's because she killed him," Peter said. While most men raised their voices in anger, Peter dropped his to be almost inaudible, Merry noticed. "A more ludicrous thought I've never encountered. She has difficulty killing the beetles that attack her roses." He paused, looking away from Merry's chair toward the moors beyond the study's picture window. He came to some decision then, and turned back to her with finality. "I know why she was drinking, Detective, and it has nothing to do with this case. I tell you this in strictest confidence, and it reflects the trust I place in you. It is not to leave this room. Do I have your assurance it won't?"

Merry hesitated, then nodded. "Yeah, sure. For now. If it really doesn't have anything to do with the murder."

"I give you my word it does not." Peter paused. "How to explain this? Lucy came to Nantucket to escape an unhappy marriage. Her husband—a man she met in Europe, she tells me, during a junior year abroad from Bryn Mawr—is what is known as a gray arms dealer."

"A what?"

"He brokers the purchase of components for deadly weapons between those who have them and those who should not. He lives two lives—one, that of an Italian aristocrat with estates in Portofino and Milano; the other, a subterranean existence bordering on the criminal. He surrounds himself with dangerous men, according to Lucy. And she lives in fear of them."

"Why?"

Peter gave Merry an appraising look. "Have you ever been beaten by a man, Detective?"

Merry recoiled inwardly, and her shock embarrassed her. Her face flooded with color. "I take it you don't mean that spanking I got when I was six?"

Again the harsh laugh. "Hardly. I mean blows strong enough to raise bruises—but never on the face, or the arm, or the leg, where they might be visible. Bruises on areas of Lucy's body she hid with her clothing. To hear her tell it, the beatings happened almost daily. The bruises never healed."

"Why'd she marry him?"

"For the reason most women marry men, Detective. She thought she could save him."

"And the day of Rusty's murder?"

"She ran into one of Marcello's thugs on the ferry. He's found out where she is. She's been run to earth. I think she's living in terror—waiting for Marcello to turn up at her doorstep. I offered to move her into the Cliff Road house, I even suggested she go to New York—stay at Sky's, or find a hotel where she could check in under another name, anything. She said it wouldn't do any good."

"I've got a better idea," Merry said. "She could go to the police."

Peter shook his head. "I told her that. She seemed more terrified of police involvement than of anything else. And in a way, she's got a point. Marcello can make life hell for her if she tries to fight him with the law. She hasn't seen his hired thug since she got off the ferry, and anyway, there's no charge to arrest him on. She's in a bind, Detective. She'll have to wait for the violence to come to her before she can ask for help."

Merry thought of Lucy Jacoby, half hidden in the vines of her loggia like a nesting bird, and felt a wave of pity for her. Peter was right. There was no way he could explain the circumstances of that life to Merry. It was as alien as a foreign tongue—as alien as Peter Mason, if she was honest with herself. Over the past few days she'd viewed his life more closely, and had almost come to believe it was little different from her own. But she was wrong. They existed on two separate planes, thrust into sharp contact by violence and death. Once she found the murderer—once the violence ended—the planes would part again. She shook herself out of her thoughts and looked over at Peter. He was staring at a spot two feet in front of him, worry alive in his face, and she knew that she had recalled Lucy's danger to his mind, at a time when he was physically ill-equipped to help her. Give him something else to think about, she advised herself grimly.

"There's one more thing," she said.

"Yes?" He looked up, as if surprised that she was still in the room, and waited.

"Rafe," she said. "The motive being money, the victim being you."

This time, perhaps because he had crossed the threshold of surprise, the idea didn't even faze him. "It's too little. Besides, I never told him about his bequest."

"Suppose he found out somehow. Never mind how, right now. Suppose he knows that he's in to make a bundle, and what's more, his current girlfriend comes in for quite a bit if you die now and leave that tuition to her son. If you're alive, the money goes to Will, not to her; so in her mind, you're better off dead."

"It's peanuts."

"People like Tess and Rafe don't think in terms of millions. They could do a lot with two hundred and fifty thousand dollars—what you've left Rafe plus the bequest to Will—particularly if it meant the difference between losing everything and survival. They could invest it and live off the income. Do you have any idea how well the Greengage is doing? Can Tess make it until next season?"

"I don't know," Peter said. He remembered the investment magazine he'd seen on Rafe's desk the night before, and thrust the image of it away. He passed his good hand over his eyes wearily. "God, this is awful, isn't it? Looking hard at everyone you know, wondering what price he's placed on your life."

"As I said, I'd rather it were about dollars and cents than about the people I love," Merry said dryly. "Unfortunately, you're stuck with both."

"That's something I live with," Peter said. He was staring out at the moors again, and his face had darkened in a way that was beginning to seem familiar to Merry. "I thought it might be different, here on the island, if I called myself a farmer. I thought I could stay away from New

York, away from the world of my father, and stop wondering if my friends are really my friends, or just people who like to be around influence and power. Stop wondering if a woman gives herself to me because she feels something for me, or because of what I can buy; stop seeing a compliment as flattery, goodwill as sycophancy, intimacy as a dangerous gamble. I was wrong. I never could trust anyone before; I can't trust anyone now."

Merry swallowed. Something in her wanted to reach toward Peter Mason—tell him that he could trust her, forge a friendship out of the brittleness of death and violence. He seemed far more vulnerable today, wounded, weak, and unhappy, than he had in the strength of his rage Labor Day morning.

Merry shook herself slightly and looked around for her purse. It was time she left. She reached for the notebook she hadn't opened, and wondered if Peter Mason would blame her for the sharp dose of reality. If he did, so be it. She started to walk toward the door. His voice stopped her.

"May I ask you a question, Detective?"

She turned to him wordlessly.

"If I'm the target, not Rusty, why am I still alive?"

"Because you're damn lucky."

"Maybe. Or maybe the murderer's had a change of heart. A really thorough one would have finished the job."

Chapter 19

WHEN MERRY HAD GONE, Peter lay back on the sofa cushions and closed his eyes. Rusty's face as he had last seen it in death—lined, emptied, and forever unreachable—hung in his mind. He had felt no sense of loss at the murder, and no rage toward the killer; those had been felt long ago, in the presence of another form of death. But in the void left by his banished love for his brother, a simple conviction remained: that in the world he had chosen to value, justice must be done. How dispassionate, he thought, how like a man of my class. I am doing the decent thing, to keep me from feeling the unthinkable—the joy of revenge in Rusty's death. To keep me from feeling at all.

He allowed himself to consider the nature of his brother's disease. He had never known someone with AIDS before, and he realized, suddenly, that this is what it meant to live on an island. There were notices, from time to time, in the memorial section of his alumni notes; but these were generally older men, from classes before his time, cut off in their forties by the swift and deadly disease. Rusty brought the illness uncomfortably into his study, as he lay caught in a shaft of sunlight, and forced him to look at it nakedly. Rusty, who had played rugby like a god, who had loved too many women to remember, who had burnished his strength like a bright shield held before the eyes of everyone—Rusty would have died a slow and painful death, turning to bone in front of them. If he had felt little at Rusty's murder, he felt a flicker of sympathy for the prospect of his slow deterioration. Peter clenched his hands as the sudden fear of dying swept over him, and the movement of his sore left arm caused him to cry out in pain.

Footsteps clattered down the hallway from the kitchen and Rebecca pushed the door open. Her face was drained of color and her eyes were wide. "Glory be to God, what's happened?" she said hoarsely.

He pushed himself upright with his good arm, holding the other stiffly in the least painful position, and grimaced at her. "Just jogged it a bit. Sorry."

She rolled her eyes and turned on her heel, annoyance in every line of her body. She hated to be caught out by emotion. Poor Rebecca. Alone in her room in the converted icehouse the previous night, she hadn't slept, and despite her obvious relief at his return from the hospital, she would probably be up again tonight worrying the gunman would come back. Regardless of the pain in his arm from the attack, and the nagging questions left by Detective Folger's suspicions, Peter believed he wouldn't. It was important for him to believe that Rusty, not himself, was the victim; and he had convinced himself the trail to Rusty's killer began in Chappaqua. He was headed there tomorrow.

He glanced down reluctantly at the typewritten sheets Merry Folger had left on the sofa next to him—Rusty's letters. He picked up the first, addressed to Sky, and wondered if the originals were in Rusty's handwriting. There was something about the artifacts of a life—a signature, a scent wafting out of a drawer, a particular pair of shoes left on the floor of an empty closet—that spoke more eloquently of a vanished face than any photograph. Pictures froze a person in time, rendered him mute and static; whereas the things he had used sparked one's memory, and unleashed a tide of images vivid with life. All in all, Peter thought, he probably preferred the letters typed.

The first one was to Sky. It was undated.

Barra da Tijuca
Rio de Janeiro,
Brasil

Dear Sky:

I know it's been a while, and I'd apologize, only why bother? We've both got our lives, and I'm sure you haven't spared much thought for mine.

Maybe I'd better start over. The bitterness is something I can't control anymore, even if I'd like to, and it invades even this attempt at writing a letter to an old friend.

I've heard about you from time to time, from chance encounters in Rio bars with people you know, or have once known. I've liked getting the occasional letter you churn out, even though I've never answered them. You've been a sort of lifeline to the past. It's good to know you're doing so well. As for me—what is there to say after ten years?

I don't know, Sky. Maybe spending a few years in a minimum-security country club would have been preferable to rotting in this beautiful hell. You tell me. Was I a fool? The only difference be-tween wisdom and idiocy is how it looks in retrospect, or so it seems to me. I've wasted a third of my life in this rancid, aching, despoiled paradise, learning that all of those qualities are what paradise really means: a dream come true has the profile of nightmare. It's time to wake up.

For both of us, Sky. Your career could end if I came back and decided to talk about how it started. I haven't decided yet if that's what I'll do. I'm going through rough times—you've no idea how bad—and while money can't solve everything, sometimes it helps you pretend. I wouldn't be above keeping silent for a price. Pretty bald, isn't it? Pretty brutal? But then, so's my life. How much is yours worth, Sky? Add it all up, like the honest broker you are—the houses, the million-plus salary, the identity that comes from dealing with power, the stature you've spent a decade building, that woman who keeps you sane. Think about it long and hard. Hire a lawyer if you can find one who'll convince you it helps. And contact me at

Peter's on Labor Day. You know where he lives; I don't. Yet. But I will.

We'll talk terms.

There was, of course, no signature. Someone from Merry's forensics team had dutifully typed the word "Socks" at the bottom, Rusty's nickname from college. He had rarely done his laundry on a regular basis, and his roommates had gone from calling him Rusty to Musty and finally to Socks. The innocence of the monicker placed at the end of such a letter, filled as it was with the perversion of Rusty's former love for Sky, jarred Peter. Or perhaps it was the vividness of memory that it brought, and the sense of youth irretrievably lost. He shrugged off his thoughts and turned to the body of the letter itself. Sky, contrary to his words, knew why Rusty had left, and that knowledge somehow incriminated him. Or so Rusty believed—enough to think Sky would be willing to pay him not to talk. What could Sky know? Was it the same as what Malcolm Scott could tell him? Should he confront Sky with the knowledge of this letter?

This letter. He stopped, his gaze suspended in midair, and saw once again the interior of Mayling's studio, the dim light of a foggy Labor Day, and her fingers scrabbling desperately at scattered sheets of paper. She had been angry, and afraid. At him, he had thought, but perhaps what he had seen was anger at Rusty, and fear for Sky. If it was the same letter. The copy Rusty had sent.

He turned to the second letter, hoping for some answers. Like the first, it had been written in Rio; but this one was dated August 20. He scanned it quickly, and stopped short at the sight of his own name. He went back to the top and read it more slowly, trying to understand what it meant.

Dear Sundance—

Bad pennies, like bad drugs, always come back to haunt you. Don't ask how I found out where you are; we'll have hours to catch up with one another when I get to Nantucket. I'm coming home. I don't expect you to greet me at the dock.

I need money; I'm sure you must have some. Sudden death has a way of making people wealthy. On the other hand, if you're unwilling to part with cash, I can offer you the destruction of that safe little world you're in the process of building. You realize that all I have to do is say a word to my brother Peter. So I think we'll have a lot to talk about.

I'll be in touch.

There was infuriatingly little to suggest what sort of hold Rusty had on Sundance, or who he—or she—was. Only that Sundance lived on Nantucket, had known Rusty at some point in the past, and possibly now knew Peter. That could be anyone, he thought impatiently. It was as though Rusty was afraid that Sundance, whoever he was, might decide to expose him to the law; and his letter, as a result, revealed nothing that could be taken as blackmail. Rusty had become careful in his last years.

Peter read the letter again quickly and pondered the final paragraph. "Sudden death has a way of making people wealthy." He shook his head. Will and Tess Starbuck were his only friends in mourning, but Dan's death had brought them more debt than wealth.

He shuffled the sheets and found the final letter, the one to George. He liked reading this the least, afraid he would discover something about the Whitneys' lives he'd rather not know. This was the worst of it, he thought; Rusty had brought discord back into his world. He read on.

My dearest George—
Lo, and the prodigal brother returneth.

Biblical words for catastrophic events. I assume that you, of anyone, have fatted calves to kill—a room, for instance, up in the eaves of that palatial house you call home. I can see it now—done up in Mario Buatta, probably, or Mark Hampton, reeking of nouveau wealth and Hale's unfortunate conservatism. I'm counting on the conservatism, by the way, to keep me healthy: make sure you tell him I'm coming home around Labor Day. You can tell him he needn't leave the country, either—I have no intention of bringing up our unfortunate mutual past. Provided I'm well looked after.

I won't bother to lull you into thinking I'm a changed man—for the better, that is—with false interest in your brats or sweet inquiries about your happiness in marriage. I never liked kids, I have no hope for Hale's, and I wrote off your marriage when you made it that summer before I left. You were always one to go for security over daring, George darling; something you inherited with Peter. Much good it may do you. You'll die well and fat and without a single live emotion in your body, your only satisfaction the knowledge you've lived a life as empty as your mother's. And Peter—Peter, who actually thought there was such as thing as objective morality, never realizing he imposed his subjective values on me, thinking they could "save" me. You're idiots, both of you, and I've never got done despising you for the safety you wrap around you like a shroud. May it stifle you as you tried to stifle me.

So I've had a bit too much scotch. I'm sober enough to know you can't turn me away, George, not if you want your home intact and your children to grow up with all the illusions you think so precious. Make sure Hale knows. He needn't throw himself off the train from Greenwich some morning, he needn't oil the old family revolver and lock himself in the library. He just needs to negotiate. Man to man. I'm ready.

And I'm coming. To take back my inheritance. You took it from me, George, you and Peter. And I'm not going to die without what is mine.

R.

Peter read the letter three times. Then he folded it carefully with his right hand, eased himself to a standing position, and reached for a buff leather briefcase that rested on the floor next to his desk. On second thought, he turned and folded the letter to Sky and placed it with George's. He would take them both to New York.

Hale Whitney was a shy, introspective, cherubic-faced forty-five-

205

year-old who had entered a new world when he met Georgiana; she was ten years his junior and socially his complete opposite. He exuded confidentiality, trustworthiness, and respectability. He had a wicked instinct for making money. But he was no street fighter—threatened with the loss of his reputation, or his home, suicide might seem like a not unreasonable option. Rusty had tapped George first, to make sure Hale didn't bolt. He had been very clever.

Peter snapped the tabs on the briefcase and stood up. Then he reached for the phone and dialed the Nantucket police station. The receiver was picked up on the second ring, then bounced painfully onto a hard surface, jarring his ear. He winced. He could hear Merry Folger swearing in the distance, and then her voice, annoyed and abrupt, came across the line.

"You dropped me," he said.

"Yeah, well, people were beginning to—" she began, then caught herself. "Never mind. You read the letters?"

"Yes. Merry—this has everything to do with family history, with Rusty's past. I may be in a position to clear it up for you when I get back from New York."

"New York?"

"Well, the suburbs, actually. Greenwich. Westchester. Rusty's funeral. And some conversation that may lead somewhere."

There was a short silence on the line. "I think New York sounds great. Sky Jackson's in New York. You planning to see him?"

"Yes, actually."

"Then I'm coming with you."

Peter opened his mouth to dissuade her, then stopped in mid-thought. He had a sudden vision of her intelligent green eyes and the way her jaw clenched when she asked her unswervingly tough questions. Perhaps that's what it would take to crack the counselor's veneer.

"We'll catch the eight-thirty flight," he said. "Pack light."

Chapter 20

FRIDAY MORNING OF A SHORT WEEK after Labor Day, and still she felt exhausted. Lucy Jacoby struggled to open her eyes at the insistent ringing of the alarm clock, sensing the dim light of five-thirty beyond the skylight of her loft bedroom. She sighed deeply and threw her arms over her head, reaching for the coolness of the empty white linen pillowcase next to her own, resisting the day and its rush of duties, tensions, and memories. She felt a profound desire for sleep, an almost overwhelming compulsion. Should she call in sick again today? Have coffee over her morning paper and then catch a ferry for the mainland? Unbidden, the face of a familiar stranger rose in her drowsing mind. Her last encounter on the ferry had been a horrible one. There was no escape in that direction.

She swung her stiff limbs out of bed in the dim, fog-laden light and padded to the small window cut in the peak of the gable. From here she could see the Atlantic off Tom Nevers Head. It stretched like a sheet of iron to the horizon, and she shivered. She had never found charm in the sight of limitless distance. Time for a warm shower, coffee, the intimacy of her garden.

•   •   •

207

SHE WAS HUDDLED IN the dew-laden grass near her roses when Peter pushed open her garden gate. The fall of auburn curls flashed around her shoulders as she turned, and fear suffused her face at the sight of the neat sling supporting his arm.

His heart turned over. She looked so much like a burdened child, playing in the dirt to keep her mind off her worries. The roses towered above her head, a dozen flaming candelabra, and their mingled scents drifted to his nostrils on the shifting damp of the day.

"Peter! What happened?" She stood up quickly, dropping her trowel in the bed at her feet.

"Somebody took a shot at me Wednesday night," he said. "Nothing serious. I'm fine."

No one would ever know what it had cost him in pain and swearing to get dressed that morning.

"Who would do such a thing?"

He walked toward her slowly in his business suit. The dew spattered the polished leather of his shoes and left raindrop-sized stains on their tips. "The roses are still blooming."

"Not for long," she said, glancing back over her shoulder. The words were laced with regret. "I can keep them going until mid-September, but after that, I admit defeat and leave the heads on to wither—it triggers their dormancy. The drop in temperature at night is doing it for me, anyway. You've probably seen the last flowering."

Peter stopped at the edge of the bed and, with his good arm, reached toward a coppery pink bloom. "This one reminds me of you," he said. "It has your fiery head." He turned to look at Lucy and saw her pallor, the widening of her eyes. She was staring fixedly at the sling.

"Whoever killed Rusty must have come back for me," he said. "But he failed. That's a good thing, Lucy, not a cause for worry."

"Unless he was hunting for you all along," she whispered, "and got Rusty by mistake. Oh, Peter, I'm so afraid."

"Don't be. I can take care of myself."

"What does—the detective think?"

"I don't know."

Lucy stared at him wordlessly, her lips working, and then took a deep breath. "That's a lie," she said. "I never thought you'd lie to me."

Peter looked away and thrust his good right hand into his pocket, turning over his keys with his fingers. He came to a decision. "I think she's always believed the killer was after me, Lucy, and this has just confirmed her hunch. But I don't agree with her. And I don't want you worrying for no good reason."

Lucy stared at him without blinking, then shook herself slightly and reached down to dust the dirt off her knees. Her movements suggested profound weariness. "That's as good a reason as any," she said, throwing a glance at the sling. "Be careful, Peter, or I'll never forgive you." She surveyed his clothing. "Where are you going in that getup?"

"New York. To see a former business partner of my father's."

"Gone long?" Her voice was trembling again, and Peter thought he knew why. He hesitated an instant, then placed one hand lightly on her shoulder.

"You'll never know I've been away. How are you feeling, alone in the house? You can move to the farm while I'm gone—Rebecca and Rafe would be some company. Not to mention Ney."

Lucy smiled a watery smile and shook her head. "I'll stay here," she said. "I've got to face him sooner or later." She jumped suddenly and glanced around for her watch. "What time is it? I've got to get changed for school."

"Seven-thirty."

"I'll be late. I always am." She turned for the door, then hesitated, and reached for her garden shears. She leaned past Peter and snipped off the coppery-pink rose he had touched. "Here," she said, "take this with you. Roses are good luck."

Peter smiled and breathed in its scent deeply. "You know, this is the one thing the farm still lacks. We should plan a rose garden this winter. What's the name of this one?"

Lucy's eyes shifted away, and she shrugged. "I don't know. Maybe it doesn't have a name. I picked it up on the Cape." She made for her back door, with her characteristic furtiveness, a small animal bolting for protective cover. At the screen she paused and looked at him sharply. "Call me when you get back."

"I wouldn't dream of not," he said to the empty doorway.

•   •   •

PETER PLACED THE ROSE carefully on the Rover's passenger seat and gingerly shifted the car into first with his right hand. He could just manage to steer and shift at the same time, if he did it slowly and had plenty of warning; but he wouldn't mind letting Merry Folger drive the rental car once they got to New York. He glanced down at the rose as he bumped over the ruts of the Chuck Hollow Road and turned the car toward Milestone. It was an extraordinary color, the orange-fuchsia of each petal's tip deepening at the base to a glorious, tropical copper. It smelled of cinnamon and citrus and the deep woodsiness of tea. He had never seen anything like it. Not that he was an expert on roses—his mother had grown them, but as a child, he'd ignored everything that wasn't a sport or a book. He glanced at it again and had a sudden, vivid image of his study at night, with Rachmaninoff playing and the heady scent of this flower drifting in through the screened windows—and made a decision on impulse. He had cut over to Tom Nevers on his way to the airport, but instead of heading for it now, he backtracked down the Milestone Road to Maplethorne's Nursery.

When the Rover crunched over the gravel and pulled to a stop near the railroad ties that served as markers for the garden center's parking, Buck Maplethorne was in the midst of hauling a garden hose down an avenue of fall chrysanthemums, set out on trestle tables to brighten the foggy morning. He looked over his shoulder at Peter, gave him a swift grin, and shoved the hose nozzle up into the outdoor spigot.

"Peter. You look like summer people in that getup."

"Blood will out, Buck, blood will out. You can buy land here, but you can't buy history."

Buck grinned again and said nothing; the old-timers still called him "that fellah from the Cape," after twenty years in business. He glanced at Peter's arm. "Need some more runners? I've got an order going out this afternoon, and you're just in time to get on it."

"Thanks, Buckie. How about another beater—a rental, maybe—in time for harvesting next week?"

"With that arm?"

"You'll notice I have another one."

"I'll put in the order and call you when the delivery arrives. You can send it back, end of next week, and that way you're only paying for five days."

Peter pulled the rose out of the car's interior and handed it to the nurseryman. "What can you tell me about this?"

Buck Maplethorne let out a low whistle. "Now *that's* a beaut," he said. "Where'd you come across it?"

"A friend's garden. I was hoping you'd know the name and how to order it."

"Can't help you off the top of my head," Buck said, "but I can find anything, if it's grown in the U.S. Give me a couple days."

·　　·　　·

JOHN FOLGER HAD HIS COFFEE MUG and his morning copy of the *Inquirer and Mirror* spread out on the scarred oak table in the kitchen. The screen door was open and the morning sounds of the island—birds, distant foghorns, and the whoosh of bicycle tires—filtered into the room. Ralph Waldo, humming over his tomato plants, was just audible.

The chief took a long draft of coffee and grimaced unconsciously at the taste; not that the coffee was bad, but he had never really acquired a liking for it. He'd given up a lifelong smoking habit three years earlier. Caffeine was a poor substitute for nicotine.

A loud thump reverberated through the house, and John glanced up at the ceiling. Merry's room. The girl was throwing shoes again. He shifted his gaze from the upstairs to the wall opposite his chair, the newspaper still in his hands and his bright blue eyes unfocused. Merry. He was uneasy about the progress of this case, or lack of progress, and he couldn't tell her that. Would he have told another detective on the force? Probably. Was it favoritism to keep his peace now? Probably. And yet, horning in on her case would seem like overactive parenting, and he was trying to reform.

The thumping made its way down the timeworn steps—the carpeting was so old it was useless as a sound barrier—and his daughter swung into the kitchen with the front pieces of her hair gathered up in one hand like Pebbles Flintstone. She was wearing her one good suit, a stylish piece with a short skirt and a long jacket that made her look like a lean and hungry executive, at least in her more composed moments. Now she was casting about the kitchen distractedly.

"Lose something?" John said dryly.

"Notebook," she said. "Barrette. I've got ten minutes to get to the airport, dammit. And can I find my notebook? Can I have a good-hair day? Not a chance."

"Check your car. And good morning."

"Morning." She fished a plastic tortoiseshell clip out of a drawerful of rubber bands and plastic-bag twizzlers, slapped it into her hair, and dashed for the driveway. John heard the Blazer's door jerk open and after an instant thump shut. He closed his eyes painfully. Every noise Merry made this morning seemed to reverberate through his skull.

"Of course it's not in there," she said. "I was reading it somewhere around here last night."

A slight thrill of self-conscious guilt rose in the pit of John Folger's stomach. He remembered where her notebook was. He had taken it after she had gone to bed, and read through her notes himself. A way to satisfy his overwhelming urge to monitor this case. The notebook was on his bedside table. He took a quick sip of coffee to hide his face.

Merry turned at the sound of Ralph Waldo's wheelbarrow, its unoiled wheels complaining and burdened, as he trundled a load of compost toward the tomato bed. "Ralph! Hey, Ralph!" she said. She shot through the screen door.

John Folger hurried up to his bedroom, retrieved the notebook, and sauntered into the kitchen just as Merry reentered the house. "This it?" he asked indifferently.

"Yes!" she said. "Where was it?"

"Dining-room table. Slipped in among yesterday's paper."

"I must be losing my mind," Merry said. "Thanks. I've got to go."

"Case got you tied up in knots?" he couldn't resist saying. He tried to look unconcerned. She studied him closely, just the same.

"Should it?" she said.

"I don't know. You haven't mentioned anything about it."

"But you've got some ideas, don't you?"

He didn't like the green intensity of her gaze. He shrugged. "A few."

"And?"

"Oh, nothing much. I just wondered why you were letting Peter Mason off scot-free. Isn't he worth a question or two?"

"No, I don't think so."

"You don't think so."

"No."

"Why not?"

"Because if he were going to kill his brother, why not do it somewhere other than his front yard? And why leave the body there for anyone to discover? Why show me so clearly that he couldn't stand Rusty's guts? And if he *did* kill his brother, who shot him Wednesday night? It doesn't add up, Dad."

"Unless you're a very clever killer," John Folger said mildly, "and you figure the best cover is to look like a knucklehead or a victim, or both. He has no alibi, remember; he's got the motive; and he's definitely got the opportunity. Look for those, and you'll find your man."

"You know that's too easy, Dad. Guilty until proven innocent. You taught me to think beyond that."

"So think," her father said. "Convince me I'm wrong."

Merry stared at him an instant, her face darkening. "The Mason bumpers were clean," she said.

"You know that doesn't mean anything."

"Oh, come on, Dad. It means that Rusty wasn't hit by any of the farm cars. Give me that, at least." She paused, considering her words. "Let's say he didn't know his way to the farm and the fog only made it worse. Let's say somebody offered to drive him to Peter's. He—or she— lets Rusty out a ways down the road, in front of the gate, and then, for some reason, hits the gas. Rusty pops into the air and falls backward, hitting his head on the hood of the car, and rolls to the ground, unconscious. The driver of the car gets out, opens the gate, drags Rusty over to the driveway, and pitches him into the bog. Then he dumps the car with the damaged bumper somewhere it'll be hidden—Gibbs Pond, say, that's close enough, or Sesachacha."

"So he dumps the car in the farm pond, and Rusty's bag over at Surfside? That doesn't make sense."

"Can't expect a car to go out with the tide; you've got to get it to sink. A bag full of clothes, now—better to let the surf take that, just in case the car's ever found." She looked at her father. "Then you head for home and lie low. End of story. Anybody could have done that."

"And Mason better than anybody. An athlete like him, he could run all over the island at night and be none the worse for wear. But it doesn't work, Merry. Nobody'd sink a car he owned in the middle of Gibbs Pond and just go out and buy a new one. It's not human. He'd keep it locked up and hope he could repair it when the furor died down."

"Like Mayling Stern," Merry said. She started to speak and then stopped, a sudden look of surprise crossing her face. "Unless it was rented."

"Rented," John said.

"By Rusty," Merry said slowly. "And he picks somebody up on the road. The somebody offers to show him to Mason's. And then he kills Rusty and dumps the car somewhere. Same script as before. Only there's nothing to connect the murderer to the murder weapon at all."

"Well, that's a relief," her father said, in the infuriating tone he reserved for children or the mentally handicapped. "There's no way Mason's in the clear if the car was rented. What's more natural than Rusty meeting Peter on the road to his farm? He could have been out running, or on that bike of his, and the two of them loaded it in the back and Peter took the wheel. He sends Rusty out to open the gate and floors it while Rusty's fiddling with the hasp. I'm just thinking out loud," he said, as she turned an exasperated glance upon him. He reached for his cooling coffee and picked up the newspaper with an air of nonchalance. "And by the way, more than one suspect in a murder investigation has pulled the self-inflicted-wound number on a rookie detective. Keep it in mind, that's all I'm asking."

"It's incompatible with the evidence," Merry said.

John looked at her over the paper. "The footprints near the body?"

"How'd you know about the footprints near the body?" Merry asked, startled, and then her eyes narrowed and she looked at the notebook. She looked back at her father. "Oh, Dad, couldn't you just have asked?"

He had the grace to hang his head.

"All right. Since you've rifled through my notes, let's talk about those footprints. In my mind, they're the clearest indication that Peter Mason didn't kill his brother. Someone else did—and wants us to think that Peter was the intended target."

John Folger sat back in his chair. "I'm not with you."

Merry glanced at her watch and hesitated. Then she pulled out a kitchen chair and sat down. "Listen. I've got five minutes to make it all the way out of town to the airport, but since your curiosity is killing you, I'll just have to speed through several lights to make the plane." She reached for his coffee mug and took a sip, grimacing as she did so. "God, that's awful. Couldn't Ralph spring for a new percolator once every decade?"

"You eaten anything?"

"I'll have plane food. Now listen." She leaned toward him conspiratorially. "The prints walk up to Peter's body and stop. Whoever shot him took the time—despite a frantic dog willing to eat its way out of the barn and Peter's housekeeper running to the scene in her nightie—to check whether Peter was dead. A real killer would have noticed he'd simply fainted—that the wound was in the arm, not the chest—and shot him at point-blank range in the head. This guy turned and walked away. Or ran. Then there's the shot itself."

"What about it?"

"Peter told me yesterday that he saw the muzzle flare and instinctively dodged left, trying to protect his chest area. He hoped the bullet would hit his right chest or arm. But the bullet went into Peter's *left* arm."

"So he misjudged the killer."

"Maybe."

"Or this guy couldn't aim straight."

"Possibly."

"But you don't think so."

"I think he—or she—never intended to hit Peter at all. I think the attack was a red herring—to make the police think Peter was the intended victim of Rusty's murder. Confuse the trail a bit and direct us away from the scent. But the killer miscalculated; Peter's an athlete with an athlete's quick reflexes and coordination. The bullet was fired well to the side of Peter, *and he jumped into it by mistake.* When Peter went down, in a dead faint, for one awful moment the gunman thought he'd killed him. So he walked over to see. Then he hightailed it out of there."

John Folger sat back in his seat, mulling it over. "That's pretty good, Meredith. That's not bad at all."

"Gotta go." She came around the back of his chair and kissed his cheek. "Do me a favor?"

"Maybe."

"How 'bout three favors?"

"Not a chance."

"Good. First, send Howie out to the rental car companies and see whether any have signed contracts with a Jorge Luis Ribeiro or a Rusty Mason. Second, send some of Clarence's boys out to drag Gibbs Pond in case there's a submerged car in its depths. If that doesn't work, try Sesachacha. Third—Howie can do this, but Clare would really love to—draw up the papers requesting a search warrant of Mayling Stern's garage. Okay?"

"You think you've got enough to charge her?"

"I might after today. I just want the warrant in case."

"Counting Sesachacha, that's four favors, Meredith."

"Who's counting? And Dad—next time you want to talk over the Mason murder, *ask* to see my notes first, okay? I don't want to have to lock them in my glove compartment."

She was out the screen door before he had thought of an answer.

Chapter 21

"How do you think flaubert feels about Emma?" Lucy Jacoby asked the room in general. She was pacing slowly back and forth in front of the rows of desks that ran from the front of the advanced sophomore English class to the back, one hand propping up the elbow of the arm that held her copy of *Madame Bovary*. Her tousled auburn curls fell over her right shoulder and the heavy bangs hid her forehead, making it difficult to read her expression, Will thought. She always reminded him of a forest animal seen through a screen of underbrush—barely distinguishable from its camouflage. Today she looked as though the sound of a snapped twig would send her into flight.

"I think he feels bad for her," a girl ventured. Lucy said nothing. "I mean, like, she's got such a boring life. Anybody'd go nuts. It's like she lives *here*."

A wave of self-conscious tittering rippled through the room and a wad of paper, tossed with precision, struck the girl on the back of the neck. She ignored it and grinned, delighted with the attention. Will raised his hand. Lucy nodded to him, and he felt a slow flush mount in his cheeks as a few hostile eyes turned in his direction.

"I think he hates her," he said.

The room fell silent. "Go on," Lucy said.

"I think he enjoys watching her sink further and further into her despair, regardless of the things she tries to do to distract herself—all the guys, the fantasies of wealth—because he knows she can't escape the way she is. He strips her of everything she cares about until she's left with nothing but herself, and it makes her sick. She's got to kill herself in the end, because death is the only way out."

"Out of what, Will?" Lucy said. She had come to a standstill, and the features of her face had tightened. Will swallowed. He couldn't retract what he'd said, so he'd have to go on. He dropped his eyes and studied his hands.

"Well—out of the loneliness—of living, I guess. Out of knowing that dreams never come true, they're just God's—I dunno, fate's—way of laughing at you for believing things could ever be different. I think Flaubert hated the fact that people kid themselves into thinking that certain things matter—the clothes they wear, the things they own—to get through the day. He probably did it himself and knew he was a chump for doing it. So he took it out on Emma. He made her pay for being human."

Lucy stared at him as though frozen, her thoughts far away. Then she shook herself slightly and managed a smile. "Well, that's one view. A lot of scholars would agree with you. Any other thoughts?" She looked around the room at the group of blank faces. "I'd like you to think about the author's perspective for tomorrow and be prepared to discuss it at some length. Consider the fact that Flaubert, like all writers, created his character out of thin air, and he made choices when he chose to depict Emma as he did. He chose to subject her to loss after loss—the particularly brutal ones being those of her own making." Her voice trailed off and she stared into the middle distance, then abruptly snapped the book shut. There was the sudden sound of chairs scraping against the linoleum flooring as twelve kids shoved themselves away from their desks and made for the door. As his classmates passed him, Will stood up and collected his books into a symmetrical pile, his eyes fixed on them as if they were the only significant thing in his life.

"Will."

He looked up. Lucy Jacoby was holding out a paperback. *The Perpetual Orgy: Flaubert and Madame Bovary.*

"I think you might get something out of this, if you're interested. Vargas Llosa's got an excellent brain and a real empathy for Emma. Well—he admits he's in love with her, unlike Flaubert. I'd pay particular attention to the first section, where he talks about the book's importance to him personally," she said. And why Emma's suicide kept him from trying it himself, she added mentally.

Will turned the book over in his hands, as if uncertain what it meant. "Okay," he said. "Thanks. You want me to write a report on it or something?"

"I want you to learn from it," she said. "Nothing more."

•   •   •

HE WAS STUDYING THE PHOTO of the author on the book's back cover as he stood by his locker later that day, figuring out what to take home and what to leave.

"What'd she give you, Starbuck?"

He turned around and saw Sandy Stewart, who had been his friend once, before his life had gotten so weird.

Will shrugged. "Book on *Madame Bovary*," he said, and made to shove it into his backpack.

"Can I see it?"

He looked up, assessing the situation. Sandy's face wore the closed, wary look he usually adopted with him these days, but it wasn't obviously hostile. He'd left his gang of football buddies somewhere else. "Sure."

Sandy flipped through the pages intently. A few scraps of paper fluttered out of the back section and fell to the ground. Will stooped and picked them up, turning them over half-consciously as he waited for the book.

Sandy's eyes flicked up at him, and he reached for the scraps. "Here," he said. "I'll put 'em back." He placed the papers carefully in the back of the book and handed it to Will. "Looks good. My mom reads a lot of his stuff. You know, he ran for president of Peru."

"Yeah?" Sandy's dad had been a political writer in Washington before he'd moved his family to the island to work on The Novel. He'd been writing it now for three years. Tess said Maggie Stewart was about

219

fed up and ready to move back to the mainland, with or without Dick.

"Can I borrow it when you're done?" Sandy asked.

Will nodded uncertainly.

"Maybe I could stop by your house on Sunday and pick it up? If you're done with it by then, I mean?"

"Take it now," Will said, handing it to him, "and drop it off Sunday," as though Sandy'd been coming by every weekend for months; and then he bent down to cinch his backpack closed. But he watched Sandy out of the corner of his eye as the boy sauntered off, and for an instant, a fragile smile flickered over his face.

Chapter 22

THE RENTED TOYOTA WAS British racing green, a color the Japanese never got right, Peter reflected. It felt like a toy after the solid bulk of the Rover, but it took the steep curve of Hamilton Road responsively under Merry's surprisingly aggressive driving. He had relaxed once he realized she was competent, and kept one eye on the windshield and the other on the ragged bank to his right. Lined with old Westchester houses set amid trees and well-tended gardens, the Hill, as it was known, seemed exhausted after a summer of heat and bloom and braced for the onslaught of falling leaves. He had immediately warmed to this town, to its echoes of his Greenwich boyhood and its train whistle piercing the air with scheduled chaos. The conviction that in Chappaqua he would find the key to the past strengthened with every switchback in the road.

"We need to talk about those letters, Peter," Merry said. Somewhere over Rhode Island, while he'd filled her in on his theory about Rusty's insider trading with ME stock, she'd finally dropped the formality of "Mr. Mason."

"I wondered when you'd get around to that."

"The one to Sundance—an unknown—I think we can ignore for the moment. The ones to Sky Jackson and your sister have me worried."

He said nothing, wincing slightly as the car cornered sharply and his weight shifted onto his left side.

She gave him a quick sidelong glance from under her black brows. "Am I going to have to draw you out in my celebrated fashion?"

"It would seem Sky stepped over the boundary of the law. I'm counting on your celebrated fashion to discover exactly how this afternoon. Rusty seemed to think it was capable of ending his career. I'll bet it involved helping Rusty on his way out of the country—but who knows?"

So they'd leave George aside for the moment. That was okay. She had all afternoon. "That'd be around the time of the indictment. Sky was where?"

"Law school."

"Guy can get disbarred just for withholding evidence," Merry said conversationally.

"I didn't know that."

"Betcha Sky does."

• • •

MALCOLM SCOTT LIVED just at the apex of the Hill where the road circled and dove back down to the train tracks below. Built in an era when ostentation was considered in poor taste, the house, although huge, had been cast as a modest country cottage with peasant shutters and used brick. When Merry and Peter drove into the gravel drive, an aged golden retriever struggled to its feet and woofed woollily in its throat.

The sound summoned Scott to the apple-green front door. Peter waved to him as they pulled to a halt, struck immediately by the change in the man's appearance. He stood upright and alone by the lintel, but his once-powerful frame had shrunk, and the sharp-featured head with its flowing mane of hair was withered and frail. Malcolm Scott was ill.

"Had lunch?" he asked testily, by way of greeting.

"Unfortunately, yes," Peter said. He braced his good right hand on the car and thrust himself out, adding the years in his mind. He had last seen Scott at Max's funeral, a decade ago, when he had just hit seventy. "This is Detective Meredith Folger of the Nantucket police," he said, nodding his head in her direction. "It's good to see you, Mr. Scott. It's been some time."

"You've grown up. I've grown old." Scott opened the screen door. Peter motioned Merry ahead of him.

She hesitated just inside the doorway, relishing the cool dimness that immediately descended on her sun-struck eyes. The hall smelled vaguely of moth and cleanliness. She took a few paces into it and looked up into second-story rafters, feeling Peter's height blocking the light behind her.

"In here," Scott said. The testiness was habitual rather than personal, Merry decided, and she turned toward the direction of the voice. Scott had moved into a small sitting room, done in yellow-flowered chintz, with wide windows that caught the afternoon sunlight. A woman in a bright orange skirt and a broad straw sun hat stood in the garden, gazing at some roses. There was a paintbrush in her hand and an easel set up nearby. Merry felt a sharp flash of her mother and stood mesmerized, staring out at the garden.

"Mary," Scott said, waving vaguely toward his wife. "Sit down."

Merry settled herself on a couch with her back to the view of Mary Scott and her Peace roses, while Peter took a wing chair facing Malcolm, who sat rigidly at his desk. He had a closed manila file in front of him, and he adjusted the edges restlessly with his thumb and forefinger as he peered at Peter fixedly.

"You've turned out a fine boy," Scott said. "It's been a while."

"Yes it has."

"You must take after Julia."

"Her father, actually."

"Isn't Max, that's for sure."

"I'm supposed to have some of his expressions."

"Haven't seen any yet."

"I suppose you'd have to make me angry."

"Well, I might, at that. Not like your brother. Now, he was the *image* of Maxwell Mason," Scott said, turning his fierce gaze on Merry.

"Didn't wait for somebody else to make him angry, either. Had the temper of a bull in rut."

Merry pulled out her reading glasses and perched them on her nose. In combination with her suit, they gave her the appearance of a sexy librarian.

"Rusty, however, is dead, Mr. Scott," she said. "His temper—or something else—got him killed."

"Not surprising," Scott said, and slammed his hand on the desktop with surprising force. "That boy lived too long."

"Maybe," Merry said, looking at him severely over her frames, "but I imagine dying isn't easy at any age."

There was a pause as Scott assessed her with his steady blue glare. Then he nodded.

"I'm finding it difficult to do myself, and you'd think with eight decades of practice I'd have a little more grace. Doctors say I've got a few months yet to learn."

He opened the manila folder and raised a pair of gold-rimmed spectacles to his nose. He peered at a document carefully, as though seeing it for the first time, and lifted it closer to his face. Then his eyes shifted back to Peter. "You're here to find out why your father gave up on living, aren't you? Your brother's just part of it. The real reason is Max."

Peter hesitated, taken aback, and considered the old man's words. "Maybe it is. I've got a gut feeling that whatever happened between the two of them ten years ago ended on my farm this week. That may seem crazy—"

"Seems like common sense. Your brother left town with his business at loose ends; he came back, and some loose ends got caught around his throat."

"You sound as if you know why he was here," Merry broke in.

"Haven't the foggiest. Nosir."

Merry shifted in her chair. Malcolm Scott was enjoying himself hugely. This visit was probably the highlight of the old man's month.

"We had hoped you could tell us something about the events that occurred just prior to Max's death," she said, and waited for Scott to make of it what he would.

"Now, let's see, that would be—oh, close to ten years ago now, wouldn't it?" He shifted the papers in the folder as though Max's death certificate were among them.

"January 1983, Mr. Scott."

"Yessir, it would be. Well, well. Doesn't seem like ten years. How far back do you want me to go? Can't exactly tell you everything that went on in the thirty-five years I knew Maxwell Mason, even if I could remember. You have to frame the questions right to get the answers you need."

A swift glance, like blue lightning, shot over Merry's face. *He doesn't know whether to trust me,* she thought.

Peter hesitated, glanced at Merry, and chose his words. "My father died a month after disowning my brother, who left the country. A grand jury investigated Rusty for securities fraud, but because of his status as a fugitive from U.S. law, the indictment handed down was sealed. My father never told us why he broke with my brother, and we never knew exactly what he had done. But when Rusty turned up dead a few days ago, I started to wonder if the past might not have something to do with it."

"Why?" Scott broke in.

"Because of the things Rusty brought with him," Merry said. "Letters, a photograph, all of them references to the past. It was very much alive for him; we think it's possible he wanted to reawaken it in a certain group of people. That may be why he was killed."

"There must be a reason why someone wants the past to remain dead," Peter said. "Since you were closer to Max's business than anyone else, I thought you might be able to shed some light on why."

"Oh, there's lots of light to be shed," Malcolm said.

"It was insider trading, wasn't it?"

"For starters."

"With ME stock."

"Yessir."

"In the midst of one of Max's hostile takeover bids?"

"If you know all about it, why are you here?"

"That's the extent of my knowledge, Mr. Scott, and to be frank, it's all speculation on my part."

"What else do you speculate?"

"That insider trading, even with ME stock, wouldn't be enough for Max to cut off his son."

"Go on."

Peter searched the line over Malcolm Scott's head where the white ceiling met a butter-yellow wall, and steepled his fingers under his nose. "If I allow myself to think like Rusty, then I decide that making money isn't the point. I go for the bigger prize: power over Max, whom I've loved and hated and striven to beat for most of my life."

"You've got that right."

"I take my knowledge of Max's plans—the time, the target, the extent of debt-to-asset leverage—to someone else." He looked at Merry.

"A competitor," she said. "Rusty sparks a bidding war between Max and his rival for the target of the takeover, drives up the stock of the target company in the process, and laughs all the way to the bank. Until the feds show up."

Malcolm Scott gave vent to a high cackle and slapped the desktop again with the flat of his right hand. A tole lamp to one side of him trembled slightly, but he ignored it, leaning across the desk toward Merry and Peter eagerly.

"Ten years," he said. "Ten years I've been waiting for one of you idiots to ask me about it." He tapped the manila file. "It's all right here. All you had to do was ask.

"Max's target was Ultracom, an aerospace firm," Scott continued. "In 1982, at the height of a recession, it was an enormous risk—the only kind Max relished. He was leveraging everything he'd got, banking on the idea that the economy had bottomed out and he'd profit from the upswing. He was right, of course. He'd have taken ME into defense contracting at the beginning of the Reagan buildup, and he'd have made a fortune."

"Enter Rusty," Merry said. "Do you know where he got his information?"

Malcolm Scott leaned back in his chair and dropped heavy lids over the furious blue eyes. Calculating what to say, Merry thought—or what not to say.

"Max didn't tell him, that's for sure. He didn't even tell me. I knew vaguely what properties he was looking at, but I never knew which one he decided to go after. Max told nobody about the crux of these things. I've wondered for some time how Rusty knew."

Peter nodded. "Let's assume, for the sake of argument, his knowledge was good."

"Oh, it was good enough to screw matters up royally, that's for certain. That brother of yours was the devil's own. I say that knowing full well he was Max's son. I repeat, the devil's own. Ever hear of Mitch Hazlitt?"

Peter shook his head. He looked at Merry.

"The corporate raider," she said. "He's doing time in some minimum-security country club upstate." Reading through those case-law textbooks had paid off.

Scott nodded. "Rusty chose Hazlitt to take on Max. Only Hazlitt had an even better idea. He decided to go for ME, instead of the aerospace firm."

Peter sat up. Malcolm looked at him over his glasses and nodded in satisfaction. "Brilliant, wasn't it? Max would be at his most vulnerable once he attempted to take over the aerospace outfit, because he'd leveraged everything he had. He wouldn't have the resources to fight Hazlitt off."

"And suddenly, Rusty was in way over his head," Merry said slowly.

"If he'd been a little older, he'd have seen it coming. Plain as the nose on your face. You give a shark your finger, and he'll take your arm. He'd handed Hazlitt ME on a plate, something I don't think even *he* intended to do."

Peter sat still, probably envisioning Rusty's panic and his father's wrath, Merry thought. "Knowing Rusty, he'd try to ride it out somehow, anyhow," he said.

"Don't think he had any other option, myself. Other than looking the fool in front of your father. Probably Hazlitt anticipated that. He made Rusty an offer he couldn't refuse."

"Meaning?"

Malcolm Scott leaned back in his chair and sighed. Then he adjusted his glasses and riffled through the papers in the folder. He was doling out the details of the past like fortune cookies, Merry thought. He looked up and over her head, seeing something beyond the image of his wife painting in the garden, something that had died long ago.

"If Hazlitt succeeded—and he would have—Max's head was to be on the block. Hazlitt told Rusty he could run ME in Max's stead."

Peter whistled—a low, bated breath. Merry looked over at him.

"The very idea. An insult. An idiocy."

Peter's interlocked fingers tightened imperceptibly as Merry watched. *The thing Max couldn't forgive. The reason Rusty ran.*

Scott was still talking. "Personally, I doubt it would have happened. The Hazlitts of this world eat the Rusty Masons alive."

There was a small silence. "Mason Enterprises was a sacred family stewardship to my father," Peter said. "The very essence of his identity. He would have dealt ruthlessly with anyone who tried to cut ME out from under him. And yet, it would have to be something like this—an unbelievable risk with an unimaginable prize—to attract Rusty. He'd have found the danger irresistible."

"And so what happened?" Merry asked.

Malcolm Scott looked at Peter and waited.

"Max found out what Rusty had done, called off the merger, and disowned him," Peter ventured.

"That's what it looked like to me."

"How'd Max find out?" Merry persisted.

For the first time, Scott's fierce blue gaze faltered. He took off his glasses and rubbed his eyes wearily. "That I cannot say, my dear, any more than how Rusty got the information in the first place. But I can tell you the day it happened. December seventeenth. Max called me into his office and sat me down. I was the one dealing with Salomon's corporate finance side, leveraging Mason Enterprises beyond anything I thought possible, and I was the one who'd have to explain to them that the whole venture was called off. Max had that look of his—like he'd swallowed a frying pan hot off the fire—and he was deadly quiet." Malcolm shot a blue glance at Peter. "Your father had a habit of holding in his rage, as no doubt you know. Made it all the more terrifying."

"You're right."

"Everything we'd planned, the months of work, went in the waste-basket."

"Rusty went to Brazil—" Merry said.

"My father went to Greenwich for Christmas," Peter added. "Salomon went to the Justice Department and launched an investigation into Rusty's activities—"

Scott cleared his throat. "—and a month later, I went to Max Mason's funeral. I have never felt so heavy-hearted and lost in my life as I did on that day. *Nosir.*"

.   .   .

PETER SAT STILL and mulled over Malcolm Scott's information. Then he rose from the wing chair and turned toward the garden beyond the window, his good hand in his pocket. The September days were shortening, and in the space of their conversation Mary Scott's easel had moved from sun into shadow. He squinted to make out the image on the canvas; she was painting her roses. Her carriage was erect, and her grace, like the house's, was built into the bone. As he watched, she reached for a blooming copper-pink rose and touched it to her nose; the color glowed on her porcelain skin like sunlight on clear water. Then she turned toward the house, feeling his eyes upon her, and smiled briefly, a smile meant for Malcolm but including him in its compass.

He felt a sharp pang of loneliness. These two had grown old together through the decades, in the certainty that their last years would be spent on these lawns, under the spreading trees and the lengthening shadows, surrounded by roses like the ones in Lucy's garden. And he had no one, no one.

"That's the hardest thing about learning to die," Scott said, and his voice cracked. He had left the desk and was standing at Peter's right elbow. Peter did not turn to look at him, afraid he would find tears dimming the blazing blue eyes. "I don't know what will become of her after I'm gone." Abruptly, he cleared his throat again and turned toward the hall.

Merry looked up at Peter from the couch, nodded once, and flipped closed her notebook.

At the front door, she turned and extended her hand to Malcolm Scott. "Thank you for being so forthright," she said. "I'll let you know what I turn up about Rusty's death."

"And my apologies for taking so many years to ask," Peter said.

Scott's face wore a listening expression, but it wasn't for their words. There was the sudden sound of many wheels rolling on iron, and an instant later, a train's plaintive blast rent the twilight air. Scott smiled the delighted smile of the very young.

"The evening train. I listen for it, any time of day. Can't get to sleep, the first week we're in Florida, I'm so used to waiting for the whistle. Used to take it into Manhattan in my foolish Yale youth, went to the debutante balls. Met Mary at one of those things, matter of fact."

He took Merry's elbow and shook it gently. "Walked down to that train every morning for forty-five years, you know, until I didn't have to anymore. First day of the rest of my life, I walked down anyway. Bought a paper from Reggie, the station newsboy, and watched the rest of 'em getting off to Gotham. Hah! Newsboy. He's seventy if he's a day. No teeth. Just a mass of purple gums."

He turned and glared at Peter. "You should take that train some-time. Some of the cars still have wooden settles. Not the new ones—they're built in Japan, all metal and plastic. Strange for a country that has no natural resources to build so much stuff out of metal and plastic, isn't it?" The blue eyes turned to Merry, and Scott's hand, frail as a November leaf, patted her on the shoulder. "I'm old. Never mind."

He started to push open the screen door for them and then stopped. "You said there were some pictures and letters," he said. "What'd they say?"

Merry hesitated an instant. "I'd like to talk to the people who received them before I discuss them," she said.

"Blackmail, huh?" Scott said, an edge of satisfaction in his voice. "Figures. He knew how to turn a trick, that boy."

Merry reached into her briefcase and pulled out the photograph that had washed up on the beach. "There's no reason you can't see this," she said.

Malcolm Scott took the snapshot in a hand that shook slightly with age, and adjusted his spectacles. Then a curiously set expression came across his drawn features. He thrust the photograph back at Merry without a word.

"Any idea who she is, sir?"

"None at all," Scott said. "It's time you were going."

·　　·　　·

MERRY SIGHED AS SHE TURNED the Toyota's hood toward Manhattan and Sky Jackson. "My mother was painting a portrait of Billy when she killed herself. It's still on her easel, in the middle of our hallway, unfinished. No one seems to know what to do with it. So we leave it there, like a postcard from the beyond." She looked over her shoulder and waved at Malcolm Scott. "He's a canny old bastard."

"He told us everything he knew."

"You don't really believe that."

"Don't you?"

"The most important thing is missing—the name of the person who told Rusty about Max's merger plans, and the one who told Max that Rusty was doing him dirty behind his back."

"The source," Peter said. "My father would have known how to repay that kind of betrayal. And you think Malcolm Scott is protecting him?"

"Could be. You can check my notes, but I think his exact words were that he *couldn't* tell us, not that he didn't actually know who it was. Makes me think he's holding out on us."

Peter looked at her soberly. "Whoever it is has a hell of a motive for murder."

Chapter 23

NIGHT WAS FALLING OVER New York City, and pinpoints of light sprang into life behind a thousand office windows. The lawyers and the bankers and the raiders and their secretaries were getting their second wind before plunging on into the evening hours; in their minds, the day was still young. Peter had told Merry he'd never taken a train out of the city before midnight without seeing an endless tide of workers borne late into suburban homes. There was no meaning to rush hour in this place. Sky understood that, and lived by the same code. He would be back to his office this evening.

They were sitting in the trim, modern, graphite-colored chairs that Mayling probably had chosen for Sky's office. Merry could barely make out Peter's features: his face and form were receding into vagueness as twilight descended over New York. They had not bothered to turn on the office lights. Merry saw a city skyline too rarely to ignore the view. But she turned around when Sky opened the door.

The lawyer hesitated on the threshold, aware of their presence in the room, his hand suspended as it reached for the light switch. His secretary, a nine-to-fiver with a child in day care, had left hours ago, and Peter was familiar enough with Sky's office to enter it unannounced. Sky peered into the dusk and cleared his throat.

Peter took pity on him. "Here like a bad penny, Sky," he said.

"Peter." Sky shut the door firmly but quietly, and crossed the room with his lanky stride. He was admirably in command of himself. Perhaps, Merry thought, he's known that he must face this sooner or later.

"I've brought Detective Folger with me."

Merry stood up and straightened her short skirt, impossibly wrinkled. Sky Jackson took her hand in his—a light, dry shake. He was like an aristocrat from a Masterpiece Theatre production, she thought: fine features and height held together by good manners.

"You've seen Malcolm Scott?" he said to Peter.

"You were otherwise engaged, I take it, when we stopped by for you this afternoon."

"A settlement conference that couldn't wait."

Peter nodded. Sky threw his suit jacket over the back of his desk chair and stood by the floor-to-ceiling glass that served as both wall and window, his hands in his pockets, surveying the city fifty-eight floors below. He had not bothered to turn on a light either. "God, it's so beautiful," he said. "I hate and love this city the way I hate and love my life."

Merry glanced at Peter, who nodded. She reached into her briefcase and withdrew a piece of paper. "I'd appreciate your looking this over, Mr. Tate-Jackson."

Sky didn't even turn his head. "What's that?"

"Rusty's letter. The one he sent you sometime last week, I imagine."

"Did Mayling give it to you?"

"So he did send it," Peter broke in. "I'll be damned. You're a better actor than I gave you credit for. When I told you he'd been killed, you had me believing you didn't even know he was coming back to the island."

Sky ignored Merry's outstretched hand. She dropped the paper on his desk.

"No, Mayling didn't give it to me," she said. "Actually, this one's a copy. It was found when Rusty's things washed up on Siasconset beach, a few hundred feet from your door."

233

"It's like him to make a copy," Sky said bitterly. "But you're wrong about the timing. I didn't read that letter until the morning after he died."

"Labor Day."

"I flew up to Nantucket on Sunday evening, if you remember. I didn't bother to look at my accumulated mail until the next day."

"That's a little hard to believe."

"The truth sometimes is. Especially where Rusty's concerned."

"It's far easier, for instance," Merry said, "to envision you receiving this letter in New York instead of on the island, flying back to Nantucket for twenty-four hours in order to kill him, and then pulling a good show the next day when Peter found you fishing for blues in the fog. Unfortunately, in a murder investigation, I have to take that scenario seriously."

"I'm sure you do," Sky said. He jingled some loose change in one pocket, thinking, and then turned to face them. "I certainly wasn't going to mention the letter's existence once I knew he was dead. On advice of my own counsel, I pled the Fifth."

"What did he have on you, Sky?" Peter said quietly.

"What did Rusty have on anybody? Our collective stupidity, the fact that we were naive enough to care about someone who cared only about himself."

"I assume it was your life at stake," Merry said, "or at least, life as you know it."

"That's a good start," Sky said. Suddenly he laughed. "God, it was brilliant."

He turned the chair toward the window, talking to the shadows behind him like a man in a confessional, she thought.

"If you've met with Scott, you know what Rusty did. Or attempted to do. He shot the moon and got himself into a royal mess."

"Did he tell you where he got his information, Mr. Tate-Jackson?" Merry asked.

The outline of Sky's head above the back of the chair moved slightly. "No. He had some sort of source within ME, that's all I know." He paused. "It wouldn't surprise me to hear it was Scott himself. I've wondered for years if old Malcolm got antsy in his twilight years and used Rusty to move against Max. It wouldn't be the first time in corporate history."

"I don't think so," Peter said. "Not after talking to Scott. He's sick and he hasn't much time left. I think he'd have told us if he had something that serious to get off his chest."

I'm not so sure about that, Merry thought. But she said nothing, following Sky Jackson's train of thought.

"Whoever it was proved Rusty's undoing," Sky said. "The guy apparently panicked when Rusty started to move ME stock before the date of the takeover, and I guess he went to Max with everything. Max killed the merger plans. No surprise. But it left your brother with nowhere to hide. That's when he came to me."

They waited. After a moment, Sky went on, his words coming more slowly now.

"I was in my third year of law school. He showed up in Cambridge in the middle of the night, without a coat in the middle of a snowstorm, looking half mad. He'd gotten himself in too deep. Hazlitt had 'lent' him the funds to buy a huge block of stock—"

"ME stock?" Peter broke in.

Sky shook his head. "The target of the takeover. I've forgotten the name."

"Ultracom," Merry said, glancing at her notebook.

Sky turned and gazed at her through the dark. "You do know quite a lot, don't you?"

"We've guessed even more."

She saw Sky swallow nervously. The aristocratic veneer had its vulnerabilities. His eyes flicked away from her, and he continued.

"A takeover bid drives up the price of the target company's stock, as you know. It usually drives down the stock of the raider company—in this case, ME. Rusty bought his block before Max published his offer to Ultracom stockholders, and waited for the price per share to rise. He knew that when Hazlitt challenged Max's offer, the stock would soar even higher. He figured he'd sell his block a few days later, at a huge profit, and repay Hazlitt's 'loan.' "

"But then Hazlitt went after ME and Max pulled out of the bid," Merry said. "The Ultracom stock must have plummeted. No profit for Rusty, no payment for Hazlitt. I wonder if the creep called in the loan."

"Why do you think he made it in the first place?"

"Sorry?"

"The loan," Sky said impatiently. "Hazlitt gave Rusty the money to buy shares in Ultracom, knowing the price was going to drop once he went after ME. He knew he'd have Rusty in a tight spot. He needed that kind of leverage in order to get Rusty's stock."

"His ME stock," Peter said, comprehension dawning.

"Exactly. The seven percent of voting stock held by each of Max's children. Max had—what, thirty percent?—and he voted your shares with his own until you reached the age of twenty-five. Is that right?"

Peter nodded. "We inherited the stock from my grandmother, split three ways. A trust. I never thought about it until Max died."

"Between the four of you, Max voted fifty-one percent of the stock—a controlling interest—with the rest held publicly. Even if Hazlitt was able to buy up the other forty-nine percent, he needed to be sure he could count on part of Max's voting power. Otherwise the whole gamble was for nought."

"Rusty's part," Merry said.

"He'd turned twenty-five that year." Peter was thinking out loud. "Hazlitt gets him in debt, and then forces him to sell his stock. It works."

"Rusty refused to sell, apparently," Sky said.

"You're kidding."

"He figured it was all the bargaining power he had. He rolled the dice, Peter. He offered Hazlitt his voting power in return for Max's job, once ME was in Hazlitt's grasp."

"Jesus." Peter's voice held shock. "He actually thought that was possible? Hazlitt would probably have cut the firm into bits, sold off the pieces, and left town with the cash."

Sky nodded. "It wouldn't surprise me. But none of that really mattered anyway. The stock, the debt—they were the least of Rusty's problems."

"Max discovered he'd leaked the takeover information to Hazlitt," Merry said smoothly.

"Max went to the U.S. attorney," Sky said, "and turned his son in for trading on inside information."

Peter slid lower in the gray chair and steepled his fingers, tapping his nose thoughtfully. "So there was Rusty: probably arrested, probably out of a job, and in debt up to his ears. With no Dad to turn to."

"He was desperate. He came to me for advice. As if a 3L at Harvard had anything to tell him. The whole thing got more and more ludicrous."

"You told him to go to Brazil?" Merry asked.

"I told him if Hazlitt didn't get him, the SEC would, sooner or later. No, Detective, I told him to make a clean breast of it and take the consequences." Sky fell silent, and Merry waited.

"I remember what he said to me," Sky said softly. " 'I'll be damned if I graduated from Princeton to rot in a federal jail, Jackson. I'll die first.' "

They sat for a moment, hearing the irony. "A lot of twenty-five-year-olds have been made idiots by a love of money and power," Sky said. "But none so completely as your brother."

That horrible year of 1982, Merry thought. *The year Peter lost Alison. And his brother. And finally, Max. He must have lost a bit of his soul as well.*

"Why didn't Rusty come to me, Sky?" Peter said.

"I should think that was obvious. Because he'd failed."

·   ·   ·

THE ROOM WAS NOW WHOLLY DARK, the floor checkered with bars of reflected light from the office windows opposite. They had all fallen silent—Sky seemed lost in thought; Merry watchful; Peter oppressed by the weight of old disaster. The wind whined around the building's height, and Sky stirred. He reached over to a black metal desk lamp and switched it on, flooding the lacquered wood under his hands with a disk of light.

"He wrote when he got to Rio," he said. "I'd send letters once in a while, although they got less and less frequent as the years passed. He'd write whenever he had a new address, which was fairly often. It wasn't until about two years ago that he started to rehash the past. Some business deals hadn't worked out as he'd planned, and the tone of his letters changed; he seemed to have grown bitter. I don't know. Maybe he realized this exile was endless."

Merry glanced at Peter and mouthed the word "AIDS." Peter nodded.

"He wrote and asked what the statute of limitations was for prosecuting insider trading, and God help me, I told him the truth," Sky said. "I told him that when the subject flees the country, and a sealed indictment is handed down by a grand jury, there is no limit on the duration of liability. He'd be picked up at any border the minute he tried to reenter the U.S. I thought he'd believe me."

"And you wanted him to stay away, didn't you, Mr. Tate-Jackson?" Merry said.

"Didn't everybody?"

She ignored him and went on. "Because whether he was picked up or not, he was dangerous. He knew you'd lied to the Justice Department investigators who pursued the case, and then to a grand jury. Even before you'd graduated from law school and passed the bar, you told no one that you knew what Rusty had done and where he was living. And then it was too late. Withholding information from federal officials is not only a punishable offense; if you're a lawyer, it's grounds for disbarment. Isn't it, Mr. Tate-Jackson?"

"I don't know why he thought he had to ruin my life, too," Sky said quietly. "I'd tried to help him. It isn't fair, dammit. It isn't fair."

"No, it's not," Peter said. "For what it's worth, Sky, I'm sorry."

"Do you believe me when I say I didn't kill him?"

"I find it hard to believe that anyone I know killed Rusty. It's not the sort of thing one imagines a friend doing."

"No, I suppose not."

"But Meredith Folger doesn't have that problem," Peter said, glancing at her. "None of the people she suspects is a friend. And her mind is turning over a lot of information about you and Mayling."

"Mayling?" Sky was startled, and, Merry thought, really afraid for the first time. "She's got nothing to do with this."

"How did she damage her Mercedes, Mr. Tate-Jackson?" Merry asked. "The front end. There's no record of an accident report. And when I checked your alibi at the airport—she'd told me she picked you up around eight—the attendant at Island Air mentioned that you'd been hanging around for almost an hour, waiting for a ride. You finally took a taxi. Isn't that right?"

Sky's face had frozen. He held the expression for the space of several heartbeats, and then his face crumpled and Merry could see him let go.

"She damaged the car that night. The night Rusty died. As God is my witness, I have no idea how it happened."

"You weren't in the car, then."

"No. No—as you said, Mayling was supposed to meet me at the airport. I'd left a message as to when I'd be getting in. I arrived at eight o'clock, and when she hadn't shown by eight forty-five, I called a taxi. I got to the house—it's only about a seven-minute drive—and neither she nor the car was there. I figured she'd somehow missed the message and had gone into town for dinner with friends or something. But when she came back at midnight, she was incoherent."

His voice faltered, and he looked down at his clenched hands. "I don't know how to explain this—she's been having something like blackouts for some time, now. She functions normally, but she doesn't remember where she's been, who she's met, or what she's done."

"Drinking?" Merry asked.

Sky shook his head. "No. At least, I don't think so. We ran her through a series of tests in the spring. The doctors were looking for a brain tumor." He looked at his friend. "I've been half crazy with worry, Peter. You can't imagine. Now they've decided it's stress." He laughed hollowly. "Stress. She's been on the island doodling in the sun for three months now, with nary a blackout, and it seemed as though rest and solitude had repaired the damage her spring collection had done. Then this.

"That night, she couldn't tell me what she'd been doing or where she'd gone—she just fell into bed. The next morning, when I'd seen the damage and asked her about it, she couldn't remember a thing. She said vaguely she'd probably hit a deer."

Peter said nothing. Sky threw up his hands and pushed back his chair, unable to bite back the words that formed his worst fear.

"Labor Day weekend, with no warning, and Rusty dead on the road. I don't know what to think, I really don't."

Merry hesitated. She had bided her time to confront Mayling Stern with the evidence she was slowly, inexorably gathering. She had deliberately withheld from Mayling her knowledge of the damaged car, so carefully hidden in the garage. By probing Sky, she could be sending his companion to New York on the next plane, and from there, anywhere on the globe. It was a risk she'd have to take.

"If she thought Rusty could destroy your life, would Mayling try to protect you, Mr. Tate-Jackson?"

"You're everything to her, Sky," Peter said.

"But she didn't know!"

Peter looked at Sky steadily. "Perhaps not. But perhaps she did."

"You don't believe me when I say I never told her a word about Rusty?"

"I believe you. I think she had other sources of information."

"Like what?"

"The letter, Sky. The one you say you received a day late."

"I did."

"Labor Day, when I came to your house to tell you the news, I walked in unannounced and surprised her reading a letter. She was so startled she dropped the pages, and when I tried to help her gather them up, she lashed out at me pretty viciously. She looked guilty as hell. Any ideas?"

Merry shot a green look at Peter. He hadn't told her this.

Sky looked completely surprised. "A letter? Mayling?" He thought it over for a minute, and his face cleared. "But even if it were *the* letter, what can that have to do with Rusty? He was already dead."

"Perhaps she was rereading it," Merry said. "Before replacing it wherever you'd look for it." *Or discovering your motive for killing him,* she thought.

"Reassuring herself that she'd done the right thing in running him over—is that what you're thinking?"

"People do strange things out of guilt."

Sky gave a short bark of laughter, derisive and angry. "I should never have told you about her—vulnerability. Listen, for the last time: *I read Rusty's letter the day after he died, and I'll swear it had never been opened.*"

"I have to consider that you're likely to say that in order to protect yourself—or Mayling," Merry said. "Do you have any proof? The envelope with its postmark, for instance?"

Sky shook his head. "You'll have to take my word. But that seems to be something no one values."

"Not exactly," Merry said. "But murder is the most human of all crimes. You have to weigh abstractions like honor and trustworthiness against the strength of instinct—in this case, to protect someone you love."

Sky hesitated, and looked at Merry. "How much of this will have to come out? About my—career, I mean?"

"I can't say, yet." She paused. "On the one hand, Rusty's dead. The indictment is useless, now. Your role in the affair might not matter anymore—but you'll know that better than I."

Sky laughed again, harshly. "Oh, it'll matter, all right. But I'm not sure I care. I've been living with it so long it feels like a happy release. But I couldn't bear to have Mayling hurt. Anything that keeps her out of harm's way—"

"In the meantime," Merry said, "don't encourage her to fly to any exotic locales, okay?"

Sky nodded, and then looked down at his fingertips, which were tracing a delicate pattern on the shining lacquered surface of his desk. "What do you do next?" he said.

"Keep hunting."

"For the murderer?"

"That. And for the meaning of the past."

"Peter," Sky said. He cleared his throat.

"Yes?"

"I just thought—it's just a thought, really—but don't you think you've overlooked something?"

"Meaning?"

"The source. Whoever gave Rusty his information about Max's merger. It seems to me the source had the most to lose."

Peter looked at Merry. "We've been thinking that, too. He'd have sold out Max, then sold out Rusty. Returning to Max with the knowledge of his betrayal wouldn't win him many points. He was probably out on his ear."

"He may have lost everything."

"The question is—would that be enough to drive him to murder Rusty?" Merry said. "Simply for revenge?"

Sky shrugged. "We can't know until we know who the source is, now can we?"

"I agree," she said, "but I'm beginning to think that's like finding a needle in a haystack. Even Malcolm Scott was no help."

"There's one person who might be useful." Sky avoided Peter's eyes, his head high, but he was speaking to him, Merry realized. "You know it yourself. The only person close to Rusty at that time was Alison."

Peter's jaw went rigid. "Keep her out of this."

"At the very least, she should be told he's dead, don't you think?"

"She reads the papers. At least, she used to."

"Are you afraid of seeing her, Peter?"

He was silent a moment. "Yes."

"I think you're being foolish. Worse, counterproductive. She may know exactly who you're looking for."

Sky's face was flushed and defiant. He was trading Alison for Mayling, Merry thought. She hated it when men personalized their battles. They took no prisoners.

"Well, it doesn't matter what you want or what you say," Sky said harshly. "I've already put forces in train to locate her."

"You had no right to do that." Peter's voice was almost inaudible.

"I had every right. What do you think I've been doing—waiting for you to figure out my alibi is threadbare, my motives just, and my opportunity better than perfect? My professional specialty is damage control. If there's a chance Alison can save my skin—or Mayling's, for God's sake—"

"You're right," Peter said, and with an effort, he forced his jaw to relax. "You're right, Sky. Just give me a bit of notice when you locate her, that's all I ask." He stood up and motioned to the detective.

Merry sat an instant longer, studying Sky Jackson. The lawyer was slumped over his desk; he looked like a man whose life was in ruins. Was he capable of premeditated murder? Absolutely. He had the brains, the will, the motive. He just might not have the strength to bear the deception once the killing was done. Like Peter. Like so many men of their class and upbringing, where personal integrity was a lesson laid down in the sandbox.

She stood up and crossed to the desk, extending her hand. "I hope we meet again in better circumstances," she said.

He was too well-bred not to shake it.

.   .   .

MERRY SLID OUT FROM BEHIND the wheel at La Guardia and then leaned back inside the car, her blond hair sliding toward him. "I hope the funeral goes—well. You know. Oh, forget it." She turned to go.

"Merry—"

"Yes?"

"Thanks for coming along. There's no easy way to tell a friend he's suspected of murder."

"It's even harder to tell your sister," she said carefully, but he saw the steel in her green eyes. "You've got to confront her with that letter, Peter. She and her husband. You sure you don't want me around?"

Chapter 24

WILL WADED THROUGH WATER above his knees, the beater whir-
ring merrily in front of him. He was completely happy. He had
biked over to the farm after school, thrown on a pair of waterproof
overalls, and plunged into the midst of the harvesting team Rafe had
organized in Peter's absence. The bog owner might have to fly to the
mainland for obscure reasons of his own, but the bog had to be harvested. After eight hours of work, broken only by Rebecca's hearty
lunch, the flooded fields lay stripped of their burden under the setting sun.

"Will!" Rafe shouted from his position by the flatbed truck. "Wrap
it up, okay? You can come back tomorrow morning."

Will waved in his direction and steered the beater toward the end
of the row. Tomorrow was Saturday, and he'd be here early on his bike.
A shadow passed swiftly over his thoughts as he remembered the last
time he'd come to harvest in the morning, but he shook it away. He
was getting better at shrugging off the darkness. There had been a time
when he could not fight it, and it had terrified him.

He cut the beater's motor and hauled it up onto the dry bank behind him, then shook himself like a wet puppy and grinned as he
caught Rafe in the shower of drops. He yanked off his overalls, which

smelled not unpleasantly of dampness, earth, and mold, and looked around. "Where's Ney?"

"Gone home," Rafe said. He was paying out the hired harvesters' wages in crisp bills, snapping each one to be certain they didn't stick to each other, and his lips moved soundlessly as he counted. "Knows it's suppertime, and Rebecca's dropping food left and right. Dog's as good as a vacuum cleaner."

"She drops stuff on purpose."

Rafe handed the last man his wad and clapped him on the back. "Probably right." He turned and scrutinized Will. "School okay today? Got your homework?"

"Heck, it doesn't have to be done until Sunday. This is the best night of the week!"

"Don't leave your books here, all the same. Where's that back-pack?"

"I left it with my bike. Don't worry. I'm not totally clueless," Will said. He gathered up his gear and sauntered toward the house, pulling his beater in tow.

The foreman's eyes followed him speculatively. Whether it was the prospect of two free days at home, or better yet, a good day at school, he couldn't say; but Will looked unconsciously happy tonight, and Rafe felt a curious thankfulness, as though a burden had lifted from his shoulders. Tess's worry was catching. He'd found himself studying Will to excess of late.

He hoisted the handle of his own beater and strode off toward the barn.

·   ·   ·

WILL'S BACKPACK, heavy with books, pulled at his shoulders as he pedaled toward home. His young body shook off the strain of guiding the heavy beater through the bog more readily than those of the hired crew, worn out by years of hard labor, and he was still naive enough to find the ache of a well-used body pleasant. He would sleep soundly tonight. He whistled slightly under his breath as the bike cut through the rough path that led across the moors to the Milestone

Road; he was coming up on the radar tower and Altar Rock. Already in mid-September the days were shorter and the color faded early from the six-o'clock landscape; the twisting path was obscured by a gray light that turned the brilliance of the fall flowers to a heathered dimness. His eyes narrowed as he peered ahead.

He stood up on his pedals and leaned forward over the handlebars, hastening the bike toward town. His fall, when it came, was that much harder.

The bike shuddered violently as its throat met the taut wire stretched across the path, flipped over, and fired Will like a projectile fifteen feet through the air. The weight of the backpack pulled his upper body mercilessly to the ground as he fell. The back of his skull glanced off a rock, and he rolled over, his brain screaming in panic even as the darkness descended. He came to rest on his back.

A covey of bobwhite rose into the evening sky, leaving a listening stillness behind them. The front wheel of the bike spun merrily, uselessly, in the air.

Chapter 25

"IT'S ABOUT TIME, Detective," Rafe said, spitting the words through clenched teeth. He stood like a commando next to Will's bike, legs spread and braced, arms folded over his powerful chest. A light rain was falling steadily, and he was soaked. A half hour of wet had plastered his dark hair to his scalp.

Merry had a headache. She had eaten only plane food all day, and the final pack of peanuts had almost made her ill. She had been met at the airport by Howie Seitz and the news of Will's accident. His second bit of news—that Clarence's crew had found Rusty Mason's rented Jeep at the bottom of Gibbs Pond—paled in comparison. The implications of it ran through her head all the way out to Mason Farms, nonetheless.

It made sense. Gibbs Pond sat between Peter Mason's cranberry bog and the cooperative on Nantucket Conservation Foundation land; it was the main source of water for both. Whoever had knocked Rusty over with the Jeep had simply disposed of it in the most likely spot. But why, an insistent interior voice asked her, hadn't the murderer left Rusty's body inside the Jeep when it went into the pond? Why leave the body at the scene of the crime? *Because he wanted it to be found,* Merry thought. *He didn't expect us to figure out so quickly that a car was involved.*

She forced herself to consider the worst. Whoever had thought of the pond knew the island and the immediate neighborhood well. Say Peter Mason had killed his brother. Would he think of hiding the body and the car together? No one on the island really knew Rusty; he was supposed to be out of the country; if Mason had wanted him dead and forgotten, he might think of deep-sixing them both. But then doubt might begin to gnaw at him. What if Rusty had talked to someone on the ferry? What if he had been seen, and recognized, in town? Peter might have panicked, disposed of the murder weapon, and left his brother to lie like the victim of a vagrant attack on the road outside his home.

Her headache had begun at that moment.

Now she slammed the Blazer's door and paused, looking at Rafe. She knew this mood. He was furious and hurt, and he'd throw it at her. And much as she hated bearing the brunt of his anger, she couldn't blame him. Will Starbuck felt as much like her responsibility as Rafe's, but the ache of anguish and nausea in the pit of her stomach must be only a pale shadow of his own. Poor Will. So fragile and so vulnerable, and always in the wrong place at the right time.

"I'm sorry, Rafe. Will didn't deserve this."

"Folks never get what they deserve, Mere. Good or bad."

She still wore her suit under the slicker she always kept in the car. She walked over to the bike, stumbling as her thin heels sank into the wet sand, and bent down to beam her flashlight on the throat of the handlebars. A faint mark of bruised paint, nothing more, and some lingering patches of torn grass from the impact with the heath. The rain on her head was chill. She thrust her hair behind her ears, pulled up the hood of her slicker, and played the beam around the trampled bit of earth.

The rain hadn't helped. The once-dusty path through the moors was a morass of wet sand and mud. Will had been taken away by the rescue squad; tire tracks and the movements of men lifting his body had obscured any of the killer's tracks that might have remained. She closed her eyes for an instant, willing the pounding in her temples to stop.

"I'm sorry I wasn't here," she said, without looking at Rafe.

"There was a sergeant out earlier. He got somebody from your crime scene division, and they worked over the whole place pretty good."

Merry nodded. "Peter is in Greenwich if you want to reach him. The funeral's tomorrow."

"I know Pete's schedule better'n my own. Let's wait until the funeral's over to bother him. He's had enough heartache for one week," he said. "Hope you got what you went to New York for." He couldn't keep the bitterness from his voice.

"Meaning, if I'd been around today, Will might not be in Cottage Hospital?"

"I just wonder if you know what you're doing, Merry Folger."

Merry stiffened at the rage in his voice.

"I think I'm going to see Chief Folger tomorrow morning—ask him what he's doing with a candy-assed little girl on a murder case. I'm starting to think I'll be next on the stretcher, and I don't like that one bit."

She turned the beam on his face, and he scowled, turning his face away. "Stop it, Rafe," she said. "I'm doing everything I can. You think I like this? I couldn't have saved Will. Nobody could. Not even you. So stop blaming yourself and blaming me."

She shifted the beam from his face to the ground, searching for the stakes Clarence had told her were there. The first one sprang up suddenly, like a hidden watcher, in the darkness at the side of the trail. She walked over to it and crouched as low as her narrow skirt would permit, shining the light on its base. The weathered wood suggested the stake had stood in the field for some time, but the earth around it was only recently disturbed. A smart move on the killer's part—a new stake would have caught too many eyes. The force of the bike's impact against the wire had thrust the stake forward, but it had held. She turned and searched for its mate, found it, and inspected it as she had the first. Then the line, taut and gleaming and deadly in the flashlight's beam. Ordinary, lead-colored wire, strong yet light, available in any hardware store.

She stood up and snapped off the light. "So much for that," she said. "Guess I've got to face Tess now."

"I think you should leave Tess for tonight," Rafe said, walking toward Merry. "She can't tell you anything about this business, and all she'll want is to be alone with Will."

"I wish it weren't my job to show up at hospitals and accident scenes. I'm always the last person anyone wants to see. That's why they have to pay you to do this, you know?"

"I know you don't do it for the money, Mere," Rafe said awkwardly. "And I'm sorry I've been so tough. You're just the one I ran into first." He pulled her toward him in a rough embrace.

She had to shut her eyes against the shock of it, thrilling through her body. His strength, the way his arms seemed to fit around her, the good smells of rain-wet skin and flannel shirt.

"You love him very much, don't you?" she whispered.

"I love 'em both. It's killing me to see Tess like this, and not be able to help. She's everything to me, Merry."

"I know," she said. And heard a door close somewhere in her mind.

• • •

GEORGE'S ARM TIGHTENED around Peter's waist as the *Seventh Wave* motored toward the channel beyond the Indian Harbor Yacht Club. Behind them, the club's officers stood at attention on the dock in their dress uniforms. Rusty Mason, an acknowledged master of wind and water, had embarked on his final voyage. Indian Harbor was speeding him to his rest. As the Mason boat slid past the vessels of friends and former crew members moored in the harbor, their flags dipped to half-mast in silent farewell. At the channel buoy, the deep boom of the first cannon fired from the shore reverberated across the water.

Long Island Sound was a flat, oily gray this Saturday afternoon; it fit the mood of the Masons and Whitneys scattered around the deck. Hale was at the wheel, his eyes on the darkening horizon, his eldest son, Maxie, at his elbow. Little Casey, almost consumed by the bulk of her life preserver, sat primly swinging her legs in the cockpit. Near her stood Dr. Pritchett, the yacht club chaplain, who had agreed to officiate over the burial—more as a favor to George and the Whitneys than from any remembered love for Rusty. He was an avid sailor himself and had lost some hotly contested races to Rusty's skill; had the younger Mason been less obviously exultant in his victory, Dr. Pritchett might have viewed him more kindly.

Julia Mason was below deck. Peter imagined her sitting there, ramrod-straight and icy in her composure, a deep furrow of displeasure etched into her brow. That line of unhappiness had probably greeted him at his birth, he thought; it had accompanied his mother through life, that much was certain, growing deeper with age, regardless of whether she witnessed her daughter's marriage or her husband's death. Josh and Abi Whitney, George's twins, sat opposite their grandmother, waiting for her to notice them. Presently they would grow bored with her stubborn disregard and come up on deck.

The boat lurched as it hit the wake from a cigarette boat, and Peter braced himself with his good arm to ride out the swinging passage through crest and trough. They were motoring across the sound to Oyster Bay, Rusty's boyhood haunt. There was no wind to fill the furled sails, nor had there been for the past week. A muggy, humid stillness had come down over the New York suburbs like wet wool, trapping the smog from the city and turning the sound the color of olive oil. The odor that rose from the waves was of heat and fatigue that came straight from the streets of Manhattan.

The metal box holding Rusty's ashes sat below on the galley table, one reason for Julia's steadfast vigil in the cabin. She had not spoken to Peter since his arrival at the Round Hill house late the previous evening. It was clear she held him responsible for his brother's death.

He had driven up from La Guardia in the desperate tug-and-hurl that was commuter traffic, clinging to the wheel with his one good arm to steady it over the potholes that riddled I-95, and sighing with relief when the Arch Street exit came into view. If he could fly directly to George's door, he'd visit more often, he thought. Gone were the days—his late teens and early twenties—when he'd exulted in speed, driven like a demon, and scorned all cars with automatic transmission. A decade on the island had eroded his tolerance for blaring horns, shaking fists, vicious cuts and weaves among the lesser cars that chose a tortoise pace. The realization disconcerted him even as he recognized its sense. He might be growing wiser, but he was certainly growing older. Perhaps with time he'd become even more eccentric, the sort of uncle the Whitney children would speak of with affectionate understanding— unmarried, childless, cultivating his cranberries and his sheep during the day and reliving Napoleon's battles by night. They would visit him during the summer holidays as they would a quaint reconstruction of a vanished settlement, for its historic value.

"There's the Sultan's," George said, pointing, and Peter looked down into her eyes, which had gone suddenly merry, and for an instant he was thirteen. The Sultan was their private joke, one of the lost pieces of childhood, the imaginary owner of a vast white abomination of a house that stood on a peak overlooking Oyster Bay. As young children, they had sailed to the bay with Max and moored overnight, the Sultan's house a main part of the entertainment. They watched lights go on in various oddly shaped windows, strained to hear the music of a harem, and craned to see the colored candles flicker across invisible lawns. George, the storyteller, spun elaborate tales of the lives lived behind the Sultan's vast doors, and once, at the age of eleven, had even tried to run away to his castle in a dory, only to be rescued by the Coast Guard several hours later.

"You know, the awful thing is, it was sold to a Saudi oil magnate two years ago," she said. "Life imitating art."

"I find that somehow comforting," Peter said. "The Whitney clan's childhood need not be impoverished. Their mother can go on inventing lives for the Sultan, and their dreams will be filled with strange music and the heavy scent of hashish."

"I hope not," George said. "You've never had to deal with four A.M. nightmares."

"I hope this doesn't cause any," Peter said quietly, nodding toward Casey.

Georgiana's merriness faded abruptly, and her lips flattened into a thin line. "I have to believe that scattering dust is less disturbing than lowering a coffin into the earth. And it's not as though they even knew Rusty."

Peter kissed her hair briefly, once, and she looked up at him grate-fully. "Thank God you're here, Packy," she said, using his childhood name. "I couldn't handle Mother alone."

"Of course you could," Peter said. "You're the one she still speaks to."

"There's one disadvantage to that," George said. "I'm also the one who has to listen to her." She dropped her arm from his waist and flapped the loose folds of her rain slicker, searching for a breath of cool-ness. "And she'll get over her silence, wait and see. Laying the whole Rusty thing to rest will help immediately."

"She'll never lay it to rest," Peter said, a trace of bitterness in his voice. "She might have to wake up and care about someone else in the family. Your kids, for instance. There's a luxury to obsession, you know. It justifies all sorts of selfish behavior."

George looked at him speculatively and said nothing. He felt him-self coloring slightly, and he glanced away from her, back to little Casey. George was thinking of Alison, he knew; his own luxury, his excuse for solitude. Perhaps he was too much Julia's son. He turned and looked out over the water, at the Sultan's house, as Hale slowed the motor.

"Okay," Hale shouted. "I'm going to idle here instead of throwing out the anchor. Doc Pritchett, would you ask Mrs. Mason to come above deck, please? With the—remains?"

"I'll go," George said. A brief, wistful smile, a smile that asked Peter's forgiveness, flickered across her tanned face as she turned toward the hatch. As if honesty should have to be forgiven, he thought. That was the essence of George: her short, dark hair; the eye-brows arched like a gull's wings; the ready smile and constant desire to please. Where had she come from in this family?

The *Seventh Wave* slowed, the throttle's vibration thrumming dully through the fiberglass hull, and its forward momentum slackened al-most to motionlessness. Peter looked toward the cockpit, studying Hale as he turned and backed the boat until it faced away from the Long Island shore. Hale was slight and trim, with a quiet, bespectacled face that suggested rock-solid predictability. His once-sandy hair was fading and thinning with each passing year, the only sign that he was facing forty-five. He seemed to bear the stress of his burdensome job and his burgeoning family with comforting steadiness. He inspired his children with confidence and respect, but not with warmth. For that, they turned to Peter.

Hale's head swiveled to the cabin's hatch, and Peter followed his gaze. George, holding the box containing Rusty's ashes, was helping his mother as she stepped gingerly from the ladder to the deck. It was the way Julia Mason allowed her driver to assist her from her car, the way she had taken the hands of a hundred servants during the course of her life. Despite years of exposure to sailing, she had never acquired sea legs; Peter thought it a deliberate refusal, as though in her world ladies did not become too comfortable with anything outside their expected competence. Her head came up as she gained the deck, and she looked straight at him, then allowed her gaze to shift without expression beyond him to the water. This was what she termed "cutting someone dead." He had just been declared *persona non grata* by his mother.

"Josh—Abi—come here, we're ready," George said, her head swiveling as she did her reflexive Whitney head count. As the children scrambled across the deck, she looked for Peter, and he moved silently to join her. She took a deep, shaky breath, as though she were standing at the top of a steep ski run, bracing herself for the descent. Doc Pritchett was suddenly at her side, lifting her burden gently from her hands, and turning solemnly toward the leeward side of the boat.

"Almighty God of the vast and changing sea, take Rusty to the depths of your great heart and keep him in everlasting light. He was a child of these tides, he was tossed by these swells, he loved their terrible power and fierce gifts. He understood the blessings You gave to those who master the craft of the ocean. Most of all, he paid homage to Your power, with his understanding that no man ever truly holds dominion over the waves, as no man can rule the Lord; but each of us can aspire to some form of joy on earth and in heaven. Amen."

"Is the sea God's great heart, Mom?" Maxie asked.

"Uncle Rusty thought so," George said.

Dr. Pritchett held aloft the box Peter had brought with him from Boston, and the wind from the sea caught Rusty's ashes and carried them in a fine veil out over the sound. For the first time since Rusty's death, as he watched his brother's dust sift into the ocean, an aching knot of sorrow formed itself in Peter's throat and would not be ignored. *Peace to you, Rusty, of late, unhappy memory,* he thought. *I don't ask for forgetting. We'll none of us have that, the rest of our lives.* He stared at the roiling water an instant and then turned back to George. Two large tears were coursing down her tanned cheeks, and her eyes were swimming; tears not for these ashes, but for him, and for herself—for the rifts that went unhealed, for their vanished dream of childhood.

He looked at his mother. Her fists were clenched at her sides, her arms stiff, and as he watched she stumbled like an automaton to the rail and clutched at the slender nylon cord. The boat rolled in the swell, and Julia Mason, disregarding her balance, leaned toward the water as if intent upon following her son into the sea. Dr. Pritchett reached for her swiftly, discreetly, as though she had stumbled and he had merely steadied her; and the moment passed. She turned toward Peter and George, her arms slack and her eyes glittering.

"From the day you were born, you couldn't stand it," she said. "That he was everything you're not. One of those the gods loved." She looked past Peter, but her words were meant for him all the same. "You pitiful, loathsome little boy. You had to destroy him, didn't you?"

"Mother!" George said.

"You burned his body. Burned!" At that, Julia Mason's face crumpled and she was wracked by a harsh, guttural sobbing that seemed to break her in half.

"What did Nana say, Mommy? What did Nana say?" Casey's hand was in her father's free one, and her eyes were solemn.

"I said your uncle is a murderer," Julia said, and she struggled past them to the hatch.

George looked after her, uncertain whether to follow, then bent down to Casey. "Nan's not well," she said. "Don't worry about anything she said." She looked up at the ring of serious children's faces and smiled at them uncertainly.

Chapter 26

AFTER DINNER IT RAINED. They laid a fire in Hale's library and sat before it, books forgotten on the leather chesterfield, gazing into the flames. Georgiana's legs, sheathed in bright red wool, were drawn up under her, and her face was pensive. Hale sat behind his desk, studying some papers. Julia had gone to her room upon their return from the boat and had refused dinner. The children were scattered about the house, and the echoes of their voices drifted faintly through the old plaster walls.

"Poor old Malcolm," Georgiana said. "He must have been wild to see you. How awful to be so old, and sick, and alone."

"Not alone," Peter said. "He has Mary."

"Oh, yes, but Peter! It's so senseless."

"What is?"

"That he's estranged from his granddaughter! Don't you remember? The daughter of his only son, the naval fighter pilot. The one shot down over Laos."

"No, I don't remember."

"Well, it was years ago," George said, "and nothing important enough for you to remember, but they raised her like their own, and then broke with her over some foolishness, and here they are dying without a word. It makes me so angry."

"How like you, George," Hale said, looking up at her fondly over his glasses, "to worry about other people's families."

She stood up restlessly and walked to the window, pressing her face to the glass. Her breath left a pale fog of condensation against the darkness. "It's just that pride is so infuriating, don't you think? Like you and Mummy. It gets in the way of so much feeling. But I suppose it's easier to be proud than to feel." She paused, and shivered. "This rain is awful. Peter—" She turned back to the sofa suddenly and huddled next to him, her eyes fixed on the fire. "Do you remember how it snowed the day we buried Daddy? Relentless, so cold and so still, as though the world had descended into sleep. I stood by the windows and watched it mount up on the hemlocks, thinking of him lying out there in the ground for the first time, lying under snow. It broke my heart."

"I remember."

"I'd feel the same way about this rain, if we'd buried Rusty."

"It seems less heartless, doesn't it, releasing him into the water."

"Air, water, earth, and fire, all the elements. Yes, it seems right. I think I'd like that to happen to me. Remember, will you?"

Peter nodded. The logs, still green, were steaming gently, and the flames were blue to their edges. He felt drained and sluggish, as though he could remain before this fire indefinitely, unspeaking, unthinking, and beyond all emotion.

"How long will you stay, Peter?"

He roused himself and looked at George. "Not long," he said, and paused. "There's too much to be done."

"I was almost forgetting, wasn't I? It's not over, even with him gone."

"No." Peter looked over at Hale, working in his contained circle of quiet, and felt his spirits sink. Why disturb this peace? Because Merry Folger's hard green eyes awaited him back on the island. "And if it's going to end, you have to tell me about the letter."

"The what?"

"The letter. The one Rusty sent you from Rio, the one you didn't mention when I called and told you about his death." There was a silence. Georgiana's face had frozen. Peter looked over at Hale. The banker continued his deliberate writing. "They found a copy in his things. Did she tell you about the letter, Hale?" Peter asked.

"Naturally. It concerned me," Hale said imperturbably, and set down his pen. He looked up at Peter and waited.

"I suppose I should have told you," George said in a rush, "but when you called with the news that Rusty was dead, it didn't seem important anymore. In fact, it seemed like . . ."

"A godsend," Peter finished.

George looked down at her fingers, which she'd locked together in her distress, and she nodded rapidly. "Lord help me, yes," she said. She met Peter's eyes, and he was torn by the pain in them. "I didn't know what the letter was about, you see," she said. "And then I asked Hale."

Hale cleared his throat quietly and took off his glasses. He passed his hands across his eyelids and sighed.

"When did you receive the letter, George?" Peter said.

"The Saturday of Labor Day weekend," she whispered. "But we didn't talk about it until after Rusty was dead."

"He was clever, sending it to George," Hale said. "He knew I'd never pay him, and he figured she'd just put up and shut up and never ask any questions."

"How attractive," George said bitterly. She unfolded her long legs and crossed to the bookshelves. "Brandy, Peter?"

He shook his head and turned back to his brother-in-law. "What'd he have on you?"

"My career," Hale said comfortably. "And the mistaken notion I'd do anything to hang on to it. Poor fool. My one rule in life has been to be able to walk away from anything. I've kept my resignation in every drawer of every desk I've ever used. That's the sort of freedom Rusty could never understand. The freedom from power." He strolled over to the leather sofa and stood staring down at the fire, his hands in his pockets. "I suppose you'd like to hear about it," he said.

"I've got no choice," Peter answered. "It has to do with Rusty's criminal activity, doesn't it?"

"Oh, yes," Hale said. "And my own. I can call it that without flinching. Seems silly to go into events that happened so long ago, and I suppose the details are irrelevant in the eyes of the law. But they make a more interesting story." He took the glass of brandy his wife handed him, and then placed his hand on her glossy cap of hair. The gesture moved Peter. Hale was such a private man.

"George and I were married the summer of 1982, you remember."

"Yes. You met at a Salomon party the year before, didn't you?"

"ME was a major client of the corporate finance department; Max came to the Salomon bash and brought Georgiana. Julia was in Capri, I think."

"Paris," George corrected automatically. "For the spring collections."

"Whatever. Max brought George. I fell in love with her then and there."

"Hale," George said softly.

"I talked to her a bit, but I've never been the most dynamic man at a party, and she was absolutely dazzling. Max Mason's only daughter, twenty-three years old and utterly unaware how beautiful she was. I was thirty-five and beginning to lose my hair, I had survived three lousy love affairs, I'd made money and I'd had success, but I was just another guy in a dark-blue summer suit and expensive handmade shoes. I hadn't the slightest idea how I'd ever see her again."

"Enter Rusty," Peter said.

"Enter indeed. The firm had essentially given Rusty his job three years before as a favor to Max."

"I thought you'd brought him on."

Hale shook his head. "Too junior, frankly. I didn't become a director until 1986. No, Rusty was a bond trader—just the sort of job a Mason would take, isn't it, a job that looked unextraordinary at the time, and a few years later would turn out to be the center of the financial markets. I was in stocks, a waning if respectable profession, but not one that made money and glamour as quickly as bond trading would, by the mid-eighties. I only ran into Rusty occasionally, in the cafeteria, that sort of thing. But I tried to strike up a friendship with him. At first he ignored me completely."

"Until I started working on him from the other end," George broke in. "What Hale neglects to tell you is that I was utterly infatuated with him from day one, and kept pumping Rusty for information. He was so—urbane, so—sophisticated. Not like a college boy. I got Rusty to ask Hale for drinks a few times so I could see him, but he was so terribly shy. He would never ask me out on a date."

"Then one day, one marvelous day, Rusty came by my desk and invited me to your home in Greenwich. It may have been his one disinterested act of our entire acquaintance."

"And you came," George said, her voice thrilling. "I thought then there might be hope."

"That weekend was like a glimpse of a dream," Hale said. "A glimpse of life as it could be—in the midst of a wonderful family, their happiness, that beautiful home—"

"You poor idiot," Peter said, laughing harshly.

George shot him a look of hurt and surprise.

"You're right, of course," Hale said. "But I didn't find that out until later."

"After you'd been married a year. When Rusty came and asked you for your stock. Or rather, George's."

Hale looked down at the brandy and swirled it thoughtfully in his glass. "Oh no," he said. "That was later. He offered me the money first—what I thought was his money. A loan to buy shares of a company called Ultracom. A company Rusty said was likely to be the target of a takeover. A sure thing. Make a profit and pay back the loan when you sell the shares, he said. What a crock." He looked up at Peter, and his eyes were flat.

"You, too," Peter said.

Hale nodded. "It seems you know what went wrong with the plan. The takeover company became the target and pulled out of its tender offer, and Ultracom's value fell. We lost our loan instead of doubling our money. That's when I found out the takeover company was ME. And that the raider was Mitch Hazlitt."

"Rusty hadn't told you?"

Hale shook his head. "He was still smart about some things. He knew I was shy of trading on his information in the first place—it was a risky business even in those days, before the spate of prosecutions—but

260

if I'd known where the information came from, I'd have gone to Max and told him Hazlitt was sniffing around the deal. I was older than Rusty, remember. I dealt in equity. I knew what a man like Hazlitt was capable of. But when it all came out, it was too late. I was in up to my neck. And I'd dragged Georgiana with me."

"I only wish you had," George said softly. "None of this might have happened."

"You couldn't have changed anything," Hale said. Then he looked back at Peter. "When things went wrong, Rusty and I were in a hole. As you can imagine. First, there was the matter of the loan—it had to be repaid, and to Hazlitt, not Rusty; neither of us had the money. We'd already taken a loss in the stock we'd purchased with the loan. Then there was the broader consideration—Max. The fact that we'd traded on information leaked from ME. I spent a whole day out of work, walking the paths in Central Park, wrestling with the mess in my mind."

"You didn't go to Max," Peter said.

"Not then. I was searching for a way out that wouldn't involve George or her father. I'd already sold the bulk of my assets to buy a co-op on Central Park South—we'd moved into it six months before, if you remember. A second mortgage on the place was possible, I supposed, but that would mean telling George why I needed the money. I couldn't ask my new father-in-law for funds so soon in my marriage. And as you know, my parents have very little." He paused. "And then Rusty asked for the stock."

"George's seven percent voting stock."

"Yes. He had a buyer, a source of funds to repay the loan. Hazlitt. I began to see why the loan had been made in the first place. And it was out of the question, of course. I could never sell George's stock without giving her full knowledge of why it was necessary. But beyond that, it was unthinkable. Hazlitt was using extortion, with George's birthright as his object. I think it was then that I ceased to be helpless and began to be angry."

"And so you went to Max."

"It was an interview the likes of which I hope I may never witness again the rest of my life. He was in a white rage. Cold, efficient, and absolutely deadly. He dealt with the matter at hand—my troubles, the loan—and advanced me the full sum, to the tune of fifty thousand dollars, so that I could repay Hazlitt. Then he went to the U.S. attorney's office and told them about his son. Me, he kept out of the whole affair. I owe the sanity of the past ten years to Max Mason. Not that I deserved it."

"It worked," George said. "Even after Daddy died. Hale was transferred to corporate finance—"

"A department considered boring, but safe," he said.

"—and he did so well that four years later they made him a director," George finished.

"Forgive me, Hale," Peter said, "but what I don't understand is why you accepted the loan in the first place. I can perfectly well see Rusty trading on inside information. But it's completely unlike you."

Hale smiled, a trifle wistfully. "Not like safe, sober Hale, is it? Hale, who can always be trusted to do the correct thing." He looked at his wife. "Maybe I was caught up in the lure of the risk, Peter," he said. "Or maybe I wanted to impress George with my trading prowess. Maybe I just wanted to be more like Rusty. But I learned. The hard way."

George lifted the hand Hale still held tightly, and kissed his palm. "My darling, idiot, Hale," she said. "Never, never do anything illegal for me again."

"Like murder, for instance?" Peter said quietly.

At that moment the phone rang, and the three of them froze, Hale and George locked together in front of the fire, Peter on the sofa, until the ringing ended. The quiet murmur of Mrs. Shallit, the housekeeper, came to them through the closed study door, and then her footsteps crossed the hall.

"For Mr. Peter, madam," she said. "A Rafe da Silva." She said the name suspiciously, its cadences strange to her, and waited for Peter. He stood up and followed her to the phone.

George looked imploringly at Hale. "Does he think you killed him to protect me, or that I killed him to protect you?"

"Probably that both of us killed him to protect everyone," Hale said fondly. "Don't worry about it, love. It didn't happen." He turned as Peter came back into the study, his face like death.

"I've got to leave tonight."

"What is it?"

"Will Starbuck. Someone's tried to kill him."

Chapter 27

RAFE TURNED HIS HEAD at the sound in the doorway. Merry Folger stood there, an expression both solemn and awkward on her face. He knew that her presence meant Peter had returned, but he felt no relief. Even Peter Mason could not pierce the coma wrapping Will in silence. He glanced at his watch as he stood up to join Merry: two-thirty in the morning. Any other hospital would have kicked them out long ago.

Tess had not looked up from Will's motionless form. Her hand held his, maddeningly slack. How much more, her rigid neck seemed to ask, must I take? She did not allow herself to say anything—no word of reproach to Merry, no wail of despair to Rafe, not even a word of love to her boy lying prone and broken before her. The muscles of her face seemed likely to shatter if she attempted speech.

Rafe placed a hand lightly on each of her shoulders as he moved around the bed to the doorway. She seemed not to notice. He pulled the door shut behind him and heaved a deep sigh as he looked at Merry. "Man, that's tough," he said.

The banality of the words struck him even as he said them, and he hung his head, hands groping over his brow.

Merry nodded lamely. "Mason's out in the emergency room, waiting. Guess they don't want more than two people at a time in there," she said, nodding in Will's direction. Her words seemed overly loud, a sacrilege. "He's pretty beat," she finished, in a whisper.

Peter stood up as they approached, the sockets of his eyes standing out sharply in his white face. It occurred to Rafe that he was probably still weakened from his own wound three days earlier.

"How is he?"

"The same. Tess won't go home in case he wakes up. But the doctor says he probably won't, for a while. Fractured skull. He could be this way for a few days or a few weeks. I've gotta get her out of here sometime. She'll fall over if she doesn't get some sleep soon."

Peter nodded and gripped Rafe's shoulder in what passed between the two men for an embrace. "You found him last night?"

"Last night, late. We didn't call you until we knew the funeral was over."

"That was good of you, but it wasn't necessary. I'd have come anyway. Tell me again what happened."

Rafe looked questioningly at Merry, and she nodded slightly and turned to Peter. "Will was deliberately thrown from his bike on the path leading from your house, Peter, through the moors near Altar Rock," she said. There was an edge to her voice, and her cheekbones seemed about to thrust through the skin of her face. She was exhausted.

"Thrown?" he said.

"A length of wire staked across the path, pretty hard to see, about waist-high. Designed to catch a bike across the throat and knock off the rider."

"Who found him?"

"Ney," Rafe said. "But not for a while after he was thrown, we figure. Dog was inside until about eight o'clock, with Rebecca. I was over in the barn, looking at some figures, and got a call from Tess. She'd just realized the kid hadn't made it home—too busy before that, in the kitchen, you know. I guess she thought in the back of her mind he was still out at the farm, and then looked up from her dishes and saw it was dark. Anyway, I got in the Rover and started driving the roads; Rebecca let the dog out and he hightailed it down the path through the moors. She thought he'd found a cat when the howling started." He paused. "Poor kid lost a lot of blood."

"Rafe called the police after he called the ambulance," Merry said.

"I didn't see the wire in the dark right off," he said, "nor the stakes. Thought it was just a regular fall."

"The ground was pretty useless by the time I got there—all those rescue squad footprints, and tire tracks. Not much you can tell except that the wire's there, and it did what it was supposed to—"

"Wait a minute," Peter said. "Wait a minute. Let's back up a bit. Why would anyone want to hurt Will?"

Rafe shot a look at Merry from under his eyebrows and said nothing. The detective looked at Peter speculatively. "Well, that's the question of the hour, Mr. Mason. Why would anyone want to hurt Will? You tell me."

Rafe saw the hardness in the lines of Merry Folger's mouth, the latent anger in her eyes, and knew Peter had better tread softly without knowing why.

Peter hesitated. "I don't know. Any more than I know why someone would kill Rusty, or shoot me. But I know the three are connected."

"There's a chance somebody decided Will had seen or suspected something dangerous. We can't know that until he wakes up. If he wakes up."

"Can I go in there now?"

"I guess," Merry said. "There's the other aspect, of course, that we can't forget."

Peter turned, his weariness in his face. "Meaning?"

"That this has nothing to do with Will, Peter." Merry's voice had sharpened, and the anger was obvious now. "Haven't you learned anything about anything? That wire was probably meant for you. It was at a height for tripping a bike like yours, and it was stretched across a path you take all the time. Just Will's bad luck he rides a bike you once owned and knows the quickest way through the moors to the road."

She stopped and fixed Peter in an uncharacteristic glare, her eyes bright green. "You're really a case, you know? All that education and no common sense." She stopped short suddenly. "Sorry. I get tense when I'm tired. I'll stop by the farm tomorrow morning and talk to you, okay? I want to hear about Greenwich."

"I'll be up early," he said.

She scrabbled her hands through her hair, which badly needed brushing, and closed her eyes. Then she hauled her purse higher on her shoulder and left without a backward glance. The two men followed her progress out the door in silence.

"The Terror of Tattle Court," Rafe said ruefully, and looked at Peter. "She thinks this is all her fault, and she's taking it hard. I made a fool of myself last night and told her she wasn't doing her job. Funny, isn't it, how when you're angry at yourself you take it out on whoever's around? And that woman has a knack for showing up at the wrong times."

"Let's see Will," Peter said.

• • •

HE HAD HATED HOSPITALS since Max's death, hated the tubes and the clinical light and the soft whirr of machines that should have made him thankful but instead made him afraid and longing to be anywhere else but here. In hospitals, death was a glaring light shining full in his eyes, driving him to blink, to tear, and to avert his gaze. Hospitals forced him to accept he was human, and a coward, and he had never forgiven them.

Tess turned as they entered the room, her face curiously blank. "They want to fly him to Mass Gen," she said, her hand reaching blindly toward them. "I don't know what it means. I don't know what it means."

Rafe caught hold of the groping hand and covered it in his own. His touch seemed to calm Tess. She dropped her head and crumpled against the side of her chair, breaking down finally into silent, racking sobs. Rafe touched her head tentatively, and looked at Peter.

Peter was staring fixedly at Will's ghostly face, at the dark, luxurious eyelashes trembling with unconscious dreams. He seemed too frail ever to have lived. Peter felt the viselike grip of love for the boy, love that had brought Will only harm, and his throat knotted with tears. Will was meant for better things than this. And he was lying in a bed intended for Peter; someone had almost sent him to a grave Peter's size. "What's the doctor's name?" Peter said.

"Westfall."

Peter nodded and ducked out of the room, making for the nurse's station.

"Dr. Westfall," he said. "Where might I find him?"

The nurse looked up, her eyes smudged with dark underlying circles. Working the night shift and probably holding down another job during the day, he thought.

"Chief resident," she said. "He's on call tonight. I'll page him."

Peter nodded and turned to look aimlessly around the waiting area. He was exhausted and restless at once, unable to sit down and read one of the helpful pamphlets on back injuries, venereal disease, and salmonella poisoning that lay scattered on tables. He drifted slowly around the room, hands in his pockets, dimly aware of the throbbing in his bandaged shoulder and wishing in vain for a shot of scotch. He could not blot Will's image from his mind, or the belief that he was responsible, even if indirectly, for placing Will in that room where machines monitored his life and his mother's words could not reach him.

"How's the shoulder?"

Peter turned. "Hello," he said in surprise. The man standing behind him had treated his bullet wound. "Not bad, actually."

"You wanted to speak to me, I think?" the doctor said quizzically.

"You're Dr. Westfall," Peter said. "I never caught your name."

"Right," he said. "I drew the late shifts this week. What brings you out here at three in the morning?"

"Another near miss. The boy lying in there was injured on my property."

"I see," Westfall said, and his tone hardened. "Two almost fatal attacks in a row. Unusual on this island."

"Very," Peter said. "The police seem to think this attack was intended, like the last one, for me."

"I see," Westfall said again. "Or rather, I don't, but never mind. You're a friend of the patient?"

268

"Yes. His mother tells me you'd like to fly him to Boston. I wanted to ask you why."

"Because we don't have a CAT scanner in this hospital, Mr. Mason, and I want a better picture of what's happening inside Will's cranium," he said. "He's got a fractured skull and he's in a coma. We could wait and see if he wakes up—that could be weeks or days—or we could know in a matter of hours whether his brain is damaged, or even hemorrhaging. It's fairly simple."

Peter nodded. "What's the risk in moving him?"

"Next to none. The risk if he stays, on the other hand . . ."

"I understand. Doctor—" He paused. "Tess Starbuck is not well off. I doubt she has any kind of health insurance. I know that medevacking someone to the city is fairly expensive. I'd like to make arrangements for any bills to be sent to me."

"That's already been taken care of, I think," Westfall said. "When the boy was admitted. Mr. da Silva has directed the bills be sent to him."

·   ·   ·

THE HELICOPTER WITH Will's prone form, Tess beside him, lifted from the helipad at six o'clock that morning. Peter and Rafe stood with the wind from the blades whipping their hair about their heads, staring at Tess, until the glass bubble beat its way into the air and out to sea. Neither of them said anything for several long moments. Then they turned, wordlessly, and walked to the Rover.

"I'll drop you at the farm, and then I think I'll be heading over to Boston," Rafe said carefully. "You get some sleep, okay?"

Peter glanced at his watch, then shook his head. "I'll run you up to the airport. I've got a date with the detective. Bacon and eggs at my place, seven sharp."

Chapter 28

MERRY HAD REACHED WHAT SHE THOUGHT of as the dry, bleached-white stage of her exhaustion, when nausea replaced sleepiness and her forehead held a permanent frown. Her body moved seconds after her mind conjured the impulse to move, her walk was a delicate balance between weaving and stumbling. She had never been so tired, she thought, and yet so beyond comprehending it; she progressed through the wee hours on will alone, unquestioningly. She had been awake for two full days, and still her bed hung like a mirage before the hood of her car, receding indefinitely.

She pulled the Blazer to the sandy verge in front of Lucy Jacoby's house and turned off the ignition. No lights behind the snug eaves. She checked her watch—only three-thirty. Not surprising that Lucy was sound asleep. Still—for a woman in mortal terror of pursuit and the unnamed horrors wrought by Italian gray arms dealers, she was remarkably comfortable in her isolation.

Merry ducked her head around the windshield visor and studied the houses on either side of Lucy's. Both were dark. As she had thought on her last visit to Tom Nevers: summer people, probably gone for the next eight months. Anybody in her right mind, who'd seen the sort of ghost Lucy'd talked about, would have cleared out long ago.

An Italian count with a penchant for playing rough. I wonder where she came up with that one, Merry thought. She scowled to herself as she thought of Peter Mason's worry, the lines deepening around his eyes as he talked about Lucy, his all too chivalrous decency in the face of the all too obvious torch Lucy carried—full in his face in case he preferred to remain in the dark about her feelings for him.

"Men are such chumps," Merry said out loud, and to her surprise, the words sounded vicious.

She got out of the car and walked around the side of Lucy's house, searching for the garbage. There it was. A stack of wine bottles next to it. Perfect. She crouched down and eyed them, then pulled the handkerchief she'd brought for this purpose out of her pocket. She lifted one of the bottles by its rim and carried it, willing herself to be careful and steady, back to the Blazer. Prints should show up all over this baby.

She turned the key and shoved the car into gear, not caring whether a light came on in Lucy's house or not. She needed coffee and a nap, and she needed to talk to the only guy on the island with any sense.

. . .

RALPH WALDO WAS WRAPPED in the faded blue seersucker bathrobe that Merry's grandmother had bought in Hyannis twenty years ago. His mug of black coffee steamed on the wooden table, burning a heat mark into the scarred surface. He had not yet shaved, and the white bristles on his chin made him look, Merry thought, like a cross between Santa and a drunken sailor.

"This case means too much to you, Meredith Abiah. No surprise. The first one always does. So what we've got is Rusty Mason's best friend killing him, or the best friend's girlfriend, or his sister, or the sister's husband," Ralph said. "Or someone unknown. We'll call him X."

"Right," Merry said. Then, almost against her will, "Dad thinks Peter did it, Ralph."

Ralph Waldo snorted, all the answer he deemed necessary. "So you've got these people who could've killed Rusty, for reasons you're not sure of."

"I'm not sure of anything," she said.

Her grandfather's turquoise-blue eyes flicked up at her from under his eyebrows at that, his expression unreadable. He slathered some butter on a piece of toasted Portuguese bread and handed it to her. "Eat that, Meredith Abiah. You look like walking death." He kept his tone light, but Merry knew he was worried about her.

She did as she was told. He watched an instant to see that he was obeyed, and then set about toasting another piece.

"I'm stuck on Lucy Jacoby, Ralph."

"Stands to reason. You're stuck on something else, young woman."

"I am?"

"Motives for killing Peter Mason, not Rusty. And the people to pull the trigger."

Merry wrinkled her brow. "They're the same bunch, Ralph. And Rafe da Silva and Tess Starbuck, the motive being money."

"How's that coffee?"

"Tastes like the inside of a trash can."

He nodded approvingly. "Good. Now let's think systematically about what you've done. You've decided Rusty was the target of the murder. You've decided Peter's attack was a fake. Now you've decided Will Starbuck was a mistake, too, and that for some reason Peter was supposed to find the wire."

"That seems fairly clear."

"Why?"

Merry hesitated.

"The false attack on Peter should have been enough to confuse the police, in the killer's mind," he said. "Why try another one? You've already worked out that whoever shot Peter didn't really intend to kill him—and I agree with you. So why try to kill him a day or so later?"

"Because maybe I'm all wrong," she said, in a very small voice.

"Trust your intelligence, Meredith," Ralph chided.

"You think Will was the the one the killer wanted?"

"I don't think you should rule it out. What could Will know?"

"Search me. And it's impossible to ask him. But what you say makes sense, Ralph." She stood up and started pacing the narrow length of the kitchen, her lanky body looking even thinner than usual.

"So the guy chooses a day Peter's out of town. To make sure it's not Peter who takes the path."

"Now you ask yourself who knew he was out of town," Ralph said gently.

She sat down and bit into her toast. "Same set of suspects, basically. Peter Mason has a small group of friends, but it's a tight network."

Ralph Waldo set his chin in his left hand and gazed at his granddaughter like a seer.

"Find out what Will might know. And another thing—find that Lucy's errant husband."

Merry dropped her toast, startled as always by Ralph Waldo's uncanny ability to read her mind. Her grandfather picked up the piece of bread and set it gently on her plate.

"It's just an idea, understand. The good English teacher runs into her ex-husband's thug on the ferry Sunday night. Let's imagine that if he knows where she lives, he knows about her life. Maybe he knows she's lost her heart to Peter Mason. And maybe he's here to strike. What could hurt her more than hurting the man she loves? He doesn't even have to go to her house to reach her, that way."

Merry sat very still, her mind working.

"There's a pattern of sorts," Ralph continued. "Peter Mason is in the company of the fellah's wife every Monday, Wednesday, and Friday—you've said he runs with her those days. And lo and behold, this week there's blood shed on Monday, Wednesday, and Friday."

"If you count the late hours of Sunday or the early hours of Monday morning," Merry said. She set down her napkin and sat back in her chair, her shoulders slumped, willing herself to think. Peter had been shot the evening after his run with Lucy; the trap that snared Will Starbuck on Friday had been laid along the path of Peter's run through the moors. It seemed too neat. "It's too easy, Ralph," she said.

He shrugged. "Well, you've picked up one thing from your father. He's been saying that to me his whole life. But you're going round and round with the folks you know. Try the ones you don't."

. . .

273

He had bought the phone-answering machine only under duress, when his friends had grown too accusatory and his lack of a message center had begun to seem like deliberate obstruction of progress. Unlike some in his acquaintance, whose answering recording was arch or cute, and changed as frequently as the weather, his was the blunt request he'd placed on the tape a year earlier—to leave one's name and number and be done with it. He hit the message button now and listened to voices alternate with beeps as he moved around the kitchen, throwing open the refrigerator door and rummaging through Rebecca's carefully organized stores. Sunday was her Quaker day of rest, and he was on his own for Merry Folger's breakfast.

George's voice, tentative and filled with affection, asking after his safe arrival. *Beep.* Walt Sargent, at the Ocean Spray depot, confirming receipt of the flatbed filled with cranberries from Tuesday's harvest. *Beep.* Peter pulled out half a loaf of Rebecca's oatmeal bread and set it on the counter, found some of her raspberry jam, and then went for the eggs. Someone hung up without a word. He'd do a Southwestern omelet with some of the salsa and cheese, throw a couple of sausages on the fire, add some of the last of the green peppers from the garden. *Beep.* A pause, some hesitant breathing, and more dead air. He stood up, suddenly alert to the silence on the machine, and looked at it—as though that might help. Lucy Jacoby shot into his brain, a sudden reminder of her fear and isolation. Then he heard the voice.

"And now what do I say?" He froze.

"It's so odd to hear you, Peter, even on a machine, after all this time." She sounded amused, distant, like a fund-raiser for the Boston Symphony. Another pause. He closed his eyes and turned toward the counter, gripping the edge painfully. "You sound so much the same. Never mind. I suppose I should say hello. It's Alison. Sky Jackson, whom it seems you now *pay* to be your friend—or is it your lawyer?—hired somebody to track me down here in San Francisco." A short laugh, of frustration, he thought. "Couldn't you call the alumni office if you needed my address? Of course not. Masons *hire* people to keep in touch for them. At any rate, he told me about—your brother." A pause, as she cast about for something appropriate to say in sympathy, and abandoned the attempt. "*Your lawyer* asked me to come back East to discuss the whole thing. I'm not sure why that can't be done over the phone, but he's good at arguing otherwise. He would be, wouldn't he? He's been trained." She paused for an instant, and Peter imagined her passing one hand across her eyes, fighting to keep down her irritation. "Never mind. I arrive tomorrow night at seven thirty-five. Island Air." There was an instant of uncomfortable silence, and then her capitulation: "Oh, Peter, I'm sorry for sounding so— It's just been—rather difficult. Until tomorrow—" And then the sound of the receiver.

Automatically, he hit the "save" button on the machine and replayed that voice—her voice, like the current of a cool, dark river, a voice drowned in calm. It had maddened his dreams through years of sleepless nights. He listened for the trace of New York that lingered metallically in her vowels, and found it. His heart raced. A shakiness in his gut that was part euphoria and part terror: he would talk to Alison again.

Not at the cost of the ground he'd gained, an inner voice said, those years of small victories and savage losses.

He listened a third time to the message and half willingly, uncertainly, copied down the time of her arrival. He glanced at his watch. Tomorrow meant today, and he had less than twelve hours to wait. She hadn't asked him to meet the plane; probably hadn't known whether he'd want to. For an agonized instant he wondered if she hoped he would skip it, then reminded himself she'd given him the information. And the choice. Very like Alison.

San Francisco. She'd gone almost as far away from him as she could go. He ran one fingertip over the trailing numbers and wrote Alison above them. Alison in San Francisco. The city—its moody weather and jagged seas, the plunges and peaks of its streets, the very shaking foundations—would suit her perfectly.

He looked up as the sound of tires on gravel filtered into the kitchen through the open back door. Merry Folger had arrived.

Chapter 29

"I T'S A SHAME YOU DON'T WRITE for television," Merry said. "Because this stuff about your family is great material."

She was staring out the kitchen window at the dog Ney, who sat under a young maple tree in the yard. He snapped periodically at the green horseflies that came in off the marshland and targeted his thin, short-haired skin. Presently Peter would whistle him inside for the remainder of a steak bone coated in sausage grease; for now, he seemed content to sit in a last pool of summertime warmth. Merry had never owned a dog. She yearned, suddenly, for something warm and contented to hold in her lap, something to put her arms around; or perhaps she yearned to be held herself. She winced, feeling an almost physical pain, and shifted away from the window. She was too tired, and she needed all her intelligence right now. "So it was Hale who told Max what Rusty was doing."

"Yes."

"But he has no idea who gave Rusty the details of Max's merger plans."

"No."

"You trust this guy? You really think he's got nothing to do with Rusty's murder?"

"By the way he acted, I'd say Rusty's blackmail threats had less impact on him than they did on Sky. His career is only so important to him. And besides, I have George's word he was with her in Greenwich the night Rusty died."

"A wife's word isn't worth much," Merry said. "I knew I should have gone to Greenwich. I'd know better if I'd seen and talked to them myself."

"Can't be everywhere at once," Peter said. "You're just going to have to trust me."

"I wish that were easy." She closed her eyes and leaned her head against the cool panes of glass that separated her from Ney's summer idyll. "We found the car, Peter."

"What car?"

He was startled, but more by her admission that she couldn't trust him, she thought. Trust was a tenet of Peter Mason's. He didn't seem to understand it had no place in a murder investigation.

"Rusty's Jeep," she said.

"Rusty had a Jeep?"

"He had a credit card. With a credit card, apparently, you can have anything."

"So it was rented."

"From Over Sand Vehicles. Under the name of Ribeiro, of course."

"Where'd you find it?"

"Wondered when you'd ask that. In Gibbs Pond."

There was a silence. "In Gibbs Pond?"

"Well, even a Jeep can't walk on water."

"What made you look there?"

"It seemed the closest place to deep-six something that weighs a ton. Particularly if you know the area well."

She turned to face him, her green eyes remote. The chumminess of the flight over water and the Westchester drive seemed a distant memory.

"Let's talk about your family," she said. "The woman in the photograph. Why would she be with your dad?"

The abrupt change of subject seemed to unnerve him, and he struggled to find her meaning. "A secretary, perhaps."

"Uh-huh. Could be."

"Or a business associate."

"At this kid's age and in these clothes?" The anger was back in her voice. "How about we try lunch date. Or steady date. Or call girl."

"That's enough." The words were sharp and bitten, like a lash across her cheek.

"Is it? You call me here to make a clean breast of the family history, but you're still trying to keep the dirty socks in the closet."

Involuntarily, his lips twitched at the mixed metaphors. But the humor was fleeting; she was too serious. "I didn't call you here. You came."

"You know what I mean. You're not helping. You're obstructing. Look at the facts. Look at the picture, for God's sake." She picked up her reading glasses, cast aside on the breakfast table, and settled them on her nose. "This is a very expensive broad we've got here. Leggy, too." She heard the tartness in her voice and despised herself for it, knowing he would hear feminine spite and dismiss what she was saying. "Your brother brought it for a reason. He was coming to see you. Put two and two together—he thought he had something to tell you about the woman in this picture."

"Perhaps. Or maybe he loved her, and kept the picture for old times' sake. How can I say?"

"He sure didn't carry this out of affection for your dad, you've got to grant me that."

"Granted."

"Taken with everything you've told me about your family, I'd say the odds are even she's the famous source you're looking for. She knew your dad; Rusty apparently knew something about her. So I suggest we figure out who she is."

He considered this a moment, the brows furrowed over his gray eyes. "Malcolm didn't know her."

"So Malcolm said. I wonder." She paused, and looked at him speculatively. "Another thing. I'd like to find out what Lucy Jacoby's real name is, and why she wants you to believe she was married to an Italian count."

Peter, in the act of opening the back door for Ney, stopped in his tracks. "Her real name?"

"Well, it's not the one she's using, that's for sure."

"You can't be serious."

"Unless she's managed to get to Italy and back without showing a passport."

"How do you know?"

"Called the Department of State a couple of days ago. Asked if they'd ever issued a passport in that name. They said no."

"Maybe it was under her maiden name."

"So Jacoby's the last name of the Italian count?"

Peter paused, and then smiled, grudgingly.

"Not bloody likely, as they say," Merry said with satisfaction. "There's a driver's license under Lucy Jacoby in the Massachusetts system, but it only dates to 1987."

"The year she came to the island."

"As far as her official history is concerned, she's been on record as Lucy Jacoby for only five years. Could be perfectly normal, as you say, because she moved here; or it could mean she changed her name. For a lot of reasons."

"Like?"

"Say Jacoby is her name: maybe there never was an Italian count. She never went to Italy, and so she never needed a passport. Or say Jacoby's a name she just adopted: maybe her husband—if she has one—is such a creep she's trying to keep him off everybody's screen by making up exotic stories and alternate personalities. Either way, something about the story isn't right. There are a lot of maybes," Merry said.

"And none of them have anything to do with Rusty," Peter said. "Don't you think you're losing your focus? Whatever the nature of her marriage, if Lucy changed her address, why wouldn't she change her name? It's probably a grandmother's, or a middle name."

"I'd be obliged, all the same, if you'd ask. She'll tell you if she'll tell anybody."

"I'll find out what I can."

"Good. Look, I've got to get some sleep. Thanks for breakfast." She pulled off her glasses, picked up her decrepit bag, cast one last look out of the window at Ney under his tree, and turned to go.

Peter was studying the photograph of his father. "You're right, you know," he said. "Rusty brought this for a reason. You may even be right about the source."

"Once or twice a week, I'm right about something," Merry said slowly, "but lately I've been hoping I'm wrong. Like today." She let her bag slip off her shoulder and waited for him to look at her. He didn't disappoint her. She held his eyes, trying to find innocence or guilt.

"The idea that you know something about this woman has been driving me crazy. I keep thinking maybe Rusty actually got to the farm, and showed you the picture, and it made you mad enough to kill him. You worry about the car being traced, so you dump it in the pond, throw his stuff in the sea, and hightail it back to bed." There, she'd come out with it. She waited for him to react.

For a moment, Peter seemed stunned. Then the warmth faded from his face and his expression grew remote. "And what about this?" he said, tapping his left shoulder.

"Maybe you got somebody to do it for you," Merry said carefully. "To confuse me. I have to think of every possibility, Peter. You understand."

"No," he said, "I don't. I thought we were working together."

She picked up the photograph. "Tell me the truth. Is this a picture of Alison?"

He threw back his head and laughed at that. "No," he said. "Alison was a pretty woman, no doubt about it, but she's never looked like this in her life. This sort of image takes a lot of money, Merry, and that's something she never had. You can see her yourself tomorrow—she arrives on a plane tonight."

"Sky's work?"

He nodded. "He's pretty desperate. He thinks Alison might know who the source is. You can show her the picture tomorrow."

·   ·   ·

WHEN SHE HAD LEFT, Peter dragged himself upstairs and settled himself carefully on his bed, favoring his left arm. He was exhausted, but

280

Merry's words were reeling in his head, banishing sleep. He picked up Rusty's photograph and studied the image of his father. He recognized the expression on Max's face; he had been happy, and amused. But whether he knew the woman well or had met her for the first time, Peter couldn't say.

He studied the leggy broad, as Merry had dubbed her, and, not for the first time, wondered what it was that he found familiar. Her form in the breathlessly tailored dress? The sleek cap of chin-length hair? Perhaps she tugged at his memory simply because he thought that she ought to. But when he tried to define the indefinable, it shifted away from him like a half-remembered name. He thrust the picture aside and closed his eyes. He needed sleep almost as much as Merry. He had Alison to face, tonight.

He had reached the semi-drowsing state where thoughts enter the mind and depart ungrasped when suddenly he shot upright in bed. Mayling Stern. Merry had found a Jeep in the pond, but she hadn't said whether the bumper was damaged. What had Mayling hit, and where?

.   .   .

THE WIND OFF THE ATLANTIC blew Mayling's glossy black hair against the grain, a faint but inexorable tug that annoyed her, like an alarm sounding repetitively in the distance. She was stretched out on a wrought-iron chaise, reading the Sunday *Times,* and her garden was filled with the white noise of surf, punctuated by occasional birdsong and the muffled roar of planes coming in from New York. They made her think of Sky, and she looked up at the arch of blue above her head whenever they passed. Then she thrust a lock of hair behind her left ear, a futile gesture; it slid across her cheekbone to her chin almost immediately.

She had spent a good part of the past hour looking down at her lap; the fall fashion supplement had arrived that day, and in it, photo spreads of her latest collection. Women with the legs of giraffes and the looks of domesticated panthers strode in her clothes before the cameras, an identical expression of solitude on their faces. There was even a picture of herself, with clasped hands and brilliant smile, in the midst

281

of a covey of girls; her eyes were opaque, unfocused, but only she would see that. And Sky. Sky saw everything. Except what was vital.

The unoiled gate in the white picket fence swung open, breaking her noontime peace, and she looked over her shoulder, her heart racing uncontrollably. She readied her face with a smile very much like the one in the magazine on her lap, had she but known it, and waited for Sky to turn the corner of the house and break upon her. But it wasn't Sky. She stood up, and the magazine fell closed.

"Detective Folger! How good to see you! I thought you were Sky, surprising me."

"He didn't come up this weekend?"

She shook her head. "I'm going home myself in another few days."

Merry's lithe frame crossed the lawn and stopped a careful few feet from her chaise. As she held out her hand, Mayling half-consciously compared the detective to the women stalking her clothing for the *Times*. The effect of sunlight on Merry's blond hair was almost blinding, a white light; against her dark skin and brows, it gave her the effect of a photographic negative. She should wear sage-colored linen, Mayling thought, but she never does. Then she came out of her dream and remembered why the woman was in her yard.

"More trouble," she said.

"May I sit down?"

"Of course."

Merry threw herself into the chair opposite Mayling's chaise and glanced at the *Times* spread. She knit her brows. "Biker's boots and chiffon over bras. None of those clothes looks real, except yours."

"I wish the people who count thought so. The reviews have been damningly faint in their praise."

"Then they're not worth counting."

"Money always counts, unfortunately. But you didn't come here to talk about the rag trade."

"I don't know enough to sound intelligent, anyway." Merry met her eyes and studied her frankly. "On the subject of your life on the island, however, I think I can do better."

"You met with Sky Friday."

"So he's told you."

"Yes. He also told me to lock the garage and fly to New York. I've disobeyed him."

"I thought he might tell you to leave the country. He seems ready to do anything to save you, Ms. Stern."

Mayling's entire form became still. She started to speak, and could not. Merry Folger was looking at her again, and under the green force of the eyes that held neither warmth nor pity, only waiting, she understood the depth of what she meant.

"Why should he be?" she said finally, each word dropping like a stone into a cold sea.

"Mr. Tate-Jackson is concerned about the mangled front end of your car. Probably about the button lost from your sweater. And the hours you can't remember, the night that Rusty died."

Merry's face, ever more intent, came toward her now. Mayling leaned away from her in panic.

"And your hands, holding the pages of the letter Rusty sent to Sky, the morning Peter found you in the studio. After he found his brother's body on his doorstep."

Mayling's fists were locked tightly over her ears, and her mouth formed the word *no* in a soundless refrain.

"Why didn't you tell me about the Mercedes, Mayling? What are you afraid of? The fact that Sky got that letter from Rusty, and you knew about it—knew he was blackmailing Sky—before his body was found, and not after, as Sky is saying?"

"No!" she said, and the word came out with explosive force this time. "You're all wrong! All wrong! I had no reason to kill Rusty, even if everything else you say is true."

"The button, the bumper, the letter—all of it?"

"All except the letter. That's where you're wrong. I read the letter you mean, but it wasn't until Labor Day. Rusty was already dead."

"Can you prove that?"

Mayling was silent.

"You were reading the letter when Peter surprised you in the studio. Rusty was already dead at that point. But there's nothing to prove you hadn't read it before. Peter said you looked like you'd seen a ghost when he walked in—as perhaps you had. You may have thought, at first glance, that he was Rusty—insufficiently dead and back for his revenge."

Mayling stared at Merry, oddly composed. She had gone so deeply into her fear that it no longer had the power to move her.

"I wasn't reading Rusty's letter. You may be right in thinking Sky got it earlier than he says—I don't know. He didn't show it to me until the evening of Labor Day. When he knew it didn't matter anymore."

"Because he knew Rusty was dead."

Mayling nodded. "He needed to talk to someone. That's when I began to be afraid, Detective. So afraid."

Merry studied her intently, the idea coming clearer. "That Sky had killed Rusty?"

"Yes. He was late, you see, the night before." She took a ragged breath and locked her fingers together over her mouth to stop its trembling.

Merry leaned back in the lawn chair, her face very still. "The airline attendant remembers him arriving at eight-thirty."

"He may have," Mayling said. "I don't remember." She paused. "He told you about my—my problem."

"Your blacking out."

She nodded. "He put me to bed when I showed up at the house, around eleven-thirty, and I fell into a restless sort of sleep. He didn't come upstairs for a long time. When he did, he gave me a sleeping pill and kissed me good night. He said he was going out for a walk on the beach—that he couldn't sleep. I knew he was upset about me; I thought it was nothing more than that. I woke up around eight-thirty the next morning."

"What did you mean when you said he was late?"

She looked at Merry, her black eyes unreadable. "I mean, late coming back from the beach. I mean, Detective, that I don't think he ever came to bed that night. And I can't stand the worry. Because he told me, that morning, that I'd crashed the car the night before. And I don't remember doing it. I've been wondering, for days, if he did it himself.

When he killed Rusty. While I slept, drugged, at his hand."

"Would Sky let you believe you were responsible for Rusty's murder, rather than take the rap himself?"

"I don't know," Mayling said. "That's the most horrible thing of all. I can't bear to be with him, Detective, because of not knowing. And I'm too terrified to ask." She huddled like a broken-winged bird on her chaise, the glossy photos in a heap at her feet.

"Mayling," Merry said, "what were you reading when Peter found you that morning?"

She hesitated, blushed, and then looked away. "Sky's letters," she said. "He gets them, from his mother, every week. He never opens them, you see, but I do."

She focused on the sea, letting the glare off the waves flood her sight. "I fill a kettle with water and wait for it to steam. Then I open the envelope carefully with a nail file, read the letter, and put it back in the drawer where he keeps all of them, unopened. I keep hoping she'll change her mind. But we'll never know, will we, if he doesn't read them?"

"Change her mind about what?"

She smiled bitterly. "Hating me. That's my life. I live with a man I've loved more than anyone—and yet think is capable of murder—and whose mother calls me a mongrel whore from the garment district not fit to marry her son. She's never accepted his love for me. She never will."

Merry sat up. "She's opposed to your marrying? After all these years of living together?"

"You'd have to know Gwendolyn Tate-Jackson. A direct descendant of the New York Junker class, the Knickerbocker Club, the Four Hundred. I met her once, you see," Mayling said, "so I know what she is capable of." She turned to Merry, a woman talking to another woman now.

"It was at the Park Avenue apartment. She made me wait in the kitchen with the housekeeper while she told Sky what she thought of our plans to marry. Their shouting came through the walls, Detective. Horrible, vituperative things. People of that class suppress feeling for so long—in the name of decency—that when they explode, their words are unforgivable. I was mortified. And the housekeeper betrayed not the slightest interest—in me, in what they said—as though she were deaf and I were invisible." She paused, her mind adrift in a familiar nightmare. "Sky never went back."

Merry thought of Sky's patrician face, the courtesy that masked profound fear and anger, and understood something of the stress that weighed on Mayling's mind. One reason for the occasional blackouts perhaps, the inexplicable dread. But she said only, gently, "I'm sorry, Ms. Stern. If I were you, I'd say the hell with it and marry him tomorrow."

"I won't do it," Mayling said. "I'll never enter a family that doesn't want me. I won't give them the satisfaction." She brushed away her tears. "And I'm afraid now, Detective. Of what, exactly, Sky might have done. The not knowing is worse than any knowledge."

Chapter 30

THE SMALL PROP PLANE OUT OF HYANNIS was the kind that didn't have a stewardess or in-flight catering; and at takeoff, the right engine tugged so wildly in a different direction from the left that the pilot aborted the attempt, taxied off the runway, and pulled down a technical manual from the shelf above his head. Alison could see all of this because there was no curtain—much less a door—between the cockpit and the passengers. She felt a tidal wave of panic surge from her feet to the roots of her hair as, his consultation with his documents finished, the pilot brought the plane back around to face the runway. *I'm going to die,* she thought. *This is how it happens. He looked at the owner's manual, for God's sake. Why did I ever, ever, come back to this coast?*

In the course of her constant travel she experienced all the stages of behavior common to terminally ill patients: Denial (*I'm not really here, I'm really in my own bed*); anger (*I'm too intelligent to be this afraid*); bargaining (*If you just let me live this time, God, I'll never get on a plane again*); depression (*I've spent my whole life in pursuit of success, and my last meal will be airplane food*); and finally, acceptance (*I've placed my life in the motor skills of a man I've never met, and that's okay, really, that's fine*).

The plane bumped and surged down the runway, both engines working in concert this time, and tentatively, diffidently, lifted into the air. Her panic increased. She gripped the bottom of her seat and wished desperately for in-flight catering. She hated flying without a drink.

.　　.　　.

PETER WAS LEANING against a pillar, losing a battle with his calm, when she appeared at the gate, and for several seconds, he looked past her. He was searching for a college kid with long, unstyled hair and a graceful dancer's frame, wearing jeans or a loose sundress with a cardigan sweater. He was looking for the past, and the present arrived.

"Peter!"

The voice riveted him, as ever it had. He cast about wildly.

"Here!"

She stood barely ten yards from him, a wide grin on her face, any strangeness banished by the sudden joy of colliding with her past. He was rooted to the ground at the sight of her. The years had dealt indifferently with Alison, writing lines across her forehead, sharpening the jut of her cheekbones, shafting her dark hair with premature strands of gray. The dancer's body looked now like an athlete's—less graceful than it was strong, less lithe than it was lean. She was dressed in black linen walking shorts and a matching jacket; her shoes were discreetly Italian and very chic. She had become the sort of woman he would admire from a distance and find disturbingly self-sufficient. More than anything, her appearance drove home the passage of the years between them as nothing in his life alone had done. He walked toward her and didn't know what to do when he arrived.

"Alison." He settled for the safest gesture of his genteel childhood—the airy brushing of cheek against cheek, as though he were an art dealer and she a very special client. He hated himself for his awkwardness. "You look wonderful."

She saw the arm in the sling then, and her brilliant smile faded.

"Take a fall from a horse?"

"Something like that. I'll tell you about it later. How was the flight?"

288

"Godawful. They always are. I'm never so thankful, or breathless, as when I emerge alive from a plane."

To his surprise, a sudden vivid flash of Merry Folger's face—excited, electric, suffused with the vicarious thrill of flight—burned into his brain. He shook himself slightly. Alison was speaking.

"You're looking well yourself. I didn't actually expect you to meet me, but it's good to see you. I seem to remember this airport isn't that far from town. I hope I'm not inconveniencing you with the drive . . ." She was speaking rapidly, trying to fill silence, a cover for her nervousness, he knew.

"Not at all," he said. "I wouldn't have left you to the taxi service for anything in the world. I'm parked right out front. Is this your only bag?"

"I've learned to travel light," she said. What he heard was, *I'm not staying long.*

·   ·   ·

SHE DIDN'T SPEAK much in the Rover, just let the setting sun strike her cheek in lengthening red rays. The soft island wind flooded the open window with the scent of the sea and the faintest whiff of pine and heather off the moors. Peter, still steering and shifting with one hand, gave her a few bad moments; but the Old South Road was straight and empty enough for erratic driving, and she relaxed. It had been so long since she had smelled these smells and felt this tranquillity emanating from the very shingles of the houses. Unbeknownst to herself, she sighed deeply, and Peter gave her a look from the corner of his eye.

"Are you worn out? It's a long trip from California."

"Made worse by fear of flying," she said. "I'm completely drained when I get off a plane. I can barely walk. But this place makes up for everything. It's so restful, Peter. I know I'll sleep well tonight."

"Where are you staying?" he said.

"I hadn't thought about a hotel, to tell you the truth—I got Sky's call and caught a plane in a matter of hours." Too late, she heard how her words must sound to him—as though she were fishing for lodging. She bit her lip and looked at him quickly. He was gathering himself to open his home to her, and she could see the effort it cost him.

"You're welcome to stay—"

"How about if we try that nice brick place?" she broke in hurriedly.

He was silent an instant, regrouping. "The Jared Coffin House."

"That's it."

Constraint fell between them. He downshifted at the rotary and struggled with the wheel; she debated whether it would bother him if she reached a hand to steer, and cursed herself for her awkwardness. "What happened to your shoulder?"

"Somebody took a shot at me," he said casually. His gray eyes flicked over to hers, carefully, to judge her reaction, and then moved back to the road. "What took you to California?"

End of conversation about the killer, Alison thought, and drew in a sharp breath. "I'd run out of alternatives. I'd tried everywhere else. And I managed to get a job, one reason I stayed."

"Doing what?"

"News reporting. For the second-largest newspaper in the state," she said, and then laughed shortly. "Trust me to choose a dying profession. Print journalism has the half-life of a flashbulb, particularly in California, where anything that happened yesterday qualifies as history. I don't know, Peter—sometimes I think about going back to school, getting a law degree, maybe—and then I wonder whether I'm too old."

"Never ask that question, Alison, it's a sure sign you're aging. Assume you can do anything, and you'll stay young."

She studied his set face an instant, wondering what nerve she'd touched, feeling absurdly hurt, and then stared out the window at the new businesses on Orange Street. "Peter, this town has grown so much," she exclaimed.

"The eighties were a developer's paradise," he said wryly. "You didn't miss much."

"I'll always miss this island," she said impulsively. "Somewhere in the depths of my soul I'll carry it with me forever."

Her words wrung Peter's heart.

"The things we've loved deeply never leave us, Alison," he said. "That's the special curse of caring."

This time, she didn't dare to look at him.

DEATH IN THE OFF-SEASON

•   •   •

A WEEK AFTER LABOR DAY, and a Sunday evening at that, Alison had the pick of the rooms at the Jared Coffin House. Peter left her there with her luggage; she was still on California time and thought it too early to eat. For his part, he was flushed with a weariness born of the previous night's stress. Exhaustion was the only name he'd dared to give the sense of loss that had crept over him in the Rover, sitting next to the woman he loved. Or had thought he loved. The new Alison was a stranger, complete in her own life, and his was gone.

An impassable ache was in his throat, blocking his breathing, and a pain was growing behind his eyes. He threw the car into gear with his good arm and maneuvered his way up Centre Street, searching for a spot to turn around. Then he idled an instant in the road, and came to a decision. He would visit the house.

Mid-September twilight was coming down over the streets of the town like fog of another order; and with it, a briskness in the air. Yellow light spilled out of a few windows, and straggling tourists—a father with a child trudging at his heels, a mother following along behind—ducked along the cobblestones in search of home. The season was finding its natural end. Houses owned by off-islanders, like children left too late on an empty playground, showed lost and darkened faces to the street. He urged the Rover farther and farther into the dusk, until the sidewalks dropped away and the terrain began to climb; he was on the Cliff Road.

The Mason house stood—as it had for a century and a half—on high ground overlooking Nantucket Sound. Lonely women had paced its hallways and hung by its windows, waiting and craning to see the first small flare of a sail on the horizon. Whale oil had paid for its wood and bricks, shipped over the seas to the island; and whale oil had filled it with treasure, a monument to the power of Nantucket's captains and the Mason name. Now his father's estate kept it from falling to wrack and ruin; only the Whitney children ran through its rooms, and then only for a few weeks. His mother had not come to the island since her husband's death and her eldest son's flight.

He turned off the ignition and sat a moment in the stillness of the place, the hedges and the height of the widow's walk dreaming in the darkness; then he got out to search for memory. The sun had gone down completely now, and he moved like a shadow, a memory himself, through the opening in the hedge and down the gravel walk. The hydrangeas—dark mounds of secret coolness—were pocketed with last blooms. Now he heard the surf, far below off Jetties Beach, and the tearing cries of gulls diving toward evening.

At the doorway he stopped, and craned his neck back to stare up at the windows: the last light was glimmering off the old panes. The keys to the house were in the Rover's glove compartment, but he had no desire to walk through the empty rooms. Instead, he turned and made his way around the house to the back terrace, and the lawns that stretched to the fence at the cliff's edge. Beyond it, Nantucket Sound swept to the horizon, alive and wavering under a rising moon.

He stopped at the edge of the flagstones and pulled up a wrought-iron chair. A flaking of rust came away in his palm. Uncaring, he turned the chair toward the sea, threw himself into it, and sighed deeply. He was alone in the midst of the world and the night, and he was at peace.

Here on this lawn he had beaten George at croquet, with the set she'd been given for her eighth birthday, rocketing her bright orange ball from the terrace to the fence until she howled with disappointment. He had trained his first dog—a chocolate Labrador named Mud Pie—to dig up his mother's roses. In the shadow of the hedge his father had taught him how to swing a golf club; he had chipped a ball through the kitchen window. He had set off firecrackers near the hurricane cellar and thrown water balloons at Rusty's head from the safety of the widow's walk. Now George's children rediscovered the rituals of generations of Masons, unaware that the endless days of their summer months were already passing into memory. He envied and pitied them at once.

He stood up and walked slowly down the lawn toward the sea. This was where the tent had stood, and the dance floor with the carefully draped tables; here the guests flown in from New York and the jazz orchestra. He ignored their ghosts and moved beyond, to the circle of moonlight falling on the grass just past the tent's farthest stake. Long after the fireworks had ended and the guests had gone home—when the others had fallen into bed and a dreamless sleep—he had danced with Alison in the moonlight, a slow, endless waltz that had ended in their lovemaking. The earth had been damp with the falling dew and tangy with salt spray; her skin had still held the heat of her sunburn. The surf had broken in tumult against the pilings of Jetties Beach, and he had desired nothing so much in his life as her skin under his hands.

The first two years after it all ended, when he was living in this house alone, he had returned to this spot as a tongue seeks a damaged tooth, probing the pain. He had never failed to find it. He shivered uncontrollably now in the darkness and turned back to the house. The emptiness of the place was too vivid. His father was gone, Rusty was dead, and his mother estranged; Alison had moved beyond him. It was time for Mason Farms, and sleep.

Halfway to the terrace he stopped, alert to a change in the listening stillness of the empty house: he was no longer alone. A finger of danger caressed his spine, and he held his breath, tensed for the slightest sound. The throbbing in his left shoulder mounted to a crescendo of warning. Someone was sitting in the wrought-iron chair he had left on the terrace.

"Hello, Peter," Alison said, her voice low and filled with calm, like darkness made human. "So you came back, too."

Chapter 31

MERRY'S BLAZER CAME TO A rolling stop next to the weathered obelisk standing in the center of upper Main Street. She jumped out, her arms filled with late dahlias culled from Ralph Waldo's flower beds. Six o'clock on a Monday morning, a bright September day by the look of things, and twelve hours of solid sleep had cleared her head. She glanced back down Main to the business district, searching for too-observant eyes; but there was little traffic abroad as yet. The town was gripped in the early stillness she loved. Quickly, she hiked her right leg over the wrought-iron chain that set the war memorial off from the cobblestoned street and laid the dahlias at its base in a plastic vase of water. Twenty-three years ago, on this day, Billy had pushed Rafe away from an exploding mine. Her father wouldn't come here, she knew; Billy's name wasn't even on the memorial, at the police chief's request. John Folger had hated the Vietnam War, and he refused to call Billy a hero. The death of his son was an unforgivable waste, not something to enshrine.

Merry had mixed feelings about the war memorial. Billy's body had never come back from Nam. This was the only grave she had, the sole object of her difficult and grudging tears, the one spot where she could throw late flowers tended by the grandfather Billy had loved. She reached out a hand to touch the rough stone briefly, her throat constricting, and then she turned to go.

She had been awakened from her nap the previous evening by a call from Rafe, holding vigil with Tess at Mass General. His voice had cracked with weariness, and his tolerance for talk was short. He needed clothes for Tess—of course, she had flown out on Will's helicopter with nothing but the shirt on her back—and a shirt or two of his own. He'd tried to reach Peter, but the guy must have taken the phone off the hook—nobody at the farm was answering. Would she stop by the Greengage and pick up some things? And then drive out to the farm, maybe, for his? Whenever she could manage it. He'd pick 'em up from the mail plane that evening in Boston. Or maybe, if Peter planned to come over to the hospital, he could bring the clothes with him. . . .

There was no change in Will.

So here she was, groping for Tess's spare key in the hiding place behind a shingle, letting herself into the kitchen of the deserted Greengage. It looked far different today than it had the previous week, when Merry had met Tess over her melon salsa and muffin tins; the stove was cold and the room unlit. Tess had been called out to Cottage Hospital Friday night in the midst of her dishes; Sammy and Regina had cleaned up after her. The large pots were upended, like discarded party hats, to drain on the counters. After the brightness of the fall day, the half-light of the kitchen dampened Merry's spirits.

A light tapping on the panes of the back door made her jump, and she turned around quickly. A boy's face was framed in the glass. At the sight of her it took on an expression of caution and reserve she recognized. He'd have seen the Blazer outside, with its Nantucket police shield.

"Hi," she said as she hauled open the door. "What can I do for you?"

"Is Will home, ma'am?"

"Nope." She smiled at him, hoping he'd relax. "Who are you?"

"I—I go to school with him. Will he be back soon, d'ya know? It's kinda important."

His voice broke embarrassingly on the last word, and he flushed. A boy on the verge of being something else, she thought, and pretty bad at it. Broad shoulders that were no match for his skinny waist and legs. She studied his face, not knowing this one, but conscious she had seen him before. Then it dawned on her.

"You're the football player," she said.

He flushed again and hung his head. "Yeah."

Merry stuck out her hand. "I'm Detective Meredith Folger," she said. "You got a name?"

He eyed her doubtfully and then took the proffered hand. "I'm Sandy Stewart," he said, and craned to look around her. "Is Will's mom here?"

"Come on in, Sandy, and have a seat." She opened the door wide and stood to one side, tapping the back of an oak chair drawn up to Tess's work table. "Will had an accident on his bike Friday night and had to go to the hospital."

"He did?" Sandy's eyes widened, and to her surprise, he looked over his shoulder. "You sure it was an accident?"

Merry's eyes narrowed, and she said nothing, waiting for him to sit down. After a grudging moment, he did.

"Actually, Sandy, you're a smart kid," she said comfortably, easing herself into a neighboring chair. "It wasn't exactly an accident. Somebody staked a wire across the path through the moors that Will takes from Mason Farms to the Milestone Road. You know anything about that?"

Fear filled his eyes suddenly, and he shrank away from her into his seat. He definitely knew something.

"Is he gonna be all right?"

"He's got a fractured skull, and he's in a coma. They flew him to Boston for tests. I don't know much more than that." She assessed his fear and took a gamble, leaning toward him confidentially.

"If he ever comes out of it, he may be able to tell us something about who did this to him. And if it's a trick, Sandy—played on Will by the football team, maybe?—a lot of people are going to get even. And it'll be worse yet if he doesn't make it. Believe me when I say that. You can tell your buddies, too."

Sandy's mouth opened and he tried to speak, but no sound came forth. Instead, tears of anger welled in his eyes, and he threw himself out of the chair toward the door. She reached for him, but he shook off her hand and pulled at the doorknob, wild to be outside.

"You're wrong, you know," he shot at her over his shoulder. "You're totally wrong." Then he was gone, pedaling furiously toward school on his bike.

• • •

"IT'S LIKE NOTHING I've ever seen." Alison was staring out over the bog's tangle of maroon vines and scarlet fruit, running from her feet to the line of marshland in the southwest that marked the verge of Gibbs Pond.

"I know," Peter said, and he was quiet for an instant, caught short by his love for this land and his way of life. "You'll have to stop by tomorrow, when I'll be wet-harvesting again, and see what the proverbial red tide really looks like. In spring, when the vines are in flower, it's spectacular in a different way."

"What color are they?"

"Pinkish-white. They look like long-necked birds—hence the name, or one theory of the name, at least. 'Crane-berries' became 'cranberries' over time."

"It's a belt of solitude, isn't it, Peter?"

"The bog?"

"All of it. The house, this land, the unobstructed view, even the distance from town. At night you must feel as if you're utterly alone on earth, and master of it."

"I do," he said. It was like Alison to see the freedom in the solitude and not mistake it for isolation, or incurable loneliness. He was suddenly thankful for that.

He had risen early to tend to the sheep, feeling Rafe's absence keenly. By midmorning he had been at the Jared Coffin House, hoping Alison had conquered jet lag and the weariness that must have come on the heels of their nocturnal walk through the back streets of Nantucket town. He had found the woman he knew again, somewhere in the darkness—not the object of his passion, but the best friend he had missed inexpressibly through the years. No one had known him as well as she, before her or since; and he knew in his heart of hearts that no one ever would again.

He had told her of Rusty's death—and of his illness, of the bitterness that had filled his letters; of his banishment and loss, the worlds he had never conquered. She remained silent through most of it, her head down in the darkness as they passed the unlit and shuttered houses. He had not known she was crying until his halting tale came to an end and, in the silence, she drew a ragged breath. He had turned to her then and held her, to comfort and not to woo her, and she had broken down completely in the middle of India Street.

"His soul was warped, Peter," she said. "Nothing and no one could ever make it right. Not even me. *Not even me.* And I thought I could take it—the lack of love, the coldness, the way he enjoyed humiliating me—because I told myself he needed me. I told myself over and over again. Why else would he have done what he did to you? Why else would I—" She looked up at him then, her tears stilled and her face composed. "Rusty needed no one."

Especially not us, he thought, *we who are so much alike, and are everything he envied, everything he despised. The ones who would have died for him. We gave our love, both of us, to lost causes, and we're finally old enough to admit it.*

"That's all past, Alison," he had said, very quietly, and they had walked on.

He shook himself out of reverie and turned to look at her now, all her ghosts banished, her face alive in morning sun. It was incomprehensible that she had never been here with him before, and unthinkable that she should ever leave. As she would, all too soon.

"Let's eat," he said.

He handed her the photograph from Rusty's waterlogged gym bag when she had finished her tuna fish sandwich. They were sitting on the wooden deck at the back of the saltbox, and Alison had discarded her sandals. Ney lay blissfully under her chair while she traced slow circles in his fur with the tip of her big toe. Whenever she stopped, Ney raised his head in outrage, cocking one ear in her direction, and then sank down with a clink of his tags as her foot resumed its perambulations across his stomach. The dog had accepted her immediately, a sign, Peter decided, of his intuitive link with his master.

Her brow furrowed as she looked at Peter's father and the unknown woman, and after a moment she grew very still. Peter let her study the photo in peace, but he saw that Schuyler Tate-Jackson was right. Alison knew who the woman was.

"Well," she said finally, tossing the picture on the table, "that's trouble."

"Meaning what?"

"I only met her once," she said. "When she walked up to our table in a restaurant downtown—and threw what your mother would term *a scene.*" Peter's lips twitched at that. "I assumed she was another one of Rusty's discarded women. We had an annoying tendency to encounter them in the most unlikely—and likely—places. But he treated this one differently."

"How?"

She took a sip of iced tea. "He was afraid of her."

"Afraid of her? Rusty?"

Alison nodded. "Turns out she wasn't his girlfriend at all. She was your father's, Peter. And I think she was threatening to confront Julia."

He reached for the photograph and looked at Max's face. He had half known this, but had refused to admit it until it was absolutely necessary. His eyes slid over to the woman leaning toward the car. She was so young. She couldn't have been much older than Georgiana at the time. He glanced up and found Alison watching him, her eyes holding something like pity. "I don't understand," Peter said. "Why would Max's affair frighten Rusty?"

"I don't really know," Alison said. "I never saw her again, and we never spoke of it. I wasn't supposed to know about Max and this woman, you see, and I think Rusty figured the less said, the better."

"But you're sure he was frightened," Peter said.

"Oh, yeah," she said. "He wouldn't take her calls, he wouldn't speak of her; and he never told me why."

"About when was this?"

"Right before I left him."

"You left him?"

"You didn't know?"

Peter shook his head.

"Right after Thanksgiving. I heard he went to Brazil a couple of weeks later, and he dropped completely out of my life. Not that I was easy to find—I was fleeing my own demons."

He said nothing, but something in his face must have challenged her to name them. She did. "Guilt. Shame. And unutterable loss. In short, the knowledge that I had been a fool, and nothing could undo it."

He looked down at Ney, feeling no sense of victory, and took a deep breath. When he met her eyes she was fine again.

"This woman," he said. "Did you know her name?"

"It wasn't a real one," Alison said. "A nickname, I suppose. Now, what was it? Something odd, something made up, like Bambi. Or Sunny. Or—no, was it—"

"Sundance," Peter said. "Right on the money."

.   .   .

WHEN THE PHONE RANG he was expecting Rafe and praying under his breath for news of Will. But it was Lucy Jacoby on the line.

"I've decided to act instead of just thinking about it," she said. "I kicked myself for staying away when your brother died. I won't make the same mistake twice. How is Will?"

"You heard," Peter said. "I should have called you."

"Of course you should have. But you've probably been trying to find whoever did it, and personally, I think that's more worthwhile." She hesitated for a moment, and he sensed how upset she really was. "There were pretty gory stories running around the school today. I heard he was in Cottage Hospital, but I can't get any details. I figured you'd know the truth. How bad is it, Peter?"

"He's not coming out of the coma," Peter said gently, "and they've flown him to Boston. I'm planning to head over there myself, later today."

Lucy drew a shaky breath. "The poor little guy," she said. "Peter—there's something I have to know. It wasn't—he didn't try to kill himself, did he?"

"Good God, no," Peter said, shocked. "Where in the world did you get that idea?"

"I'm so glad," Lucy said. "Listen, I have something for Will. A book of Flaubert's short stories. They say it's possible that people in comas hear what's said to them. Tess could read these stories to Will. It might help—to bring him back."

"That's very good of you, Lucy. Drop the book by after school and I'll take it over tonight. In a few days, if we're lucky, he may be able to read them himself."

.   .   .

MERRY FOLGER HAD HER FEET up on her desk and her chair at a dangerous angle, rocking on two legs. Clarence Strangerfield's forensic report was spread before her, and it told her things that, unfortunately, she already had guessed. The footprints taken from Peter Mason's driveway matched in size, although not in shoe style, the prints left two nights later under the tree near his house, where someone had waited for him to walk the dog to the barn. Any closer identification—without a pair of suspect shoes—was impossible. She reflected on the sloppiness of this particular murderer, and wondered what it meant. Were the prints someone else's, left by the killer to frame an innocent person? Or did they betray a serendipitous quality in the attacks—an unplanned series of opportunities seized, without time to prepare or cover one's tracks, as it were?

And then there were the fingerprints.

"Yo, Merry!"

She looked up. Matt Bailey was shouting at her from the doorway. "There's a kid outside wants to see you."

Her chair came down with a clunk. "Threats, unfortunately, work better than promises," she sighed, and walked to the door. Beyond it, squinting in the sun of the firehouse driveway, Sandy Stewart was straddling his bike. *He must feel more secure when he's sitting on it than he does inside*, she thought. She opened the door and walked over to him.

"I think I know why they hurt Will," he said, without preamble. His face was stony and his voice flat, signs he was here because he had no choice. He reached around for his school backpack and swung it off his shoulder. "They made a mistake," he said, pulling out *The Perpetual Orgy*. "It should have been me."

Chapter 32

PETER HAD LEFT THREE MESSAGES for Rafe over the course of the morning, and none had been returned. He told himself that meant nothing—Will might be just the same, and Rafe and Tess taking some much-needed rest. Or Will could be in the midst of the tests the Cottage Hospital had flown him to Boston to receive. He pushed aside the thought that Rafe was riveted to the boy's bedside, unaware of Peter's calls, because Will was fighting for his life.

So he leaped for the phone when it rang again, and again he was disappointed.

"Peter!"

"Buck," he said, his voice flagging.

"Well, am I ever the consolation prize today," Buck Maplethorne said, nettled. "You'd think I was trying to sell snowplows in June, with all the response I've been getting."

"No harm meant, Buckie, I'm just waiting on someone else's call, that's all."

"Well, I won't keep you. Just called to say your beater's in, so you're all set for harvesting tomorrow, and you can come by anytime to pick it up."

"Thanks," Peter said. At least driving was preferable to waiting.

He left Alison on the deck with a book and Ney settled at her feet, took the battered Ford that served Mason Farms as an all-purpose hauler, and drove off without a thought.

. . .

MONDAYS IN MID-SEPTEMBER were quiet at Maplethorne's, with the summer folks gone and the island hunkering down for wet weather. Peter found Buck unloading ficus trees bound for his greenhouse.

"You *are* Johnny-on-the-Spot," the nurseryman said. "Things must be real slow up t'a farm. Hey, I've got a great snowplow I can sell you. Cheap." He grinned, his broad face betraying none of the financial worries that had beset his life since starting the business. Peter was one of his best customers. He placed orders in winter, when the off-islander petunia market was long gone.

Buck led him to where the yellow metal beater sat under a tree, awkward and purposeless on dry land. "It's a beaut. And you're only paying the five days. Have it back to me by noon Friday and we're set."

"You're a godsend, Buck," Peter said, "but you're going to have to help me get it into the truck. I can't lift it alone with this arm."

"Hey, you're not lifting it at all. Daniel!" he yelled, cupping his mouth with one hand in the direction of the green house. Buck's seventeen-year-old son came at a trot. "Let's get this eggbeater into Mr. Mason's truck."

Daniel nodded abruptly in Peter's direction and bent to his task, with utter disregard for his back or the proper mechanics of lifting. The yellow metal frame rose triumphantly into the air and settled onto the floor of the old Ford. Buck winked at Peter. "Wouldn't want you to have to get it off the truck when you get home, either. You wait for one of your crew, you hear me? Say, how are you driving that thing with one hand?"

"Recklessly," Peter said. "Thanks a lot, Buck. I'll see you Friday."

"God Almighty," Buck Maplethorne said, slapping his forehead as Peter climbed carefully into the cab. "I'll be forgetting my name next. Almost slipped past me. I found that rose you're wanting."

"You did?" Peter's head came around the open window.

"Yep. Least, found the name. The rose'll be a bit of a job."

304

"If you've got the name, we can order it."

"If it were a commercially grown hybrid, sure. But it's not."

Buck was intent upon enjoying his tale. Peter turned off the ignition and opened the truck door. "Go ahead, Buckie."

"Well, first I tried comparing it to the commercial catalogues—and it didn't match any of the pictures. So I looked at it some more—started comparing leaflets and thorn patterns—and decided it wasn't rightly a hybrid tea. Looks like it's got some Hybrid Perpetual in it, and that scent—well, you know as well as I do that a hybrid tea doesn't smell like that. There's Musk rose somewhere in that flower's ancestry. So I looked in the classic rose catalogues for some of the antique varieties. Came up short there—yours didn't match any of the old ones, the color's too unusual—and that almost stumped me. Then I thought of calling the American Rose Society."

"Something that would never occur to me."

"Well, exactly. And guess what I asked them."

"I haven't the faintest."

"For a description of recent hybrids of your color, thorn patterns, and leaflet, probably crossed from a modern tea—say, Tropicana—and an old rose, probably itself a hybrid from the true Musk. And they got back to me this morning. I think we've got it."

"A remarkable piece of detective work and dedication to my garden. I wouldn't know where to start."

"Sure you would," Buck said comfortably. "You'd call me."

"A new old rose," Peter said thoughtfully. "Sort of like Mason Farms. I like it. It fits. What's its name, by the way?"

"Sundance," Buck said. "But the pip'll be to find it. The old lady who cultivated it has never put it on the market. There's probably only one or two of these bushes in the whole country."

"You know who cultivated it?" Peter said, as nausea began to well in his stomach. He thought he could name the woman himself.

"Lady by the name of Mary Scott," Buck said cheerfully. "Lives in Westchester County somewheres."

"I know," Peter said. "I'm sorry, Buck, but I've got to get back to the farm."

He was gone before the nurseryman could answer.

305

. . .

MERRY PULLED UP TO THE saltbox on the moor and scanned the blank windows. Rafe was right. Peter wasn't at the house—probably somewhere in town with Alison Miller. She stifled a vague sense of unease and told herself that there was nothing unusual in Peter's sightseeing with a friend. But the short hair on the back of her neck was tingling uncontrollably.

She had come for Rafe's clothes and should have headed straight for the barn. She was bound for Lucy Jacoby's house as soon as she got the clothes to the mail plane at the airport. But she followed the tingling on her neck and walked around the back of the house, searching for some sign of life, something she couldn't identify.

Ney pulled himself to his feet, stretching luxuriously in greeting as she mounted the three steps to the deck. She saw the emptied iced tea glasses and the deserted chairs ranged around a mortally dangerous photograph. They had been here not long before, and they had left in a hurry. With a sense of foreboding, she pulled open the cover of the book of Flaubert's short stories, left carelessly on the table near the snapshot of Max Mason and the woman he had loved; she saw the name on the flyleaf and began to swear.

She ran back to the Blazer, heart pounding, and threw it into gear. *Lucy Jacoby.* Whose letter from Rusty—addressed to Sundance—had been inadvertently left in the copy of *The Perpetual Orgy* she'd given to Will. Who had knocked Will off his bike that same evening, desperate to search his backpack while he lay concussed on the moor nearby. Lucy, who hadn't been able to find the book, and had probably spent a weekend of suspense and remorse, wondering who had it. Lucy, whose fingerprints on a bottle of wine matched the prints left on a wooden button, from a sweater she claimed to have given away. Lucy, who stood, dressed to the nines, against the door of a car owned by Maxwell Mason.

Lucy, who had stopped by Peter's house, and found Alison Miller—the one person who could positively identify her as Sundance, link her to Rusty, and define her motive for murder: revenge.

If only she wasn't too late.

Chapter 33

U P IN THE COOL DIMNESS OF her loft bedroom, Lucy had Rafe's nine-millimeter Browning—the one she had taken from the barn the night she shot Peter—trained on Alison, whose hands and feet were bound. Lucy had recognized her as soon as she raised her head from her book, smiled a greeting, and said, "You must be Lucy." But she had forced down the hysteria that had gripped her at the sight of this face from Peter's past, from her own recurring nightmare. Alison had offered her iced tea. She had accepted. The two women sat and chatted about Flaubert, about Will, and about the island; and then Lucy suggested that since Peter had abandoned them both, they should take a drive through the moors. There was a pumpkin farm out toward Tom Nevers. Had she seen Tom Nevers? Alison couldn't remember. There was no time like the present, after all. Lucy dropped her copy of Flaubert on the deck table, so that if Peter came back he'd know she'd stopped by; he might think Alison had returned to town, or simply wandered off. With luck, he wouldn't look for the woman for hours.

It was only later, in Lucy's car, that Alison realized who she was.

• • •

"I'M NOT GOING TO HURT YOU," Lucy said now, laying the gun down on her bookcase. "It's just that I need a couple of hours. To pack. So I can get off the island before anybody knows." She turned to her closet and pulled a suitcase down from the top shelf.

Alison shifted slightly to ease the strain in her shoulders. Her wrists were painfully snug in the small of her back. "But I know, Lucy," she said quietly. "And I doubt you'll ignore that."

Lucy's hands stilled for an instant, and she looked at Alison nakedly, her eyes wounded and cloudy. "I know you think I'm danger-ous because I—because of—Rusty. But that has so little to do with me. It was just a moment that happened." Her voice faltered and broke. "You don't have to be afraid of me."

"Will Starbuck wasn't afraid of you," Alison said, "and he's in a coma. Explain that one."

Lucy flinched and dropped the pair of jeans she had been distract-edly folding. "It was a mistake," she whispered. "How cruel of you to say that. How cruel of you!"

"You're telling me you didn't set that wire on the path? You didn't intend to knock Will off his bike? Or maybe you expected it to be Peter."

"No!" She sat down unsteadily and put her head in her hands. "Nothing's worked right since the night Rusty came back. Before then, really—since the night I got his letter."

"Rusty blackmailed you."

"Yes," Lucy said distractedly, and glanced up at the skylight and then over to the window. Fearful of discovery, she had drawn the shades down tightly. "Or at least, that's what he intended to do."

"He came here, to your house," Alison said.

"I ran into him on the ferry from Hyannis. I hid in the women's room, and when the boat docked, I thought I'd lost him. But he must have followed me straight back to the house, after he picked up that rental car—he had my address, you know. He'd sent the letter here."

"How did he know you were on Nantucket?"

"I don't know," she said. "Sky Jackson, maybe. He was in touch with Rusty, I think, and he may have given him news of Peter, and Peter's friends. Rusty would have known the name Lucy Jacoby. It's part of my full name—Lucy Jacoby Scott. It wouldn't have taken him long."

"All those years ago, Lucy—why did you come here?"

Lucy stood up and walked to the window, blind now behind its shade, and looked toward where the sea should be. "I wanted to be close to places Max had loved," she said, "and New York and Greenwich were out. And then there's the real reason—you can get completely lost on an island this small, or so I thought. You can be the person you decide to be. You can have a private life. I so wanted those things, desperately. My father had left me some money—even Grandpa couldn't take that away—and I could live well here. Quietly. With my books, my garden, and my classroom. Five years—I had almost begun to heal.

"And then he had to come. It was so like him. He couldn't stand to see anyone happy."

"Did you plan to kill Rusty?" Alison said.

Lucy stared at her an instant, as if seeing again Rusty's silhouette in the fog. "I didn't mean to," she said. "When he showed up here, at my house, I offered to drive him to Peter's house, where he could spend the night. I couldn't bear to have him in my home. My car was in the shop—I'd ridden my bike to and from the ferry. But Rusty had a Jeep." Her voice quavered momentarily, then recovered, and went on. "I drove, since the fog was bad and he didn't know where Mason Farms was. He laughed at me all the way over to Peter's, saying he had half a mind to tell him who I was that very night—that I'd been in love with Max, and now I was in love with his son."

Her eyes flicked to Alison's, and then she started, as if remembering time was short, and scooped a heap of T-shirts and shorts into her arms. She threw the clothes, willy-nilly, into the suitcase and looked again at the woman on the bed. Tears were welling in her eyes. "He called me Max's mistress. It wasn't like that—it wasn't some crass exchange of sex for money. But Rusty had a way of making everything dirty, even memories."

"I know," Alison said, almost inaudibly.

"He got out to open the gate, and as I looked at him in the headlights, I thought of all I'd lost because of him—Max's love, and then Max; my old life with my grandparents; and now my peace of mind and the quiet friendship I'd found in Peter. I'd never wanted anything more than that with Peter—there was a restraint between us he may never have understood, but that I had consciously constructed. I wanted to be *Lucy* to Peter, not Sundance, not someone who'd caused his father pain, not someone connected to Rusty—sullied by him. I couldn't have Rusty telling Peter anything about me. My sanity was too precious."

She laughed suddenly, bitterly. "That's rich, isn't it? My sanity was too precious, and so I destroyed it.

"I knew that I'd never be able to get away from him. He'd extort every last nickel I had. He was standing in front of the car, in the head-lights, unlatching the gate to the farm. And I . . ." Her voice trailed away, and then became stronger, with the memory of violent anger. "I just hit the gas. As hard as I could, as if that would make it be over faster."

She threw her hands up to cover her eyes. "Oh, God! It was horrible, so horrible. He flew into the air and landed on the hood of the car, like a—like a—*dead body*—and then he rolled off. I screamed. I almost drove off, right then, but I knew I couldn't. He'd recover and he'd prosecute me, and it would all come out anyway. Somehow I found the will to open the car door and—and look for him. He was knocked out, lying by the side of the road. I couldn't lift him; he was a dead weight—" At this, she giggled hysterically. "So I—I dragged him by his ankles up the driveway, terrified somebody from the house would hear the noise and come running—and then I—put him in the ditch. With his face in the water. I pushed it down, so that the water came up over his hair.

"And then I got the car out of there as fast as I could. I still had his luggage in the backseat."

There was a silence. "I understand how you must have hated him," Alison said.

At that moment, they both heard the quiet scrape of metal on metal. Someone was working at the back door's lock.

Lucy gave forth a stifled whinny of fear, her hands stuffed into her mouth. Then she bent to her drawer, picked up a cotton running sock and a scarf, and gagged Alison.

• • •

MERRY HAD HER SERVICE REVOLVER cocked as she inched her way through Lucy's back door. She threw a glance around the kitchen alcove, felt rather than saw the stillness of the empty main room, and flattened herself against the wall of the loft stairs. She began to creep toward the lowest step, holding her breath, sensing the bodies listening in the silence above her.

"I'm armed," a quavering voice called out. "I know you're there."

Merry came to a halt, her black brows crinkling. She said nothing.

"I have a gun against Alison's head. I'll kill her if you come any closer. Come out where I can see you."

So Alison was still alive, then. Merry's stomach muscles, tensed in an agony of apprehension, relaxed. "Don't make this any uglier than it has to be, Lucy," she said quietly to the empty space in front of her.

Overhead, a bedspring creaked. Merry listened for the direction of the footsteps, one set pulling, the other dragging, and knew they were nearing the edge of the stairs.

At that moment, the doorbell rang.

All three of them froze. Merry recovered first, seized the moment, and swung around to the bottom of the loft stairs, her gun trained on Lucy Jacoby's surprised head.

"Lucy! Lucy, are you there?"

It was Peter Mason's voice.

"Peter!" Lucy yelled. "I've got Alison and I've got a gun."

"Don't listen to her, Peter!" Merry called over her shoulder. "I've called for backup. We'll get 'em out of here." To Lucy she said quietly, "This can only end one way, you know. Make it easier on all of us, Lucy."

A debate was raging in Merry's mind. There was no place for bystanders like Peter in the line of fire. Then again, he had a special hold on Lucy Jacoby. Maybe he'd do more good inside the house than out. If things blew up in her face, and Peter Mason got hurt, it could cost her her job. She decided to take the risk. With the gun still trained on the English teacher's head, Merry backed toward the door. She fumbled one-handedly at the deadbolts Lucy had installed on the front door and pulled them back. Then she turned the knob and slid around the open door, using it to shield both her body and Peter's.

Peter stuck his head through the opening and, following the direction of Merry's pointed gun, saw Lucy standing at the edge of the loft, and Alison, fear suffusing her face. He inwardly cursed the day he'd bought the Browning.

"Let her go, Lucy," he said carefully. "This ends here."

"Oh, Peter—to lose you too," Lucy cried, her voice rising hysterically at the end of the phrase. She was near the breaking point.

Peter stared up at her ragged face, her flowing auburn curls, and felt a rush of pity. She had been hurt too young; she had survived; and finally, she had struck back. Through it all, she had held fast to her courage. And his father had loved her. But there was Alison—the gag around her mouth, her eyes wide and staring, the gleam of cold metal lodged perilously close to the delicate bone above her ear. He felt his entire body thrill with rage and fear.

"What do you want us to do, Lucy?"

"I want time to pack and the freedom to catch a plane."

"You want us to let you go," Merry said. "You know we can't do that."

Trembling, Lucy released the revolver's safety catch with an audible click. Alison swallowed and almost involuntarily strained a fraction of an inch away from death. That was enough for Merry.

"You're better than this, Lucy," she called to the woman. "You can't rewrite the past, but you can stop being Rusty's victim. You think he isn't loving this? He's looking down on us all and he's feeling pretty good. Because you've got his brother right where he'd like to have him. You're finishing the job for him, Lucy. But you don't have to be his pawn. You can let it all go," she said, as Lucy Jacoby's arm—the arm that held the gun—began to tremble, "and be free of him at last. Really free. Free as you haven't been since the day you met him, or the day you killed him. Let Alison go, Lucy. Nobody's going to hurt you anymore."

Lucy dropped the gun from Alison's temple and shoved her toward the steps. The woman, her feet still bound, hobbled helplessly. Merry tensed, pushing Peter behind her, uncertain whether Lucy Jacoby would use Alison's body as a shield for gunfire or let her go. In a half-crouch, her gun trained on Lucy's head, she scrambled toward the foot of the stairs.

It was then that they heard the report of the gun.

Chapter 34

LATER, WHEN LUCY JACOBY'S BODY had been taken away and Alison had been driven to the station to deliver her statement, Merry found Peter at the back of the house. He was standing next to the roses, and she didn't like the look on his face.

"Hey, Peter," she said.

He looked up and nodded curtly. "Thanks for being there when we needed you," he said.

Typical. Polite even when he believed she'd driven Lucy to her death. She thought of the woman lying inert in the body bag, felt herself grow faint, and shut her eyes. Another life ending too young, for no purpose. She should have prevented it. She should have known. Maybe if she'd had backup; or if she'd left Peter Mason out of it—

"How did you know she'd done it?" he said, breaking into her thoughts.

She opened her eyes. "Couple of things came together. I finally found a Lucy Jacoby in existence earlier than 1987—by searching computer records under partial names. Found out her last name was Scott, and her license was from New York. I remembered how Malcolm had looked when we showed him that photograph."

Peter nodded. "Max and Lucy must have met through Malcolm, that summer before Max's death. And Rusty found out. He followed them, took that photograph, and threatened Lucy with exposure—to my mother, to her grandparents. And then he used her fear of losing Max to get what he wanted—advance knowledge of Max's plans. And so Lucy slid more and more into a double life, yielding to Rusty in a desperate effort to cling to Max, fearing the uses to which Rusty would put his information, and dreading Max's wrath when he learned of what she had done."

"Until Hale decided to tell your father everything," Merry said. "That must have been a lousy day for Lucy."

"Because Max would never have forgiven her." Peter's face was harsh. Looking at him, Merry imagined she knew how Maxwell Mason must have looked on his bad days.

"There's no doubt, I suppose?" Peter said dully.

"Her fingerprints matched the ones on the button we found near Rusty's body. That alone wouldn't be enough—we knew she'd owned the sweater, and she could have lost the button at any time earlier than the day of the murder. But then there was Sandy Stewart."

Peter looked blank.

"Friend of Will's," Merry said. She took a step closer to him, disturbed by the remoteness of his face. Instead of reaching for him, she ran a thin hand through her thick hair. "Lucy gave Will a book in school on Friday, but she'd left something in it—the blackmail letter from Rusty, addressed to Sundance. It was the final version of the one we found in his gym bag."

"She gave that to Will?"

"She had to get the book back, Peter," Merry said. "That's why she knocked Will off the bike. Only she got it wrong—Will had given the book to Sandy without even reading it, poor kid. And Sandy read the letter. He came to me this afternoon."

Something in Peter's face stirred. "Had any news of him?"

Merry brightened. "Will? Rafe called a little while ago. He's come around. In all of this mess, I completely forgot to tell you. There's one thing." She hesitated, wondering if this was the time to tell Peter, and deciding she had no choice. "They think he's got some minor brain damage. Nothing that'll affect his intelligence," she said quickly, not wanting to cause him any more pain, "but he'll need some rehabilitation. Motor skills, stuff like that."

His face remained expressionless.

"The kind of thing you'd be great at helping him with."

At that, his eyes finally met hers, and she was pleased to see some life return to them.

"Run you back into town?"

He shook his head. "I've got the Rover here."

"Look," she said, groping, "I'm sorry it all had to work out this way."

"I am too," he said. "She was someone who deserved to be left in peace."

His voice cracked, and Merry, unaccustomed to emotion in Peter, felt her stomach lurch. She reached tentatively for his sleeve.

"She is, Peter," she said. "She's at peace. It's you who has to find some."

He laid his palm fiercely on hers, holding it fast to his sleeve, a shock. She felt a thrill course through her body and fought the impulse to jerk her hand away.

"I thought, for one instant, that she had fired at Alison. Then I thought that she had fired at you. And I was as destroyed by one possibility as the other." He could not look at her, and she stood, dumbfounded, willing the moment not to end.

It did. He released her hand and shook himself slightly.

"You didn't do half badly for your first homicide case, Detective. I think you've got a career."

"I hope not," Merry said, trying to find her voice. She cleared her throat. "I'd be happy never to handle another murder. It tears me apart."

"That's why you're good at it, Merry." He turned and looked at her intently. "You feel things deeply. You've forced me, despite myself, to feel as well. Nobody ever said it'd be easy. The hard things in life are the ones worth doing." There was a challenge in his eyes that she thought was meant for her, a challenge that ignored the past and looked toward the future.

He reached for the roses and, ignoring the thorns, tore off one of the last perfect blooms.

"Lucy believed that roses were good luck," he said. He handed the bloom to Merry.

Lucy's shattered skull and sightless eyes rose before her, a bloody reproach. She was dead, and it was Merry's fault. She backed slowly away from Peter Mason, away from the rose garden where he stood stock still, watching her.

His face settled into a careful mask. "I'll be down to the station to give my statement, Detective," he said gently.

•   •   •

LATER, AS SHE SAT SLUMPED over Ralph Waldo's intense iced tea in the kitchen of the house at Tattle Court, she cried. Ralph had one large, gnarled hand in her hair and the other supporting his chin. He sighed.

"Sounds to me like your father should be proud of you, Meredith Abiah."

She said nothing, her face buried in her arms.

"I'm proud of you," he said. "So enough of this talk of transferring to New Bedford. It's not where you belong."

"But Ralph," she said, lifting a tear-stained face, "I can't bear to stay on this island."

"And what would you be free of? Your family? Rafe da Silva? The messiness of murder?" He studied her an instant. "Or Peter Mason?"

She shrugged and buried her head.

"Meredith Abiah," he said sternly, "look at me and stop acting like Lady Macbeth in her last act. Lucy Jacoby ran from living. That's something no Folger does. She chose to take her own life, and nothing you said or did could make any difference. You know that, I know that. We're put on this earth to take what comes bravely, and you're no exception."

"You think I'm running away," she said quaveringly.

"I do indeed. And I'm shocked and saddened."

"Running away," she said slowly, "because I'm afraid of living. It's *too easy*, isn't it, Ralph?"

"What's too easy?" John Folger asked, stepping into the kitchen through the back door.

Merry brushed one sleeve across her eyes and smiled damply at Ralph Waldo. "This job you've given me, Dad."